AARON SMITH

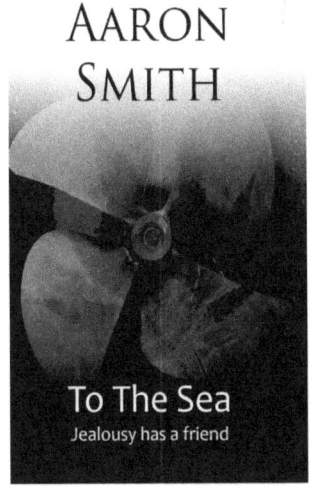

To The Sea
Jealousy has a friend

First Published 2015 by Penrose Publishing Ltd, York House, York Road, Felixstowe IP11 7QG, www.penrose-publishing.co.uk

ISBN

Paperback 978-1-909879-41-6

Paperback Larger Print 978-1-909879-43-0

eBook-Kindle 978-1-909879-42-3

To the Sea

"Too heavy is the load. I fling it down"
Amy Levy

Part One

Chapter One

Cosmo lay there on the soft sand, bare-chested, barely conscious, and illuminated by the Eastern sun in a hazy, glorious glow. His brown hair, colour like the sand it rested on, flapped gently in the breeze and his eyes, usually light and piercing, were sheathed behind black aviator sunglasses. Our train was taking us back in an hour.

"I'm not sure…"

He spoke in his deep, rolling-wave voice. He kept pausing like this:

"I'm not sure if I can exactly… help you…with your whole father-issue-thing." He strained as he got up to readjust his shorts, slightly miffed that I was involved in a situation that required his attention. "But mate, sorting out this mess with her… with your girlfriend I mean, is soooo easily done."

He looked satisfied with himself.

"Ex-girlfriend," I corrected him partway through another slug on my can of Foster's.

Fittingly, my phone lit up; it was Ashley.

I chose to ignore it. The morning's incendiary incidents told me it'd only be another mad hail of abuse. Cosmo grinned and inclined towards me from his camp of towels, magazines and beer as if about to say something, then went quietly back to his catlike resting position.

I was in Bridlington again for only the second time in my life. The glamour almost killed me.

If you want to understand Bridlington then you have to get so close to the bricks and mortar that you can smell the ancient salt which makes the town. You have to scratch with your own fingers the seventies shops with letters hanging off their signs, forming strange unfinished words like 'Ho sons Too s' and, more recognisably, 'oolwort s'; scratch the small, half-abandoned train station with its perversely beautiful garden at its dusty entrance; the dingy sand-filled pubs patronised by bald or bearded men donning blue sailing sweaters and baseball caps, leaning on the sticky bars and leering at newcomers; the streets which cannot escape the clouds; and the nightclubs, dry-ice-filled and seedy, packed to the rafters with inbreeding and resignation.

The town itself had a strange, inexplicable draw on me. At first Cosmo was intrigued by my sudden desire to hit the rails and escape to Bridlington. I explained, once I'd finished my laugh, "Going there is just something I feel we need to do, you and me." There were grains of truth in what I'd said, but if I had been totally honest I would've said there and then that I had to get as far away from Ashley as practical, to somewhere so obscure and anonymous as Bridlington as to make my getaway, even for just a weekend, complete. So I sorted it with my mother's friend to stay in her disused flat on Cardigan Road and bought Northern Rail tickets from Knaresborough to York before hopping on the Transpennine to wind up in that lost little town at four o'clock in the middle of July.

It was refreshing, cathartic even, to watch the agricultural wasteland tumble by as we rode on the train through the East Riding cornfields and pig farms; and when we were almost halfway there Cosmo had looked up at me from his magazine and said the most life-affirming thing I think I've ever heard.

"Gene, y'know when you were young…did you ever just want to jump out of the car and run and run and keep on running into the fields outside? Did you ever chop the corn in them with an imaginary scythe as they sped by?"

And I knew exactly what he meant; gazing through child's eyes at one of those crisp, end-of-summer fields and inventing deep tales in a passing moment, before the wind-whipped grain would disappear behind the whoosh of an oncoming lorry. I replied without hesitation, "I still do."

It was one of those moments, those perfect moments, when two people understand not only what the other is saying, but also exactly who the other person is.

Then to the mither of the passengers around us we started jawing loudly about exactly what alcohol we were going to throw down our necks and how many girls we were going to sleep with.

That night, as the sun lowered itself slowly landwards and the salty breeze drifted in through the flat's open, wood-framed windows, we sat in the old woman's long-disused wingbacks drinking Tesco's own vodka from her vases and, after splashing out on the voddy, eating the only food we could afford—frozen supermarket pizza—off her good china. We were seventeen years of age in the summer between the first and second years of sixth-form and we were unburdened with care or knowledge. A complete adventure in that Eastern-town.

We skipped out on foot into the buzzing sea-air feeling pretty on the way. After passing the giant Spa, with the last suggestion of light fading from the sky, we found a strip of bars and dived into a half-empty club filled with small-town teenagers drinking VK's through straws. The DJ was wreathed with smoke in the corner and running the latest Pop Idol crap through the speakers. Those grinding or head-nodding on the floor looked uncomfortable, numb as though they couldn't tell whether being drunk was something to be enjoyed or endured; we were that far gone that we didn't care.

We made it to the bar and I looked again at the dance floor. There, dressed head to toe in denim, like in those Western films where the town-whore is entertaining the saloon, was a rough, sketty-looking woman rolling her round bum against her next victim.

We bought drinks. The undiscerning barman, eyeing me with a crossed look of derision and amusement as I 'shhhed' on the 'S' of 'Stella', ignored his duty to

ID me—as he had with everyone else there—and passed two bottles across the scratched, gum-pocked bar.

I cursed how young I looked then, my soft cheeks mixing unfavourably with my patchy stubble and wide eyes. Cosmo was undoubtedly better looking though I'd never admit it. He had those pinched dark brows like a fox's which, when mixed with the sandy hair, I always thought made him the obvious choice out of us for girls. He'd been watching the denimed woman closely.

"A tenner. Go on."

"What, pay you? For that? No chance," I laughed. "You'll probably catch something… and get twatted by whoever's pimping her."

"Bullshit. Bullshit, my friend. I could take anyone in here," he half-shouted, casting around the room and expecting a response.

I looked around. He was very wrong. "How many pints?" he continued louder as he slopped lager on his aztec-patterned Topman t-shirt.

"She's a ten-pinter, honestly," I replied gravely. He gave a look of disgust and finished his beer in one, as if to show off how combatively he believed in her beauty; then, forgetting me altogether, he made for the exit shouting, "Bye bye Denim Girl, we'll miss youuuu…" as he fell over his own feet and back into the yellow, phosphorescent street outside. I downed the hoppy, nasal contents of his half-finished bottle and followed.

We'd only staggered 50 yards up the seafront before we found another club, reached by some stairs which resembled Mount Sinai. I fell against the handrail while Cosmo, like some soberer Moses, gained the summit, in which position he turned and hollered and screamed, questioning my shaky limbs and my manhood. Well, I was fucked if I couldn't match that idiot's achievement of reaching the top, so I clambered up, on all fours most of the way, paggering my shins in the ascent.

I wondered, honestly, if we were going to meet any women at all that night, and then I remembered that I was purely out drinking to forget. At the bar we discussed the merits of moving back onto spirits and I made us a quick decision. With the backs of two shirted men turned, and the barman disappearing swiftly off to the next customer, I swiped two vodka cokes and headed straight to the narrow, steel-girdered smoking terrace with Cosmo in tow. We were down to our last twenties already, and poverty, I reasoned, warps people's morals.

The terrace was suspended a full thirty foot up the side of the building and had a punch-holed steel base. We looked directly out onto the black sea, with our faces licked by the wind and our chests pressed against the railings. A tall, short-haired fella lit up Cosmo's cigarette at his request and the two had to crouch down to keep the sea-breeze from extinguishing the flame. But just as he held his lighter out and the flame touched the tip of the cigarette, two men started shouting off to our left and Cosmo and the Tall Guy flicked their eyes upwards. Suddenly, two factions began scrapping along the three-foot-wide gangway, fists flying like helicopter blades. More were entering the melee from each side and it was a minor miracle that me and Cosmo could duck and dodge the boozy roundhouses and not lose a drop of our chawed drinks.

Diving quickly back inside, we threw ourselves on some dark-purple sofas near a huge, circular mirror in the corner. The club, which in one vast sweep held the seating area, a dance floor, the bar and the bogs, was bedecked in purples and reds; the bar was backlit by a neon-blue glow, and the walls, unmirrored in places, were smothered by textured wallpaper patterned with classical images of jugs, boats and fleurs-de-lis racing along its sides. Everything about that room felt fabricated, unreal, as though every façade covered mould and decay.

"C'you believe 'at?" slurred Cosmo. "Look at 'em!" Outside, a whole squad of bouncers were now prising the men off each other.

"I know," I replied, stretching out like a tired dog on my two-seater sofa. "They should have thrown each other off that platform, then there'd have been a real fucking mess."

Cosmo sat to my left on a sofa at right-angles with mine, copying my reclined position by hanging one of his legs off the arm, with the other planted on the grape-coloured floor. We had been sat there perhaps a minute or so, just looking round with curious glances and glossy eyes while listening to the DJ when a black, built Spice Boy, replete with those multi-pocketed G-Star jeans and a fist full of gold, walked up to us with a look on his wide face that said, "You're in big fucking trouble boys."

I straightened back up in my seat as he loomed over me.

"Get the fuck out lads. These are ours," declared Spice Boy, gesticulating aggressively as he bent down to pick up Cos's dangling legs.

"Fuckoff knobhead!" ejaculated Cos instantly, kicking his legs free of the man's grasp. As Spice Boy prepared to make a second grasp, two women, one blonde, the other a kind of attractive reddish brunette (in truth, I couldn't tell. Every woman who wasn't fat looked distinctly shaggable in this half-light) appeared at his side, along with a much more sinister, older, I've-got-at-least-two-knives-on-me White Bloke. This fella wore a black jacket covering disproportionately broad shoulders, had slicked back his salt 'n' pepper hair which looked straight out of seventies Peckham, and kept a mouth which shimmered with gold like that on his friend's bling-encrusted hand.

I really couldn't be arsed with the Bridlington Mafia on our case so I tried to calm things down.

"Fellas, fellas," I began in what sounded like a diplomatic voice. "Listen, I know these are your seats usually and I get that you probably haven't seen us here before, but why don't you let us stay here and you could pull up some seats and have a drink with us?"

Fuck. Now I'd done it.

Cosmo was still on his guard staring at Spice Boy, who didn't look so angry anymore. The broad White Bloke revealed his glimmering teeth in a sick grin.

"Allraht then, boys," he drawled deeply and slowly, smiling all the time. "Ernly if yeh dern't mahnd lahk?" It was a rhetorical question.

"No, go ahead," I said.

"We're off ter't bar ladies—glass-o-vino?" He made the last part rhyme; fairly clever, I thought, for a man who must have beaten one of his teachers up to get through primary school. The women, who I could see were drowned in fake tan now they had moved closer, nodded their assent with a smile and the men strutted off in the direction of the bar.

The blonde instantly schlooped down in between Cosmo's legs, revealing a flash of tiny white knickers. She was shaved. My heart skipped a beat and I felt the blood rush downstairs.

"Whoah" said Cosmo, trying to sound casual. He swung his left leg over her head and sat upright while necking his drink, all in one fluid movement. He banged the empty glass down on the plastic table. Then the brunette sat next to me, her thigh tight to mine.

"Do you boys come 'ere often?" she purred.

"No no, we're from near Leeds."

"Well," she said, lowering her mouth to my ear, "yeh're proper sexeh."

She ran her elaborately manicured fingers through my hair. It felt good. I could see that the blokes were at the front of the bar, about to be served. What the hell were these women *doing*? There was a train wreck approaching and our continued survival lay on the line.

"Ta," I awkwardly replied.

The blonde whispered something in Cosmo's ear. He looked at me, bewildered and fearful. Then my girl laughed and put her hand on my erection, which was pretty visible under my shorts even in the dusk of the club. The music reverberated all around, from every direction, rattling my head. We were trapped. We had to do a runner, right now. Then came an earth-moving roar.

"AH'M GUNNA FUCKIN KILL YEH!" Spice Boy smashed his metal-studded fist down on the bar. Dropping the wine glasses, the White Bloke charged forward with pure venom, no, murder in his eyes.

"You are fuckin dead, fuckin' dead boys!"

Simultaneously, me and Cosmo bolted from under the women's grasps, vodka and coke and god knows what else flying everywhere, vaulted over the low-level table, and legged it at full sprint for those stairs. I led the escape, cascading down six steps at a time and somehow staying on two feet despite my intoxication, wondering how the hell we got up the stairs in the first place there were so many of them, knocking past the people ascending, bouncing off walls and sending some badly-positioned plant pots and loose handbags cartwheeling downwards. I hit the bottom and used my hand on the floor to avoid going arse-over-tit. We burst through the double-doors together, then passed the single bouncer before he could react to what was going on and sprinted down the sloshing seafront in a blind direction, not daring to look behind.

Luckily for us, a young man with a semi-active lifestyle and a strong will to see the dawn is a better runner if not, sadly, a better fighter than a gnarled, middle-aged bloke with a forty a day habit, a spare tyre and seven pints of lager in his stomach. So, by the time we had got about a quarter of a mile up the road, having taken one or two snickets and a couple of left turns away from the front, we were well out of sight and range. We each put our hands on our knees and drew some breath back.

"Fuck's… sake!… huh… huh," Cosmo panted next to me, his breath shaking like a rattlesnake.

I turned away to check again that no-one was there and spat on the floor, holding onto a railing for support as I panted too. Cosmo fell into a noisy coughing fit that got more theatrical as it beat the oxygen out of his lungs too quickly for him to catch his breath so that it forced him onto the floor in a ball against the wall.

I burst out laughing; I couldn't help it. Then I couldn't catch my breath any longer and we both ended up in a state on the cold stone floor, coughing, laughing and gasping for air like two landed fish.

After a couple of minutes we recovered and locked thumbs to get to our feet like footballers do.

"Jeeesus Christ," he began, "you could see they'd set that up. Fuckers wanted that fight."

I nodded, exhilarated from the chase, as two seagulls waddled over into our snicket and inspected the goz I'd artistically left on the floor.

"Well, what d'yeh fancy doing now?" I asked.

"Aw man, we can't go back to the flat, not yet anyway. I need 'nother fucking drink, that's for sure." I always admired Cos for his simplicity.

And so we set off again through that little town. We'd been walking for perhaps five minutes when, in the short distance, there appeared a chilled-out looking bar adorned with red chilli pepper-shaped fairy lights and vines which hung around its large front windows. Outside there were tables around which groups of people, distinctly better dressed and more peaceful-looking than the previous crowd, sat chatting. We got in, ordered two pints and sat down in the surprisingly large upstairs section. The DJ and his decks were crammed in at the back between two six-foot speaker stacks. He was spinning some deep house, a fact I only gathered from reading the flyers that were plastered on the walls and doors in there; the crowd he had dancing away filled the room's wood-panelled floor.

"Cos?," I asked in a wide-eyed shout over the music, "are you still completely buzzing with adrenaline?"

He nodded vigorously.

I felt that this was what going out on drugs was supposed to feel like. I was about to tell him so when, with sweat breaking on his forehead and permeating his fringe, he shouted back the simple words: "Let's dance." He took a massive gulp of his San Miguel and then flicked his head sideways.

Only on the dance floor did it become obvious that there were some insanely beautiful women in the room and that they were outnumbering the men. They were the kind of women (and they were mainly women, not girls but women who were in their prime—around twenty-five or twenty-six, I guessed at a glance) who had that mature, sassy, confident aura about them and looked as though they could teach a seventeen-year-old some tricks. They dressed differently; their bodies were more developed, stacked head to toe with beautiful curves; some wore fishnets, others secretary-style jackets and pencil skirts.

I turned to Cosmo as we reached the floor and saw that he was having a genuine drop-jaw moment. He had gone quiet, like a kid in a giant toyshop who can't believe his luck; and he looked predatory, as though there weren't humans in front of him but targets.

We started busting the few moves we had. And we didn't care if we looked younger, freer and inexperienced. We just wanted to show these women that we were brimming with energy; and that always puts you in with a chance. The music was new and perfect, the near-opposite of the chart which infested everywhere that had come before for us. All this time I could only think, How did we find this place in Bridlington?

So Cosmo, with all his bombast, got chatting away to one of these mature stunners near the speaker stack. She didn't have a friend there which he could palm off to me. I headed out to the tables at the front to give the young wizard space to cast his spell.

As I settled in a soft wicker chair some distance from the entrance, I meditated on the forays we'd been on before. Back home it was a case of scrounging someone else's ID (which happened sporadically at best), get leathered, get on the train to Leeds—whatever night of the week—and try to pull girls who would be semi-respectable and not leave us dying of shame on the morning ride home. More often than not though we wound up sharing our beds the next day with takeaway boxes and each other.

Tonight was starting to feel different.

As I pulled out a cig and avoided the potted shrubbery which lay near my out-splayed legs, my mind also cast itself back to Cosmo's usual pulling technique.

It was all about the ironic dance and making sure he was as tall as he could pull himself up to—around 5' 9' in 'big shoes'. Like I say I was convinced his light hair stroke dark brows combo had a lot to do with it; anyhow, once he had grabbed her attention he would slide in behind her for the grind, and whisper creepily through her hair, "Do you fancy a drink?" I'd always been against the grind, but then what did I know?

Here in these new, luxuriant, adult surroundings, he had clearly changed his tack: I was perhaps halfway down my Marlboro Red, deeply contemplating the various retro aluminium advertisement plates on the wall opposite, when Cos and two women, one taller and one shorter than him (the shorter one a striking blonde and the taller having the look of a well-preened Malaysian beauty about her) came bursting into the still-warm night air and out of the beat-filled interior. Cosmo was laughing loudly with his arms around their waists. My eyes bulged.

"Gene! Gene you legend, meet the girls!" Cosmo boomed, like an overexcited tourist.

"Sasha. Sasha, this is Gene. Gene, Sasha. And this, this is, erm, this is G…"

"Georgia," the striking shorter one interjected with a warm, sexy smile, her eyebrows raised behind her thick-rimmed black glasses.

"Hey, nice to meet you. Come to save me from myself out here, hey?"

Georgia laughed at this. A small switch flicked on in my head. I just hoped that

Cosmo could keep his cool and not fuck things up.

This was exactly what I'd wanted to come out here for, to get away from all the stresses at home which had multiplied recently, and if he dropped a clanger now like he was prone to I was going to kick his arse.

"So, Georgia, what do you do?"

I decided to take it easy on the San Miguel.

"Oh, I'm a schoolteacher; I teach up at Headlands—you know where that is?"

"Oh no no, I'm not local. In fact, we've just come over today."

She raised her eyebrows again behind those glasses, put her straw in between her two red-painted lips and sucked up her cocktail as I spoke.

"Oh really? That's exciting! It's a bit quiet here in Brid, as you can probably tell."

Sasha, tuning into our conversation, added something in her low, rich voice. Cosmo reclined contentedly as she spoke; I felt like I was melting into my chair. It was obvious from both their voices they were from the South; they'd studied in York, we learned, and ended up as teachers in Brid almost by accident.

Me and Cos went on to regale them with our experience of the club on the seafront. We also weaved a yarn about us being students at Leeds Met, Cosmo taking the lead and me cottoning on soon after until, with four empty glasses lying on the table, it was time for us poor sixth-formers to get the drinks in. That was it as far as money was concerned for me.

At the bar, I grabbed Cos.

"Mate, how—genuinely—how did you manage to pick up those incredible women? You are a fucking genius, a god amongst men, a bona fide player... I'm just... I'm speechless."

He grinned and reminded me to play it cool.

"And we have a place to take them back to, so just keep them talking, keep them in the drinks and we're in there Genie."

"You got any bar on you though? I'm out."

"Aye, got another twenty out earlier."

"Oh, and how did you end up with the tall one?" I asked perplexedly.

"Big shoes," he replied with a wink.

Chapter Two

The next morning I awoke hungover to a banging on the tiny side-door of the flat. I had been dreaming about my father again, imagining him leading me up the stairs of his office and showing me into a room in which my mother was sitting. Next to her had been another man; and then my dad had sat down too, the three of them forming a line. Then without a word the mystery man had left, and an ear-splitting shouting match erupted between my parents as they stared eerily at me, necks turned jauntily as if they were two wide-eyed owls. I remembered the word 'covered' as clear as day, as if they had just shouted that one word on repeat.

The din of gulls replaced their shouts as it bled in through the open window, mingling with the persistent banging from the door. The sunlight hit my eyes ferociously. I groped for some clothes from my sideways position on the bed. The clock, hanging lopsidedly on the bare, stripped wall, confirmed that our train back was due in two and a half hours. I looked over and saw the soft, pale shoulder of Georgia poking out from beneath the covers, her lovely long, blonde hair tumbling upwards from her head. A momentary thrill went through my spine and down to my testicles. So, *that* hadn't been a dream. I cracked a smile. My head began to hurt even more. Then I looked quickly to my phone, the pounding at the door getting heavier with each hit. I had thirteen missed calls. Cosmo, hair sticking out at right-angles, hobbled over to the door in his twisted boxers.

"Who the fuck is that?" he shot croakily towards me on his way.

"I haven't got a clue," I moaned, puzzled and suffering. Suddenly, from outside, a female voice shrieked, "Gene, you prick! Open up! Open the door!"

Oh God. I knew now, and at that instant I bolted upright from my semi-foetal position and plunged my legs into the jeans in my hand in one lightning movement. It was her. I hadn't believed she would come all this way, hadn't thought she might have been let into my house, checked my search history and seen 'Knaresborough to Bridlington', hadn't thought she might have been told the address by my own mother—but it was her.

"Oh shit, shit…" I repeated frantically, "don't answer it!"

It was too late. Cosmo had already turned the latch and the full fuming form of Ashley came bursting irresistibly in. Her long brown hair juddered across her tanned face as she steadied herself and took in the room.

I looked at Georgia, who still slept hidden beneath the covers, then at Ashley and noticed the difference. Ashley still looked like a true sixth-former despite the fact she was a full year ahead of me, her New Look dress sense lacking the maturity of Georgia's wardrobe which lay messily on the floor.

"Where the fucking hell have you been?! D'you know what today is?!" she screamed at me, storming into the living room and looking like she was about to vent out a scalding steam. She hadn't seen the clothes—not yet. I tried to edge them under the sofa bed with my foot.

She grabbed the nearest object—one of Cosmo's battered old white Converses— and hurled it straight at my head with unerring accuracy; I ducked just in time, holding my head as the glass of the clock on the wall behind me shattered all over the bedcover-lump of Georgia. She jumped up with a girly scream, her pert breasts hanging out and nothing else other than a black thong on. My God, what. a. body. The shards of glass lay to rest in the troughs of the duvet. Ashley paused for a second and took in this naked girl who was on her knees.

"WHOTHEFUCKISTHAT?!!"

The decibel meter had gone off the chart, her arms scrunched up right into her sides, fists balled and raised, her entire torso bent forward to lend the scream more violence. In an instant, she seized the large vase that I'd been drinking out of the night before and drew it above her head, ready to launch. Cosmo, who looked wretched and nonplussed next to her in his boxers, instinctively grabbed her brown arms to prevent her from killing one of us.

"What are you doing?!" he hollered, "Ashley, maybe, maybe give us ten minutes?"

There was a charged silence as me and Ashley both looked from Cosmo to each other, then her back to him.

"Are you fucking kidding Cosmo? Are you taking the piss, seriously? WHO THE FUCK ARE THESE GIRLS?"

Cosmo's woman, Sasha, had also risen up and begun to get hastily dressed. I saw that Georgia too was frantically scrabbling around for her bra and other clothes, trying to escape this mad house.

"Maybe we should just leave, eh?" said Georgia diplomatically, her blue eyes darting up to her friend from her bent posture. "Clearly not a good time."

"Yes, maybe you fucking should, slut," she spat. "And as for you," Ashley's tone began to rise again and in her voice there was a catch, like tears were battling against fury. "YOU'RE FUCKING DEAD GENE!"

It was the second death threat I had received in twenty-four hours and was no less terrifying than the first. She wrenched herself free of Cosmo's grasp, pounced on a pile of cutlery left out amongst the disarray of the abandoned flat and advanced towards me. Cosmo had given up any attempt at restraint and watched the scene in silent amazement as it unfolded. She let loose her volley, interspersing words with missiles: "You… cheating… lying… sack of shit… scumbag!"

A lightbulb smashed under the impact of a teaspoon. "We were supposed… to be celebrating…" The wingback chair went flying sideways across the floor under the impact of her heel. "Our fucking… ANNIVERSARY!"

Ouch. The weight of this new piece of information hit me simultaneously with a small fork.

A book violently whistled past my left ear as I was struggling for balance.

"Ash, look, I'm sorry, I'm sorry, I really am. I just…"

"Sorry? SORRY?!" she yelled, the sound reverberating off the narrow bare walls. Her face was streaked with black streams of water like a rain-spattered window pane. "Two years, Gene! Two years! What did it mean to you, eh?"

There was silence. "Nothing," she replied for me through her choked voice. And now that she was stood in front of me, defeated and humiliated, I felt the first pangs of guilt creep into my stomach. Guilt for the cheating, back home and here. Guilt for the tears and for the human wreckage.

She seemed to have steadied now, gained control even, but still I remained tensed, ready for another missile.

"Why did you drive all the way out here, Ash?" I embarrassedly asked. I saw Sasha quickly peck Cosmo on the cheek, and the two half-dressed girls vacated the flat by skirting around the back of Ashley, whose welled-up eyes followed them intensely.

"I came…" (and now she really choked on her words) "to find out… where you'd gone. I wanted to be together… today… it was bad enough you'd disappeared… and now I find this."

A fresh wave of loud sobs. She slumped against the wall, still looking me directly in the eye. Then she cried quietly. "You bastard, I can't believe you've done this. That you could have done this to me." There was torment in her soft eyes. Tears streaked aimlessly across her cheek, her neck, onto her hands too.

She stumbled upwards, using the wall to support her. I suddenly felt very naked and exposed and I fumbled around for a t-shirt. She went for the door looking spent. Then, with an air of regained composure, she said:

"Don't ever talk to me again. I'm leaving for London, now."

There was such finality to that last word. My mind worked slowly, but my heart still beat two to the second.

"So, so you got the offer?" I replied, feigning an inquisitive, hopeful air. God, did I feel like a complete cunt.

"I don't ever want to see you again," she said quietly. She gave me one last look of utter, pitiless contempt. And she left.

Me and Cosmo listened to the sound of her Toyota engine juddering into life outside the front of the flat in an almost-dignified respectful silence. It rattled back onto Cardigan Road and was gone.

I inhaled deeply; it felt like the first breath I'd taken in hours. I heard Cosmo hoot softly behind me.

"I'm really sorry about that mate." We stood, both in silence again. I cracked the knuckles of my tensed feet, and a fork fell off the mantelpiece. I looked at the open door which was letting in a soft breeze.

Then Cosmo, still a way off at the other side of the kitchen, looked at me with a grin lighting his face; a bizarre, wide, out-of-place grin. It got wider. And suddenly we were both laughing—walking towards each other across the cold kitchen floor and laughing like madmen.

"Oh for fuck's sake Gene, you naughty boy!" Cosmo hollered as he held me at the shoulder and shoved his hand through his hair, his eyes looking almost hysterical. Then he hopped over to the radio on the kitchen windowsill and turned it on.

I felt strange. We were laughing hysterically, as if this something was all simply a game that I had invented to amuse us both. I had probably hurt Ashley more than I could comprehend. She'd just had her heart broken by me, but, inexplicably, I felt like a huge weight had been lifted, like a sword had just been withdrawn from above my head by some merciful hand. I felt free. Finally and irreversibly free.

I don't think I'd ever loved her. You see, she was the one with the plan, the plan to move out from our little town and begin her adventure keeping me at her side as I dropped out of my failing A-Levels. And I had simply nodded along because I could not work out what else to do with my life.

I'd had these feelings from time to time, these nagging doubts, these flights of fear that I had no destination, nothing to strive for, no aim at all, but I'd been choosing to utterly ignore them. I had let her take control and lost it in my own life; I realised it only now, only in the cold-floored kitchen of a Bridlington flat on a summer's morning with Cosmo, my best friend at my side.

Paolo Nutini blasted out of the radio and met the energy of the sun's late-morning beams.

"So, you got caught red-handed then eh? Faaacking hell! Ha! Ha!" Cosmo barked amusedly above the music.

"Yeah," I began, raising my eyebrows, still not quite believing it had happened. "What a balls-up. What a scene…" I turned to Cosmo trying to gesticulate this soaring feeling, unable to do anything to communicate it properly.

"On the day of your anniversary too man. What a love rat! Ha! Haha!"

"I blame you, you were the one who found those two, Cosmo."

He raised his hand and gave me a benny round the back of the head. "I'm not the one getting caught cheating on my girlfriend!"

"Not that any lass'd have you for longer than a night. Oh God," I continued, feeling the pain shoot back to my head and wondering what the financial damage was. "How much did we spend on them?"

"Oh don't, don't remind me how empty my wallet's gonna be, I don't even want to look. And don't take any of the glorious shine off last night! Or off my skill."

I nodded in agreement and put the kettle on with a flourish, as Paolo sang "And best of all, I've got my baaaabbbyyyy," with Cosmo wailing along too.

"So what were you going to do with Ashley if she hadn't finally caught you in the act?" He grabbed at some popped-up toast. "And I thought you were sticking around at home? She made it sound like you two were about to bugger off together or something."

I hadn't confided in anyone that I had planned to move away.

"Yeahhhh…" I sighed, "stupid really. I just didn't know what else to do. She was off to uni, I was just going to follow her y'know? Find a job down there or wherever else she got into, or summat or other."

Cosmo looked up, knife in hand. "You didn't have a clue, did you?'"

I shrugged. He gave a bassy laugh. "I can't believe you were going to divorce me," he smiled, buttering up a slice each.

And that was his quality, Cosmo. Never a hard feeling. It's why I couldn't stay away from him. We popped out into the brilliant sunshine on the balcony and ate. After breakfast we cleaned up and packed our things, ready to hit the beach before catching the train.

And that's how we came to be lying there that afternoon in the middle of July on a bed of soft sand, killing time before the 13.05 train to Seamer for the first of our connections. My phone lit up—a text from Ashley, the woman who had driven out of my life down the A1.

I put my aviators back on and walked down to the sea, the sand becoming wetter by grades as I stepped along its sidewinding ridges. I let the water reach up to my knees and stopped. The sun overhead was hot and dry on my shoulders; the land and cliffs looked parched. It was the perfect day.

I turned seawards; the curvature of the Earth along the North Sea looked supreme. Above the waterline there were vapour trails crossing and intersecting in the blue sky; leftovers of flights that would go on to span the world. The same vapours inhabited tropical Indian skies, icy Canadian mountain ranges, endless Chinese expanses, just as they occupied mine, and I felt alive. I looked down to the sea again, and I fell in love.

And I knew then that Ashley hadn't deserved me. I had spent every day for two years with her and had felt hardly anything, yet the sea had taken my rudderless heart instantly. And I can't explain it, but I was seized with a desire, no a need, an unconquerable need to get on those waves and just go in whatever direction they took me.

But Cosmo's voice echoed from the shore. He was tapping his watch. It was time to go.

We strolled the ten-minute walk to the station, browning in the hot sun. Halfway there, just beyond the giant, lonely-looking Tesco that stood next to the acres of waste ground in the middle of the town, I turned to Cosmo. He'd been talking about getting back to his summer job at Curry's when we got home, and there was something about a Cubism book; I hadn't been paying attention. I wanted to know something of him instead.

"Cos, what use is there in staying in one place, in being fixed, stationary? We only live once right? Shouldn't we be squeezing everything we can from life? What use is a job when we're only going to die? What do you think?" My words tumbled out in a heap. All my vistas had changed since the morning and I still struggled to articulate it all.

Cosmo stopped and turned, maybe detecting the hint of desperation in my voice. He was looking up at me, bag over shoulder, his tanned face wearing a confused expression.

"Mate, what are you on about?" he replied savagely. "Don't be stupid. What's that even supposed to mean?" His voice had got higher. The usually laid-back

Cosmo was looking genuinely agitated. "That you want to be Kerouac? That you want to spend your life at a Beat party in New York, or San Francisco, and talk shit and get high?"

"Yeah, I know, I've…"

"It doesn't pay for itself, nothing does," he went on, "in this life you've got to graft." He slung his bag across his other shoulder with an effort-laden sigh. His momentary animation was over now that he had a foothold in the conversation. "I don't mean to burst your bubble, like; I know I fuck about all the time, we're seventeen, nothing matters at the moment. If we had some bar we could go up and down the country, over hill and dale if we wanted to," he laughed deeply; I nodded along. "But you just know that that thing called 'real life' is gonna be snapping at our heels sooner or later."

He sparked a cig as a full stop to his sentence. He was saying exactly what I'd predicted he was going to say, what I wanted him to say to me, because I felt like I needed some sense knocking in to me to fight my giddiness. But now, the truth was I did want to be like Kerouac. I really did want to be on that proverbial Greyhound bus, crossing the awful continent in the inky night.

We went through the station's open foyer, with its weird little garden and Victorian stone offices and hopped on the waiting train. Despite all the windows being flung open it was still mafting. I stuck to the seat through my shirt. After a minute, a man sat down opposite us on the cramped little table. He was wearing a beige hat which bore a thin black band around its rim and a matching beige suit, and he was peering through his tinted spectacles at his magazine. It was about boats—a sort of members-only glossy with the Rotary Club logo sat in the right hand corner of the front cover. It reminded me of something I'd noticed when we'd been eating our fish and chips at Bridlington harbour the day before. There, I had seen something that took my fancy—a tiny white fishing boat with sky blue edges to it, the kind with an upright cabin in the middle of its compact deck. I'd even said to Cosmo, "Wouldn't you just love to have one of those?" but he was too busy mopping up his curry sauce to bother noticing. I loved the proportions of it, crammed in amongst the macho yachts, polished catamarans and souped-up jet-skis in the harbour, its minuscule hull and bulldog stern giving it a defiant look. I think above all it was a boat that one man could tame, manage and maintain. A project. One man could get lost on that boat, alone, with a stack of food tins and a long-wave radio. My thoughts had drifted, just like the white wisps of cloud travelling across the sun just then, as I'd looked at that boat.

The present caught up with me. The pig farms and agricultural hinterland played on loop again. The sun sent ochre beams past the rubber window trims and onto Cosmo's gently swaying face as we sped past the Wolds' Ryedale foothills travelling westward. That same sun would soon be rising for the world beyond.

Chapter Three

Back home, I got an exciting message from Jack, a friend who was studying down in Birmingham. Cosmo had disappeared for the last fortnight, either playing videogames and drawing away in his garage or working his job at Curry's. Meanwhile, I had taken his word—at least for now—and had been labouring for my uncle outside of town. His fibreglassing company had received an order from a Norwegian firm who wanted giant containers to be manufactured and shipped over. My pay was £60 a day and my job was to clear the warehouse of the tiles and wooden carcasses that had been left behind after its previous incarnation, a bathroom showroom, which (so Uncle Dave said) had had HMRC on its back. We saved all the MDF and chipboard and screws for the office that my uncle was going to have built in the corner. The rest of the warehouse was the factory floor, and we shovelled it mercilessly clear in those two weeks. It was a ten-mile ride on my bicycle to get out there though I took the bus when it rained. It was still summer and although the route was long it was a good breeze-in-your-hair ride on the dry days. I would set off at half past five and would sleep like a child when night came.

Jack was a Birmingham University student, older than me and Cosmo by two years. We knew him through Cos's elder brother, who'd gone up to Newcastle to study. When we met at Conyngham Hall by the River Nidd, Jack had instantly become good friends with us; he loved how we would give up everything at the drop of a hat when fun was available over work.

That was the gist of this message. He was organising a 'mad weekend' down there for 'Dan' and 'Cam', two of his friends from home who were driving down and eager to fill up the car. Me and Cosmo fit the bill.

I had also met this Dan down at Conyngham Hall and in fact I'd been working with him: he was Uncle Dave's right-hand man, often seen looking over plans with the boss at a desk in the corner, poring over blueprints and order forms. Despite this I'd rarely spoken to him. He rolled up to work everyday in his clapped-out '93 Ford Fiesta which had virtually no exhaust pipe and a cracked chassis.

It was because of Jack's call south that I organised a pint with the otherwise elusive Cosmo.

I met him at a low-ceilinged real ale pub some way up from the river. I'd biked straight from work still dressed in my dust-covered cut-off jeans and a torn Primark t-shirt which was rigid from all the plaster it had collected. He was late, as usual.

"Guess who, gorgeous?" he muttered with his bassy voice as he shoved his hands over my eyes. I looked up through his fingers at his grin-filled face.

"Heyyy…" I said excitedly, bursting to tell him the news. "Take a pew. How's tricks?"

He joined me on my seat, which due to the crowded beer garden was simply a low, hot stone wall that overlooked the distant rockface at the side of the Nidd. Shuffling to get comfy, he trailed off into a delineation of the last week or so while I nodded along, not really paying attention. Instead I was taking in the glorious evening with the pure, true relaxation that only physical work brings. People milled around outside the pub in its extensive, lush beer garden, dressed to keep cool in the early evening sun. Birds swooped and called out loudly; a barbecue crackled on the patio nearby.

Cosmo paused his story to let out an approving call of 'Every pint is sacred!' as a table near the barbecue let out a loud beery cheer for the man who'd just eased some drinks down without a drop lost. "Speaking of which mate, pint time?"

"Yeah, get us a bitter Cos, I'll save the seats," I smiled, patting the baking stone beside me.

I looked back across the river. The old steep banks stood agelessly still, the sun nestling in between the arches of leafy trees which hung languidly in the air. Two swans sauntered on the water in the rock face's shadow. Ten minutes later the swans were still slowly dancing with each other and Cosmo had returned with a beer in each hand.

I gulped the first half of my pint down without thinking. "So, I have exciting news, sir," I began.

"Oh aye?" he said slowly as he slipped his brother's driving licence back in his wallet.

"It could be high time for one of our little jaunts again. Jack's got in touch."

He looked quizzical behind his glass.

"You know, Birmingham Jack…"

His face lit up. I proceeded to inform him of the vitals. Cosmo appeared as enthusiastic as I had hoped, nearly spilling his beer across my lap in his haste to exclaim "How long can we stay there, Genie? I'd love to go out and get lost down there for a few weeks, wouldn't you? Let's do it." He threw the rest of his dry-roasted nuts down his neck and continued crunchily, "I can get my brother… oh this is genius, he's just been sacked from Argos, he can take my job… we could spend the rest of summer down there…"

"Well," I began. I was worried he would say something like that.

"What, what's up?" he crunched quickly, wide-eyed.

"Remember that thing I told you I thought I'd found out, in Brid? About my dad?"

"Ohhh…" he breathed out, slowly tilting his head. "Shit, I'm sorry mate, that should've been the first thing I asked you…" He fixed his eyes on me, like he could when he had to be serious. "What's happened there then?"

"Well, pretty much as before mate, I've told you most of it already," I said gravely.

"She actually walked in on you while you were reading it?"

"Pretty much, yeah. The first act of getting caught," I laughed bitterly. "There I was, off for my breakfast, and I saw Mum's Facebook page up on the computer downstairs, so I just had a nosey, y'know?"

Cosmo nodded along as I reiterated the events before our dash out to Bridlington.

"As you would."

"As you would, exactly. Well, I just couldn't fucking believe it. And I didn't tell you exactly what she said, did I? She called him a 'secret', called me a 'happy lad without him'. And now I'm asking myself, who the hell is Darren Bradley? Who is this…."—I struggled for the words—"…random bloke who's brought me up! I mean… who the fuck…" Cosmo put his hand on my shoulder and squeezed.

The Facebook conversation page flashed up clearly in my head - the page that had told me that my real father was out there somewhere, unbeknown to me for all these years.

"Did you catch his name? Your real dad I mean… if you don't mind him being called that!" he added quickly.

"Yeah, we might as well call him that," I said looking him back in the eye. "No, no I didn't."

"How come?"

"She walked in, didn't she." I felt hot fury rise up in my chest and spat.

It was hard to convey any of it, the sense of betrayal, the sense of living a life not entirely mine. We sat there in another silence, watching the water below. The swans were still there, preening each other now.

"She shouted up to me," I began again with my eyes fixed intensely on the water, "the morning of the day we went to Brid, just before I saw the message. She said she was off to Newcastle to see dad." I swallowed the word bitterly, wondering as I said it who the man who had brought me up really was, he who had lied to me every day since I was able to listen. "Because… because he'd forgotten some files, or some bullshit lie. And I can remember how she slammed the door. She never slams the door…" My mouth curled in self-beration—"She was clearly off to have a crisis meeting instead."

Cos got out a cigarette and lit up. 'Two's. Here you go. So what about the last two weeks? Hasn't it been a nightmare?"

"I've just… kept my head down with work," I started. "We've not said a word about what happened since then, not a single word…

"I've been trying to think of how I can get out of the house, y'know, actually move out. It's a relief that Jack's got in touch. I need this."

"I'll bet."

"And you're game?"

"Absolutely."

We both reclined and fell silent like teenage lads do in a lot of their conversation, supping at our beer. Then Cosmo asked,

"Are you going to go after him? Your real dad?"

"Yes. Yeah, I am," I replied quietly. Cosmo was looking intently at me; my eyes followed the swans below. "But I don't know how I can. I know nothing about him. I can't work out what mum's password is, so I've got nothing to go on. Only the knowledge that his name is in her messages somewhere."

Cosmo drained his glass and held it forth.

"They're not friends?"

"I've checked them all. He's definitely not there, most of them are family or workmates."

I'd so nearly given up on finding him.

"So. He's just a password away." There was a determination in Cosmo's reckoning which I hadn't expected. It was touching. "You better be on top form for Birmingham still Genie; I'm relying on you."

I felt myself break into a big smirk.

"Hell. Yes," I replied above the noise of the busy river bank, "but like I said when you asked if we could stay the whole summer... if I find him, you know..."

I tapped my empty glass on the cool stone next to me.

"I know you'll be straight after him." He picked up the glass. "Same again then?"

After a couple more pints I was drunkenly treading my way home again. The path by the river was the same as always: same geese, same car park on the right, same giant trees lining the flat bank opposite the face, and the same wet smell of mown grass, synonymous with the time of year.

Every summer it was the smell that made me think of what I had been doing exactly one year ago, reminded me of how quickly time goes by, how quickly things change. I had already begun to feel old in my late-teens. It felt like an age-old tragedy that I'd be jaded and sore with the best years of my life in full-swing.

The path up from the river was the same, but somehow this walk felt different to the countless other times I had made it; the distant glorious setting of the sun, now blood-red, seemed changed from the way I used to think of it. The sun lay in the South-West; and it was in that direction that the weekend beckoned me.

Chapter Four

Two days later I was sat alone in the house when I heard the rusty clatter of Dan's knackered '93 Fiesta approach my house, bringing with it memories of the early mornings working out at the warehouse. I listened nervously to the wheezing, coughing engine and hoped it would last the journey.

Anyhow, I trusted the driver. The few times I'd spoken to Dan he'd seemed dependable and cool-headed. He was also in my uncle's confidence. What seemed more impressive was that he was only twenty.

A bright yet overcast cloudscape greeted me as I carried my giant travel bag through the wooden front door of my house and down the three steps leading onto the street. I'd packed everything I could physically take; I had no plans to return. A breeze carried the sweet smell of potted lavender plants from across the way.

Some Radio 1 tripe tinnily blasted forth from the car, and like a dog Cosmo was sat in the backseat with his head poking out of the window, his sunglasses some appalling shade of orange, topless despite the clouds. Dan and Cam sat in the front looking amused to see me struggling. The former had his thick hands resting on the steering wheel, the latter with his legs up on the dashboard, smoking a joint and reading the Sun.

"Gene's coming out, we're off away again. The party begins!" Cosmo screamed over his shoulder like a madman as I waved with difficulty at the cohort and then loaded up the pitifully inadequate boot. The suspension looked offended that I'd added to its already heroic workload and seemed on the brink of collapse. I gently replaced the boot catch and then plunged my hands through Cosmo's window to violently massage his bare shoulders, telling him to be quiet because if he wanted his laptop, it was in my room still.

He burst out of his door hooting "Oh yeah oh yeah!" and jogged through the open front door of my house and up the green-carpeted stairs with the noise of a pack of hyena.

"You need a muzzle Cos, honestly. I'm worried for when we get there and you actually try to talk to people," I called as he retrieved his laptop.

"Yeah yeah dad, gizza break. Ouch! Where'd that come from?" came his muffled reply through the unexplained bangs and scrapings emanating from above.

"Have you sorted it all out with work and that?"

"Aye, yeah brother's taken it for a month… he was well happy… all done and dusted."

His face appeared as he came thudding back downstairs, legs motoring wildly. "I'm free Gene m'boy!"

"Good good," I replied, following him to the door.

My nose enjoyed the soothing aroma lavender plants again; I felt almost sorry to be leaving. And as if reading my thoughts, Cosmo stopped halfway down the steps outside and swivelled on the spot, suddenly becoming hushed in his tone:

"Oh mate, listen. Have you cracked the password?"

He had once again slipped from delirium to sincerity, and it threw me for a second.

"No. I've been trying again, but no luck"

"And nobody in the house's said owt about the whole thing?"

"The only words between us have been that I'm leaving for a while. I could see the relief in their faces."

There wasn't much more to add to this summary of my dealings with my parents. They had been lying for the past however many years and it didn't look like they were going to be any less deceitful now.

I had been obsessively mulling things over: A-Levels, my real father, abusive texts from Ashley, this feeling of imminent flight—in short, my place in the world. Only the distraction of work—the smashing and the riving, the Glasgow hankies and the mindless chatter from the lads, only those had kept me sane along with falling into bed at the end of the day and letting the white noise in my head fizzle out. Jack's house in Birmingham shone in my mind like a lone beacon. I knew it was time to leave.

"Fair play mate. Shall we?"

Cosmo jumped down the remaining steps, almost losing his balance and his laptop. His house had been on the way for Dan and Cam and the three had evidently become quickly acquainted judging by the smile on Dan's face as Cosmo threw himself full-tilt into the backseat. I fixed Dan with a knowing look, shook his hand, and took my place behind him.

Dan was a stocky lad about the same height as Cosmo. He had dark, almost Turkish features. His chin stuck out further than average, steely, squared and strong, and his solid-brown eyes were overhung with large, heavy brows. He had a face of two-day-old stubble as if he had lain under a pepper-mill. At the warehouse he had won the 'beer for beard' competition, where we'd gone unshaven for a week, with ease; my inconsistent patches had been nothing on his impressive black face-scarf. He wore a customary polo shirt, striped on this occasion with blue and orange.

Cam—short for his surname Cameron—with his knees pushed up almost past his head and his skinny shoulders angled in at the newspaper, cut a pretty different figure. I had met him only briefly when he had come to the warehouse one morning while catching a lift with Dan to Wetherby. He stood at about six foot four and had equally dark features but longer hair, short at the sides but with a massive floppy fringe cast over his forehead that somehow managed to suit him, and a narrow face like a crescent moon. He'd worn (ironically, I presumed) unfashionable jumpers on both the occasions I'd seen him, the type of eighties sweaters with Native-

American motifs. Today he was wearing one with wolves in a moonlit foreground.

He was looking intensely at the paper. In a flash he folded it up with a rustle and turned to look at me with the same furrowed expression, as though I was an unplanned addition to the schedule. He stretched his hand out and shook loosely.

"Now then mate, good to see ya, doing good I hope."

He kept the stern look but gave his words a strange warmth despite their abruptness; equally abruptly Dan revved up the engine, threw the radio on even louder and barrelled round the street's corner while Cam began filling me in about where he'd been the day I'd seen him last.

"I actually ended up in Leeds that time for some reason or other. Christ, the amount of buzzcuts and tracksuits you see around there. Just chavs filling the city centre, you know," he complained vehemently, shaking his head. "I'm sick of idiots just being a waste of space, filing down Briggate like zombies, you know? I mean, just fuckoff, why are you here? How can you have stayed like that? Fair enough, you get a bad upbringing…"

"Well," I began without thinking.

"It's not so bad around here like, but you really see it as soon as you go into those big cities."

"I'm not sure it's that bad; I mean, we all dislike those types, but the fact is you don't have to worry about them," I contested, trying to be as diplomatic as possible. "Surely people like that, you know, the chavvy skinheads, you don't have to deal with them directly. Just leave them to it, why worry?"

"But then the problem's still there, the crime and the violence; you're just ignoring it," he spoke quickly, "That's not dealing with the fact that society still produces people like that."

"But is that ever really going to change?" put in Dan as he turned the radio down. His voice was quiet and level as still water.

"Well, it should!" said Cam loudly, glaring at him. "Dan, come on, we were talking about this before, how can't you see that things need to change?"

I took Cam rounding on Dan as an opportunity to look away. I found it hard to care that much about what he was arguing for, or why; my mind had been focussed on getting out of that street and away from that house, not the world's problems.

But as if to illustrate Cam's point, a police car doing fifty wailed by on the other side of the road. "See? Probably off to deal with some crackhead who's beaten up his girlfriend."

"Well then, isn't that… erm… Cos…"

I'd stopped because firstly I didn't really have much to add to the tiring conversation, and also because I'd realised Cosmo was shuffling around next to me with one earphone in, singing along to The Cribs. Cam seemed to calm down as he inspected the stoppage in the rear-view mirror. "Isn't that us dealing with the problem right there?" I resumed, "Isn't that the solution in progress?" I raised my palm as though to indicate my logic.

"Thh," he hissed with his tongue between his teeth, "None of you get it—I give up." He was trying to joke, but his words had a turbulent undercurrent of annoyance. "By the way, it's Gene isn't it?"

I was to learn over the next few days that this was Cam's style; interrogative, provocative, and always on the trail of 'the big issues', trying to work out what was for the best in the grand scheme of things. He was an armchair revolutionary, and despite his appetite for conflict he wasn't, as I first thought, an annoying prick. Through our subsequent conversations Cam became instrumental in the formation of my own opinions, tapping in to my insecurities about where I was moving towards in life; and it gave me the glimpse of a feeling that for the first time I was arranging things in my head, one by one, in a linear, coherent way. But I'd only begun to learn all this after surviving a terrifying trip down the M1, Dan an unmoving figure at the wheel, a determined Ahab—a journey which somehow ended with us driving unscathed round the dusty, sunny side streets of Selly Oak, Birmingham.

Chapter Five

The journey down had taken about two hours, including a prolonged break at the services to let the struggling Fiesta's radiator cool from its molten state. Jack's neighbourhood was made of packed-in terraces with jungly front-gardens off a busy road where his local pubs and shops were based. It had the spine-tingling feeling of being right in the middle of everything, students criss-crossing around in twos and threes laden with booze, shopping and homeware, and traffic passing back and forth. It sat near a crossroads where an imposing, sharply-sloping church and a large, disused public building stood. As I looked upon the little house for the first time, I bristled with the possibilities unfolding like umbrellas in my head.

The street was constricted by cars on either side and Jack's house proved impossible to park in front of. Dan wrestled the Fiesta into reverse and expertly shot us back down towards the main road with his chunky arm wrapped around Cam's headrest and his unmoving eyes on the road behind. In one smooth movement he slowed and slotted us into a space outside the dilapidated Bournbrook & Selly Oak Social Club.

We crawled out of the car, grabbed our gear and headed straight back up the road. I turned and saw an oddly futuristic figure looming over the packed neighbourhood, a kind of government building or maybe a hospital looking like a landed spacecraft. Its roof was made of three grey, swooping u-shapes, which seemed to suck in the cloud behind them as its white flanks rose high and wide.

In a garden to my left a king-size mattress sat proudly behind a wall, beer cans strewn around its edges. In a concrete tree-pot on the corner of one of the streets, a white plimsoll had been wedged toe-first into the soil and around it lay small plastic bags with weed leaves emblazoned on their sides.

"Looks like the landlords are doing a roaring trade round here," remarked Cam.

"And the dealers," laughed Dan in his quiet, measured voice.

"You'd do well, wouldn't you?" Cam continued obliviously—"if you could buy a few houses in an area like this and do them up, rent 'em to students."

I looked at the piles of tat—old plasterboard, half-smashed sinks—that littered some of the gardens and guessed he was right. I would've liked some of those landlords' profits myself. I'd saved up around 300 quid, and thought of it running out and leaving me high and dry wasn't a palatable one.

As the house numbers got higher and we approached the church junction, Dan was talking about how he could only spend a few days here before returning to the factory. Then he asked me about my plans.

"Erm, I'd like to stay for longer. I'll have to play it by ear," I evaded. I felt uncomfortable going any deeper into my real plans with someone so close to my uncle, who was in regular contact with my parents. I changed the subject. "So, you're getting a lot of responsibility with this job eh? Seems like Uncle Dave's putting you fairly high up." I instantly regretted using the word 'uncle' before his name; it sounded childish, but Dan took no notice.

"Yeah, I can't believe it. But we've done quite a few jobs together now. I just don't want to let him down." He was looking at me with his brown eyes, fishing for reassurance. "It's been dead interesting, but a lot harder dealing with the paperwork as well as the usual stuff. Your uncle really knows his trade…" he trailed off, turning away from me abruptly. We had reached number 100.

Jack's house had a small, concreted front garden which was blanketed byhad accumulated the usual urban debris—colour-drained crisp packets and so on—and a foot-worn front step which rocked as we each stepped up to his front door. Bassy, thunderous dubstep was shaking the window panes.

Cam knocked loudly shouting nasal insults through the letter box; after a few seconds the sound of pounding steps could be heard from within and a shirtless Jack flung open the door with a toothbrush sticking out of his mouth.

"Lads! Come in!" he bellowed through bristles and paste. A huge bubbling smile lit his narrow, clean-shaven face.

"You look a state Jack," shouted Dan dryly, grabbing him with a rough hand.

"You could've made some effort mate," I added.

"Sorry, sorry fellas'," he said in a tone of mock conviction after removing his toothbrush and raising his hands like the victim of a dawn police raid. "Just woke up, dinna?" He smiled again, revealing his wide set of gappy teeth.

"Alright for some innit?" spoke Cam, bennying him round his black-haired head in greeting. Cam was the only one tall enough to do it

We passed by his lanky figure into the hallway by the stairs. The air was surprisingly fresh, feminine even, though it was hard to notice much else with Jack jumping about like there was no time for anything in the world, let alone us being there in the hallway.

"Don't make yourselves too comfortable guys—we're off out! Now! No, now!" he squawked while we filed further in. This was his birdlike 'excited' voice; his other calmer voice was smoke-affected, like water running constantly over large pebbles.

"What, dressed like that?" said Cosmo laconically as he snapped off a bit of a gummy snake with his teeth.

"I'll be five minutes," he spread out his upheld hand to indicate the "five", as if to emphasise that it was a realistic target, "And then we're out of here." He chuckled gleefully. Without another word he bounded back up the stairs in a bizarre gorilla-like sprint using his fisted hands like pistons on the steps and we were left to our own devices.

"D'you reckon he's got stuff for a cuppa?" asked Cos loudly as he tramped off across the bare floor towards the kitchen, which was flooded with light at the end of the short, murky corridor.

"Er, Cos, I'm not sure if we should…"

"What's the problem? It's Jack's house…"

Just then, Jack stampeded back downstairs and streaked past Cosmo.

"Almost forgot to make you all a brew boys! Sorry sorry, you all fancy one right?" There was a general nod. "And Dan—it's one sugar, Cam—two… am I getting it right? Wow, even after however long it's been I can still remember. I can't remember shit for essays and exams but I can remember how you take your tea. And Gene, Cosmo?"

"Two please."

"One for me please mate."

"Okay okay," flustered Jack in the kitchen, dropping the kettle in the sink and kneeing the door to. He reappeared almost immediately.

"Oh, and keep an eye out for my housemate, she's kicking around somewhere." He shut the door again.

Right on cue, a short, dark-brown haired girl popped her bemused head around the nearest door, which I guessed led into the front room where the looping bass-heavy music was coming from, its low frequencies causing the surrounding floorboards to reverberate like a big, flat electric razor. She was holding a bottle of Becks and would have been attractive were it not for her eyes being so close together and the presence of a massive dimple right at the bottom of her chin, both of which somehow combined to make her look like a squirrel. Her hazel eyes carried a look of delight, and as they flashed to my own brown eyes there was, I thought, a hint of inebriated, darting lust in them.

"JACK'S FRIEEEENDS!" Her set of lungs were more capybara than squirrel. A faint laugh came from the kitchen. She threw her small hands in the air and, having relinquished her grip on the doorframe, tumbled through the door, bouncing back off the bottom banister. Cam jumped forwards like an angular spring lamb, dropping his duffel bag in the process of steadying her.

"Christ, we've got some catching up to do!" he joked, turning to us. His face was at first upturned in laughter, but it quickly shifted to one of unimpressed vitriol. She looked at him like he had never made sense in his life.

The two parties stared at each other awkwardly for a second or two in the silence.

"Whywon'tyouhaveadrink?" She offered her bottle to me, speaking with an impressive slur on her words for five in the afternoon. Without waiting for a response, she rested her denim-shorted bottom on the second last step of the bare stairs, taking inefficient drunken care to straighten her shirt round her petite waist. "Where'd'ye get them, sweedart?"

She trailed off while she stroked Cosmo's glasses, her head lolling slowly, slowly down past her outstretched arm, which was barely managing to support her small body as it held to the banister. She sank slowly, inevitably, until her arm slipped onto the bare, dusty floor, the dead weight of her body swiftly following like a jack-knifed lorry heading into a pile-up.

Cosmo nonchalantly walked past her into the front room; the rest of us stood over her collapsed form like mourners at a dimly-lit church funeral, with our baggy shorts and sunglasses replacing the usual sombre togs.

Cam turned the top half of her body over and spoke to her, tapping her tawny, hair-covered face. She was completely out of it. I watched with my hands on my hips, accidentally amused as after a short heated debate with Dan he began to carry her up the stairs across his arms.

"Stick her in what looks like a girl's room Cam," suggested Dan with a quizzical, best-guess tone. "There's only one in the house, I think."

"Yep," Cam wheezed back, his skinny arms hardly coping with the load.

With a few snickers we filed into the front room. Cosmo was slouched happily on the sofa nearest the wide, sun-filled bay window. Against the far wall there was a large low-lying wooden table with all sorts of paraphernalia on it. I walked over; covering some of it was a battered copy of the Guardian with all its component pieces: magazines, paper sections, a wall chart depicting the different British mushroom varieties. It was all dog-eared and tea-stained, the circular brown shapes of the mug bottoms interlocking on top of the type like skewed Olympic rings. There were grinders on the table too and the same weed bags I'd seen on the street, and from them my eyes worked up to the top of a giant Turkish shisha pipe, its ornate form dominating the entire room.

The television sat on an old stool in the corner, a stool which looked like it'd been made use of in a painter's workshop or art college judging by the pretty pattern of multicoloured splatters on its legs and seat. The television itself, I noticed, was a tiny square-backed lump which reminded me of the one we had when I was growing up, before we moved up the hill.

"Haha, what is that telly?" Dan barked. "Looks like a piece of shit."

It had been left on and was delivering a fuzzy old spaghetti western.

"I know, it's great!" I shouted back without thinking.

Jack entered balancing a tea tray laden with mugs filled to the brim. He sighed in his calmer, pebblewater voice.

"Cosmo mate—batman mug, Dan—the white one, Cam—red KitKat and Gene—the smaller red one. Right, down in five."

I looked back at the table, which also had on it a deck of cards, two £10 notes trapped under a Zippo lighter, a stack of board game boxes, guitar plectrums scattered across the surface, a pair of boxing gloves, a pair of sunglasses and some socks intertwined, a ball of string and bent-looking scissors, and a large tin containing packets of weed and bags upon bags of unknown white powders. On our arrival, I reflected, there had so far been a paralytic girl, thumping music, and drugs all around. A nervous excitement tingled inside.

Cam bent down and adjusted the volume on the amp next to me and the room seemed to calm. Some noisy passers-by ambled past the front window chatting animatedly.

"OMFG," one girl squealed, "Gatecrasher's gonna be so sick tonight. Can't fucking wait." The group laughed and made noises of agreement as they carried on up the road.

"How very bloody student-y, have you heard anything more Rah in your life?" asked Cam, to a general grunt of agreement. Then he coughed, and added, "Does sound interesting though."

I agreed.

"Don't worry Cam, Jack'll deliver," Dan said.

Cosmo had found the remote and flicked from the old Western film to 'Deal or No Deal'. Cam and Dan cawed a 'here we go' noise.

"Check out that smug twat Edmonds," sneered Dan. "I mean I love the show but, by God, he gets on me tits."

"I know I know, the way he always makes out he knows exactly what's coming next," added Cam.

"And I'm sure it's all a set up. Million Pound Drop—now that's a game show… but that arse Edmonds, Gaaad…"

I'd never really thought badly of Edmonds in my life, but now Dan and Cam mentioned it, there was a kind of pompous, irritating air about him. "And if… IF Rosemary can turn her game around and produce a blue AT THIS STAGE, then that dream she's always had of seeing the Pyramids might, might just be achievable." Rosemary smiled at the camera and then at Noel Edmonds, clasping her hands together like she was praying. "We've been enthralled, I think you've been enthralled," he stumbled, "and we hope, for that reason, you'll be sticking with us after the break—don't go away."

"What a pre-drink eh? A brew and 'Deal'," I said to the group. I looked nervously again at the table. The others chuckled. Rosemary, to her dismay, revealed the £100,000.

"Eh," began Dan standing up, "gents, here's to getting here in one piece."

He came around the room clinking our mugs. "Not as likely as it sounds with that heap of shit outside I know…"

He was cut short by the door swinging open, and in its frame a now fully-dressed Jack stood tall, wearing skinny blue jeans and a purple hoody with 'Hospitality' written across the front. He leaned into the room by hooking his fingers on the door's architrave above.

"Gentlemen, if you'd be so kind as to slip on your shoes, Jack Lawrence is ready to take you on the lash of your lives." In his grey eyes was an almost ominous, wicked playfulness.

"Such a lame line," I said to him.

"Not got much to work with here have I?" he rejoinded. He bounced across the room and ruffled Cam's shaggy hair so hard that his scalp began to move.

"Get off you sallow-cheeked prick," Cam's voice rang irritably. There was a high-pitched "Oooh!" from Dan and Jack. "Bloody juveniles. Plebeians."

"I'm at university, and I don't even know what that means."

There was a general murmur of consent, and we went into the hallway to throw our shoes back on. Jack spotted the bottle of Becks that had been left on the floor. "Bex's been on the piss again. Always at it that girl."

"Tell me about it; she was a bloody handful."

"Where is she now, d'you know?"

"Erm, well she passed out just here," Cam theatrically outlined the spot in which Bex had lain collapsed, "then I lifted her up there and shoved her on somebody's bed. I assume she's still alive, but you know…"

"Meh don't worry about it, she's usually prostrate on somebody's bed."

"Oh aye?' chirped in Cosmo with his pinched brows now raised high. He had been unusually quiet for the last five minutes. Dan grabbed him, roughly massaged his shoulders from behind, and whispered loudly:

"Bit old for you lad."

"Get out. Doesn't make any difference once youre past sixteen, does it?"

"Ooh I dunno, you know these uni girls—they want someone mature, articulate, strong…"

"Everything our Andrew here embodies," I said, veiling the sarcasm.

"Mate don't use that name, I fucking hate it. Come on," he shot back. There was laughter amongst the others, who were now stepping out the door.

"Andrew eh? Not as cool as we claim to be!"

"I had no idea that you even had a real name, I thought your parents just had a death-wish for you."

Cosmo looked at Dan for the next comment.

"Hey, I'm not saying anything."

We shut the door behind us and leapt out into the hazy summer's evening. Everything was new to us, and we were relying completely on Jack's skittish stop-start lead.

He led us as if back towards the main road but instead took us left at the disused public building and past the smashed-in Selly Oak 4x4 shop. We turned sharply under a maroon railway bridge and then up hill. Traffic, motorised and human, dashed everywhere. Then we passed a sign announcing 'Bournville Village', cut into some woodland, and found ourselves walking across a small field.

We stopped at a forgotten, fenced-off piece of waste land at the bottom of the field and looked down. Birmingham stood partially visible below like some vast, pointed mountain range. I jumped on top of an overgrown concrete bunker to gain a better view.

In the foreground a red-brick clock tower dominated. I asked Jack what it was.

"Old Joe," he called from under a broken floodlight, "my timekeeper on the way to uni."

Cosmo joined me on my perch. Behind Old Joe lay the city beyond, giant, square-shouldered hotels and office blocks kneeling in their claustrophobic tightness underneath the white, syringe-like prominence of the BT Tower, staggered walruses in the heat; and in the hills a heaving hum, all the time a heaving hum as though the bass from Jack's amp was somehow still reverberating around the mass of the city. Jack saw the look in my eye as I took in the scene and wandered over with his lanky stride. His gapped smile told that he'd been getting pre-heated for our visit for a while.

"How's it looking from up there Gene m'boy?"

"Not half bad mate," I replied in a kind of awe. "I'm here, I'm finally here."

Cosmo span around. "Not half bad?" he squeaked, incredulous, "forget Sixth Form man—fuck it. When do we get to move here? Look at this!"

Jack made an odd, excited noise pitched between a dolphin's call and a badly oiled door and grabbed Cos by the ankles.

"Yes Cos, yes! My neighbourhood. This is it. This is where you wanna be. This is where it's all happening."

Cosmo hopped off the bunker, grabbed Jack's shoulder, pulled him down to his height, and moved his mouth close to his ear whispering clumsily the words, "Jack, are we er…do we get to do some illegals tonight?

"…I've heard stuff," Cosmo was yapping now, "about pills and powders—stuff that makes you feel just…I dunno…good."

Cam's and Dan's interest seemed to match Cosmo's all-too-obvious enthusiasm, and I noticed with some self-comfort that they seemed less clued-up than I'd guessed. I watched the circle of them.

"MDMA is my main drug—it's what I sell and what I tend to get mashed on," said Jack, enjoying the curious faces around him.

"So, what does it actually do?" Cam asked. He then pulled a pre-rolled spliff out of a battered Hendrix tin and lit it.

"Weeell, it's hard to describe… it just opens you right up, y'know? Really gets you talking and experiencing things." Cam and Cosmo answered with an "mmm," and Dan stood with his arms folded. "It has you going from one person to another just saying the right thing, being THE man, y'know? And then when you feel like half the night's gone you'll go back to find one of your friends—like, Cosmo," he grabbed Cosmo by the shoulder loosely and Cosmo, strangely I thought, looked back at him and copied the gesture. "If you imagine just coming back to Gene after what feels like aaages, and hugging him and both realising at the same time that each other is the best human in the world EVER, then both realising it's only, say, twelve o'clock and you then spend the whole of the night just doing…"—he fished desperately for the right word, couldn't find it and gave up—"perfection. Just perfect things like that."

Jack had looked up to me by now. I felt a little odd wave of contentment wash not through but almost in and then past me once he'd finished speaking, and I hopped down from the bunker.

"Fancy some bifta?" asked Cam, and I took it from him and dragged deeply.

We tramped down towards the gate at the bottom of the field, Jack waxing about the experience. We were enraptured. He had worked himself up into a bundle of energy; and slowly, everybody seemed to build the same energy inside them. Jack cut his narrative short and snorted as though he knew something so simple that the only way he could communicate it was through laughter. Everybody wore a massive grin on their face and even as I tried I couldn't wipe mine away.

Then without any warning Cam howled and he and Jack, both huge, thin figures, threw one arm around the other's shoulders and seemed to lose it completely. As

I focused on them and felt a dislocating confusion I also felt a growing, swoopy, nervous sickness hit my stomach.

I looked at Cosmo and suddenly needed reassurance. I felt a flash of the brotherhood I'd felt so strongly in Bridlington, as if this perfect drug had somehow hit me. I had this feeling, as we trod quickly, irresistibly down the hill to God knows where, of ecstasy. Then I realised.

"Jack," I blurted, partly in amazement at his audacity, partly in mild anger and partly in sheer thrill, "Jack, I know what you've fucking gone and done. That tea, that tea... did you? You put it in the fucking tea!"

As the truth of this dawned on me, Dan, and Cosmo the tall, maniacal figure burst out into loud, ecstatic chuckles and shouted "Yes boys, yes!" throwing his clenched hands into the air. We all laughed in raw disbelief. Cam slapped me on the back, his face screwed up in raptures of hysterics. Cosmo was bent double, first losing his stupid but brilliant day-glow glasses then retrieving them from between his feet, nearly falling arse-over-tit in the process. Jack looked like a victorious lunatic with his hands now on his hips and his sallow, devilish face with its wide-toothed grin looking over us in sweet delight. Cosmo raced over to him with his typical energy and bombast, but this time it seemed intensified, out of proportion but right on. He shook him by the hand. His glasses were off again and now I looked on his face I saw it was a complete picture. It was the first time I'd seen his eyes all day, and they glowed golden orange in the sun. These warm thoughts kept hitting me.

"Jack, Jack, please tell me we're off to a party," said Cosmo, "because I feel high." His voice rose like a swallow's call on the last word.

"That," began Jack, "is exactly where we're going."

Very soon we were deep in Bournville suburbia, walking five abreast along the sun-scorched road. I gazed wide-eyed at our surroundings.

"Hey man," Cosmo called, "you look like a fucking owl."

"You too! Seriously, try squinting." He did and I laughed.

"Go on, you too." I did and then inspected them in the wing-mirror of a green Jag. They'd got smaller, but I could still see the barely restrained ripples of excitement which ran through them.

"I can't, I can't carry on doing this."

He finished off his cigarette and sent it spinning to the foot of a little purple-leaved sycamore in the vast garden across the path.

"Give us a cig Cos," I said feverishly.

The flame from his Zippo seemed to be perfectly defined in the fading light of the late afternoon, and I could feel its comforting warmth on my eyeballs. I took a deep pull on my cigarette. Fuck, it felt good.

And now a pulsating bass beat seemed to be shaking the shimmering pieces of loose gravel on the pavement. We strode—no, we bounced—down there double-pace: five kangaroos bouncing along in the Brummie dusk. And there it suddenly was, the party house. Mock-Tudor roof dormers jutted upwards like turrets on both sides of a central alleyway leading inside. The whole building had been opened up for the arrivals, two houses converted into one for the night. A beautiful green creeper wrapped its limbs like dried clay around both bay windows; and as I gazed at these weaving arms, a black Volkswagen van pulled up. A group of guys started shifting musical equipment and crates of Red Stripe into an open garage.

"A second rig!" whooped Jack. "Mischa told me there was definitely one in 205's front room: this one must be for 206."

"What…" Cosmo began, awestruck. "I thought you lot lived off beans and Basics Cider?"

"Cos, look at the place. Just look at the fucking place! Mischa's fucking loaded. Parents bought the pair of houses and she's been here since first year."

As we approached the archway Cam turned to me.

"Is that a feckin' bouncer? No, two bouncers. What? Have you ever seen this, man?" Cam's tone had changed from its usual distaste; there was a silvery-topped edge to his tongue, and the way he added 'man' at the end… God, it felt like we'd been friends since the maternity ward.

"Nah, what the hell?"

Two bouncers, one about 5' 10" and the other well over 6' 6", were commanding the way. The passage beyond them gushed with sound, sound owning a weird organised vigour; and through that passage was a new world, this previously inaccessible Mecca, this escape from reality. My nervous system gorged on the thud of the beat and the breeze all around and cast off the shackles of worry I'd worn for far too long. At that moment I saw everyone around me feel their knowledge of the real world slip away, us stopping short of the bouncers and grinning at their strangely regimented vibe as though they were characters on a page, virtually immaterial. Jack stepped up.

"We're friends of Mischa's, mate," he said calmly and authoritatively to the tallest one, who Jack was more on the vertical level with—a rarity. The bouncer flicked through several pages of a checklist attached to a clipboard and his hulking figure seemed to pop back into reality. Cosmo caught me with his ice-blue eyes excitedly. 'Play it cool' I was reminding myself like a mantra. I frowned, trying to narrow my eyes. "Mischa" Jack repeated.

The bouncers parted. We walked through the arch and into a central yard that separated the two houses, Jack's tall frame leading the pack.

"Now you lot have come up early, so…"

"What do you mean—that you haven't Jack?"

"Oh no, no definitely not. I had to see this with sober eyes," he grinned. "The Knaresborough boys on MD! No my friends, that's way too good to miss. Listen, like I was saying, when we go out we tend not to drop until like twelve, so you need more to keep you going all night 'cause it's gonna be a long one."

The inner yard was circled with seats made from anything Mischa had got her hands on—tree stumps, hay bales and old TVs. The walls of the yard, hung here and there with picture frames and long, coloured bits of material which had been trapped in the windows above, looked like they were quietly waiting to watch the night unfold from within their clutch.

Jack carried on through a door and into one of the kitchens.

"Fuck, this is like a palace," Dan gawped. His eyes seemed to drink it in. They were wide orbs of suggestibility underneath his strong brow.

Every work surface of the kitchen was glossy black marble and the ceiling extended some sixteen or so foot into the air. In the middle was a centre-console which alone would have filled the front room I had left behind in Knaresborough. Me and Dan stared dumbly as Jack began talking with the few people who'd also arrived early, speaking with an energy that made me wonder... but then his eyes looked relatively normal compared to the other guys', without unbridled wonder. What was it about the eyes?

"Ah, where's Khan got to?"

"He was getting a taxi from Bullring last time I text him, shouldn't be long."

"He'll be carrying yeah?"

"Yeah, course," laughed the big, blond Rah that Jack was speaking with, "when doesn't Khan carry?"

"Fair point," laughed Jack. He opened the can of Heineken that had been offered to him.

"Boys?" intoned the blond Rah deeply. We each accepted a can and as the pressure was released in unison from their tops a glorious tingle ran through me.

A mixture of male and female students dressed in checked shirts or tight skirts were stood in a crescent eyeing us newcomers with interest.

"So Jack, come on," started a tall, kind of gawky grey-eyed girl whose skin looked like it hadn't recovered from major secondary-school acne—an appearance that jarred with her low, sexy voice. She swept her hair off her cheeks. "Is this the famous crew from back home?"

Jack jumped with that steam-train energy. "Oh God, yeah, sorry! Completely forgot about this lot,"—shouting above the music while clapping Cam on the back like he was a horse—"Right then," he rubbed his hands, "guys, this is Mischa, who's on my course—great girl as long as you can resist her vixen-like charms," (even through the rushing waves of soothing energy I couldn't help but think a bit less of Jack's estimation of women as he said this), "Douglas," punching the big blond lad on the chest lightly. He stood at about 6' 2", with a fleshy, broad build and spoke, I thought, like Daddy had paid for his Harrow creche sessions with a gold American Express card. His hair was white blond, and his Neanderthal brow hid large, watery eyes giving him the unseeing, greedy look of a prehistoric reptile. I clocked this while attempting without success to replicate the pressure he was exerting upon my right hand.

"Hey," we all said in turn to him with dead indifference. The rest of the semicircle were girls, and as I looked at them glimpses of our success in Bridlington drew close around me, filling me with confidence. Two of the girls were blonde, their hair done-up with what must have taken hours of attention in front of the mirror—they were neat, as the lads would've reckoned back at school. The other was a tall brunette who, while not as immediately stunning as the two blonde girls, carried an unknown, strong attractiveness that washed the efforts of the lasses next to her down the sink.

"Hey. Joanna, or Jo if you like." She smiled, and it felt like she was looking directly into me. My God, what was it about her? The look on her brows, the shape of her shoulders? I felt ready to love, not just like but love everything she said and did. That intelligent, half-curled smile, that unknown quality, both whispered to me she was a girl who wouldn't take any shit in the chase I was about to give.

Jo, I repeated internally, conscious not to lose the name. I loved it. That was the word subconsciously flowing through me, love popping out of everywhere and everything.

"Jo," I repeated, this time out loud. "Hey. I'm Gene, as in Simmons, if that helps you remember. A bit less make-up, but…" A warm, amused noise; I was back in there before it could stop—"Incredible place Mischa! We all thought uni houses were in the slums, but this is something else, it really is." She laughed a 'thank you', before beef-arsed Douglas shot back in.

"Yeah, truly sick place Misch, we've all been saying it since you moved in. Sorry, where are you guys from?"

"Knaresborough in Yorkshire, same place as Jack—that's why we're here," Dan pretended to laugh.

"Oh yah, sorry dude! Mind not working," he laughed with nervous loudness, gesturing to his head then sweeping his blond fringe sideways. "Yeah could I, uh, borrow that boddle-opener man, cheers." His eyes flicked downwards.

"So Jo," I couldn't stop repeating her name, "Could we, ah, put our beers in that vast fridge of yours?" There was a connection, I felt it rushing in; she smiled, took the beers, put them in the fridge and said something about her not really living there. As I listened to her silky voice I homed in on the beat from the invisible speakers; I realised I could use that rhythm tapping up through my toes and skywards up my leg to keep her gassing; I said something of an apology, and she gave this "tsk!" with a flash of her eyes and a gorgeous smile and I melted, my heart hammering like a hummingbird's.

"We're gonna go and chill upstairs until the party arrives guys, if you wanna come?" Mischa was hanging her thin frame from the cream-coloured bottom banister of a long flight of stairs. She stared and chewed on something; we made our way towards her. Looking upwards, I noticed a chandelier with teardrop-shaped glass, bluer even than Cosmo's eyes, which were staring upwards too. Cam trotted up from behind dangling beers in front of us, three in one hand and two in the other.

"Just thought," he said happily as he passed them around one by one, "that we could do with a few more." I looked up at him: our eyes locked. And he gave a broad smile like he really knew me. It was the same type of connection that Cos'd fired across riding to Bridlington; I saw a flash of the cornfields once more.

My feet were on autopilot. I was hovering over soft strips of silk.

My mind's eye drifted back to one hot afternoon spent at a river in the South of France with the family. A fifty-foot high stone bridge plunged itself at either end into sheer faces of rock. I looked up at the bridge, looked at the locals screaming in French and fearlessly dashing their semi-naked bodies off the bridge's midpoint, cascading down into a deep patch of water and I was terrified. But shit, I wished I could do it. I wished I had the courage. Dad, with his hairy chest and brown skin had been sat at my mother's back slapping suncream onto her, pushing his sunglasses back from the end of his nose every once in a while. He looked up at them and then at my excited face and said, "Not a chance, son. I'm not taking my boy home in a coffin." Then I remembered, recalling his face again: that man is not your father. You shouldn't have listened to him. You should have done it.

I'd been lost for so long in the pool of my memories that I had forgotten what we were doing, and when I snapped back I wondered why I was stood over Cosmo, who was sat on the edge of an impressive, padded bed with a huge ornate steel headboard.

"Go on mate, you gonna sit down?" he asked.

"Ey, how ya doing?" was the only response I could think of.

"Yeah mate how's it going?"

"Feeling good?" asked Cam and Jack in turn, nudging me from either side as they went to sit down too.

"Yeah good, good," I said automatically, still slightly trapped in my daydream. "Feeling very good indeed. Jack…" I was grinning and shaking my head slowly, remembering the revelation on the hill and feeling the full, unbridled and fantastic effects of it now. All of our group laughed and huddled in, repeating "Jaaack…" in mock sternness, each clutching at their beer cans. The momentary upsurge of hatred I'd felt for my 'Dad' had dissipated, dissolved by this thing, this new mode of being, which was coursing around my body and in and around everyone. Mischa and her friends fumbled around on the floor gathering some plush beanbags to form a circle, Douglas giving a big masculine sigh as he plunged into one and looked around the room, nodding his head to the house soundtrack coming from Mischa's Mac. One of the blonde girls, whose legs I noticed were long, smooth, brown perfection, went over and crouched by the Mac to play dj. Jo took the furthest beanbag from me, but I knew it wasn't a refusal, knew not to let my mind get too far ahead. I just licked my lips again and chomped from right to left on my teeth, and the old foot tap was back, unstoppable.

The remaining blonde girl asked in a sweet, summery tone what our names were again; after my answer, I asked for one of the giant cushions in the pile next to her.

"Oh, could you make that two?" added Cosmo. The others then made noises for one as well. They were big and soft and great for back supports, so we each laid backwards on them, still upright enough to talk. The girl who'd passed us the cushions sank back down and blew her hair from underneath, sending it shimmering across her forehead.

Mischa's room smelt of vanilla, a scent which fit perfectly with her soft white bedding and cream sheepskin rug. Underneath us lay varnished floorboards the colour of molasses. The walls around us were covered in posters for nights spanning the country, from Bristol to Sheffield to Newcastle. The long sash windows had cream curtains semi-drawn over them; beyond, dusk was setting in.

"So how was the drive down boys?" Mischa asked, racking up lines of something.

"Yeah, not too shabby at all, I pretty much did all the work and this prick," Dan prodded at Cam who I saw was laying back on his cushion staring at the ceiling, "just got high basically. The kids here," he pounced over onto me and Cosmo, "just fucking yip-yapped nonstop and talked shit the whole way down. Took forever too in my shitty little motor. '93 Fiesta, pride and joy I suppose, but she don't run like she used to haha, oh no—had to make a pit-stop at Ashby services like, just to cool the engine down and top up the radiator…" Dan trailed off like he'd realised he'd said too much and he took a slurp on his beer. I smiled thinking of how the drug was taking him away on his own little thought train. He was licking his lips every few seconds and chewing with machine-like concentration on some gum.

I decided to try and save him with a comment on Mischa's magpie-like poster collection. She laughed and proudly started taking us through each night—"…Oh yeah, swimming in the dock at Bristol at 6am, M-Kat mishaps in Manchester…"

"So long's you got a good amount of weed at the end of a night, anything goes," put in Jack. The group continued to talk as I leant over Cam to see what was up with him. He was staring up at his free hand, completely awestruck, lost—the very definition of the word—in his own universe. I saw that his already dark eyes had become wide black mires rimmed with creamy narrow bands, just pools of distant knowledge opening up as if for the first time and taking in more than just wavelengths and bits of broken colour, more than just the shards of what was in front of him, and that, more than chewing on his teeth like I was, he looked as if he was gasping for air, as a fish in the mud of a dried-up lake. I tugged at the shoulder of Jack's purple hoody and worriedly whispered,

"Jack man, what's happening to Cam? Look at him!"

"Oh he's fine," responded Jack in a voice that you'd give to a pet dog, rubbing Cam's belly. "He'll be fiiine," he carried on, "you say he's been battered since the drive? Yeah, powerful combination that, no wonder it's hitting him harder than the rest of ya's."

Jo yakked about uni work with one of her friends and I looked around at the room. It'd become a part of me; not in a psychedelic sense but in the sense that the floors, the rugs, the pictures, the tables, the pillows, the sounds, the lights, the air, all were behind me, pushing me up, ever present as part of everything I did and felt; and the people, leading me to a human plane, a plane that stretched for miles as I could see it, the people conversing with precision and rapidity and it. However long I sat there doing my thing and amusing Cam and trying to imagine what plane he was on I don't know, but I realised that I had finished what I needed to say in that womb of curtains, drapes and rugs. I heard voices outside and felt instead like it was time for me to wander off right into the party.

So I said my goodbyes to the circle and left alone, which I knew would somehow seem strange to those around but which felt perfectly normal and natural to me; yes, it was perfectly normal and natural that Gene Bradley should want to shake these legs out over the carpets and floorboards of the entire vast house in and among all the people who, above all, wanted to talk.

Talk!

I flew through the door, closing it behind me with a 'click!' that signalled yet another new beginning. I existed through this landing leading to the staircase where there was a throng whooping and roaring in the vacuum.

I rounded into a scene of banisters, Red Stripe cans and beautiful apes all walking upright; and there were so many, I lifted off another foot, a peroxide-blond Londoner with a clown-painted face cried out, "Has anybody got a nose like me? No-one has a nose like me!" At the giant Ming vase on the landing one lad in braces, beard wrapped around his neck, and another with a mandolin slug around his back were taking it in turns to snort lines and shout "To the regiment!" with each hit. Indecipherable conversation rang around me mixing with the bass and beat, where the bass and beat were coming from I didn't know; I squeezed past one couple chatting and then felt a clap of thin hand on my back. It was Cam.

"Mate, I had to come and join you!"

"Yeah you did!' Without thinking I grabbed at his hand on my back and squeezed it like trying to wring a towel dry. "Look at this, when did they all arrive?!"

He nodded. "Want to go and see what's going on in here?" He pointed through the nearest door to a melee of bodies, bottles and animated faces, whose voices ebbed and flowed like the side-flows and currents of a dammed river, the air lyrical with its slosh and spatter, its ride and gush.

The half-circle of people dangling off the side of the bed looked up at us standing near the door and one girl called, "Hey! Come over! Who are you? Where are you from? You at Aston?" She shuffled aside as Cam and I recounted our pieces—our origins— with childlike zeal. We told of the trip down, of Jack's house; I mentioned something about gap-yearing at a Leeds newspaper in order to gain some experience on placement, or some lie like that, and Cam, cottoning on straight away and looking old enough to pull it off, said he was a fashion photographer who had been called back early from a shoot in Madrid for the birth of his child. It was all games—harmless, hilarious—and the group, bohemian, beaded and rapt, lapped it all up. Each smile, each person who engaged with my avatar was fascinated and became trapped not in a web but in a pool I was constantly creating, correcting, warming and treating with new facts and revelations.

I sat tall, kneeling on my shins, demonstrating everything with my zooming hands. Cam bounced off me, picking up the thread every time I was about to drop it, rushing in there with just the right amount of haste, forcing laughter out of the five or six people sat around like juice out of a halved lemon.

In the middle of one of our short rests, where one of the others would hold the floor with matching energy about their lives to date, I heard a big roar from the crowded guys near the laptop as a new track came on—"Rusko!"—and people started to move slowly and methodically to the dark beat. It coursed its way through my body and before I knew it me and Cam, both still on our knees, were dancing at the guy in glasses who was talking to us. Damn, what was his name?

He fished in the breast-pocket of his checked cotton shirt and pulled out two bags—one containing weed and the other half-filled with white powder.

"What's that?" I asked clumsily. Luca! That was his name. I knew it was something unusual. Luca looked up and smiled as the small dark girl next to him— his girlfriend, I guessed— picked the bags from his hand. He replied in a curious voice.

"That's MD guys. You've taken some?"

"I think so." I explained the tea situation on the hill. Luca fell about laughing as the girl did something strange with a few rizla and the MD.

"That's fucking hilarious," he gasped, "so you've basically been drugged? Priceless! Enjoying it? You guys seem so, I dunno, up for it!"

"Really?" said Cam. "That's good! Yes yes that's good, we like it don't we Gene? Already man, already we're just like, buddies, we kinda seem to have just hit it off, don't you agree?" he gushed looking at me. "I mean, don't get me wrong, the other guys—there's more of us in some room round the corner—the other guys—Dan (beating his chest), respect to that man, he's top, he's just sensational—always be top mates—the rest of 'em too, what a bunch! We've all come into this together, bombed down the M1, said fuck it and come down—they're all top! Just, wow, and yeah, me and Gene, What a combo! Just in a day, just in a day…"

Suddenly Luca was offering up a palm, and in that palm were two small wrapped-up packets.

"Seeing as you're new to the game *ragazzi*, here's a bomb each." I took one of the packets from his palm and eyed it.

"You just swallow them?" He nodded. "What do we owe you man?"

"*Nonulla*, boys." He continued to smile.

This high was going to be extended to a distant future I thought, holding that little ball twisted at the top in between my thumb and middle finger.

"Although I don't suppose you got any smokes?"

We washed down the bombs, which stuck to the back of the throat, and then me, Cam, Luca and his girlfriend lazily removed ourselves from the room and passed through the crowded hallways out into the central yard.

I felt mashed by now. Giant white diamond-shapes and endless series of fairy lights danced on the yard's walls in a shimmer, casting shadows behind the figures which stood and sat around. There was a cabal of young blokes to our left, all huddled and sat like American Indians on their 'hams'— I'd read that somewhere— "And what was the crowd like Ste?" "Insane—the whole room went ballistic. I was only getting paid fifty notes and I was worried about my equipment. But it was just insane."

Was that a flash of purple? It was! It was Jack in his big grapey jumper, squatted down there with them. He looked up at us in a haze of smoke and revealed his big gappy grin again.

I had a cigarette with the guys and went to get a drink of water.

I agreed to meet the others in the big front room-cum-dance floor which I could see in the adjoining house. Fuck, I was thirsty. I found a cup and, seeing that the sink was surrounded, went to the nearest bathroom.

I gulped down two cupfuls, felt the burning need for a piss, and unbuttoned my jeans. Then I jumped, and even stifled a cry. What had happened?! My cock! It'd almost retreated inside me, like a frightened tortoise. Fuck! What if I was to get lucky with Jo? I was grateful that it still delivered a slash. I washed my hands and looked into the mirror on the cream cabinet above the marble sink. Then I looked at my distorted reflection in the round brass handles of the cabinet.

"Your eyes shine like brass, sweetheart," said Mum on the Isle of Wight, 1999. Thoughts and images whirled suddenly in the brass like a thick mist. The eclipse had just been and gone. We couldn't see it because we didn't have the glasses, so we sat in a café on the Isle's north tip at Cowes, and I peeked, trying not to let my mum see because she said it would damage my eyes. And it did hurt, but I had to see. Even as a child I knew the gravity of the occasion, knew that history was being made. I saw the bright disc covered by the dark one, burning away at its peripheries. Afterwards the sun came back out and my eyes looked like dark brass.

I looked at them now. Brown but with yellow flecks, yellow rimming the iris, eclipsed by the chocolate centre. I visualised the golds and browns of an eagle taking flight, talons hidden from the ground, kept close to the body. The bird soared to its eyrie behind the figure of the wolf in Cam's sweatshirt. The world around me closed off, and I was in the eyrie.

I put my water down. I saw the picture of Dad—Darren Bradley, the man at my old home—above the telly. He had those same eyes—but how? Yellow and brown, brass handles, golden eagles, eclipses—they were almost identical. I had mum's nose and lips yes, everyone said so. But the eyes, how could they be so close, almost-matching, when I knew he was the false father?

I wondered and wondered and lent in far, so far, almost at the glass, seized in the pools of my own eyes, sucked in, drawn magnetically to the field of the parallel pools, swirling, closer, yellows and browns, closer… then a deafening crash made me snap my head back in shock.

Two people, male and female, burst through the door—which I'd forgotten to lock—and tippled over the rim right into the bath, taking the shower curtain with them as it pinged off its rails. I leapt out of the bathroom, still dazed, and bounded off for the dance floor. Then the second wave hit me.

Chapter Six

It was unclear how exactly we made it back to Jack's humble little house. There was a chatter of taxi's followed by a long, optimistic walk with Cosmo down a semi-lit road bordered by small corner-shops with Indian-style fronts in search of some cigarettes, down which we held the most intense, whispered discussion about the state of life in the city and our roles in the up-and-coming world. Then we went back to the spot with the bunker and caught a glimpse of the stars in all their limited ethereal city-glory. But make it we did, and before I knew it we were all sat cross-legged chattering like birds in a bush as Cam picked out the music for the scene with his eyes cross-haired on Jack's laptop screen, cool vibrations slipping out of the speakers which had kicked out the music we'd heard on our entry to the house the afternoon before—

—*The afternoon before?* It felt eternally longer ago; already the first creeping suggestions of dawn were weaving their way into the fabric of the curtains, but this made the scene all the more exhilarating, because here we were all cocooned in the warm bowels of Jack's, music still igniting the senses and tapping out a rhythm for all the disciples to latch on to. There were the boys—Cosmo, Jack, Cam, and Dan—all flapping about in intensified conversation and shuffling on their cushions whilst rolling joints and digging about for weed paraphernalia, Jack searching through magazine articles to illustrate some point or another. Then there were others—Jack's remaining housemates, Kerry and John, who we'd met at the party; I had vague recollections of dancing feverishly with them in the front room there. Mischa and Jo had stayed, I remembered that; abject heartache in the kitchen as the two revealed that they couldn't come to the afterparty, the beleaguered acceptance and then the rush of ecstasy as Cosmo swept me up and we strode to the dance room lost in the energy of one another. And there were, unexpectedly, the two blonde girls who at the start of the party had sat in the circle in Mischa's room, now sitting with each other like before as they observed the quick chatter of the lads and occasionally spoke up in their sweet honeyed voices. Cosmo, I thought, was trying to get in with one of them—Rachel. I was wishing him all the luck my heart could hold; she looked incredible right at that moment, indie head-band and golden blonde hair seemingly melting into her brown shoulders. She held one of the bottles of Becks that Dan had brought through from Jack's fridge. He handed one to me laughing, thick eyebrows raised.

"That was unbelievable Gene, that party. Worth the drive?" he asked in a high-pitched voice, scrunching up his chin and knowing the answer I would give.

"Not half, not half Dan man. Best decision I've ever made. Ta for the beer."

"No problem mucker. You lighting up?"

"I was actually gonna wait while they rolled one, know what I mean?"

I heard Jack chuckle 'not long now' as Cosmo made Rachel gurgle with laughter after a gulp of beer. "So, any luck with the ladieees tonight?" Dan poked me in the ribs and repeated "eh, eh?," nearly making me drop my beer. I swivelled round to him as he crossed his legs and gave an involved, detailed and glossy-eyed explanation of Jo, the girls in the second room and then those in the yard outside, but each time I mentioned the others I couldn't help winding up back at Jo.

"…a benchmark, y'know?" I found myself finishing. Dan's dark face twisted with amusement.

"Ahhh," he said long and loud with a knowing look in his eyes. "I had no idea you were cracking onto her that bad. At least, you didn't let on."

"It was kind of… odd y'know? When we were in that circle, she started talking away with her mates and it was like… with Cam on the bed, and all of us feeling this," I grabbed my head at the sides and then pulled my hands away and upwards, "it was like… maybe I have a feeling that I'll see her again. Almost like it would have been wrong for me to try anything in this state."

"You mean it wouldn't have meant anything?" His head was nodding like a Churchill dog.

"Perhaps, yeah. That's it actually. Like it would somehow have ruined it, tainted the whole thing, you know?"

"Yeah yeah, well maybe you're right Gene. We could see her again. Now let me tell you about this leggy redhead, my woooord…" and off Dan galloped into a delineation of the girl he met on the dance floor, his hands flashing wildly.

"I take it you got somewhere with her?"

"Ah well, this is where it gets interesting!" He laughed for a few seconds and took a big swig on his beer. "You know how packed the stairs were? Well, we fought through all that and she was up for it, I mean, really up for it. I dunno if she was on MD too but anyway, up on like the sixth flight or summat daft like that, you know how big that bloody house was, there was this weird cupboard, and…"

"Ha! Good work!"

He basked in my all-hail-Dan routine, guzzling on his beer and fist pumping in hilarious mock-celebration which, I'm sure he would've conceded, was just a little bit serious. His unshaven face creased up with delight as I laughed and pounded him on the back. "I hope you're not having me on."

"No no, honest to God."

Just as he said that, Cosmo clasped me on the shoulder and proffered a smouldering J. After a few tokes I was lying back, mesmerised by the world. I closed my eyes and little scenes unfolded behind my retinas—vast chasms of space opened out like ice tunnels into entire hollow glaciers. I would zoom in on one from above and observe sketches of faceless people boarding escalators and passing over into other glaciers that revolved off the last as though they were separate universes.

These vivid imaginings flowed on and on, a constant gust of snow, while the voices of the others mingled with dub in the background, becoming stronger, raining down until I felt Cosmo lie down next to me with his back turned. I peeked an eye open and saw only his Aztec t-shirt and slim shoulders; I craned upwards with a strain from my stomach and looked over him to see Rachel's tanned face locked to his.

With slightly muddy eyes I sat up fully.

"How are you buddy?" Jack had his arm around the other girl. I smiled back at him.

"Good. Good man. I'm thinking of bed now, though."

"Yeah, we were thinking of leaving them to it as well." I realised that Cam, Dan and Jack's two housemates had left the room. Jack had a face of total contentment, charcoal hair and brows sleeping peacefully on it.

I lumbered to the corner of the room where I'd left my sleeping bag among those of the others.

"Along the landing and straight in front of you pal."

I thanked him and said my weary good-byes, grinning for a second as I saw Cosmo lying on the floor repeating the success of Brid. How long ago that felt, like an age. I shuffled off upstairs and fell into the most vivid dreamscape I'd ever experienced.

The morning, or afternoon as it was, brought with it sausages, eggs and brews. We gathered in the kitchen, standing with our plates in hand, radio on, talking and enjoying the breeze through the wide-open windows. Cosmo was telling us all about his dad's music collection, saying how his vinyl took up too much space in the shed where he went to draw when it was warm. I looked to the blue sky blanketing the West Midlands conurbation, with its wisps of white far in the distance, and heard the hum of the city mixed with the bumbling music of insects and birds. A nest of birds somewhere above, probably a family of house martins, had left an entire section of the window covered opaquely in their droppings. I chewed on my sausage, savoured the breeze and recalled lining up at primary school between the red-brick wall and green iron fencing near a sloping, sleepy Knaresborough street, getting my name read out and looking up at the round, dam-like nests that the martins had assembled against the walls underneath the overhang of the roof. One day Nana told me all about those house martins, how clever they were that they picked up mud and dumped it in layers until the nest looked almost like a beehive.

The door to the kitchen squeaked open. Jack plonked his plate down on the table and started towards the small figure entering.

"Becky Becky, where've you been ya little scamp! What's wrong with you eh?"

"I know, I know!" the brown-haired girl from yesterday, who was now enveloped in the lanky arms of Jack, replied sheepishly. She looked embarrassed but smiled all the same as she came into the kitchen towards the line of boys in front of her, leaning onto the worktop with her hand. "I just want to say that I am so, so sorry for the state I was in yesterday afternoon," she addressed the group.

"It was impressive," Cosmo's deep voice said simply. "I just don't understand how you could have been that arseholed that early. Top marks, like." All Becky could do was laugh and say in her small, distinctly Brummie accent, "sorry, sorry. And who was it that took me upstairs?" There was a surge of voices as Cam raised his Batman mug in the air and smiled.

"You were quite light, don't worry."

"Bloody hero this kid," said Dan passionately as he slung his arm around Cam's neck. "Heart of gold that lad."

"Oh thankyow, really, thankyow."

"Come here Becky, I'll pour you a brew," said Cam warmly.

"A what? Oh, a cuppa, yeah that'd be lovely."

"A brew for Becky," Dan re-asserted, filling up the electric kettle and handing it to Cam. The boys were putting on their best behaviour now that there was a female in the room.

"Oh ta, you boys are good to me aren't they Jack?"

"Yeah. Dunno why, you mess. You missed an absolute belter."

"It wasn't so bad round at Claire's—that's where I went after I woke up! I feel alright this morning."

"It's afternoon y'know. We've got a proper excuse," Jack joked batting her long, straight hair. The dazzling chestnut of some individual strands caught the light and blinded me for a second.

"Oh, it was one of them was it? Well, you know I wouldn't have bothered." Her tone had changed. "You lads all took part as well I suppose?"

"Erm yeah, last night was the first time actually," Cosmo replied.

"Jack!" she exclaimed, turning to him and trying to contain her disapproval of the man in front of his friends. "It's bad enough you doing it, but getting your friends to as well?"

Immediately Jack shot back, "We've been through this time and again, Becky, I'm not talking about it. You can tell Kerry and John off too in a bit; they're upstairs doing the usual business, managing worldwide drug rings from their Hushmail accounts and all that." There was a breathy grimness in his voice that I'd never heard before; the room felt like it had darkened.

"Okay whatever."

I shifted uneasily, forked the toast and egg on my plate, and eyed the two of them. The last thing I needed was a potential powder keg. The kettle clicked off.

"Do you have normal?" Cam asked diplomatically.

"Yeah, yeah thanks." She seemed to have snapped out of a reverie and appeared dull, blustery and cold like an autumn day. "Milk and one sugar please. What's your name?"

Cam explained how the 'ph' in his first name, Stephen, was the biggest embarrassment his parents had ever bestowed upon him and how he'd managed over the years to convince those around him just to shorten his surname. In this way he was amusingly similar to Cosmo I thought, almost hiding behind an extra identity. But that suited Cam well. I remembered his expression on the stairs of

Mischa's house, and even now when the effects of the drug had worn off, I felt an extra surge of affection, a deeper understanding of this individual, this man who for a second on the stairs had opened a little of his soul up to me through those owl-like eyes… It felt a little like the beat was still with me. I chewed down the last of my egg, savouring the first meal I'd had in about 18 hours.

After a brew, we found Jack's half-pumped football and walked down towards Bristol Road to have a kickabout in the Bournbrook & Selly Oak Social Club car park. It was long-abandoned, the signage around the square, squat building reminiscent of the seventies-style boards and shop-fronts we'd seen in Bridlington. Between the boughs of one of the trees which bordered the road, a doctored 'To Let' sign had an 'i' added unsubtly to it; across the road a pensioner was suspiciously twitching at her net-curtains and eyeing us with a grim scowl. It was another hot day; I'd dressed in a bog-standard white t-shirt, Cosmo a green wifebeater, and the others in their usual togs except Jack, who wore a different hoody this time.

If I'd wanted to fully paint everyone's character there and then I would simply have described their kick-ups with the sagging ball: I tried, met some success, and quickly failed with the left leg; Dan was the master of control, trying not to show off; Jack flailed a foot in the wrong direction, toppled over and then hooted like he meant it; Cam stopped the ball dead, letting it bounce accurately onto his planted foot to then roll off (until we stopped passing to him); and Cosmo, well, he let it smack his chest, pop awkwardly off his knee, and then belt it into the shutters of the Club hollering 'Gooal-Lazio!'

The day brought a re-arrangement of sleeping quarters. Me and Cosmo were put in the room I'd ascended to in a warm haze the night before, and it was only now I remembered Cosmo's apparent success.

"So what happened there then, player?"

He was pulverising a vast dust-filled cushion out of the window. "Erm," he began, laughing with an inflection of frustration, "Well, that didn't actually happen my man."

"Ahh, gutted. How come? What did you do to put her off? I know what you're like. Jumping on 'em before the kettle's boiled."

"Nooo, it wasn't that—she was on the rag."

"Oh."

"Yeah." We rustled about with the cushions on the floor, arranging them into two small beds. The cream-walled room was hardly more than a cupboard, but it was going to be home for the foreseeable. "So fucking frustrating."

"She was fit too," I added. "I mean, banging."

"Don't rub it in." Cosmo lifted up his sleeping bag with a shake. "We stayed downstairs, just spooned on the sofa, and when I woke up she'd fucked off."

"As had her mate," said Jack entering the room with more cushions. One was huge and square and we both grabbed for it like two fledglings competing for food. He won.

"Blonde beauties never stick around eh?" said Cosmo ruefully.

"All too true," replied Jack, "at least I haven't been able to hold one down for long here. Although it's worth being single even with the pitfalls. I can't imagine what it'd have been like if I'd stuck with Caroline, her going to Brighton. Fuck. That."

"Don't dwell on that shit, you got some last night." Cam was leaning in the doorway with a paper under his arm.

"True, true."

"Wait," I began, "Jack, you had a girlfriend in Knaresborough?"

"Aye, a Starbeck lass. Never saw her?" I wondered for a second, curling up my mouth in amusement. Somehow the image of Jack with his long arms draped around a girl walking down by the Nidd at Conyngham Hall and in love on a Spring afternoon didn't quite fit with how you perceived him. He was a bit like Cosmo: too mad to settle with one girl, too lovable to be ignored. What about the others? Cam was someone whose women would have to meet strict intellectual criteria. Dan was a man who you could see settled down in a few years' time, content to nick a weeknight at the pub with his single mates and live the good old days, then steal back inside to watch The Notebook and be either granted or denied sex. As for me, I didn't have a fucking clue about where I was going with women or who'd have me...

"Who was that Jo girl?" I blurted out suddenly.

"No, her name was Caroline. What are you on about?" Jack looked puzzled.

"Oh nothing, nowt. Just... something from last night."

"Oh," he purred, twigging, "I know who you mean." He let out a high 'twooo' tin-whistle sound. "Dark hair, patterned sort of leggings? Don't know her at all. Friend of Mischa's I think from home; I'm not your man to ask really, but hey, we should see her again." I nodded and tensed my lips in agreement.

"That'd be good," said Cosmo.

"Oh, you were a fan too?" asked Jack.

"Most certainly," he smiled.

I hadn't seen him look at her all night, and now he was officially after her? Then I supposed that Cosmo had also been roaming about and doing his own thing when I wasn't with him, and that the night had been one big flipbook of scenes, faces and occurrences, none of which I could've monitored simultaneously. And then the sickening sinking feeling came where gravity became stronger and my windpipe became hot as I realised that Cosmo might well have been getting somewhere with her without my knowing. "She seems fair game. No boyfriend, pretty fit. I know this sounds odd, but there was just something about her, y'know? Like, okay Rachel was fitter, but I wish that it'd been Jo back here and not her."

"And not just for the fact that she could have put out?"

"Not exactly. I mean, no," getting Jack's criticism, "not because of that, although that would've been nice too. Just... well, we'll see," he trailed off, laying his sleeping bag down with a flourish. "We'll see."

Jack clapped his hands. "Well, it sounds like the boys from the borough are going to be competing for the girl's affection. It's all about the giiiirl," he sang to no tune in particular, waltzing off through the door to the top of the stairs.

"Nah, maybe it was just the way I was feeling," continued Cosmo, perhaps sensing the movement of ruffled airwaves. He looked up with a completely altered expression and repeated: "The way we were feeling, eh…"

We started to trade stories excitedly again about the night while messing around with our bags. I'd brought my old giant cricket bag from when I used to play with the local under-13s side, into which I'd thrown my life as the old saying goes, while Cosmo'd opted for an undersized duffel bag and to compensate in his usual disorganised way, a load of carrier bags bearing the slogans of several different supermarkets. We carried on until we heard the bounding thud of Jack again. This is how Jack goes up the stairs: in that same bizarre gorilla motion, fisted hands pounding the staircase and jumping up two steps at a time with his hind quarters, holding his breath, slipping at least twice and then hauling himself up with a weightless swing on the rounded top banister and panting at the top. It was an action which told a thousand stories about him, about the man who once climbed a huge oak by the Nidd and stood up on a bough with just his legs for support, shouting, "Look at me, look at me ye mere mortals!" before overbalancing and falling twenty foot into the cold, silty waters below, about the man whose moped had literally fallen apart on his first big ride when we were fourteen on the corner of Gracious Street, gashing his leg and him running inside the Sainsbury's for some blue roll. Jack was, all in all, the jumpiest, most borderline-neurotic friend you could have, and that was despite spending most of my time with Cosmo.

He stood there again on the landing and panted breathlessly,

"Come on, we need to pick up." Without knowing exactly what this meant but having a vague idea we followed him downstairs.

We entered Selly Oak station from the road leading to the maroon-coloured bridge.

"Just a short hop up nearer town fellas," said Jack breezily as he hammered at the 'Five Ways' button on the ticket-dispenser's touchscreen. We each bought a return; the train was ten minutes late.

"Bloody London Midland," grumbled Cam in every accent from Inverness to Falmouth.

The ride into town followed a canal for stretches and I could sometimes see the red-brick splendour of the University of Birmingham peeking through walls and trees. We got off at Five Ways and wound through a few packed-in streets in the wake of Jack's once again skittish lead until we stopped abruptly at a corner. There we loitered for a minute or two. Jack explained we were there to see his dealer.

"Picking up, you see, is a term derived from the toilets and bars of America, where the dealer would literally put your gear on the floor and you handed him the cash as you picked up." Jack took £15 from each of us while we whistled around on the corner kicking at the cracked and upturned pavement. I'd already begun to wonder about my money. With the little packet I'd made from my uncle I was safe for now, but who knew when the supply was going to run short and I was going to be begging my mother to come back home. That would never happen though, I told myself sternly. That couldn't happen.

A short, badly-shaven guy, a student I guessed, joined us on the corner. He wore a Wu-Tang Clan hoody that was about four sizes too big for his stubby frame; it must have had him sweating rivers underneath. He nodded energetically to everything Jack said, which seemed to centre on everything but drugs, and then they closed their bodies together and did an exchange which was masked from the road, and the Wu Tang man backed away still nodding intensely with his hands in the big hoody pocket and saying his happy, sincere goodbyes to all of us, whom he'd never met and would probably never see again.

Chapter Seven

The rest of the day brought nothing of note except the emptying of Dan's car, during which Cam dropped his laptop onto the tarmac and chipped its bottom-right corner, sending him into a crap mood until tea-time when fish fingers and beans reanimated him into his old interesting self. Becky wandered into the front room now and then, barely less mardy than before. We also got to know Kerry and John, the other housemates, over a happily administered DJ-session from Jack during which he pointed out particular artists and gave their short histories, imparting his encyclopaedic knowledge to us all as if he was the documenter of dubstep himself. Cam took it all in with knowing nods and little 'ahs!' at the bits he didn't know; and from that short session I too felt my knowledge expand like a balloon. Dubstep was clearly his genre, but his library didn't stop there; he took us through his deep house and chillstep collections, taking the same care and dedication in backgrounding each artist as he had before.

The evening provided a monetary lesson in the price of drugs, Jack confirming that the 15 quid spent earlier in the day had been an all-inclusive kitty for tonight. Cam cracked his fingers in contained excitement; I kept drumming at my knees, just as nervous from knowing the thrill waiting to burst through my synapses, hovering in the space of the evening like a kestrel poised to strike.

This time the party was nearer, in the same neighbourhood, and the house much smaller. The place was packed; I saw familiar faces from the night before, all madly crowded, in communion—but no Jo. The music was different, more indie, and that made it feel like the house parties of old back home, but of course, with this new, expansive edge. I had the same sorts of visions as the night before, minus the visitation of my family; I stayed up for longer until it was just me, Dan, and John watching snooker highlights on that ancient telly on the stool in the corner while puffing away at some spliffs. The pale dawn strengthened as the effects of the drug wore off into a quiet, battered sort of bliss; we habitually brought up new conversation subjects, new ideas with each other we could never have thought of sober.

"Dan, do you suppose humans will eventually regress into an animal state, like in the beginning? And which company invented in-car cigarette lighters?" John would ask. Neither of us knew, but there'd inevitably be an in-depth analysis of all the considerations relevant to the point, Dan often picking up objects from around the room to illustrate the dynamics of his half-baked idea.

After Dan had gone to bed we turned off the TV and I spoke to John, another Social Science student, about care and about the visits I'd had in Year 8 from my social worker after the first time being caught riding one of the many mopeds I'd stolen. He said he was reading about stop-off houses for young offenders for the upcoming uni year, and said I should be glad not to have ended up in one from what he could tell.

When I crawled up to the cupboard room I found that Cosmo was still awake copying pictures of women out of a Cubism book that was splayed next to his pillow, and we chatted for what felt like hours about his drawings and girls from school; we even talked about Jo. All the time we were happily munching away on our shivering jaws like two dumb animals compelled by the drug. Now it was just the two of us things didn't seem so heated, so strangely disconcerting. We set each other the target of finding Jo and taking her out, the cost of which the loser would have to cover. Cosmo claimed he was going to wait outside the university every day with fresh flowers in the hope that she would be heading in to take a book out or something—'the learned angel'—before realising how expensive and tedious that exercise would be. I wanted to win now for financial as well as emotional reasons— but still I had this urge, this prowling urge within me that I should keep him far, far away from her.

Cosmo's casio watch beeped and told us it was nine a.m on the first of August 2010, and we took this as a cue to fall unconscious until late in the afternoon.

I woke up feeling utterly drained of all the goodness of life, and I noticed that Cosmo wasn't there. I shoved my hands roughly through my hair, lurched up onto my teetering feet, and zombied downstairs. It felt as if my brain was a flat car battery desperately trying and failing to give charge.

"Alroight kidda?"

Becky had joined me in the kitchen.

"Knackered," I answered; even speech was exhausting. "Never felt like this in my life." She looked up through her own bleary eyes as she pierced the film on her microwave curry and told me about her night out in the city-centre, adding reproachfully,

"The way Jack does his nights always leaves him in too much of a state. That's part of the reason I tell him not to."

I wanted to ask why else she told him not to but instead muttered "aye", suppressing my curiosity for the time being and adding insincerely, "I've sort of been missing having a proper drink."

"It's the ownly way to do it, love."

I don't know who she thought she was, telling a stranger what to do with his nights, but there was a strange, disarming, motherly charm about what she said; I told her that her 'o's' sounded funny, and she said the same to me. "It sounds like you're saying er, y'know? Everybody in Sutton would think you're hilarious." We carried on making fun of each other's accents until I realised dimly that we were flirting. The line was thin—thin between conversation and something more. I felt sure she was giving me the eye as she stirred the sauce and peeled the film all the way back, but was I being arrogant? Anyway, even though I'd been on a dry spell since Brid I knew without thinking that there wasn't a chance in hell that anything would happen between us; I swiftly poured a glass of water and made an excuse.

I entered the living room and stood above Jack, who was lying down under his duvet and looking like shit warmed up, as Deal or No Deal flashed up on the telly again. He looked up and asked, "Alright mush, who you been chatting to, Becky?" He lifted his arm feebly out of his blanket and tugged at my jeans leg, pulling me in closer. He whispered "She's got the horn for you, you know," grinning with eerie similarity to the Cheshire Cat. Dan and Cam, who sat on the sofa I was facing near the window, shouted hoarsely in unison, "Player!" undoubtedly audible in the kitchen. There was a strange muted jump in my chest as I realised I'd been right. I feigned disinterest and slumped down into the free armchair.

"Where's Cos?" I asked.

"In t'other room on the internet, he's plugged his laptop straight into the router," came the delayed reply from Cam. I sat there for a few minutes watching Norma's game turn itself on its head thanks to a succession of blues, then went to find Cosmo.

He was in the storeroom, a kind of cupboard where the broadband router was kept amongst ironing boards, clothes-horses and the hoover, a cupboard lit well enough thanks to the small window looking out onto the path down the side of the house. We were checking the cricket and football news, laughing at Sol Campbell's—that old warhorse—move to Newcastle United, when we heard two doors shut and the voices of Jack and Becky as they bumped into each other.

"Oh, ay up duck," I heard Jack say wearily but affectionately.

"Hey," answered Becky tonelessly. A longer pause than usual passed.

"What's up?"

"How long are the boys supposed to be staying Jack? They've been a couple of nights already."

"As long as they need to, I thought that was okay?" Jack was trying to be diplomatic but already you could hear the strain in his voice.

"Well, I don't mind Gene so much, he's a nice lad, but there are a lot of 'em and…"

"Oh we know you like Gene," chuckled Jack, trying to make light of the situation. His words, however, had the opposite effect.

"No, it's not like that," she growled. "Just, just think about others in this house for once." We heard a rustling and then Becky thumping up the stairs above our heads. The smell of curry wafted in. We heard the closing of the living room door again and exchanged raised eyebrows.

"Looks like you might have to keep her happy, if you know what I mean Genie boy." Cosmo's mouth curled as he shot me a look, like he had down by the river a week ago. I brooded ominously on this possibility.

Chapter Eight

Cosmo went back to bed saying that he felt worse than I did, and I found myself left in the room with the laptop. The first thing I considered was porn: going onto Redtube or some other free site and satisfying that nagging urge at the back of my mind. It'd been a few days. But I threw out that tempting thought; as far as I knew, Jack, Dan and Cam were still in the next room, and there was no lock on the door. So I just surfed around, hitting the sports news and then Twitter. I was following, amongst others, Alan Sugar, Charlie Brooker and David Mitchell, and by the looks of Mitchell's latest tweet a fantastic three-way argument had erupted between them: 'Sugar and Brooker: two utter fuckers.' Brooker, I recalled hearing vaguely amid the showbiz news on the radio yesterday morning, had tweeted something to the effect that Amstrad was a bigger joke than Alan Sugar's beard. I checked on Brooker's tweets—yesterday: 'Watching The Apprentice, 'bearded get' would be the kindest way to describe Sugar. He does angry like a David Mitchell character: badly'; Sugar'd replied, 'Nice to see the gutter press of the 21st Century are still around'; and Mitchell had weighed in with, 'A David Mitchell character doing angry badly? Sounds as improbable as a Brooker screenplay that doesn't rely solely on innuendo'. Mitchell had been a bit of a knob since Peep Show I thought to myself.

Brooker was my idol; I read Screen Burn when I was twelve. I brought it into school one morning and began reading it during form time, a period when Goughy (or Gough-syrup) would twattishly enforce silence after the register, and we hated him for it. I think it was the bright colours on the cover that attracted Cosmo (or Andrew as he was known back then). He read the book and loved it. Then he got me into Kerouac. When we weren't reading we were either playing on Pro Evolution Soccer for money, double or quits, or out by Conygham Hall hoping somebody older would be there to buy us cider. And that's how I met Cosmo's older brother and how we in turn met Jack.

It's not that Cosmo had always been my inseparable, unshatterable mate though. I'll never forget one thing he did.

We'd agreed to meet in the car park by the Nidd; we spent most of the evening kicking at the bark at the bottom of trees, failing to complete pull-ups on sagging branches, and throwing sticks into crusted cowpats. As the light was failing, and as that cold rush of air which happens near rivers at nightfall was gusting, he discovered a backwater down a slope which was held firm by the roots of some trees. "Look, look Gene!" he yelled over in his as-yet unbroken voice, "tadpoles!"

I think my response would've been 'Cool!' and before we knew it we were bursting our lungs back up the hill to find a container for them.

A few days later we'd both set up tadpole labs at our homes; mine was in the garage with a bit of light, and consisted of an old, clear packing box which my mum had reluctantly parted with, and some small jars with muslin over their tops. I fed mine boiled cabbage and checked on them daily—Cosmo threw in mealworms from his dad's fishing supply and looked at them when he could be arsed . When October came I put a heater over them, but it was a disaster; by November all our tadpoles were dead—all except one from my lab. Cosmo wouldn't believe my word and so he came round after fifth period for me to prove it.

Its tail had undergone apoptosis (I'd been reading about the metamorphosis—a lot) and its little back legs and even littler front legs were clinging to a piece of concrete I'd put in the packing box. "See? It's virtually a frog now."

"As if!"

"Anyway, mum asked if you wanted a brew."

Cosmo peered at the tadpole again with a strange, quiet look in his eyes and thrust his finger in the water. The froglet scarpered. "Alright, yeah," was his abstracted reply.

I went off to the kitchen. When I returned, Cosmo wasn't in the garage. I went through to the garden. He was sat on the lawn, and in one of his hands was a yellow screwdriver.

"It, um, it had a spaz out! I didn't know what it was doing." He muttered something about 'misery' as I threw down the brews and rushed over. I was appalled when I saw the mangled body. Not only had Cosmo killed it, but around it lay its tiny lungs and all four of its severed limbs. He'd butchered it. Of course I didn't believe his excuse and got my mum to throw him out. We were friends again by February, but that grisly episode soured things for a long time.

It seemed like a faint echo of a nearly lost past, now that much sourer things had taken place.

Being on my tod in the cupboard provided the perfect opportunity to try and hack my mum's Facebook account and find that address, the address of my father, the address that had eluded me on that fateful morning weeks ago.

I immediately logged out and contemplated the task ahead of me. I typed in her email address, j_bradley64@googlemail.com, and began to think of possibilities. I needed a pen and paper. I left the cupboard quietly and found a piece of junk mail from a local gym on the kitchen table and a pen from above the microwave, not wanting to have to make excuses to the boys in the front room.

It only then occurred to me then that there was every possibility he might not have given my mother his address. What reason would he have to? Maybe, I reckoned, in case he wanted to tell me where he lived. He wasn't aware of the situation: he didn't know his old love Jane Ross, now married and with a different name, hadn't told their son about him. I clung onto that thought, and remembered that even if I couldn't find his address I could at least have another look at those messages, see what had been exchanged between them, see his face again.

I wrote down the bands she liked, realising at the same time her awful taste in music— Lionel Richie, Bryan Adams, New Order, Depeche Mode, Take That - then the names of all our pets, including hers from childhood whose names I'd memorised through Nana's constant storytelling—Jojo—the West Highland Terrier, J.R—the cat that ran away, and Besty and Charlton—two goldfish named by Grandad Alfie who'd been a Man U fan until forty a day and old age caught up with him. Then in our house we'd had Bugs—the bunny, Simba—the cat who'd also run away and then returned much thinner a year later, and Pinky and the Brain—two mice who hadn't lasted long up in the loft after I left the hatch open one day and, like the fags for Grandad Alfie, Simba had done for them as well. What a great sense of humour my family had.

What else, what else? In all probability the password had nothing to do with any of these things, but they were a start. I tried all of them with no success. Each failed attempt was getting me more and more radgey. Now I'd started, I was *bent* on this password. What to try next? She loved her work, but that wouldn't be it. I scribbled 'work' on my piece of paper as a last-ditch reminder. I tried my own name in its various guises: gene, genebradley, genealfredbradley. No success there either. I began typing random places in Knaresborough, TV shows, food, anything, but I was beginning to feel my eyes droop as I stared horse-faced at the screen, aching from the night before. I sucked back up a bit of dribble that my lips had been too tired to hold in. All I had in my field of vision was the terrible, bright white and blue of the Facebook welcome page.

I decided that I couldn't do this just now; the last two nights had purely floored me. There was no fuel left for the pistons to pump. Without looking I folded up the piece of paper feebly with my left hand, shut the laptop down and slipped it onto the floor next to the dozing Cam on the sofa. Jack and Dan groaned goodnight as they watched a repeat of Take Me Out. Then the stairs, then sleep. Blissful sleep.

My time in Birmingham was moving quickly. Over the next couple of days, Jack spent a lot of his waking hours in the library reading up on social policy in preparation for his third year, and spent the rest of them small-time dealing in amongst the bookshelves, as he informed us one morning once Becky had left the kitchen. Becky, I noticed, was being shy with me. We were enjoying the sun in the middle of Birmingham with Kerry and John; and only once or twice had I caught her looking at me, when she'd half-jump, avert her squeezed-together eyes and then smile to her hands. The group of us wandered around the Bullring for all it was worth. There was a small church down a sweep of steps nearby and I suddenly felt like a real tourist; I'd been drawn to churches for a long time. I found myself suggesting we go in and take a look. John admitted he hadn't even taken so much as a second look at the building.

I led towards the big oaken doors flung open for the visiting public to scour its insides. Dan's phone went off loudly and without a word he snaked off towards the steps to sit down. The rest of us walked slowly on past the threshold; I had to dodge a shuffling North American couple who twanged in their nasal accents about 'grabbing coffee someplace'. Cam sniggered to Cosmo on how you could spot them a mile off. "It's the raincoats, the macs you know? And the bloody size of them."

Cosmo agreed. "Rainmacs and BigMacs."

We moved further inside, our heads lifting with soft mechanical movements to take in the new, rich interior, the flashing advances of the stained glass windows changing with each step, and to take deeper breaths of the new, stony air. Cameras clicked all around. Japanese tourists looked almost worried as they shifted around on the aisle and into the pews, as if they were confused by the church's existence. 'What is this giant draughty place; who would live here? Thank god the English are a crazy lot. Someone has to do these things so we don't have to! No no, delete that one, my rain hat's still on...'

"Oh, I can't believe we haven't been in before, it's beautiful!" breathed Kerry. "Look at those windows! And these paintings..." She walked off towards the paintings she'd seen, her arms wrapped about herself.

"Oi've always hated churches. We were made to gow to the one rewwnd the corner with school for all thowse little events they put on at proimary. Always cowld and dirty," Becky droned. I'd inadvertently ended up alone with her. The light became stronger by degrees, poking through the windows and casting itself brightly on the altar, as I walked forward with her in tow. A man sat slightly hunched on the front pew, a tattered coat visible across his shoulders. As we got closer I heard that he was muttering softly, unintelligibly to himself yet with a certain care and attention. As with every one of those situations where you quickly realise that there is something wrong with this person so the best thing to do is to leave them alone, I looked away sharpish and filtered deliberately to the other side of the pews.

"It's a bit of a shame, Becky, that you don't like churches. I've always been a bit of a fan."

"I know I know," she replied quickly, "it's just... bad memories, that's all. I got sick a lot as a kid." She paused.

"Really?" was the only response I could think of.

"Yeah. Well, we had to do a performance in one once—St. Hilda's—and, well, I choked on my line—it was my one and only line. I was so nervous before, and I just sort of threw up everywhere."

I smiled, biting my top lip, trying very hard not to laugh while also being thankful she stood a couple of paces behind me. I heard sniggering from the back of the church. I turned to look and saw John gesticulating as he and Kerry stood close to some Christian trinkets. Cosmo was nowhere to be seen. "It sounds weird but when it happened it koinda tasted loike church dust. Loike, loike neww." I grinned at her; right then I saw in my peripheral vision the hunched man on the pew stand up and look towards us. Then he said in a loud, deep, damaged voice:

"Oi! 'Ope yeww've got permission to be in 'ere, yeww two! They put me in charge, they put me in charge y'know..." He had his arms raised, a water bottle clasped in between the black fingers of his left hand. The tourists at the back went quiet. The man was big: tall, broad but hunched. There was power in his shoulders;

he could've been an athlete as a lad I thought, visualising him breasting the tape with a strong chest in the sun. All this was hidden away now beneath an oilskin coat, dirtied by the years, but not all was lost. I watched anxiously at him approaching.

He stopped a few metres short of me and Becky. His mouth spread into a broad grin, revealing big, white teeth, some marked with disease and some inexplicably untouched. "Eyyyyy. Eyyyyy. It's always been moi motto, y'know? That if yo' in the pews, yow gotta share d'news! Sow what's going on young 'uns? C-c-courtin' is it?" He hopped about, crackling the 'c' sound like the static of a radio through his elated mouth with his eyes lit up like yellowed balls of smoke-stained wallpaper. He giggled and kept on giggling, sounding like a child as he twisted and turned and repeated 'courtin', occasionally stuttering and crackling the word again.

He calmed and sat his large frame down. His face turned solemn and troubled. "Some of the things y' see thow, eh, eh, some of the things y'see y'know—but," and he looked up first to Becky's face, which she cradled with one hand as she looked down in pity, and then to mine. "Nooo, you'd be too young." He clicked. "Sow many songs to be sung." He clicked again, as if gathering the words to his mouth. "Down't end up loike me, eh, will y'kids? Down't be loike dis, a poor owld church-keeper, keeping d' peace, please please…" he trailed off slowly. Then he quickly scratched his head and barked at himself to shut up, just shut up!

Becky stifled a small shout and ran to the exit holding her mouth. I was glad to be shot of her.

"Little missy, probably going to… now, I wown't say it," he went on, smiling almost fatherly. He leaned in again and, mouth shuddering like a washing machine, whispered: "Sometimes, I have to tell the pigeons to go away! Shoo, shoo! Loike that! Eh, Eh!" Then he stood up, flipping the back of his hands upwards in a shooing motion from the end of his long outstretched arms and stamping his feet on the floor exclaiming 'shoo, shoo!' over again, lost in his own little moment.

John's voice sent a quick jolt through me from the aisle behind.

"Doing a good job there man!"

I was unsure whether John was saying this to me or to the nameless man—his eyes were on neither of us but on the stained glass—but anyway the man kept shooing obliviously, apparently seeing pigeons on the steps to the altar and playing a little game, talking to some of them, asking them kindly to leave and then flicking his hands into the invisible flock once more. John turned as I caught up with him and said, "Well, you never know. Maybe there really are pigeons there, and we're the crazy ones."

Outside, Dan asked why Becky had run around the corner to be sick. I explained as best I could and we waited for her to emerge. Cosmo sauntered out of the oak doors in the meantime, claiming he'd 'just found God but then lost him somewhere'. Cam followed, newly-bought candles in his long, slim hand. Kerry went off to find Becky (as girlfriends caringly do), and after a couple of minutes the pair returned, the latter looking rough as arse with her hair mussed and greasy and her cheeks mascara-streaked like a zebra's hide.

Cam and Dan had already strode off down the hill towards the giant indoor markets. Twenty minutes later we'd all bought towels stitched with Birmingham landmarks; to boot Dan had bought a cut-throat razor, Cos'd bought 3 knock-off DVDs and a sketch of a water-mill, and John was laden with a half-size banjo. We took a walk down by the canal and then at Cosmo's jumping, elfish request, we took the train back down to Selly Oak and crossed the canal to visit Cadbury World, which was conveniently close to Jack's house. We got funnelled around the bowels of the attraction by droves of fellow tourists and didn't stay for long. Drizzle set in quickly as we left. Cam wanted a bottle of vodka; suddenly we were all in the local Aldi and I'd picked up a crate of Galaghad. I waited with John, Cam and Becky at the packing bay while the other three dicked about in the booze aisle.

"Bit grim on a dark day, isn't it?" sniffed Cam as he stroked his neck.

"Can be here, but they call it the Black Country out boi Dudley for a reason, you know. The soot from the factrays," chipped in Becky. "Bloody yam yams."

"But mint parties, eh?"

"Students," sighed John happily in his deep, rolling Rah accent.

John was one of the likeable Rahs though, completely different to Douglas who we'd met at Misha's. He stood at about six foot but stooped forward with a straight back; on his head was blond hair that was cut very short at the back and sides with a long, straight fringe on top. Cosmo described his dress sense as 'quelque chose arthouse': he wore jumpers with elbow-patches, t-shirts with sailor stripes and chinos or skinny jeans whenever he could, complemented by the occasional scarf, or cravat as he referred to them.

Kerry, a darkish redhead with freckles, big breasts and a boyfriend, talked mainly to Becky but threw the occasional question towards us. She remained distant. Dan, who'd grown the beginnings of a dark, Turkish beard, was told by Kerry that he was starting to look like a younger version of Jack Dingle from Emmerdale. He came downstairs the next day neatly shaven. As Jack commented, it had taken years off him and made him a much more attractive mate.

"No, I just wanted a shave," he lied. We were in the front room listening to some music while playing Trivial Pursuit. Every incorrect answer demanded that 20p be put in the middle for the eventual winner. Me and John, his semi-stained teeth poking out in a smile above his prominent ginger-stubbled chin, looked up from the board at each other in amusement.

"Bollocks," I said looking at Dan's bald neck.

"Alright, I just wanted to look a bit nicer that's all, and if Kerry'd noticed then all the better," he conceded softly, fiddling around with his board-piece to avoid looking at us. Cam had been keeping his laptop close to him, constantly on music or news websites which he would read snippets of every now and then to anyone listening. He'd fall into an argument with either Cosmo or Jack about some small point, especially Cosmo; Cos was an indie boy through and through and couldn't take Cam's sniping about the genre lying down.

"It's dead, it ate itself and created a landfill site where it buried all its shite spin-off records I'm afraid Co-co-cosmo," coughed Cam, belting his chest with his fist and punching the husky on his t-shirt at the same time. "Don't get me wrong, I loved all the early stuff—the Libertines, Cribs, even the Arctics for a bit, but it's gone nowhere since then."

"It's still the music that gets most people going though—that says the most about life," Cosmo hotly contested.

"I disagree. You need to broaden your taste, listen to some more folky stuff, something out of the ordinary. And I don't mean Mumford."

That was his golden rule, not Mumford. They carried on like this back and forth for a while. I saw that Cosmo had at least taken Cam's character, with all its confrontations and contradictions, with a pinch of salt; to be brave enough to question every bold statement he made was to prove yourself. Cam responded to assertiveness and argument, not meekness, and respected people for it.

The next morning it happened to be just me and him munching on some cornflakes we'd been out to buy, when on the radio came the announcement that three British soldiers had been killed in a roadside bomb attack in Afghanistan. He sniffed, then said before the report had finished, "It was a mistake putting so many soldiers over there, and I can't believe the people up top can't see it. I'm not having a go at the fact we're there in the first place, although the politicians could do themselves a favour and come clean about all the reasons we're over there for, don't you think?"

"Go on," I said.

"Well, we're over there to stop the Taliban getting back into power, who amongst other things would let Al-Qaeda build training bases, yeah? But if they actually listened to the experts, they'd find that even without any presence from the West, it would be virtually impossible for the Taliban to get back in anyway."

"Hang on a second, surely that's not true? Afghanistan has no defence, and the Taliban are brutal, they'd take power easily."

"Not true." He shook his head while relaxedly pouring milk into his brew, from which he'd just taken the teabag. The table beneath the mug was smothered in stickers from various clubs and bars in Birmingham. The leg nearest the fridge was too short and I, finding myself in the chair next to this leg more often that not, was constantly kicking the folded-up newspaper under it to balance the table out. "Need some?" He poured milk into my mug too. "The other thing they need to come clean about is the fact that while they're keeping—and I fully admit and accept this—an awful, vicious ideology from getting into government by using ground troops they're also securing the massive natural reserves the country has, which includes— and here's the important one—gas." He took his first slurp of tea with a satisfied expression that instantly transformed into a grimace.

"Hot?"

"Just a bit," he croaked. "I could talk about gas and oil all day—huh-cough-aack!—Because they should be investing in renewables. But back to the troops— the people who know what they're on about, who have their heads screwed on straight, know that what's called a 'light footprint' is a much better approach than a heavy one. The government just panders to the press though and sends more out when stuff like this," he pointed to the radio, "happens. What they don't grasp is that their deaths are caused by there being too many of them there in the first place."

"But where's all this from? For all I know you could just be saying it Cam and not actually having any concrete evidence."

He put up his long skinny finger and pursed his lips, flipping open his laptop.

"You need to see this site, it's got stuff on everything you need to know. Facts can't hide now like they used to." He coughed again. "Fucking burnt the roof of my mouth. Anyway, the net's got it all. Just look at the alternative sites for the real news Gene. The BBC just don't cut it anymore." The kitchen door, which was covered in photographs of everyone in the house in various states, swung open and in swept Jack.

"Shouldn't guzzle like a sodding elephant then Camshaft," he said, slapping Cam on the shoulder.

"Where've you been?"

"Oh just down the library again, clocked off early."

"It's only eleven now!" I laughed, though impressed at his motivation. At sixth-form, mornings off equalled my warm duvet pinning me down helplessly, when not even a JCB could lift it off. How does anybody get up with nothing to do? All the unemployed, all the permanent students of this world?

He lay down some shopping on the side and produced a big clear plastic bag from his wallet which didn't have powder in it, but some lumpier stuff

"Good news. There's a party in Wolves we can go to tonight, if you fancy? Another cheeky one," he said wagging the bag. I felt a shock of excitement. I'd missed that rush over the last couple of nights, and now that I was fully recovered...

"Wa-hey," whooped Cam.

"Sounds good. Very good."

"Good lads. Get rounding up. We'll go out about ten—it's a bit of a trek up that end."

With a day of sunbathing, drinking, and a fat barbecue ahead along with the night in prospect I was seized with the idea of trying to hack that Facebook account again, not wanting to let it slip out of mind.

"I'm off to the cupboard for a spell."

"Alright geezer, and check out them videos on that site I put up," Cam rushedly replied, turning back to Jack to talk about the night ahead.

Turkishdelight, I tried, remembering her love of it. No. Scratch head, pull hair. Desperatehousewives. Again, denied. Curl up fist, tap table. Minutes pass. Jontysboy, I typed in feverishly, congratulating myself on remembering the name of the horse on which she had won a grand at Wetherby in May. My heart pounded in my ears as the screen took longer than usual to load. This could be it. This could be it! I gripped my fists, leaning into the screen on which the little egg-timer was sifting through the milliseconds. Then a red-rimmed box appeared saying 'Please re-enter your password'. My head slumped.

"Fuuuuck."

I was convinced I'd found it. But then another thought occurred to me, one completely unconnected with my father. I signed into my account and clicked on the search bar where I typed in Jack's name and went to his friends section. There I typed in 'Mischa' and clicked on her profile photo, that of a picture of her and a girlfriend kissing. I raised my eyebrows and thought of having a closer look but shook my head and remembered there was a task at hand. Her account and friends I saw, thanking God (a strange enough experience though that was), were unlocked and so I typed into her Friends bar the name 'Joanna'. Three options came up. Straight away I recognised the Joanna who'd got me enraptured the other night. Her second name was Briers. In a second my mood of despair and frustration had shifted to one of exhilaration, and with a quick plume of breath directed up towards my fringe I clicked on 'add friend' with a flourish and pm'd her with what we were doing tonight and my number.

Buzzing from how, out of the blue, I'd found her and from thoughts of the coming party I leapt off for a shower to wipe away the layer of nervous sweat I'd gathered. For now Birmingham was allowing me to keep my 'father-issue-thing', as Cosmo had called it, somewhere deeper and darker.

Chapter Nine

Jo hung inescapably in my mind like a vivid, silvery fog as the five-seater taxi screamed along between the never-ending traffic lights on the road north-west to Wolverhampton. Each screeching take-off from the next set of lights seemed to be quicker and more violent than the last, slamming us back in our seats. The driver looked over his chunky, fattened shoulder and told us above the metallic squeak of a woman talking on the radio that he was trying to get us there as Bullet as possible, Bullet being the Steve McQueen film. He gripped the wheel tightly and leaned into the receiver with wide eyes. "If 'er on the radio shuts up, we'll get there Michael Schumacher, eh, eh!"

"Doesn't mean he needs to throw us around though," put in Kerry, her straightened red hair slipping across her forehead in tumbles. She sat across from me, knees nearly touching mine, in an exquisite little black dress.

"He is letting us drink though I guess," defended John. He belched as he polished off the bottle of bourbon being passing around.

Jack and Becky were also in the taxi. The remaining three lads sat in the taxi tailing us, along with an Asian fella called 'Khan' who had turned up twenty minutes late to Jack's house and jumped in with them just as they were setting off. I vaguely remembered his name from Mischa's party but couldn't remember his face.

"How much are you doing tonight?" I asked Jack, eager to sort out the bombs.

"A half mate." He paused, stretching. "Why, you feeling up for a half too?" There was an element of hope in the sound of his husky, watery voice. "Oh, that reminds me—you three —I need the cash if you don't mind… just before I forget."

"Yeah, yeah," I replied whilst nodding my head as the other two shuffled about for the money. I fished a twenty out from my wallet. "Will that be enough?"

"Yeah pal, spot on, spot on. We'll sort it out at the place and I'll show you what to do." Kerry and John handed Jack their money, ten from Kerry, twenty from John. Becky stayed silent.

There were twenty-five minutes more of the dark bumpy taxi ride. I saw through the window uncountable anonymous faces—all straining at something, straining to stay, to leave, to get out of or into the night, thronging and massing and then ebbing. The streets were a fairground mural waiting to be packed away come morning-but first, the night. We arrived at our destination with a crunch of brakes and loose tarmac. It was not too dissimilar a house to that of Jack's in Selly Oak, smallish from the front, white window-frames, an un-looked-after feel. We paid, knocked and arrived.

The time was eleven. All being relatively sober, we filed into the loosely populated living room and sat down in the small available gaps. The flavour and translucence of incense could be smelled and seen, the lights were dim and the room had something of the East about it—a gathering under yurt-top. In the corner a television stood low with a tarpaulin-sign draped over, on which I partly read 'ee Sky he'. Some people, guys in Obey caps or with their unfaded clippered sides on show and girls with top-knots and vampire-esque make-up, sat on the windowsill outside smoking. I sat down staying quiet, sipping my last beers from the barbecue. I listened to the different and at times competitive voices tackling items ranging from the football transfer market to politics. I understood much and said little, looking forward to Cam's arrival. My eyes and arms felt tired as I sipped away; I looked at Jack expectantly.

There was a loud knock on the door and the others entered. I shuffled and made room for Cosmo next to me. We just chatted insularly until Cam joined in with a debate to our left. Then Jack tapped me on the knee and said, "Time to sort this stuff out."

He turned towards the small, brightly-lit galley kitchen through the back, raised his crossed arms above his head like a runway controller, and shouted: "Oi, Nugent. Got a baking tray? A dark one?"

A strained, high voice shouted back, "Yeah, two secs though mate!" The shortish, beanie-hatted guy called Nugent eventually side-stepped and tip-toed in past the ever-swelling numbers of people, carefully passing over a tray. Jack gave it two metallic knocks and breathed "Right, upstairs then chaps."

Jack slid the tray onto a small desk he'd pulled up to the edge of the bed and me and Cosmo sat either side—leaning over eagerly like two schoolboys at a pond, jealous of their mate's catch—as he plucked out a couple of bags of the rough, brownish crystal MDMA. Jack went straight into his walkthrough.

"So, here's the actual stuff, it comes in crystals and you have to crush it up," he said in a patronising teacherly voice. Cosmo oohed at the process. "And to do that it's best to pour it out —this surface best not be greasy—pour it out onto a dark, flat surface." He poured happily and the grains pattered energetically down onto the dull aluminium. "Now, the best thing for this is an old receipt," and he pulled one from his wallet, "This one I kept from a transaction earlier today. Ooh! hula-hoops. Put it flat on top of the whole pile and then get a bank card or some kind of card, doesn't matter really, can be a uni card, plastic gift card, railcard, loyalty card, any type of card lads, and place it on the top and crush it downwards, first like that," the grains crunched like cinder toffee, "and make sure there's nothing spilling out of the sides, and rub it back and forth—ooh matron!—back and forth on the receipt, lifting it up and chopping it into a flatter pile every now and then. Soon, you have a little white pile." After about thirty seconds he tapped his card down and smiled. "There, look. Now have I put you off drugs yet?" He turned to me and raised his eyebrows.

"Have you put us off yet…" Cosmo stretched upwards, his denim shirt creasing and lifting up. "Imagine if my mum could see me now."

"Stop being such a Nub," snapped Jack with fake condescension. But when I looked at him in the pause after I saw that, despite his gentle ribbing, Jack was wavering, his eyes looking up through his brows and his lips shifting to a fan of unsettled flatness. He sighed, "If your mum could see you now! Hahum…Oh boys, what have I done… are you angry at me? You are enjoying it, right? I've not just dumped some terrible evil on you? Have I?" His voice shrank.

"Jack, if I'd have had a problem with it I would've said straight away back on the hill, right?"

"Oh, but I'd made you all high! Don't you see? What was I expecting? For you to turn round and tell me off? I don't think you could've if you'd wanted to. But it was good right?" And in defeat, he added "It's only just occurred to me I could've fucked things up for you two."

Cosmo bent his arm around his slouching shoulders, "Listen, we are having an amazing time down here. Don't believe for a second you've fucked things up." I listened to Cosmo's words and took them in for all they were worth. Then I glanced over to the white pile, only my eyes moving.

What were we doing? Was this the right path?

I was experiencing realisations while on this stuff, escaping, doing the job I'd set myself, but even now that sounded mechanical, wrong. I wondered for a second. What was the meaning? Was it only artificial? Were the feelings and urges that washed over me while I was in the chasms of its high just magnifications of feelings I already had; was it a vehicle for my articulation, a path to the stars where I could once and for all know everything I had wanted to know…

Cosmo asked from far away what we did now. "What do we do now? What do we do now? You look like you've seen a ghost. What's the matter?"

"Nothing's the matter mate." I shook my head and took a long glug of beer.

"Good, I'm glad you two are cool with this. I just got worried, for a second," continued Jack, ripping some Rizlas in half. Expertly, he sorted the powder into piles and then, using his bank card and the rail ticket into town from the other day, he picked up each small pile and tapped the powder into each skin.

"And that's how you make the bomb, I'm guessing," coming out from my slumber of thoughts. I saw my pile—five big ones—and a smile flickered back onto my face. The two battling sides of me which had been delving into the ethics of the whole situation flew together again in one last airborne flurry: the winged proverbial 'Yes' threw down its opposite. I dropped the bombs into a bag and stood up, triumphant.

We bombed straight away, Cosmo Jack and me, and looked at each other. The room was still. Then Jack led the way downstairs. The scene had completely changed: an army of people had arrived and there was loud drum'n'bass roaring out of some speakers in the now opened-up front room. A strobe flashed fast. Of course, I couldn't feel anything yet, but the sudden up-step in the party and the knowledge of having a half in my wallet cocked my synapses like a thousand trembling rifles.

"I know it's not actually happening, but it feels like it's happening. Throw this down your neck," I shouted into Cosmo's ear as I passed him another Foster's.

"Yeah, yeah: placebo. It'll come soon." And it did. I began telling Cosmo how much he meant to me, how we'd met, what all of my impressions had ever been about him. I told him of my dream last night: visions of Ashley, visions I hadn't had in a long time, visions of her when we first started to go out, looking into her pure eyes and not seeing a single demon; visions of a cycle track, a race against myself, and occasional near-misses as I sped along, then pulling up just short of a huge cliff, only the sea beyond as the waves crashed around the deadly rocks below.

Cosmo's dream was even weirder. The way he told it was as though he was lost in a wilderness close to home yet somewhere completely foreign—such a familiar thread. "And I was travelling through these woods, scared shitless, completely shitless, and there were only the sounds of the owls and this strange hum humming away in the distance. Then… then I became proper aware of being in the Wolds, somewhere on the way to the coast… Foxholes, that's where I was. I'd been transported, or something, somehow. The hum was louder, then… oh yes, that's it! The hum was really loud and I could hear the exact direction it came from—straight on, from the direction of the sea—and I ran along the road at that sort of double speed you get in dreams when in front of me this massive black panther appeared. But, get this, I didn't stop, I just jumped straight over it like some sort of Olympic athlete, hit the top of the hill and started to run down the other side, and just then dawn broke over the top of the sea. And I woke up."

The music thudded on. It was still only quarter to twelve. I came up fully at quarter past. Girls were whirling around like the mini-tornadoes that pick up leaves. At some time between this and one in the morning, Cam collared me outside having a smoke and told me that we absolutely had to go now because there was this amazing club that everybody had been raving about and everyone was going to, and I looked behind him and saw that he had indeed gathered a group and, despite obviously not knowing Wolverhampton, that he looked in charge of its organisation. I thought only briefly about my money and the sting in my wallet from earlier in the night and then burst back inside to grab Cosmo, Jack and Dan. I found Cosmo coming on to a Scottish girl and convinced them with almost zero fuss to join.

I found Jack and Dan, after a while of flurrying about and popping my head into various upstairs rooms, sitting down on a bed with a couple of others and the strong smell of skunk in the air. They admitted that they were far too battered to do anything of the sort.

"You have a good time though mate, it'll be ace. Misch might be there, she goes sometimes," Jack grinned with his elbows barely propping him up through the haze.

So we had our group. The taxi seemed to take us in and then out again of Wolverhampton city centre. I got suspicious of the driver and started telling one of the new people—a nameless man with a black leather jacket and hood combination, and a monkeylike flash in his Asian eyes whenever he looked up—that he was trying to fleece us, when we pulled up outside an abandoned-looking warehouse. I saw Cam, who'd got there in the taxi in front, shuffling round the building in a party of semi-familiar faces, and I led on after. I still had three bombs left and the second was just waning. The trail led down some dusty steps to a basement. The noise got louder as we descended hushedly. Then I saw the queue.

"Ah, I thought there was just no-one in here—how wrong I was!" I said with a leap of excitement to the still-nameless little man. He giggled along nervously and told me limply, "It's busy here. It's good."

After a long wait and seven pounds payment we entered the hot, low-ceilinged room and danced solidly, me dropping my third and fourth bombs along with Cosmo. Cam looked over jealously then steered us to a juice stand by the corner.

"I only bought a quarter! I'm right in the middle of being up right now but could do with some more for later, y'know?" His face was glistening.

"Well, you could try find someone selling? It could be dodgy in a club and that, but if you fancy some…"

"Wait, isn't that Khan fella here?" chimed in Cosmo after wiping his sweat-riven forehead with his shirt.

"Is he?"

"Aye, aye, I saw him jump in the taxi behind us. And if you remember, there were three of them." Cam had already handed me his drink and commanded: "Look after this, mate, while I go and find him." He turned, then wheeled back round, bellowing through the thick air, "Do you think I can trust him though?" I thought Cam could well be throwing himself into deep water, while the thudding of my high heart pushed me to say;

"Yeah, yeah, absolutely mate, Jack knows him well doesn't he? Should be fine, it should be just fine." I let Cam disappear into the madness of the dance floor, using his craneish height like a watchtower to seek out Khan. It was me and Cosmo again. I became shot through with the surge of the latest bomb when there was a changeover of d'js. Things hit an entirely new level. The bass was pounding from all sides, the drop was coming, just hanging as if behind a veil, the most beautiful thing about to come and an explosion set to rip through me, when Jo cut through the crowd and ghosted her way to my side; I turned and there she was, an apparition dressed in a black jumper, straw in her mouth, a soft, girlish smile on her lips. I forgot about the music, fumbled hellos, gave my leave to Cosmo (who got it) and we walked off outside in a heap of conversation as the rain fell. I forgot about Cos, I forgot about Cam, I forgot about everything I'd ever experienced in the world before tonight.

I didn't notice the figures of the two fellas until one of them came steaming into me with a staggered weight. There were screams and shouts, I saw Cosmo's arm pumping into the top of a man's head, and I flew from Jo. I landed a punch in the man's exposed side; he backed into a wall under the gravity of Cosmo's push, then he lashed out, cracking Cosmo on the chin and laying him on the deck. Cam squared up to the man—and it was only then that I realised that the face of the fighter was that of Khan's—and reached out with a hook, but Khan was too quick.

He grabbed Cam's arm and sent him spinning to the floor too. Oblivious of me, he walked up to put his foot in Cam's side as Jo shrieked. I brought my fist down with all its force on the back of his shaved head, and he collapsed on top of Cam, his Timberlanded foot flicking up in the process and scraping me on the neck. Cam pushed him aside with a strained effort. Khan moaned and whimpered with his face pressed down to the ground. There were other shouts ringing around the yard now; my arm was caught by Cosmo as he threw his head around and shouted in an exhilarated frenzy, "Run! Come on, go!" I caught Jo and we threw ourselves back through the wooden doors and through the swathes of dancers in the club, and we didn't stop running until we'd made it up the stairs and back out again into the open air. We walked quickly down the street and into the next.

"Thank God the bouncers... hadn't realised... at the front," I panted with my hands at the back of my head sucking in masses of warm air, looking round all the time to see we hadn't been followed.

"We should get a taxi back to mine," Jo suggested as she held her phone in her trembling hand. "Come on, let's keep moving." We walked and talked. We were going to Jo's. It felt like a strange sponge, that had temporarily sucked up my high in the moments before, had been lifted and squeezed, and now the adrenaline and the MD-high coursed together through my blood passages in one unified procession which seemed to rattle my skull. God, I had never felt so good in my life.

We entered a quiet square with a few shuttered bookies' shops lining its edges and some litter circling pointlessly in the middle of it, rising and falling lazily with each pump of wind that caught it. Soon a black cab pulled up.

"Jow?"

"Us." We climbed in and sped off to Birmingham.

Chapter Ten

Jo didn't live in a house but a flat off a main road which, despite all the ramblings I'd taken in the area, I didn't recognise. We entered through a heavy-looking red door with a small buzzer and a list of tenants at its side. I peeked inside the window of the cafe next door. There was a huge, twisted iron stand in the shape of a cow; it was a kind of French sculpture, one that had to be displayed in the windows of shops in a French seaside village, in every one of them, because what a joie de vivre in its shaping: exquisite, joyful, French, so bovinely French. Jo was calling.

We ascended the stairs in single file and I saw her fiddle with her keys next to another red door with both a Yale and a mortice lock.

"Are you three still all high as fuck?" she asked while turning and gurning and looking at each of us, queen of the stairs and the house.

"Well I bloody would be if I'd been able to get any more drugs!" laughed Cam resentfully. "All I got was a bloody black eye!"

"Aw, shit! Yeah, yeah, so… what the fuck happened back there? Why," Cosmo wheezed in a laughing fit, "why… on earth… were you fighting Khan? What'd happened? You not pay him or summat?"

"No! Not at all man, not at all. He would've been justified in going after me if I'd done that. No, no. It was all him man, the fucking psychopath. Basically what happened, if I remember rightly—and I'm pretty sure I'm not going mad here—is that I needed more drugs, right Gene?"

I nodded as we entered and I slid onto an obscenely comfortable low-down futon settee, closing my eyes whilst keeping an ear on Cam's story and another tuned into the internal bliss washing inside.

Hypnotic, trippy beats began to drift from the corner of the lounge; a weight settled to the left of me. I felt the as yet invisible circle of the four of us form in Jo's living room.

"…And so there he was, demanding payment off me for what Jack owed him. He was already charging twenty quid for a quarter, so I looked him square in the eye," I heard Cosmo chuckle constantly as Cam spoke, "I looked him square in the eye, up and down then square in the eye, and told him he could go and fuck himself. Well, I think you pretty much saw the rest."

"But how did you get outside?" Jo asked from somewhere close to the left of me.

"I think he dragged or pushed me; we were pretty close to the smoking exit anyway, round some corner trying to stay secret."

"Mad of him, wasn't it? To get involved in a scrap when he was carrying."

"Yeah, yeah."

Cam and Cosmo got involved in another conversation. I turned to Jo and opened my eyes. She had her legs tucked up on the settee with the rest of her body.

"Hey… thanks for bringing us back here, for sorting it out back there. It's a great place you've got. Where the hell did you get that old globe over there? It looks like it could be straight out of a Victorian politician's office."

"Haha, oh that ridiculous drinks globe thingy? Hmm, yes, in the flush of first loan payment of the year I think we all pitched in down at the market. I love it."

"Yeah, yeah, it looks mint. In the days of all the pink bits on the map…"

"Exactly, a piece of imperialism in your own front room, like some guy said. You know, one of my granddads was in charge of an area of India in the old Raj era….." We talked on about history. I told her about the giant encyclopaedia I had at home when I was a bairn, the one I couldn't even lift but would work through page by page until I reached the end and started again. I found out that she was from Coventry: a final year Geography student. Final year!

"That must be terrifying, knowing you'll have to get a job come next summer," I whispered.

"Yeah, tell me about it. Although I know that I have to go abroad. Have to as in want to I mean. I just want a new perspective on the world. I can't stay here my whole life." She asked me about where I came from and I gave her a full description of Knaresborough, its beauty, its ugliness, its boredom, its homeliness, what we did as kids, what we were doing here. I came straight out and told her everything, my dad and all. The failed hacking sessions. Cosmo looked up when I said this but he was too involved in his conversation with Cam to comment.

She told me how she was adopted but had seen her biological mother since she was seven; she was in a care home. Her biological father had died from an overdose when she was born.

"I always say biological, even though its tempting to use the word 'real'. But of course they're not my 'real' parents to me. I had those already, you see."

I paused. "I don't know what I'm supposed to be feeling right now to be honest. It's good being down here." I saw the pitying look on her face and it made me feel instantly and uncomfortably young. "But don't worry, I'm not fishing for sympathy! I'm doing fine. Just support me in my quest," I joked raising my eyebrows. Jo smiled; she knew alright. Cosmo pulled out a cigarette.

"Oh, boys, I'm really sorry but my flatmates are dead funny about smoking inside, would you mind going outside? You can just buzz straight back up," she said apologetically.

"Fancy a smoke, geezer?"

Not really realising what I was saying, I replied,:

"Nah, I'll stop up here ta mate." Cam and Cosmo filed out, still chuckling and chattering away. They had become quite a force, those two, I thought as I saw their backs disappear.

My heart spiked jumpily as I realised we were alone. We talked about the music she had on, some Groove Armada. I confessed I'd heard nothing of them. She went into raptures talking about their discography, all her associated memories. But the only sense that I had turned on in that moment was vision. I looked into her delicate gooseberry-coloured eyes.

Now she'd slid her tucked-up bare legs towards me, into the space between us. She rested her head on her palm, arm bent and resting on the top of the futon's backrest. She was looking directly at me. Her lips seemed to purse in expectation.

"Jo," I began. I was supposed to know what to say on MD. "You look… stunning tonight." Like a slow descent into a warm, perfect sleep, our heads nodded together inch by inch. I switched to autopilot, semi-anaesthetised. I put my hand to her face, her soft, cool hair brushing my knuckles. There was a pause, feeling like an eternity, as our lips stopped millimetres short of each other. Then I slid forward. She slowly lay back and I put my arms either side of her, balancing above. Our crotches touched; she thrust upwards gently. With a slight sinking feeling in my stomach I remembered that I couldn't get hard. But it would keep the night clearer, purer. We were both there on a settee in the middle of Birmingham, MD'd off our faces, feeling one another for the first time. I knew then that it was better, infinitely better, to save sex. For the first time, I thanked the mysterious biological force known as druggie-dick.

There was hammering on the doorbell and Jo started from under me and slid out to buzz the lads back up. I saw her straighten herself out and I did the same, sweeping my hair over and pulling my shirt back down. She smiled at me and bit her lip, her hair sliding down over one of her bright eyes.

They entered, Cosmo first, bursting through the door. He had his hands in front of him and was twirling his index fingers around in opposite rotational directions with a concentrated, serious look on his face. He was talking about how to draw propellers. For once, Cam, bringing up the rear, seemed to be listening to an extended explanation from someone else. He drank in everything Cosmo had to say as he resumed his position opposite me.

The conversation changed course a few times over until light began to seep in through the blinds. Jo looked tired.

"I'm off to bed boys, but feel free to stop here; it's a fair old walk to Jack's, and you don't know the way," she announced.

"What about your flatmates?"

"It'll be fine. I'll text them all now so they don't get a fright! Just use the futon and whatever else you can find." Jo passed by Cosmo and Cam and through a door to the right of the TV. "Night guys." She sank away into the dimness of her room, legs turning from white to black. The conversation turned back to the fight with Khan. I stroked my neck and felt that it'd begun to crust up, the long shallow gash running from the side of my Adam's Apple up to my jawbone. I retold the story from my perspective, reminding Cam of Khan's arm twist on him. Like only feeling the pain of a naked stove-flame when you look down at your arm, Cam realised his shoulder was in a bad way.

"Yes, he went ninja on your arse."

We talked and talked some more and wound down the night. When we were ligged out on the sofa, Cosmo asked softly,

"Anything happen earlier?" I stayed silent for a second, distractedly thinking about how I had held her.

"Maybe." There was the sound of the breeze outside and of the traffic too. Cam gave a quick exhalation, like a laugh, through his nose.

"Oh, right. Nice one. Nice one."

Cam was evidently a light sleeper given that he claimed to have met Jo's flatmates that morning while I was still passed out. It had just turned one o'clock when Jo made us a cuppa each. Cosmo started chatting to her about a book he'd seen on the worktop.

"Back to Jack's after this then?" Cam yawned to me.

"Yes, yes, we need a full de-brief."

"Mmm. But, you know, I've been thinking about the situation for us at his. Do you think it's true that," he stopped. "Do you think…Argh…do you think you'll have to keep Becky sweet for us? Because I understand mate, it's totally not up to you and it's unfair; none of us would want to be in your position man, but…"

I laid my mug down on the side. "Yeah, I know," I said, rubbing my nose and feeling mithered. "I'm gonna try and keep us there as long as I can, that's all I can do really." I sighed in genuine despair. "Come on, I need a cigarette I think." I lumbered downstairs in my t-shirt as Cam grabbed his jacket. I poked my head out of the red front door. The cold wind hit me with a short sharp spray of vapour and the road was blaring with the sounds of traffic and roadworks.

"Fuck, it's freezing."

"Grab your hoodie."

"Oh God," I groaned. "I can't be fucked."

"Here's a light." Click, click. "Pissing impossible in the wind, man. It's unlike you, isn't it, having one in the middle of the day?"

"Very. Feel like shit. No offence, but reminding me of nightmare Becky hasn't helped."

"Sorry mate."

A procession of empty buses passed by, a peeling advert flapping about madly on one of them. "I know, let's get a fry up on the way back."

"Deal." We smoked silently for a while, until Cosmo and Jo both pulled themselves through the doorway. Jo had a big bag slung over her shoulder.

"Jesus Christ!" shouted Cosmo. "Feels like Flamborough Head out here!" Me and Cam laughed. Flamborough Head, officially windy as hell, I remembered.

"Are we all leaving?" Cam enquired, looking at Jo's bag.

"Yep, library. Third years never rest," she grimaced.

"Dedication to the cause. Are you coming the same way as us?"

"No, the opposite actually I'm afraid. But if you go down that way," she pointed with her right hand, "and follow signs for the hospital, you should recognise the streets. Well, that's the theory anyway. See you all soon; I'll message Misha at some point and we'll go to the pub or something, eh?" A wave of warm embarrassment flickered up my body as I thought of asking her for her number, but some irresistible force inside me stopped me from forming the words with my mouth. Why was it that the magic of the night before had gone? I felt numb as she hugged Cosmo, who seemed to try and keep her in his arms for longer than was necessary, and then Cam. Then she came to me and I felt her hand reach into the back pocket of my jeans. "See you soon Gene," she said quietly into my ear. "Bye all." And she turned her back, starting up the pavement leading left out of her doorway. Cosmo slung me my grey hoodie, and I pulled it on thankfully to guard against the bitter, unseasonal wind. Then I felt my way into my back pocket. There was a slip of paper! I considered taking it out, just to check, but thought better of it. Best not to flash it in front of prying eyes.

"To the greasy spoon!" exclaimed the windswept Cam, hair flicking about like dark tongues.

Chapter Eleven

We settled in a cafe on Bristol Road and called up Dan; in a few minutes he'd arrived. Then he dealt a blow. He got a call from my uncle. It was time for him to go.

"Your Uncle Dave says everything's ready for a half-six start tomorrow," he said looking both sad and serious. He loaded some beans and toast onto his fork and lifted it to his disinterested, stubbled mouth. "Damn it, I don't want to go. I don't want to leave. This has been the best extended weekend ever." He smiled, then he shrugged. He shovelled the beans into his mouth and glanced out of the window into the spray. Cam, who sat next to him, grabbed Dan's shoulder and said softly, "Fibreglass needs you. I release you Dan."

It was sad to see him go, but it was no great surprise that he'd been called back home. He wandered around the house checking he had everything and threw all his stuff into the boot. We sat on the tailgate for a while in the chilly wind, talking and waiting for Jack. Becky, frowning, said he'd stopped at Nugent's. She spoke matter-of-factly, not looking at any of us but down the road, her hair sticking out in places and her hungover eyes suggesting she'd been chopping onions.

"Jack was too whacked out when I left. John too. I got a taxi with some other girlfriends. But he said he would get back earlyish. Probably to gow and deal more drugs, but hey…." She shrugged and turned to take a seat on the sagging tailgate. There was quiet between us. A lorry beeped as it backed-up in the distance, a can clattered as it blew along the grey pavement. I looked up the road, squinting against the brightness that was still there even through the blanket of cloud above. Then the lank figure of Jack turned the corner from the main road up ahead. He had his hands tucked underneath his t-shirted armpits, and as he got closer I could see the grimace on his face and his shaking body. He turned up into the house with only a glance to us, demanding,

"What's happening here then? You all abandoning me?"

His loud voice echoed in the hallway as he rustled about for a coat. He came outside again zipping up what was clearly a small woman's duffel jacket.

"Oi yow, down't bloody break that! Cost me a fortune. Oh Jack, it's too small. Bloody hell." Becky remonstrated but didn't move, except to sweep her hair out of her eyes.

"Sorry chaps, was bloody freezing," he said ignoring Becky and still shaking. He stood and looked at us in turn sitting forlornly. "So what's going on?"

"I've gotta go Jack, I'm sorry mate. Back to the slog up North."

"Back to the grindstone, eh?" Jack echoed looking into the distance with a tone suggesting that what Dan had said was somehow an important philosophical issue. "Well, had to happen sometime didn't it?" He parked himself next to Dan on the small space available above the rear lights.

"Aye, well I'm all ready to go now. Boot's packed, and I shouldn't have left anything. How are you feeling after last night anyway?"

"Oh, you know. Sideways, as always." Jack chuckled to himself.

"Where have Kerry and erm… John got to?"

"Erm, I think John pulled, at least, I couldn't find him this morning. Kerry's disappeared to her boyfriend's—he turned up eventually last night. I'm guessing you wanted to give her a big snog goodbye?"

"Fuck off. Although that would've been nice."

Dan left after embracing all of us one-by-one. I was sad to see him go, but took a pleasure in the fact that his departure was a reminder that I was here to stay for the foreseeable future. Then I remembered the antagonism of Becky, the will-she-won't-she-chuck-us-out; but she looked in no fit state to attempt turfing us out today at least. As that knackered Fiesta coughed into life and pulled away down the street, Cam exclaimed,

"Fuck, I love the guy but I'm freezing my tits off." There was instantly a low noise from everyone, and as one we all turned to the door to get out of the wind. Little spits of rain began to fall again; inside, I saw them getting bigger against the window-pane of the front room. We flicked the little telly on.

Cosmo was fiddling with his phone, texting someone. It triggered me into fishing out that piece of paper from my back pocket. On it was Jo's number. The others were transfixed by the home-improvement shite that had come on, and I quickly added the number to my phone without them noticing. I didn't know why I felt it necessary to be so secretive. I slipped the note back into my pocket.

"Who are you harassing Cos?" He looked up like a surprised rabbit.

"Oh, erm… you remember that bird from the other night? Rachel? Yeah, just her." Cam was chewing on his shirt and laughed.

"Oh really? You dark horse. Bit awkward though; thought you couldn't, you know, get it up?"

"What? Piss off! She was," his eyes darted towards Becky's presence, "erm, you know. On. It weren't me."

"Oop, my mistake, sorry pal."

"Yeah, I should think so!"

"So you're trying to set up a candlelit dinner with her?"

"Don't call it that."

"She weren't bad at all, mate. Good on ya," I opined. His phone went off. "That'll be her saying no then." Cosmo read the text. His face was triumphant.

"Ah, ha! Fuck the lot of ya. I have a date tonight." There was a small round of applause at this news.

"Looks like it'll be her place not yours, if you manage to get her smashed enough. You're not shagging next to me, sailor. I'm gonna need my sleep."

But then surely my own date with Jo could be on the cards? To hell with sleep. I sat down in the kitchen and spent a long time agonising over the wording until I felt the text would make her smile and let her know my intentions. I made a brew while I waited for her to text back, humming and tapping the teaspoon on the worktop as I studied Jack's cork notice board. 'Rubbish Tuesday nites'; 'Everyone owes John £21.30 for internet'; a photo of Jack paralytic on a sofa, hair bunched up by bands; another of Becky in the same position, slices of ham covering her face; and a gas bill (last reminder). I sat back down and picked up the phone. As I did it buzzed. I fumbled in my excitement. Then, disappointingly I read that she already had plans for tonight. The door swung open and, completely unnecessarily, I stuffed my phone awkwardly back into my pocket. It was Jack.

"Alright geezer, texting someone? Double date with Cosmo?"

"I don't think so. Texting my uncle."

"That's just weird. I've never been on a date with a man."

"Or a family member, I hope." He sat down with a groan, his creaky posture accentuating his delicateness from the night before. "Tell us about your night then, while I stick a brew on."

"Ooh, ta. That'll sort me right out," he sighed with gratitude. He stretched his arms behind his head. "Not much to tell really, just hung around and got stoned. Got quite trippy for a bit. Ended up like Cam was at Mischa's—childhood shit, very strange. Did I see you? Where did you lot go?"

I took my time explaining everything that had happened, mentioning the kiss. At this Jack looked up.

"Get in there son. Shag her?"

"Oh but you know, it's not one of them. I know I just sound naïve but… well, she seems special. Like, I didn't mind that it didn't happen, because it just wasn't right. D'ya get me?" He shook his head slowly, blowing his tea.

"Nah, I'm just playing, of course I do. But it's early days, y'know? Just don't get too… involved. That's all I'm saying. I mean, you're welcome to stop here as long as you need as far as I'm concerned, before term starts anyway. But you've gotta bear in mind that you don't have a place in Birmingham."

"Well, maybe I'll get one," I said, surprising even myself. "I mean, I don't think I can go back there. You guys are here, Cam and Cos could stay… we could get a house together sooner or later."

"You'd need a job of course."

"I know I know, and a few GCSE's aren't exactly gonna look dazzling…"

"Plenty of bars and supermarkets round here mate, you'll find something. Did you know, I'm hoping to get a job in London after this year: trainee government adviser…" Jack went on. I envied him. I envied that he had it fixed. I was happy for him. But all throughout, I could only think: what are you doing, what are you doing Gene? It nagged like a persistent, itching fly on a boiling day. Another itch was the question (if I couldn't get work stacking shelves in Aldi) of how I was going to get a job in a bar when I was only 17. We shot the breeze for another half-hour and then, by nodding half-eyed mutual consent, crept up to our beds for an afternoon nap.

I awoke at 5.30. The clouds had begun to clear away but a few still lingered, isolated and blue, in the cold sky. I sat up, rubbing my head. Fuck, I was worse than when I'd gone to sleep. Mouth dry, cheeks chewed up to shit. It felt as though I had a cold but I knew full well I didn't. Aching, retarded movements coupled themselves with an unwelcome fuzziness as I slunk slowly down to the front room sofas, dragging my sleeping-bag along with me.

Cosmo, that energetic bastard, looked as fresh as a newly-printed banknote. He'd dressed up (as far as was possible for Cosmo) in a plain purple t-shirt, a grey cardigan, and skinny jeans. He'd even attempted something with his hair, though whatever it was I couldn't discern; it'd been flattened and straightened somehow. He was a lucky, good-looking bastard. Jo hadn't suggested another date for meeting up as I hoped she would. I wasn't ready to give up, but I felt it was a bad sign. Everything felt hopeless. I started to think about tea.

"Maybe we should have something healthy; I feel like I need some brain cells back," suggested Jack. I concurred. Cam, who was kneeling by the object-smattered table with his MacBook, chimed in without looking up.

"But who can be arsed to cook?" No one responded.

"Right, curry it is then. The chilli powder gets the endorphins flowing again…" Cosmo objected on the grounds that he didn't want to smell of Indian before a date, so he went out and bought a ready meal, then left the house looking nervous. I was ravenous and made light work of the curry when it finally came. We watched films and played Nintendo 64 games until I gave up, returned to bed, and descended into an intermittent night's sleep, punctuated by strange, arid dreams.

Chapter Twelve

I awoke as the sun rose early in the morning. Cosmo was hunched in his sleeping bag at the other end of the cupboard, evidently having made it back from his date in one piece, and shagless. I opened the bottom of my sleeping bag with a crackly rustle, stuck my feet through the hole, and trudged downstairs.

I could barely hold my eyes open, but I was ravenous. Whose cereal should I steal this morning? I felt a small pang of guilt and resolved to go out to the shop when it opened and get my act together and buy some real food of my own. John's Cinnamon Grahams looked the most tempting. I shook them: weighty. I knew that if I was the owner of a packet of Cinnamon Grahams I would be keeping a close eye on them, so I shook out as many as I thought I could get away with, like a burglar taking the telly but leaving the remote. I poured the milk with an ineffable feeling that there was something wrong. I felt miserable, yet knew that I had no reason to be. It was the hangover not of the party but of the dreams I'd endured in the night. I remembered that I'd woken suddenly, that something had been wrong just before I had opened my eyes. I had searched a church on an island but couldn't find what I was looking for; there had been a woman on a station platform, trying to pickpocket me. I'd been alone.

I left the kitchen and walked past the closed living room door. Then, I stopped. Taking two steps back, I looked at the door again. There was a female voice behind it. Who else was up at this time in the morning? Slowly, I pressed my ear to the door. It was Becky.

"Yeah, I'm foine mum. No, no. I am. I will." Her voice was strained. It sounded like she was sat on the sofa nearest the window, judging by how hard I had to press my ear to the door to hear her. I held my breath though Becky couldn't possibly hear it. My heart rate rose, ready to fly at the slightest suggestion of getting rumbled. 'It's just not fair that he thinks he's allowed to keep them here loike they're not in the way or anything, and…yeah, the bills. Exactly. I'm just fed up.'

Immediately I heard a shuffling and a thud on the floor, and I jumped back noiselessly from the door. I stalked silently with exaggerated footsteps back up the stairs and into mine and Cosmo's cupboard before Becky opened the door downstairs.

I stared into space and plotted the next move. That was what it had come to now: a game of moves. Becky was ready to make hers. Those strange dreams had been forgotten now. Without thinking, I leant back down and quickly regained unconsciousness.

My dreams had been so pleasant that I woke up for the second time at half-past eleven feeling like a completely different person. My limbs felt full of life, my head a hundred times clearer, and there were sounds of multiple voices downstairs. I threw on some fresh clothes —the last in my bag—and went to join them. The day felt set up for a fresh start. But this was to be the day that it all fell down.

"He's eager, isn't he? Can't leave her alone!"

"So he definitely didn't stay at hers?"

"Who's this we're on about?" I cut in.

"Oh, only Cosmo. He's gone out to see that bird again this morning. Ah Gene, you'll know: did he stop here last night?"

"Aye aye I saw him."

"There you go Jack."

"Fair play to the lad, fair play. To be honest I know nothing about her, I just recognised her face at Mischa's." Jack looked to the window. "Give her one from me, son!"

"For fuck's sake, stop trying to be such a lad," Cam berated Jack. "You sound like such a bellend."

"But why has he gone out so early?" I asked, checking the clock on the wall behind Jack. "He's keen, isn't he?"

"Yeah, it is early. Probably wanted to enjoy the weather."

The weather, however, did not last long. The sky slipped from blue to a wood-pigeon grey without the semblance of a warning and it began to bucket down, stopping all talk amongst us of going out for the day to somewhere in the country. Jack, though, was the first to come up with an alternative.

He pulled us all into the front room and said he had a great game we could improvise. He cleared the table of its various bits of rubbish: ash trays, drug bags and magazines, standing up tall occasionally and grumbling something like, "For fuck's sake, why can't I just give up smoking, give up drugs? Look at all this shit!" Once the table was clear he got me to grab the far end of it, flip it on its long side and shift it round so that it faced the sofa nearest the window. As I looked at the rivers cascading down the window's pane I saw a figure streak past outside.

"Cam, can you shove them sofas into that corner there?"

There was first the sound of the whoosh of the front door being opened and the rain falling on the stone step outside, and then the clatter of the door and the letterbox as somebody entered. There was a loud, depressed groan in the hallway. It was unmistakeably Cosmo. He took some seconds in the hallway rustling about and swearing and then trudged through the front room door like a drowned dog, sopping over the floor and looking thoroughly pissed off. The sight was too comical for us to contain ourselves.

"Nice date then?" snorted Cam. Cosmo threw himself onto the edge of one of the moved sofas and looked at Cam with an expression of utter contempt, exploding off into a diatribe about nosey fucking people and the wankingly shit weather.

With everyone now in one room I was about to tell of what I'd heard Becky say. What was going to happen? The situation felt pressingly real again and I needed guidance.

But I'd stalled too long.

"I'm just off to find that plush ball then we can get started," shouted Jack, and then my thoughts were lost in a rifle-like stream of interrogation from Cam, who was almost bearing down on Cosmo in his agitation to hear some news. I followed Jack upstairs and went for a piss. We had to keep on our best behaviour, that was all. Naïve, maybe, but better than nothing. The other option made me shudder. Instead, we could make her enjoy our company, keep her sweet, and the first thing to do was to break up the game downstairs, tidy up, and then get her involved in something. As I patted down my wet hands on the way out of the bathroom I nearly jumped out of my skin. Becky was there, waiting for the toilet.

"Oh, hello stranger! Feels like I've not seen yow in aaages," she drawled sleepily, beaming up at me with her small mouth and hemmed-in eyes. Her hair was tied back I noticed, sadly revealing more of her oddly-proportioned face. Around her torso was a simple jumper, pulled over her hands, and on her lower half she wore a stonewashed pair of jeans. She rested her hand on the banister, slipping it out of her jumper sleeve as she did. "Sow, whatcha been up to? Did you enjoy the party in Wolves?" Her bright face was flushed and happy, and dark speckles of freckle seemed to have been given permission to camp themselves across her cheeks since I last saw them. I wanted desperately to get away from the face and down the stairs and set the front room straight again, but her arm formed a barrier across my path.

"Erm yeah I did actually, started off quiet dinnit?"

"Yeah but didn't end that way! So is he gone, whatshisname…"

"Dan?"

"Dan, is he gone?"

"Yeah, he had to get back for work." I considered saying 'bit of a shame' but thought better of giving her an opportunity to voice her displeasure.

"Sow, where did you stay?"

DON'T SAY JO'S.

"Erm, oh we just ah ended up on a wild goose chase looking for this club and then ended up at this bloke's. Pretty crap really. Would've been better to stay here to be honest."

"You should've done! It would've been better with yow around, everyone likes it when yow are." I couldn't help being flattered and I eased up a bit, leant against the wall and started picking my nails. "Think I drank a bit too much though." She made a very obvious flutter of her eyelashes. Oh, anything to make it stop! My whole body was starting to recoil, even panic.

"Ha, you and me both Becky. Oh, has, erm, has John got back yet?"

"Yeah yeah I've seen him round."

"He got lucky I heard."

"I'm surprised you didn't to be honest." At this she flicked her odd dark eyes up and twisted her finger round on the banister top. I felt a flash of what was to come and wished to avoid it more than anything in the world.

"Listen Becky, we were…" She moved forwards quickly, drawing herself up onto her tip-toes, breathing upwards into my face. Why did she have to smell so nice? Why would I have to focus on a thing like that now?

"I don't know if you've been able to tell, but I like you, Gene." Her voice was just a whisper. "I like it when you're here." I saw her eyes flicker down, look at my lips. My back had straightened, arching against the wall behind. I felt a sharp pain as my head jerked backwards onto the plaster. She stopped short of contact with my lips; she was too short. She lowered herself and grabbed my hand, brushing my crotch and causing a swoop of pleasure to judder upwards through my stomach. Even in the middle of this awful situation I had somehow managed to get a semi. "Come with me Gene."

I tried to stop my legs from following irresistibly along after her towards her door, but something was blocking my brain. She pulled with unusual strength; I felt powerless. Soon she had me on my back on top of her bedcovers.

"Oi've waited sow long for this Gene, sow long." She giggled like a drunk girl. Her leg swung over and placed her crotch on mine.

The devil inside me cackled "Gene, this feels ni-ice, let it happen." I grimaced, barely offering back the kisses she was covering my lips with. Gene, this is wrong. Don't let it happen. I closed my eyes but that made it worse; she moved her kisses downwards, lifting up my thin t-shirt, moving over my stomach. I could feel my erection was at full-tilt, hurting as it pushed into the hard edging of my boxers. She undid my trouser button, slid down the zip, slid her fingers along the shaft. I shuddered. I thought of Jo, screwed up my eyes, remembered her beautiful face, remembered that she might have been the one doing this. Her wet lips took in the end. For the boys, I tried to scream at myself, for the boys. But no!

Disgusted, I threw my knees upwards and accidentally hit both her breasts, barking "Look," then an apology for kneeing her. I pulled up my boxers and trousers, feeling sick and looking straight at her. Bollocks to the consequences. I was not going to be the bargaining chip, however much I wanted to stay in this house. I muttered "For fuck's sake"; she half-shouted my name in horrified desperation and I twisted and stumbled out of her room, knocking my wrist awkwardly on her wooden door.

My head was completely fried. I buttoned up my trousers and, without knowing what else to do, pushed open the door to the living room. I could hear the shouts of the lads and the crashing of things being thrown about, and sure enough the entire room was upside down. The still dripping wet Cosmo was wedged in a corner with his mouth gaping open and a small ball in his hand, the ashtrays had tipped everywhere, the little television was hanging off the edge of the stool by its cord and Jack was stood on top of the small slither of table which lay horizontal next to the wall.

"Gene! Where the fuck have you been?! Duck!" I threw my head downwards as the ball headed for the patch of wall next to me and dropped in between the two table legs that prayed crossways in the air like a mantis.

"Two points, that's two points!" declared Jack flamboyantly throwing two fingers in the air. Cosmo screamed and whooped like an American-Indian riding to war, and music blasted in the background, completing the din.

"Shut up, just," I turned and slammed the door shut, "Just shut up! Something bad has just happened, something really bad."

"What's happened Gene? You look like a fucking gunman's just tried to mug you," said Cosmo, trying and failing to extricate himself from the corner he was wedged in. I spoke through my teeth.

"Fucking Becky's just happened, that's what!" All Cosmo could do was put on a giant retard's grin as I looked back at him.

"What, you shagged her?"

"No, I didn't fucking shag her, I just had to force her off my cock, that's what, and she's gonna go psycho if she comes down and sees this, mate."

Jack moved across me and said bitterly, dropping his tone,

"Oh, she'll be fine, forget her. Sick of it, just sick of it." Even so, he went to return the table to its four legs, pulling hard at it to bring it back off the wall. I went to help, then a hammering came from down the stairs.

"Gene, Gene, I'm sorry!"

"Becky, it's fine, don't come in!" I shouted while I desperately tried to make it to the door before she did, but I was too late. She threw the door open with her odd, hare-like strength, and looked at the scene before her.

"What… what's happened here? What the fuck?!" Her voice rose. She looked at me, embarrassed, and then at poor Cam, who I'd barely noticed standing to the left of me. "Moi work! It's everywhere!" I looked down to see sheets of paper scattered across one half of the room, each marked with cramped, typewriter-style handwriting. She stomped forwards and pushed her hands upwards into Cam's chest.

"Roight… that's…. it! You can pack your bags! You've got to leave! Jack, your friends are leaving. Today!" Her eyes flashed round at me, the amber flecks in amongst the darker brown of her irises glowing now with anger and passion. Her hair flew across her, her fists clenched. She looked overcome with hate. "YOW LOT HAVE BEEN NOTHING BUT TROUBLE! I WANT YOU GONE!"

"Becky, oi, come on…" Jack's voice sounded weak and ineffective in the wake of Becky's vitriol.

"No Jack, no fucking way. They have to go. This is moi house too, and all you've been is selfish for the last week. They have to go." She jabbed her chest forcefully as she spoke. Cam looked at me with his mouth slightly open, at a loss. Jack looked as though he could not argue further with this livid woman. In the lengthening silence he looked defeated. I urged him desperately with everything inside me to convince her to change her mind, for the magician to say his words, make the anger disappear under the cloth, shout 'Tadah!'

But she stood firm, and Jack stayed quiet. Cam was the first to break.

"Becky, we're sorry. We'll pack straight away."

"Becky," I cut in, "Listen you can't take it out on the other lads if I didn't…" I stopped as she advanced at me.

"Yow," she whispered through gritted teeth. "I don't want to ever see yow again." Her frown, so ugly, so accentuative of her strange, dark eyes, quivered and then fell. She began to sob hysterically in the middle of the upturned room. No one moved to comfort her. She stood there, convulsing, breaking down for what felt an age, the rest of us standing clear like ramblers too afraid to undo the trap from the whining bear, until my own anger at her and at the ridiculousness of the situation convinced me to pound up to the cupboard upstairs and begin packing. What else could I do? What else could we do?

We would have to get the train to Leeds. But Leeds, then home… that was impossible. I couldn't, surely not after everything—but what else? Stay at Cosmo's a few nights I supposed, try and sort something out from there. But not home. Not now.

On cue, Cosmo entered the cupboard as I looked about it, not registering the objects within. Before I had a chance to speak he declared,

"I'm gonna call Jo. I think she'll be able to sort us out for a few nights."

There was an unnerving new suppleness and sureness to his voice.

"Mate, you can't… what are you on about?" Confusion and anger was rising. I knew Cosmo. He was being an idiot on purpose. "For a start, you haven't even got her number! And you don't even know her! Even if you did what makes you think we'd be allowed to stay? You do realise that was a one night thing, right? That we were there because it was an MD comedown, that no normal person lets people crash at theirs who they barely know?" There was a heat prickling my neck; Cosmo didn't know about Jo's rejection of me but now suddenly it was his fault; or maybe somehow he did know.

"D'ya think it's funny, do you?!" I screamed at him.

As he held his phone a few inches from his ear, there was a look of disgust on Cosmo's face that mirrored my own.

"What's wrong with you? Don't fucking shout at me. Be quiet." Not able to think of the words that could express the way in which I wanted to punch him square in the mouth, and knowing how I would regret it if I did hit him, I thundered out of the room onto the landing, kicking instead a railing clean off the banister. There was nowhere to go.

Chapter Thirteen

Jack slouched in a chair looking once-and-for-all defeated, his eyes now stripped of basic confidence. I saw him as a lamb abandoned in the darkness and rain; in the corners of his stone-grey eyes were weird twitches, and each time they twitched he rubbed them and made the corners red beneath his black eyebrows. It took some effort, a strained apology on my part, to say goodbye to him. It was not one of those apologies a person says to express regret: it was one that expressed all the thanks I could put across, and, as I choked through my departing words, I realised that the gratitude did indeed run deep.

I'd seen this emotion in Jack only once before. The Wolverhampton party had shown his parental face, his deep self-dissatisfaction; I saw this in him now just like then, and my heart fell.

I re-threw the strap of my bag across my shoulder and then patted his, slumped and bony. The embarrassed, apologetic murmur of 'goodbye' came once more from our lips and we filed out unaccompanied into the wet afternoon, navy-blue clouds streaking by overhead.

We walked down to the main road. My comment that Jack would pick himself up was followed by silence. I was still processing the revelation that Cosmo had, beneath my nose, not only been texting but also seeing Jo over the last few days.

"Those times Gene, when I said I was seeing Rachel," he was explaining unselfconsciously, "Well, you know."

Everything made unsettling sense now. He had me and I had no choice except to play his game; turning on him now would've spelt self-destruction, not only because the iron in my mind was still hot and only partially formed from the closeness and the suddenness of the news, and would brand on Cosmo something I'd later regret, but also because, temporarily, I was homeless and cast adrift again. And he was the only raft in the sea onto which I could cling.

He remembered the walk to Jo's with only a little deliberation on our route; perhaps I shouldn't have been surprised. We wound through narrow streets looking like pack-laden trekkers and hit the next main road. A familiar red doorway and French Restaurant jumped out from the side of my vision, and as fan belts slipped and faint sirens wailed in the background, Cam rejoiced.

"Door to door in…let's see… twenty minutes. Nice one Cos. I mean it." He smiled sincerely at Cosmo who had an ill-fitting, serious expression etched on his face. He shrugged quietly.

"I just hope to fuck it's the last one we have to go through for a while."

He rang the bell.

Jo answered the door in a bluster of smiles and hugs and talked us all the way up the stairs, expressing her condemnation of Becky who, when Cosmo mentioned her, had become 'that stupid bitch' and who, Jo agreed, needed her head looking at. There was a creeping, sour familiarity between the two of them. I felt like spitting to try and get rid of the taste.

As we crossed the threshold I could see that everything looked the same except for two figures in the kitchen to the side of the flat. They were standing behind a breakfast bar and were stuck in discussion whilst chopping and washing with their backs turned. Both were women: one tall, with wide and gawky shoulders covered by a thin, hanging blue cardigan and sweeps of brown hair; the other much shorter, proportions almost dwarfish— an over-lordosis of the back, stumpy legs—and wearing a mustard-yellow t-shirt, nearly the same colour as her hair. They turned and looked up just as the door swung shut. Jo flourished round and held her hands together.

"So, erm, guys, these are my two flatmates, Genna and Kat. Gen, Kat, this is Cos, Gene and... Cam. It is Cam, isn't it?" She indicated each of us, narrowing those gooseberry-green eyes.

"Yeah that's right. Just a nickname. Parents called me Joseph, but keep that under yer hat."

"You know, I never knew that," purred Cosmo in his strange, new, supple voice.

"Well, we're both living under assumed identities eh, me and thee?"

"Cosmo? Where have I heard that name before?" wondered Genna aloud. She was the short blonde one who was picking up some salad leaves.

"I'm just a massive fan of women's magazines, y'see," replied Cos relaxedly, the joke apparently becoming the cue for him and Cam to slip off their bags and thunk them onto the floor. I followed suit hesitantly. "I just want to say," he continued, "That we're really thankful you've let us stay, and that we'll try to keep out of everyone's way as much as we can, we will."

"Oh don't worry, sounds like that last place you were at had a real headcase in it."

Cosmo, it appeared, had laid it on dead thick in his phone call to Jo. Christ, he could be wiley when he wanted to that lad; he could be all screams and lunacy, and then... in what felt like a muscle-twitch something in the nature of mine and Cosmo's friendship had inextricably changed, like one of those tadpoles we'd raised being bitten by a cruel late frost. He stood there confident, almost impressive, and even as I knew we could be best mates again there would forever be the taint of what'd happened, of what was happening. And of course, it was made all the worse by the fact that I knew he'd barely done anything actually wrong.

In the meantime, we were being told where to sleep.

"I was thinking, under the window? What do you reckon? I mean, God I feel terrible, you'll all be huddled up together, but I guess that is the best place, isn't it? We can get some cushions and covers and..." He interrupted Jo with a touch on the shoulder.

"Jo, that'll be more than fine. It's amazing you've given us a roof over our heads, and at such short notice." The two exchanged a glance. They stood at nearly the same height; he knew what he was doing, holding the stare just long enough and then turning to the kitchen. Yes, you fucker, you agree that we can sleep down there because I'll bet you think you'll be sleeping in her bed in a few nights' time don't you? "So, what time is it? Ah, only half two, sound. Well, don't let us get in the way, are you cooking lunch?" he called over to the kitchen.

"Caesar salad, since you ask. It's looking, well…"

"I haven't got a Fanny's Aunt how we can't follow a recipe Kat, I really don't. You guys could probably have done a better job without one!"

The politeness flew back and forth for a while longer. I sat down.

"You okay Gene? It's good to see you again…" Jo asked softly. Her words made me jump slightly inside; that shot of saccharine warmth headed up through my body again.

"Yeah yeah, I'm really… fine. Not bad at all. It's nice to see you too," I added.

"Really? Well, I suppose you're just in a bit of a weird place at the minute. Do you want a cuppa?"

She made her way up to the kitchen (which, I now saw, was reachable by three miniature steps to either side of the breakfast bar), her black leggings stretched finely over her full, long legs and her tantalising arse. She asked the lads, still in filler conversation with the two other flatmates, if they wanted brews and took their orders: Cam—two sugars, Cos—lots of milk. They joked about Jack's surreptitious brewing method and went off into a description of the night. I sighed and collapsed my knackered body onto the biggest sofa, its back turned to the kitchen area and stared blankly ahead at the empty TV screen. Only a week or so before I would have probably cut my little toe off to be sitting where I was right now. But I'd been saved, saved, and yes it was just I to my mind, because they weren't in flight, they sure as hell had places to go back to. The North didn't repel them; all it would have meant for them if there was no longer a place to stay would have been a ticket at New Street or a Megabus along the A42 and hey! Back in Knaresborough, bored but not finished.

Though the flatmates, Kat and Genna, had appeared normal in the sense that they seemed like the kind of girls who got up early, did their work (whatever it was they did; their uni life had apparently been covered in the earlier conversation with Cam and Cosmo), cooked healthy food, kept their flat tidy and maybe ate chocolate while watching an E4 comedy in the evening; though they appeared like this, we soon found out they were far from the straight-edged young women that I'd thought. For the next two hours, news rolling on in the background, we talked about drug habits, their sources, their effects, the dealers, the scene, the music. Some of their knowledge was fascinating, some flakey, superfluous, self-involved. This uni year, they both agreed, was going to be the best; they now had the experience and know-how of the last two years, knew when to stop and take it easy and when to get royally fucked up. Some of what they said amused me with its misplaced faith, and some made sense—made taking drugs every weekend seem a necessity, something to be celebrated. It'd become clear that these girls had returned to their sheltered Surrey suburbs each summer with a fresh outlook, imported knowledge, changed minds.

Casually Genna, the more confident, brasher personality of the two flatmates, grabbed her handbag from the Ikea coffee table and pulled out a bag full of white powder.

"Right, I know it's got a bad name for itself, but you really can't beat a bit of ketamine for a chill-out sesh," she said, leaning back into her chair and sweeping her short fringe from her forehead. Her voice was assertive, almost aggressive I sensed, and it was soaked with—what was it?—that kind of London council estate speak where accents collide.

I inwardly rolled my eyes. Ketamine. Even in my limited knowledge, that was a dirty drug.

"Horse tranquiliser. Really?" asked Cam.

"I know, but really, there's so much other worse stuff people put in themselves. Don't knock it until you've tried it, eh?"

What I truly wanted was a drink, a good cold pint down my throat, something familiar. "Wanna try some?" Genna addressed Cam. Cam looked expectantly at Cosmo, knowing that he would as usual be more than willing to give something new a go—but he looked almost parental as he surveyed the bag with distrust.

"Horse tranquiliser?" he repeated, "Come on…"

"What if we'd said that about MD though mate, eh?" Cam cut in. "We've got nowt else to do this evening," Genna grinned. Then Kat chirruped,

"This is pretty much just what we were gonna do anyway, you know. Uni doesn't start for ages yet, and no-one's got work tomorrow."

Cam nudged, at first gently and then more violently, at Cosmo until he began to tip over from his cross-legged position. "Gah, go on then, what harm could it do?" He wasn't looking for an answer. I could think of lots of reasons not to, but at that moment all I wanted was something to take me out of my pounding head; so, as the dwarfish, devious Genna racked up the lines, I counted myself in.

In the haze of the hours that followed I had so many lines that I was walking up the miniature steps to the kitchen like a crab that'd been hit by a mallet. If the image seems ridiculous, that's because I'd slipped into a garish world where time was standing still and movement felt stupendous. All of my anger about Cos's supposed disloyalty had been dissolved. We'd sent Jo and Kat to get a crate from the shop; at the same time, Genna was Skyping her boyfriend.

When I finally staggered back from the kitchen, crisps in hand, I saw Cam shifting around to the left of me. He was swirling his finger around a green glass jar.

"Look at these Gene," he trilled impishly. He tilted the translucent jar towards me. "Pills. Check 'em out. Me and Cos are gonna drop when he's back from the pisser."

"Sound," I croaked. Cosmo returned and we swilled the little yellow tablets down, one each, with some vodka from the fridge and lay back again. The curtains were drawn, day had passed outside and none of us had any interest in seeing the night. Kat returned from the shop with beer and Lambrusco. I registered my disgust at the last item as she offered me a swig from the fat, baby-sized bottle.

"Oh, you keep your park-bench tipple to yourself, cheers. I didn't realise we were chavvy thirteen-year-old girls talking about Cheryl Cole. Hang on, I've got some trackies in here somewhere…" As I rummaged around in my bag and Kat tinkled a laugh, Genna squealed:

"Ooh! You've found the house apothecary I see!" She snatched up the little jar and hugged it to her head; next to her, I thought, it seemed disproportionately big. "Have you boys dropped then?"

There was a feigned look of surprise on Cos's face as he answered, "No, no we were just admiring the contents, that's all."

Genna looked at us with one sweeping, authoritative glance and replied, "Now, boys, come on, we don't mind if you have. In fact we expected it. Woulda been disappointed if you hadn't."

She lifted the little lid off the jar by its teat-like handle, which protruded upwards like a mosque minaret, and peered carefully inside. She extracted three more pills.

"Last of the li'l yellow uns."

They dropped one each and settled comfortably back.

The come up was different to the pure MDMA we'd been taking, more mellow due to the surroundings and also more focused because of the numbers. Two fellas came round, but only on a brief stop on their way to the next house. Dealers—alright too. I'd realised from knowing Jack and his dealing activities at the university that not all of them were pimps in Range Rovers, but that most were just normal people: Max in his cap with his physics degree on the way, Darren who'd finished school at sixteen and who worked down Curry's on commission, purely making a few more notes and keeping his mates in gear.

The pill knocked my head back into shape and I regained my motor skills. Jo and Genna were fishing something from a cupboard—this bizarre silver contraption that had an inlet where small zeppelin-shaped gas canisters were fixed and an outlet where the gas flowed furiously into the attached balloon. We took a balloon each. Jo instructed us to breathe in and out of it until it was spent. Kat put something clanging and jumpy on the speakers and as I breathed, the sounds digitalized, broke down and formed themselves as constellations in front of my eyes. Each second felt like a lifetime which I would never leave; each vision felt like a truth reached which would never be proven wrong.

We didn't fall asleep all night, not as, one by one, the girls disappeared to their rooms. We ended up rat-arsed on the Stella Kat'd bought, a random assortment of films playing in the background. The sun was beginning to make its morning skirmish into the folds of the curtains that covered the large double windows. The boys rolled over into their bags. I stared at the now-muted screen, where a naked man and woman were drowsing peacefully; and as I looked at them I realised that

I was falling hard for Jo. Earlier that night she'd taken me through the star signs. She talked of ours, Scorpio and Virgo, and the strong bonds of friendship that grow between them. I'd always thought astrology was fantasy. But here, with Jo sat cross-legged opposite me, her cheeks and chin glistening with the high and her hair falling like dark beech leaves around her neck, I was prepared to believe anything.

I sat alone, listening to the sounds of the two fellas sleeping. Quietly, I picked up a laptop from the floor and went on Facebook. I knew what I was going to fill my morning with.

Chapter Fourteen

No success. It'd reached twelve in the afternoon and nobody had shaken a leg in the flat. I'd been trying to get onto Jane Bradley's account for the best part of the morning. For the last half an hour I'd begun looking for jobs in Bristol Road's pubs and restaurants, while also wondering blankly about how I was going to pass as 18 to work there. And still I didn't want to sleep.

I was stiff and unused to movement sitting down there on the floor. I sniffed my armpits, concluded they were okay, grabbed Jo's key which she'd left on the side—reckoning that she would probably not be up by the time I returned—and left the flat.

Outside, the day was breezy again—fuck, this West Midlands breeze! It blew and blew as though there was a giant fan away in the distance launching the air Eastwards, wrestling my lengthening hair around my head. I sprang on to Bristol Road where the students mixed with the permanent residents outside the cafés, and where mothers pushed prams along the warming pavements, stopping now and then to tell their bairns off or to root around in their purses. In my own wallet the last twenty was a shitty reminder of the need to find a job. I walked into the local that'd come up on my right, vaguely recognising its odd name: 'The Gun and Albatross'.

On one side of the arched door there was an 18th century sailor dressed in a blue longcoat and aiming a musket, and on the other a giant albatross with its wings outstretched and beak opened looking ready to receive the bullet. The doorway was wide; there'd been enough space for the artist to use spray paint, and his Twitter handle had been left at the bottom in black:@cydeworks. Transfixed, I managed to miss a step on the threshold.

I was spooked from the sudden drop. There was no-one around the pub's wide dark floor. I backed up, deciding against asking for a job until I had slept on it; stupid idea, now, without a C.V.

As I left I saw a chalkboard sign waiting to be put out on the street that read 'Pound a Pint Tonight From 6.30—Carlsberg, Fosters, John Smiths and Strongbow. Gitcha Quids Out'. I carried on up the street to nowhere in particular, talking to no-one and nothing except the breeze as it laughed sweetly around me.

There was still no life back at the flat. I placed my hands down on the kitchen worktop and contemplated hitting myself with a sugared coffee to sustain my sleeplessness. As the kettle light flicked on, a soft knock came at the door. I wandered over and took the latch off cautiously.

In the doorway stood a man so striking and so incredibly similar in facial features and size to me that, for a split-second, my entire insides plummeted towards my feet as if I'd missed that step again, and I swayed backwards. Cheeks, mouth, eyes— here he was: my almost-double.

I took a moment to get my head in gear.

"You okay, mate?"

I shook my head and felt the back of my eyeballs burst as quickly into a jet of pain as they subsided back to normality. "Yeah, yeah... I'm fine mate. Just a bit of a late one." I did my best to hide my shock. He grinned.

"Sure, sure, know exactly what you mean." He winked mid-sentence; he hadn't seemed to notice our eerie similarity yet, or if he had, he definitely seemed unfazed. Cam ambled over from behind me as I heard the kettle click off.

"Ello ello, y'alright fellas? Morning," he yawned, lifting his sleepy, wild-haired head to the stranger in the door. "This your brother turned up or summat Gene?"

The new guy's features remained unmoved; having got used to them, I could now see the obvious differences: the extra covering of freckles he had; the longer upper lip, pulling his face downwards slightly; and the shade of hair, which in him contained none of the slight traces of ginger mine had in a certain light. I suddenly remembered that whoever this was, he'd knocked on the door and presumably wanted to come in.

"Are you after someone, then?"

"Er, yeah buddy, after Jo. Said she'd be in."

I left him at the door, expecting him to stay; however, after I'd given Jo's door a solid rap I turned to find that he'd gone to the kitchen to pour himself a cup of something with the freshly boiled kettle. I saw that his shoulders were more slouched than mine inside his too-tight, black crew-necked jumper. Still, I simply couldn't help staring at him. He looked up.

"Sorry mate, is yours the coffee? I'll pour it for ya." He flaunted his West Country twang.

"Aye mate, ta."

"Jared." Jo had come into the living room. She wore a t-shirt, no bra and a pair of back-to-front shorts. Her dark hair had slipped across her face, and as I noticed this and thought how good she still looked, she swept the hairs aside. "After your stuff."

"Yeah," was his uninterested response.

Not only did he look like me, but he was apparently part of her history. Jo left without a word to either Jared, me, Cam or Cosmo, the latter of which had now also sat up, bare-chested and with a paggered look on his face.

"She isn't too good with mornings then, eh?" Cam chirped. Jared laughed.

"Not 'alf mate, she's a bleddy nightmare. Believe me. Oh, fancy a cup of sommin' by the way?" he asked, brandishing the kettle.

Cam asked for a coffee. "So you're a D'n'B man?" he asked, pointing to Jared's jumper. It had a big 'H' printed on its front. "Our mate's got one of them, loves the merch."

"Yeah boy, it's the only stuff for me, y'know." Jared suddenly became more animated as he threw the coffee grindings into a mug, like a puppy around new company. "Much of a scene up North? That is where you're from?"

Cam replied and the two went off into conversation, like only Cam could with a stranger.

I became distracted by the beep of my phone and its lively rattling in my loose pocket. It was Jack. The text read:

Alright guys, just wanna say really really sorry for yesterday, hope things are cool at Jill's. I'm busy tonight but wanna do summat tomoz night?

I laughed, thinking how fitting his mistake was. I sat down on the sofa, forgetting about the coffee I was craving lying on the worktop over which Cam and Jared were now yapping away. I texted back simply:

"No problems here, sorted for a place. Don't worry not your fault. Defo do summat tomorrow night"

I pressed send and simultaneously heard Cosmo's text alert go off. He'd collapsed back down into the mound of bedding near the window, which had begun to look like an Eastern divan. After a few seconds he groaned over and read the same text aloud.

"Jack seems fairly cut up over the whole thing, eh?" I said.

"He needs to stop crying about it, dunnee?" came the bleary reply. "We're alright now. Anyway, it was definitely your fault, weren't it, not shagging that strange little woman. Knob."

"Yeah, what a dick Gene," I smirked, "That was not going to happen. Not a chance in hell. There just seemed to be… I dunno… something wrong with her, you know?"

"Odd little woman, but shaggable. Especially with those eyes. Cyclops, Brothers Grimm fit. You're just too picky Gene."

I got my coffee and as I took my first scalding sip Jo stalked through her door again, banging the television table. In her right hand were two scrunched up t-shirts, one white, one black, and in her left a can of deodorant; on her face was a look of deepest displeasure. She dropped them at Jared's feet.

"Oh, make yourself comfy! There's more. Find a carrier bag." She left as abruptly as she had entered. I looked at Jared again with fascination, watching this strange little tale unfold.

"Is the scene much the same in Bristol?"

"Strong as ever bruv."

Cam paused, then ventured, "I'm guessing you and Jo have a bit of history, if you don't mind me saying."

Jared also paused for a moment, picking his words.

"History… yeah, you can say that. Didn't end too well, you might be able to guess," he gestured towards Jo's shut door. "Girls mate, just…girls. One second chilled, cool, you know? Next it's 'Where you been staying? What you been taking?' Girls."

He blew out of one side of his mouth. Girls, I thought; well, they have good reason to be suspicious. For the first time in what felt like forever I thought of Ashley. Her fuming face in the Bridlington flat suddenly flew to the front of my mind like a terror from a distant age. I'd been a cheater; Jared in all likelihood was a cheater. Young men cheat. And as hypocritical as it was, my dislike for Jared was growing stronger by the second.

"But that's a long story anyway. Yeah, the scene mate, the scene—it's killer in Brizzle. Same up here," he continued, "Loadsa label nights on around the country in fact; you mentioned the jumper. It's all kicked off. Man, I wish I was like you boys again, just getting into it. Hey," and at this he lowered his tone and leant in towards Cam as Cosmo passed by in the background to go for a piss, "D'you know if Jo's got any pills or such? I'm itching for some tonight, you get me? Or you guys?" Cam looked politely back at him and replied tactfully:

"Not a clue fella, you'll have to ask her yersen. None on us I'm afraid."

"And speak of the devil! Cheers for that Jo," Jared twanged chirpily as she entered with more of his belongings. She stood with her legs next to my face. I did my best not to get caught staring.

"You done now Jared? That's everything." She thrust a pile of CD's and books into Jared's hand.

"Cheers, nice to have them back girl. There was actually one more thing. You selling any pills, girl?"

Jo folded her arms violently.

"You can pack that in, calling me 'girl'. I'm not your girl Jared, get that in your head. And as for pills," she said, her voice rising, "Why not tap up one of your maggoty little friends? I'm not a fucking dealer."

"Alright, alright Jo," he shot back. "S'just asking, no need to get skirty love."

I was getting as irritated as Jo, and the creepiness of Jared's features was getting to me. "Gen and Kat'd sell to a mate."

"Yeah, well I'm not exactly your mate now, am I?" She moved off to the kitchen. "Enjoying your cuppa by the way? Nice of you to have let yourself in."

"I was jest 'avin a chat with one o' your mates Jo, I'll be gone in ten."

She pulled out a bag from under the kitchen sink and stomped back to the sofa.

"Ten? You can fuck off now. Go on. Chuck your stuff in and get moving. And run off and tell your mates I'm still a bitch, like I know you will."

Jared, seeing how things were set to go from the wildfire in Jo's stare, made a point of finishing his cup and standing up slowly.

"Cheers for that Jo, top girl you are." He threw his few possessions into the bag she had in her hand. Then he leaned in deliberately, "Keep up the good work, 'cause yeah, everyone will hear about what a sour old cow you've got to be." His voice had lowered to a whisper. "Enjoy 'em while they're here, eh." Then he looked me straight in the face and went to move backwards, lightly pulling the bag away.

His mouth twisted into a smirk of triumph as he backed away, and I hated him all the more. Then his face made a shift and it was like for the first time he'd realised our uncanniness: a bewildered, lost look, a look unable for a second to make one plus one equal two. He paced backwards a few steps, breaking his gaze with me but still scarred by that same expression, until he finally turned and made the last few steps to the door. It clicked shut softly as he pulled it to from outside.

Jo carried on as if nothing had happened, except for muttering the word 'wanker' as she went back to the kitchen. Me and Cam exchanged a glance. Cosmo returned from the toilet.

"I miss the fireworks?" he asked laconically.

"Just a few." I got up to join Jo as the telly flicked into life. "Are you alright after that? The guy seemed like, well… a prick."

"Yeah, I'm, yeah… listen, Gene, do you wanna come outside?" she tremored. "I'll just put something on."

She returned in a pair of green joggers and led me down the stairs to the front door.

"It all got a bit crazy it did," she was explaining, her voice back to its normal strength, "Mental actually. He'd be off getting completely wasted on everything he could get his hands on. And I know I've given a few things a go, and still do, but he'd just get out of his mind, like foaming at the mouth out of your mind, you know? Just scary stuff. I just couldn't deal with it. And I had no idea what was going on behind my back. It just wasn't a real relationship." She paused every so often and stared at the off-licence across the road. "Shit in bed too," she added, "after the comedown."

I laughed, but only outwardly; inwardly I recoiled at the thought, conjuring itself grimly, of another man on top of her.

"Gene," she began, "I, you know, well I've… known you for a, and you know we… oh, just come here."

She grabbed at the back of my head and her face leapt upwards. Instinctively, I grabbed her waist. The kiss was intense, then soft; she lowered herself from me.

"I feel safe with you, Gene."

She led me by the hand back upstairs but broke the hold as we re-entered the flat. Cosmo and Cam had found a board game from somewhere and were setting it up whilst sat on the floor, and Genna had awoken, looking rough.

"Alright guys, I'll cook lunch if you want? I have bacon and salad and bread," sang Jo. My stomach felt starved.

"Wanna join in a game of Frustration?" Cosmo asked. He had, by now, put on a tatty trademark vest with stars upon it. "Quids for sixes." I looked at the board with the dice-popper lying in the middle and two sides set up opposite each other ready for play.

"No," I replied abstractly, thoughts shifting, "Actually there's something I want to do. You go ahead fellas…" I trailed off as I walked calmly across the room.

There was a job to be done. And there was a tingling travelling down my spine and up and across my face. I'd cracked it.

Chapter Fifteen

The blue-and-white screen of the Facebook login page shot into life again. I'd set myself down at the small, empty, bricked-over window on the other side of the room, as far away as possible from the game of Frustration which was beginning away to the left. My vision tunnelled. I typed in the address again, j_bradley@ googlemail.com, and tabbed over to the password bar. The excitement mounted in my veins, my breathing, which had barely recovered from the moment downstairs, suddenly deepened and quickened, and I quivered slightly as I held my hands, smooth and white, above the keyboard.

The albatross of that morning's pub wasn't just part of an amusing name, no: it was part of the answer, the answer I'd sought for weeks in vain. I tossed the word around in my head, done over by my own stupidity. There it was and always had been. 'Albatross.' I mouthed, rolling the syllables. 'Albert'. 'Ross'. There the clues ended. Albert, that old sod.

I'd never met Uncle Albert Ross but had spent many a family gathering, where drinks would flow freely as the night wore on, hearing about his remarkable life. (Yes, I did find the parallel with the Only Fools and Horses character hilarious.) Albert, as I well knew, had been an unusual man. Born—not quite on the eve of war as the movie might have gone—more dead than alive, 'A little blue thing that the doctors gave up for dead and left with our Grandmother in the Liverpool Docks Hospital,' so auntie Deborah claimed. Of course, it hadn't been a hospital because it was pre-NHS, but the Liverpool docks had had such an influx of Irish immigrants that year that a local woman, who must've had a fortune sitting dormant somewhere in a Merseyside bank, had opened up a small hospital for the pregnant immigrant women to give birth in. This I learned from my mother during a sober moment; I laughed now to think of how fussy she was with the past which did not belong to her, yet so careless with that which did.

The Irish side of the family moved to Leeds and Albert grew up along with my Grandad, Stephen, the younger of the two by one year. After they left school at 15 and both had gone into the markets to earn their living, Albert broke the mould. He set off for Malawi and founded one of the biggest English-teaching schools in Africa. Where had he got the money? No-one knew. Throughout the 50s and 60s he became famous in Leeds for shepherding groups of 20 or 30 Malawian children through its streets in order to show them the people and the culture of the land they'd heard so much about. Like an albatross with its broad wings bearing smaller birds, Albert had flown these kids back and forth between continents and, more, become a success. And then, with his thirty-first birthday just around the corner, Albert disappeared in Malawi never to be seen again.

I'd had the arrogance to try my own middle name, Alfred, in the last hacking sessions, but I'd never thought of trying the name of the missing uncle; and now, like hitting my head on a low-standing door frame despite taking the effort to stoop, I felt a stupid tosser.

My head filtered out all sound except for the relentless, ever-increasing 'Pop! Pock! Pop!' coming from wherever it was. I typed the names in and, taking in a solid lungful of air, clicked the 'Sign In' button. And I was through.

All noise rushed back: the sizzling of bacon in the kitchen, the murmur of Cosmo and Cam and the beginning beat of whatever Genna had put through the speakers, as I looked upon Jane Bradley's newsfeed in triumph. The blue-and-white dopamine page stood with its feed. I fumbled to open up her messages. After a few scrolls I'd found it. My heart missed a beat. Finally.

As I read slowly from the start of the conversation I began to see for myself the pains which he'd gone through to try and get Mum to forget about the past, about the fears he'd had over my birth, that they were too young, that her post-natal mood swings had got too much, that he had to leave because he couldn't cope with it all. For the last 17 years he'd been subject to a court order that she'd managed to obtain, keeping him away from us indefinitely on grounds, I found with disbelief, of attempted rape. My feelings had suddenly become torn in two. His leaving and alleged attempted rape? For the first, well, I didn't know what the situation had been and it seemed forgiveable, if weak. The second... I imagined it to be false, knowing her falseness; but what if it was true? How could I want to find him then?

And his name? His account had been deleted. How and why, I didn't know. All I knew was that his address was the only thing I could use now.

As I travelled further and further up the conversation the mystery of the court order was revealed. Message after message he'd repeated the words: Admit it to me that you lied to keep me away. She resisted, I saw, for over ten replies. Then, on 02 August at 19:40, Have it your way then. I suppose we both know that I tricked them, and they fell for it. And it's kept us happy for all these years.

His reply to this, now five days old, ended the conversation; it told me exactly where I could find him, the man I'd spent these exiled weeks obsessing day and night over, his location now in my grasp.

Jane, you have finally had the decency to say what for seventeen long years I have known all along. I hope that, by admitting what you did, you have entered upon a world of guilt and soul-searching, and that it will haunt you like it has me.

I don't expect you to do the decent thing even now, but hopefully your conscience won't allow you to do otherwise. Please pass my address on to Gene:

2 Nordre Skansemyren
5019 Bergen

Norway

So there it was. A death-blow to my ambitions of finding him, just as a switch flicks on a momentary light and then… poof. The filament expires. I had uncovered my father's whereabouts but felt now immersed in the dark, and not simply wading in the shadows' shallows. What could I do? What could I do with just twenty pounds to my name?

I hovered mutely and gormlessly for half a minute. I pulled my phone out of my pocket and drafted the address. I quit the browser and went for the kitchen where Jo was plating up the food I'd forgotten about. My appetite, though, had evaporated and in its place was the need for a good, long drink.

"I fancy a pint with that," I said to her before thinking.

"Oh? Really?" she replied, clunking the pan into the sink behind us. "Why, what's up?"

"Oh, nothing. Nothing at all. Just…"

She quickly glanced over at the group, then held my arm gently. "Still a bit spaced out, love? Don't worry, you know you're welcome here as long as it takes…"

"As long as it takes to do what?" I blurted.

"As long as it takes to find yourself a place. Are you sure you're okay, Gene? Here, you look pale, sit down. I'll bring your lunch over, and you'll have a cuppa?" She led me with her hand resting on my back to the sofa and then fetched my plate.

"No, only a beer would do, I think."

"Just sit there. Eat something."

"Okay."

I was conscious of my voice sounding distant and of my face feeling cold as I touched it. I began on the plate of food slowly. Jo served the others their portions in several trips. Everyone praised her selfless generosity.

"I meant earlier, as long as it takes for you to find a job, get on your feet, get your own place…" she repeated. "I wasn't trying to sound…"

"I know, I know Jo, I don't know why I snapped at you. Sorry. I'm feeling better now."

"Mmm, you do look and sound a bit more lively." She hummed while chewing her bacon until she pushed too much in her mouth; her lips stuck outwards like a cavewoman's. I caught her eye and laughed until my ribs hurt.

I finished my plate and rapidly stretched myself out as if passing my regained strength to my limbs; then I said to the room:

"Alright everyone, I've been out today and it's bloody wonderful. I've seen a pub round the corner that's doing pound-a-pint tonight. Is anyone interested?"

I felt the strengthening continue as I spoke, and quickly after there'd been a general murmur of positivity Cam's sharp, dry voice shouted out,

"That's it! The Jean Genie's got it! It's time for the pub tonight then folks—first, twenty minutes till roll-call and then out, out!"

And we were back on the roundabout.

Now the sun had begun to lower a little. I staggered upwards from our camp on the grass inside Cannon Hill Park and crab-walked to the bin. Ducks were circling noisily in the pond; on an island near the middle some lemur-like animals were yapping their feline howl. I looked around me, at Cosmo in his Hawaiian wifebeater, the girls browning in rolled-up tops, Cam all in black flaunting burnt arms and a doggy grin, and at myself in green-stained shorts and my sailor-striped tee; all were soaked in summer. The evening sat up expectantly, like a great animal sniffing at a scent, hungry for its fun.

"The Gun's not had this one before, has it? We'd have been, surely," enquired Jo to the girls. We waltzed back down a road with columns of huge lime trees standing like legionaries, occasionally twirling past sunburnt strangers.

Selly Oak was thronging with the thirsty and the already-pissed by the time we got there, so I offered to jump quickly on one of the unsanded, lichened benches away to the right of the Gun and Albatross's beer garden. Not that you'd call it a garden; it was a patio pockmarked with the occasional wide, depressing pot of cigarette-burned and unwatered petunias—the ideal surroundings for a cheap and nasty drinking session. My tongue clicked dryly onto the roof of my mouth. They pushed their way inside and as they did so I turned and shouted 'Strongbow!' to Cosmo, who had to throw his head back against the inward surge to catch my order.

They returned what felt like an age later. Three different groups had tried their hardest to sit themselves on my patch. The first, two gorgeous, black-wavy-haired temptresses, the ones with a slightly hoarse voice from the night before and a fiery attitude. The other two were groups of five and four—Doc Martened, denim jacketed, burglar-hatted hipsters who I swatted away. The din of drinking and laughing was amplified by the encasement of the walls; you had to shout to be heard. The girls, still battered from earlier, sipped at their drinks, while Cosmo and Cam were throwing down their pints with gusto.

We chatted and watched the swarm around us. The girls, as is their way, rose from the table with a clasping of their handbags and a smoothing of their hair and said they were off to the toilet.

"Just what is it they do in there? I mean, what requires three of them and about twenty minutes?" asked Cam with his usual ire as they disappeared into the throng.

"Plumbing," hazarded Cosmo.

"Chatter," I said. "It's obvious, isn't it? They go to swap notes, have a chin wag. I imagine they've got a lot to talk about."

The pair, sat opposite me now that Cos had shifted round, threw each other a look of apprehension and hugged their hands to their fast-disappearing pints. I drained my glassful relishing its cheap dryness and rose at Cosmo's suggestion that it was my round.

After the hell of getting served at the bar I returned to see the two in full-flow, broken only by a quick nod from each to acknowledge the receipt of lager.

"But of course, they don't want you to believe you don't actually need these products, these throwaway items. No, not at all. Advertising is subtle; governments, if you're not looking, are subtle."

"It's simple economics."

"Exactly. Live on credit, pay a mortgage that grossly overprices the home you live in so you're saddled with it— for life—and have a full replacement of everything you own every five years. When I get out there and—no, I'm telling you—when I do, and when Jack's on that advisory committee, and I'm heading these pressure groups and marches and so on at uni, well, I'm not saying they'll have to listen, but…"

"I know. But remember, you're just one person Cam."

"Aye, I know, think global and act local and all that."

"Mmm. There's a storm there now though eh, credit, mortgages… world's gone mad."

"Yes. And we were too young, adults too busy, and professionals—politicians, bankers, economists—too lazy or greedy to prevent it. It just leaves you speechless doesn't it?"

The pair looked at one another, and for a moment it seemed that Cam's closing words were going to become a self-fulfilling prophecy.

"You're going to be a credit to your establishment Cam, I'm sure."

Cam raised his glass, slopping the beer over its sides.

"To that then," he called cheerfully out. I met my glass with theirs in the void over the table and took another powerful slug on its contents. "But gents," he continued, "I'm afraid I have to see a man about a dog."

"Eh?" Cosmo snorted. I translated, then asked,

"What do you mean?"

Cam had half-risen, but his long, skinny hands still both rested on the table.

"I've just got this thing where I…" he mumbled as me and Cosmo leant in to pick his words out of the surrounding din. "EH?"

"I just have this thing, y'see, where I can't go for a shit in anyone else's house. I've just never been able to. I get spooked."

The two of us, who had been shitting every morning in the various houses we had called home in Birmingham, bellowed with laughter.

"What?! We've been here a whole week! Don't tell me you've just put a plug up there and sat tight…"

"Like a hibernating bear," I added.

"No," he replied slowly, as if calculating a difficult sum. "Let's see…I had one in Cadbury World. And then one at that café when Dan left."

"Ah, that one was obvious," said Cosmo, kicking himself for missing this vital clue. Cam shifted about.

"So if you don't mind, I'm going to take my leave and go and lay a log."

He made to turn around and then shot across his shoulder, "If the girls come back any time soon, tell them I've only just left." He span and floated his lanky form through the crowd.

"Maybe we should buy him a shit diary. When's his birthday?"

I took another drink. "Back to the original Brid bunch then."

Cosmo weighed this up for a second, and then, like he was in amazement at the situation, replied, "Yeah, yeah it is! Wow, as if... Brid feels like... years ago."

"We're getting old mate. I feel two or three years older from this last week alone."

"Yeah. Fuck. Everything feels... different now. Knaresborough could almost be a foreign place."

"Lost in the mists of time."

"And now it's just me and thee again."

"For the length of Cam's shit anyway."

He laughed. "You don't think the girls'll be back sooner?"

"No... like I said, they've got a whole heap of stuff to talk over, and you know women eh?" He sniffed and grunted mutual approval. "But when you think about it, we've been lucky with the people we've met, don't you reckon?" For the first time, like a suppressed image of something evil and rupturing, the thought of Cosmo's involvement with Jo flashed across my mind as I waited for his response.

"Aw, they're the best, honestly. I mean how lucky were we, just as we thought we were done for with nowhere to stay, out of the blue Jo comes through for us. And for her housemates to be as sound as Kat and Gen are... yes mate, lucky."

"I know. I'd say I'm sorry for not shagging Becky to keep a roof over our heads... it would've made quite a funny story in a few years' time."

Cosmo looked preoccupied as he nodded and nursed his pint. 'I'm the victor now, out of us two,' said a heavy voice in my head. And I realised with these arrogant, self-absorbed thoughts that this was the reason why I could forgive Cosmo. It was astonishing really, and yet it didn't matter. I enjoyed the selfishness.

Cosmo resumed, bravely, "Well, 'course, we'll avoid the unhappy housemates thing if we can stay away from Jo, you and me!"

"True."

"I mean, that sort of threatened to fuck things up for a minute, didn't it? Look," he said, beginning to sound uncomfortable, "I never meant to annoy you by what I did, I sort of just assumed you weren't too bothered about her."

"Really? So that's why you covered up that you were seeing her by saying you were off seeing that Rachel?"

His tensed lips and slanted brows were uneasy. I carried on. "Look, I'm glad you noticed the—I dunno—the frostiness between us since it happened. But I'm not going to go on holding a stupid grudge about a girl. There's no point, not between us." Then, as if to fuel my own smugness and in a deflection of the attention from me and her, I added, "Are things moving forward there?"

"Well, I had a crack; and before we moved in, I dunno, she seemed game. And yeah, like things were moving forwards. But since then I've just had the cold shoulder. I don't think she's interested. The unattainable woman!"

"Isn't she just."

I shifted my gaze to the group who were standing immediately—too immediately—to my left, and conjured up the strange mirror-like image of Jared and the scene outside once he'd gone. "But let's not talk about her, eh? It's water under the bridge, innit? Let's talk about your four o'clock."

Cosmo was one of those useless people who couldn't work out their clockfaces, and so it took me several obvious nods and flicks of the eyes to make him notice the girl I meant.

"Ah, the redhead? A bit of a flat arse, but you would. Yeah, definitely you would." He spoke with the same kind of predatory hush as you would hear from a poacher operating in the dead of night: the kind of tones which women are never ever let in on when the two sexes are together in a group. "Got those do-me eyes. And... dyed red?" I nodded in answer. "Always game. Something about that colour, makes them look like they're..."

"In season," I colluded.

"Nose is a bit narrow; a nice pair, though. And a nice dress."

"Comprehensive assessment. Well, we can dream."

"We can. God I need to speed up again, look at your pint."

"I'm celebrating."

"Celebrating what?"

"Cosmo, earlier today I hacked into my mum's account on Facebook and found out where my real father lives." At this I saw Cosmo's eyes bulge and heard the loud clunk of his glass being brought down on the table. "Yes, I did it. I've been trying to for over a week, and I finally cracked it this afternoon."

"How did you manage that?"

"Well, it was thanks to this pub, strangely enough."

"Go on."

"Well, I felt so stupid after I'd done it—for not trying it in the first place. I was thinking about here because I came here earlier, when everyone was asleep, and thinking about the name."

"The Gun and Albatross."

"The Gun and Albatross."

"I still don't see the connection."

"Never mind; the point is Cos, I did it, I did it."

"And now what? Where is he? Oh Gene, this is brilliant, fucking excellent!"

"Not exactly. He's a long way away. He lives in Norway."

"Norway?"

"Fucking Norway!"

My frustration burst forth all at once, like a shower-head accidentally flicked to the jet setting. "What was he thinking, moving there? I have his whole address but no money to go and find him with. I'm down to my last twenty Cos. No, seventeen now," I corrected myself, waving my battered old wallet.

"This last week hasn't been cheap," he agreed, "God knows how much I've spent... Look, let me be your beer money."

"No, it's a necessary expense. No really mate, I'm more than happy to pay for my own stuff. And anyway, I was talking to Jo earlier about getting a job. I'm gonna go hunting tomorrow, but who knows how long that could take. If I was to save up enough, it would probably mean giving up this extravagant drugs-fuelled lifestyle."

"Surely—and I think I've solved this for you mate—you could just look up his number and explain the situation to him. It'd save a lot of hassle. I'll even give you the coin for the call. There."

"Wish it was that simple. No number and no name."

"Just an address? Oh. A letter then?"

I thought about it for a second. "That's it."

"Tell him what's happened, send him your number. In a few weeks you'll be there."

"Yes, yes, yes. But ah them few weeks! I want to see him now, Cos! I wonder if he'll recognise me when he sees me. Before I say who I am, obviously. Give me that pint!" I'd finished mine already, thoughts racing like comets, and needed his. It, this whole thing, this victory, felt like coming up harder than any drug.

"Yeah! Standing there in arrivals fresh off the plane, looking like a little toe-rag. Oi." He took my hand off the glass that was rattling in its grasp. There was a long pause.

"It will literally be a completely new feeling. I mean, how do you anticipate any of it? 'Hi Dad, I'm your 17-year-old long-lost son'. It's mad, isn't it?"

"It is." Another long pause.

"What we gonna do tonight, Cos?"

"Anything you fucking want. The parties, the scene, surely we can find something. There are people out there who just don't stop… whose job it seems is to just get fucked-up whenever they can. D'you know, I quite like it. I'm up for all that. I don't want the party to end."

"I feel differently about everything in life now."

"What, from this party or from your dad?"

"Do you get it," I went on, oblivious, "Just where you're in the middle of the trip and you just think: I've got it, I've solved a thousand little stupid problems that should never have been problems in the first place. They were only problems because you weren't using your mind properly. I'm in the middle of the trip."

"I do get that. It happens every time. And there's this whole body of people around you who are getting it too…"

"Do you have doubts?"

"About all this?" He blew into his fringe. "When we're on MD, I'm just in the moment, loving it, feeling everything. I don't think I stop to think."

"I've only stopped to think, to assess, a few times… I dunno, I question the actual truth of the realisations you're bombarded with. Because you can't recapture it when you're sober. Except now."

"No, you can't get it back. But this is a pretty exceptional sketch, Gene."

"All I'm saying is, maybe there's something in that."

Cam returned, declaring how many pounds lighter he felt.

"Girls still not back?" he asked, looking relieved. "Thank God."

"Owt interesting happen in the bog?"

"Actually, I had an excellent conversation with this— I dunno, maybe you'd call him hippyish—this hippy fella in there."

"What, cubicle to cubicle?"

"Glory hole to glory hole?"

"No no, I'd just finished a very satisfying session and was washing my hands when he—Damian was his name—said to me that I'd make a great apple picker."

"Why?"

"'Because you're so bloody tall!' is what he reckoned. Yeah," he added after catching my look.

"Makes perfect sense."

"So this is how the conversation started, and as you can imagine it just got more bizarre from there. Ah, there he is now. I won't call him over, entertaining as he is: he'd scare off the girls."

I followed Cam's gaze to somewhere in the middle-distance behind me. He wasn't wrong. At the periphery of what looked like one of the burglar-hatted groups I'd fended off earlier was a man of medium height, with a swirling, wriggling, crooked gait. His height was the only average thing about him. As I observed him I heard him say quite audibly:

"What you ladies and gents need to remember, is that if your brains overheat, you can't think!"

He clearly meant that their silly hats were unsuitable for the weather, but the group looked at one another with uncomprehending faces. "Take it from someone who's taken too much LSD! Ge-hah!"

He spoke slowly with a strong voice, and there was something harmless and innocent in this voice, in the notes and loops it would make. Now he'd turned a little I could see his full body. He wore a black hat with an even blacker ribbon rimming its circumference and a lone pheasant's feather leaning backwards. A mid-length brown tunic with leather lacing on the chest covered his torso, flowing over his baggy, striped trousers which seemed to flow around in great swoops as he staggered around like a moth battering a lightbulb.

"Complete lunatic! Brilliant!" came the condensed response from Cam. "To think there are people who just roam the land, following the harvests, living at subsistence level. I thought that all died in the Nineties."

Cam had not yet finished his first pint when Cosmo brought back our third. We kept up our pace as the conversation turned to Jack, and then came the return of the three women.

It was around four hours and many pints later when I found myself struggling to stay upright as I stared at Cosmo's turned back.

"That's a shop front Cos! This is a main busy road! They will catch you!"

"Nah... n-nah they won't; stop, stop WORRYING Gene!"

I heard him struggle to zip his fly as he tottered dangerously backwards and I clung on to the railings outside Santander for support. A thick line of slightly frothy piss felt its way roadward across the tan-brown paving stones, like a lumbering arm with probing fingers. Then I heard Jo's voice call from behind.

"We're, we're stopping here Gene!"

I looked first at her stumbling form, hair slightly draped across her face like she had just got up in a fluster from giving head, and then at the square lit sign above her, reading: Ajmal's

Burgers
S.F.C
Pizas

"Wanna takeaway?" I muttered quietly to Cosmo, who had reappeared at my side with half of his face looking like it was sliding downwards.

"Nahhh…"

Jo had already passed through the door, bringing up the rear of the group.

"See you at home!" I shouted redundantly.

We made our way back towards the flat like two braying idiots falling over one another. Then Cosmo soberly pointed out that we lacked the keys to the flat door, and that he'd run back to the takeaway while I stayed and found some girls, adding that we would have to keep them a secret from Jo, Kat and the Other One. He went and I decided it would be better for my health if I sat down on the kerb. The heat from the pavement and that woody summer-night-time smell convinced me I was one of those people you see on a BBC3 show, the ones sat on a pavement in some Mediterranean destination with their head in their hands having overdone it. Cosmo returned quickly.

"Fuck me, you can't move in there; they had to throw me these from the front o' the queue."

If the flat pavements of Selly Oak were behaving like the deck of a ship in a storm then each of Jo's stairs had the temperament of a bucking bronco. Cosmo hung off the railing above me like a stranded gibbon; I hugged both of his legs and tried to force him upwards. I saw his elbows bend, but then with an irresistible force, like a toying, invisible finger poking me off-balance, I started to pull backwards on his legs and heard him let out a yelp before I crashed back to the foot of the mountain. I felt a numb thump in my back.

"You okay?" Cosmo asked without looking down at me, thrusting and scraping at the Yale lock. I grappled with the handrail again.

Somehow we got inside and, as Cosmo flung himself down on the sofa and I raided the fridge's contents, I had a terrible realisation.

"Cosmo, something awful has happened my son. There is no beer. The beer is gone. There is no beer. What do we do."

Cosmo groaned loudly and fiddled with his trousers, clacking around until I saw his Marvel comics wallet on the end of his wavering upstretched arm.

"Money, Gene. Here is money. That Costcutter round the corner'll still be open. I don't think I can move just yet."

I snatched the wallet out of his hand. "Always doing your dirty work. Always on… errands."

He grinned upwards, and then took his top off and put his sunglasses on. He began a slow, undulating laugh and repeated the word 'errands': a sound that faded off like the end of an old record as I left and staggered down the flight of stairs.

My walk to the Costcutter followed the road round and crossed a long, narrow park for most of the journey. As I neared a fountain about halfway through a path diverged either side and I saw a group of three or four tracksuited and tucked-in-socks teenagers ahead, each with a crew cut and swinging shoulders; I stiffened, like a fox upwind of danger, until they'd passed.

Just as I loosened my shoulders once more and began to dream of the booze-laden shelves of the glowing shop ahead, the worst unexpected feeling of dread spread like a rash across my neck and descended through my body. I felt like running home, back to Jo's; the compulsion was so strong that I'd actually stopped and turned. Had Cosmo burnt the flat down? Had someone got in a fight at the takeaway? But I was fucked and feeling the sting from the ket earlier, that was all, and Cosmo was relying on me.

The smiling Nigerian security guard seemed to notice my staggered gait as I went into the shop, stood aside from his already unobtrusive position and finally cracked out a brilliant white set of teeth as I made eye contact and strode past his spot. Other pissheads were browsing the booze aisle in the shop, some of whom I recognised from the Albatross. The whole of the shop smelt of bleach with bursts of crisping pastry from a hot counter away to the left. A flashy yellow £10 sign hovered above a pillar of Foster's fridge packs on the end of the aisle nearest my tottering body and, seeing Cos only had one orange note in his wallet, I picked up a pack and headed to the empty counter. A mute South Asian man of about 40 laboriously craned his wide, creased, moustached face above the counter and served without looking at me, instead fixing his eyes on the pack of beer like it was a child he didn't want to hand over. I looked past him and onto the shelves of tobacco products - they were shining! Calling out to me like a separated mistress! I half went to check my wallet to see if I could afford a packet that could be shared but then stopped, remembering that thanks to the earlier liver-abuse (and to a stupid bet with Kat: I was convinced that lead was heavier than gold) I had only a shade over a fiver left in the entire world. There were to be no cigarettes tonight. I handed over Cosmo's tenner (accepted coldly) and seized the precious crate.

I decided to walk the extra distance around the park, joining up with the main street sooner. I didn't feel like passing over that spot again. I opened up one of the cans and took a healthy glug on it to try and banish my returning sense of unease. As I passed the posh French restaurant and approached the door to the flat I saw that it was fully ajar and open to the street. I was sure I'd shut it. Maybe the girls and Cam had come back and been forgetful. But as I shouldered my way clumsily around the angle and tripped over the first step a faint, ghoulish sound, like droplets in a tub of water, floated from above. In that split second an indescribable pain whirled around my head, one horrific shot of comprehension.

Illuminated at the top of the stairs was Jo, lying on her side with her hands between her legs, softly sobbing. Her other hand lay near her mouth, quietening the stuttering noise yet further so that it was barely audible. I dropped can and bag and leapt up the stairs. Her white top had been ripped down the middle; her cheek bore one long scratch; a rapidly-swelling cut arced around her left eye socket; and her underwear had been pulled down to just above her knees. She did not look at me as I knelt over her from my position a couple of steps down, not even when I stuttered,

"Jo… Jo, what happened?"

But of course, I already knew. She offered nothing in reply except for a tightening of her body, a strange tension, like that of a near-petrified animal trapped in a corner. I looked at her, helpless and violated, and all of my inebriation seemed to leave as I rose slowly to my feet. But this couldn't be true? Cosmo? My closest friend?

"COSMO!" I bellowed, "Come out here, you bastard! You fucking bastard! Get out here!"

I shattered some of the plaster off the flat wall as I smashed open the door. I was transported from my body with rage. I hardly heard Jo's sobbed frantic words as she entered the room and I began sprinting from door to door, flinging each one open and screaming into their empty spaces. After the last door had been torn nearly off its hinges I pivoted wildly round; in the peripheries Jo pulled her underwear back up. It was then that I caught the final three words I was ever to hear from that beautiful woman's lips: "Gene, he's gone."

With my whole body pumping up and down I streaked past her through the door and down the stairs in one complete jump into the night.

Chapter Sixteen

I ran and ran at a pace beyond anything I'd done before—drunks, taxis, kebab boxes all flew past me like ghosts.

I was going in the wrong direction. As I caught myself I whipped out my phone and hammered it. Bur-bur, bur-bur, bur-bur, it rang. Six, seven, eight times. A heavy rustling, and Jack's voice materialised through the tinny speaker at my ear.

"Gene, what's…"

"Jack! Listen! Is Cosmo there? Is he there?!"

"Gene, just, just calm down a second. What is all this? I've got no idea what you're on about. Why would Cos be here?"

He sounded hesitant as he spoke.

"Jack mate, I'm coming round to yours now. You'd better not be covering for him, you fucker."

"Gene! What! I'm… what are you on about? Seriously? He's not here! What's going on?"

"Jack, you don't know what he's done, you don't… don't fucking lie to me mate, don't fucking lie."

"Gene, I SWEAR…"

I cut him off mid-sentence in disgust, and carried on running in what I thought was the right direction. But I'd taken a wrong turn; the dimmer street lamps looked wrong, the hot smooth pavement looked wrong, nothing held any familiarity. I retraced my steps and got nowhere.

I looked around and saw only streetlights and dark velveteen-purple sky. Maybe a person walked out of their front door further on. I panted loudly. And then without warning, I felt the sweat on my entire body burn like brimstone, snaking downwards and back into me. I began to cry uncontrollably. I cried and I shouted out and I put my hand to my eyes and threw myself on the pavement, where the loveless bricks and mortar met and scratched my skin. I thought of everything, all I'd endured in the last month, all the deceit and upheaval, then all the beauty, the incredible high nights, this bustling city where I had believed that I would float up there with the birds and the water vapour forever, coming down with gentleness and regret, regret that it could only ever be a passing thing, down to shaking, changing reality; and I thought again of the betrayal of my mother and father and wept and wept; and I thought of her face, that of my mother, focusing on her image which I still loved like the image of Christ to a faith-forgotten worshipper, the image which I still loved and would always love because despite everything she gave me life and protected me, protected me too much from too little; then I thought about my father, how little I had blamed him, my unreal father, throughout all of it, and I wondered why, although I knew it was because he had never truly felt real. Then I thought about Cosmo, the boy and the man I'd thought to be my one true friend, my brother-in-arms, and my stomach turned, lurching like a storm-bound ship while thinking of his betrayal, of his monstrosity. And finally, I thought about Jo. I thought about her beautiful face and those bright green eyes, her long brown hair flowing in the breeze outside the flat, her face close to mine as we kissed on the sofa for the first time; and then that terrible, terrible image, unforgettable, of her lying there at the top of the stairs, her humanity stripped, looming into view like Death, and out went the light into nothingness.

All of this flew around in my head like birds after carrion, ripping out chunk after chunk until I was bare, as I sat there broken on that warm August night.

After a while I looked around. My breathing settled back into a normal rhythm. There wasn't a soul wandering down these streets. Then I dragged out my phone, which had been on silent: it'd reached one o'clock. I had six missed calls, all from Cam.

Should I get up and find Jack's? Now, after everything, it seemed like a pointless exercise. The fire in my belly was gone. If Cosmo was at Jack's and I went there now, I couldn't have fought him. My only impulse now was to run, and carry on running.

And then I had an idea.

It didn't seem crazy at first; in fact, it felt like the most logical thing in the world. Only later, as I struggled to hitch-hike in the dark with dawn still an hour or so away, dim on the Eastern horizon, did I start to feel uncertain, and only much later on would it feel like lunacy.

I rose from the ground. I was still only wearing a t-shirt and a pair of jeans, but the night was warm and I didn't care that I now had no other possessions to my name.

I mapped out Birmingham in my head and planned the route northwards. It would involve first going South. I breathed in a calming lungful, two lungfuls, of my first reinvigorated breaths, and imagined I could hear the motorway humming through the night air.

Here was my plan:

My destination was Bridlington, right where the saga of finding my father had first begun. That was the first leg; I intended to sail to Norway after finding me a boat that could do it. To get there I had to seek out the M42 running south of Birmingham, which I recognised both from the Radio Two traffic reports at my old work and from the map I took a look at in the car on the way down. I had to reach the motorway and then thumb a lift northwards, ideally to York.

From York it was simple: hitch the Bridlington road through the Wolds and, under cover of darkness, I would steal that boat in the harbour to which I'd taken a fancy almost a month ago.

I couldn't help swaying into a wall or tumble over a curb as I struck out to find Bristol Road, which I knew ran South. There, looking left as I passed under the maroon railway bridge, I bade Jack and whoever else was in Selly Oak tonight a final goodbye. Then I went up through Bournville again, sticking close to the bright main road.

I checked my phone. I regretted that I'd chosen not to call Cam back. They would find out the whole truth soon enough anyway, him Kat and Genna. Guilt beat hard at my insides as I trudged on, guilt at the thought I'd left Jo, that there was simply too much happening in one moment for me to stay. I hoped the others were looking after her, that they'd called the police, that they could be more constant and dependable than me.

It was hard to leave behind a person like Cam. His teaching and expanding my awareness hadn't been his most important gift, nor the fiery temperament that you expected at every corner to turn around and bite your head off and those of any around you, only to flop over and let you rub its soft belly afterwards, or be met with your own flak and grenades. And, though I valued it just as much, it was not that he had shared in the adventures that the MDMA and everything else had taken us on, there at the comeup and comedown. It was that I'd met him an almost-stranger and in little over a week I counted him as a best friend, one who I felt would forever be loyal.

And so I said to myself that I was not really worthy of his friendship; I had failed the test he had wordlessly put down. I had failed the test with Jo too. I was running, running, and it was disloyal and it was selfish, but it was what I had to do.

The road to the M42 was long and by the time I reached the cutting that it lay in, having taken a left at some point and cut through Crofton Hackett and then Barnt Green, the time had almost reached 3.30am. When I saw the darkened landscape ahead of me, finally free from the West Midlands glare that lasts almost forever in every direction, I felt a blazing anticipation. Movement was gearing up again, like the first pistons firing above the hulk of the steam train.

I looked down on the motorway, three lanes stretching out at either side with shimmering white cat's-eyes dividing each, and two large steel barriers dividing each highway. The slope down to the road was wild. There were growing assortments of tall and wild weeds bearded with seed and litter, and unwanted saplings sprinkled in amongst them too. Not thinking with a straight head, I began to walk in that bounding walk that irresistibly happens when you set off downhill. After only a few steps some loose stone gave way from under my right foot; I shouted and went arse-over-tit. Dried maroon dock leaves scratched me as I tumbled gracelessly down the embankment; occasionally I found my footing, only to be carried sickeningly over again by my momentum. The flora gave way to chalky stone which cut at my exposed arms, and then… thud.

I got up, sighed, and brushed myself off, feeling foolish but injury-free except the cosmetic mess of my forearms. I looked down the open ink-coloured road from the hard shoulder. On the other side a lorry groaned by.

A wait of about five minutes in the dead of night feels like half an hour; a wait of twenty minutes as though a pictureless film has been put on loop. Two back-and-forth calls from owls in the distant fields were the only things that pierced the senses; but after a while, gradually, so gradually, peering round the bend almost like a child in a game of hide-and-seek who breathlessly inches sideways to see their seeker, was the light of a large vehicle beginning to illuminate my patch of the night. As it rounded the bend its distant droning noise became a roar and split the night in two. I ran out to the middle of the hard shoulder, afraid to venture much further, and threw out my arm for him to see. He bore down on me without a hint of slowing; I twisted backwards as he went past with a deafening roar, desperately hoping to see his left indicator flash on at any moment. But I was disappointed. It rolled back into the night.

"You fucking twat," I muttered to myself. I retreated back to my spot.

But then, no sooner had I resumed my position when two articulated lorries followed, one overtaking the other, and I sprang back outwards with a mad leap. As they passed I could see that they were neck-and-neck so that the shine of two lights became the raw blare of four. They crawled like two half-sprinting sumo wrestlers and when both passed by without indication of stopping I started to swear again. But then the overtaking lorry dropped back, and now in file with the other it flicked on its amber indicator—which had already grown quite small in the distance—and pulled slowly into the hard shoulder.

I let out an unexpectedly loud and joyous shout of 'Yes!' and fist-pumped, then thought to look back to my spot but remembered that, of course! I wasn't carrying a thing in the world. I turned and ran quickly to the giant red tail lights.

Chapter Seventeen

It was parked a long way up the motorway, much further than I'd anticipated; I was out of breath by the time I caught up with it and read the giant words: 'MOOR VIEW HAULAGE' on its rear. The cab door swung open for me and for a second I caught a flash of chubby, exposed arm. The unknown driver remained silent.

I clambered up the sheer set of steps. Sat there in the driver's seat was a man who, if I'd been asked to paint a picture of a stereotypical lorry driver, would have fit the bill near-perfectly. He had a short, fat head that was bald except for flashes of greying hair round the sides which glowed like white bike reflectors in the illumination of his dashboard. Wisps of blond eyebrows which, along with the skin, looked like they'd spent a lifetime getting damaged in the sun—a deep, dark, sailor's tan. Small, light blue eyes were set in deepish sockets; a wrinkled and almost delicate nose which sat above an out-turned and small mouth and a heavily dimpled chin; and a light but even coating of grey stubble, pocked occasionally with black, from ear to ear. He had an old baggy black vest on; scrunched up by his left leg was a high-vis vest with a big brown sauce stain pooled in the middle.

His bulldog mouth smiled at me as I tried to make my ascent look struggle-free.

"Yeh've no bags'r aht?" came his first loud question. His voice was rich and coarse at the same time, like a bow saw cutting through wood.

"No, no," I replied, still catching my breath, "It's just me."

He made a noise of interest, flicked his head up, grasped the steering wheel, and fired up the loud engine. I slammed the door shut, almost falling out in trying to clutch the handle, and the chugging roaring noise cut out to a whisper.

We were silent as we pulled onto the empty motorway and picked up speed. The driver sighed grainily.

"Graveyard at this tahm o' naht. An't ever picked someone up actualleh, but ah thought can't leave yeh standin theeya freezin yer chebs off, nah."

"Well thank you, thank God you stopped," I poured.

"Nay worries lad," he quickly threw back, waving his small, broad right hand. "Wheeya yeh goin to?"

"Erm—well where are you heading?"

"Ah finish in Sheffield this mornin son. Then ah'm drahvin back to Hillsborough."

"Hillsborough," I repeated softly. "I've heard of it, but..."

"Aye, so's everybody aftert Eighties. Still dealin wit reputation of that day, and still there's bin no justice..."

He looked off for a second distractedly, then returned to look at me.

"Where'd yeh say yeh're off again?"

"Well, ideally York, but Sheffield's great for now if you can take us that far."

"Aye no prob." He sniffed and scratched at his black-clad chest.

"Do you know if it's easy to hitch-hike from Sheffield to York at all?"

"Well, yeh'd ave to get on't M1 but from theeya shunt be a problem. Can't remember ow far York is nah."

"Don't think it's too far."

"No. BUT… unfortunateleh we've a drop-off in Burton and then Buxton and from them two places we come in Ecclesall Road way."

I had no idea what any of this meant but nodded along and listened carefully as he explained to me that he'd drop me off at 'Hunter's Bar', not being able to take me to the M1 because he was too busy at home, and from there I'd have to make my own way to the motorway on the Eastern side of the city.

"Long rah'd ahead ah'm afraid."

"That's alright with me. Time doesn't mean a thing at the minute. I'll get some kip in a bit, perhaps, if that's alright."

"Aye, maht as well," he chuckled laconically, "Maht as well. What the chuff were yeh doin, anyow, thumbin int middle o't naight? Ont run 'r summat?" He continued chuckling; evidently, I'd seriously brightened up his night. That bow saw voice, the whistling wind cutting through a slice of the window; both infected me with the same laughter.

"You could say that… yeah, y'could say that," I replied. "Nah, just needed a lift sharpish. You were a lifesaver, really. Listen, I'm sorry but I might as well say now: I can't give you any money for the lift mate. I'm broke…"

He opened his eyes wide at me in a moment of anger and my heart did somersaults; what the fuck was I doing, I panicked, risking losing my ride?

Then, just as suddenly, he melted into smiles and rhythmic laughter and said:

"Don't worreh 'baht that, boss, it's mah pleasure: alwez nahce to ave someone to talk to. Meks the job move quicker. Ah've been on since midnaight at Bristol an we won't b' done wahl orf eight, if we're luckeh. So don't bother thissen—just get comfeh. Lahk coffeh?"

I took the flask he was offering from across his body and unscrewed the top. It was dinted all over, with the occasional dribble of white paint streaked down it, or small oval Union Jack stickers that you get on apples stuck at all angles. The fresh smell hit my nose, mealy and hot; it was a reminder of the world around and beyond and the morning to come. I was on the road, and the faintest beginning of the ochre sunrise lay ahead.

I looked at my cross-country chauffeur—there was something in this bloke, a kind of charm, ease of speech, humbleness, something in the placative way he gestured his hand or occasionally leant slightly towards me from across the cabin as if what he had to say would only ever privilege my ears; and the combination of these things, added to the strong, thick draught of coffee I'd just thrown down my neck, made me forget all thoughts of sleep. The talk turned to Hillsborough—the disaster at the stadium—then to Sheffield and Knaresborough. I told him, "You can calcify everyday objects at Mother Shipton's Cave. But it's an expensive trap to snare tourists."

"But when yeh've lived in Sahth Yorkshire all yer lahf, there's note better than bein a tourist," came his simple reply. "Ah tell yeh what," and again he put in that little friendly lean, "Ah drahv arahnd t' country evreh single naight. An ah never get to see ote of it. Ah rareleh gerraht of Illsborough int day 'cept sometahms bobbin dahn t'ill to Sheffield, an, an…" he struggled for the words—"An it jus gets yer dahn, y'know?"

He looked at me with an expression, only for a moment, that was almost pleading, as if I could make things better. "Ah wonder sometahms if ah cunt jus pack irrall in, start somewhere new."

I nodded along, studying his face and in its crevices trying to find clues of the life behind it. He'd quickly changed his tone with these last words, casting off the vulnerability of a second ago. He sighed and pulled out a packet of Golden Virginia with a plasticky crinkle and cleared his throat—I'd had him down as a Drum man. "But we get to see some o' Dorbyshire this morn, which'll be loveleh. Went campin as a lad. Good fish in them rivers theeya."

"How come you haven't been since?" I couldn't help asking. "Can you not get the hours off?"

"Corn't afford to tek em off. Ah've fahv kids, three grandkids'n a wahf to look after. That's why ah've been at it wee'aht an oliday fo' fifteen years."

"You're kidding?"

"Not me. Me day off's me holidays."

He raised his half-rolled cigarette to his lips and gave the paper a lick, rolled it into one, then swapped it about in his hands until his right was free and wound down the window.

"Y'see, what politicians," he continued, exploding the 'p' from his lips, "And employers, and people in this country need to realise is, ordinareh folk orn't the enemeh, we're not somethin that's that's gone to the edge of societeh, that dunt exist anymore. We're still ere! We aven't changed! We are who we alwez ave been. The shock, when ah tell em dahn t'playgroup on a Wednesd' when ah pick up our Matteh thar'ahm off to work again later that naight, an that I an't ad a naight off for fifteen year! My area's turned middle class—not that ah lahk to label people, but appen that'd be what you'd say, to ear em an to know what the' do for a livin', y'know. Lahk ah say, ah'm not aht to judge anyone, onleh to stop em judgin me. An ah'm not angreh or ote. When people say, 'Oh, well yeh shunt ave ad bairns when you were seventeen!' well, all's ah want is t'chance to tell em, 'Eh, sometahms it's not as simple as all that.' Folk tend to think that it's as easeh as gerrin an abortion an usin yer ead—but what if there's a reason you didn't do that? What if you cunt bring yersen to tek away that babeh's lahf? Or what if you never ad the schoolin, or that yer parents weren't theeya when you were young? Norr everyboddeh gets born into a family that's there for em through thick'n thin; we're not all so luckeh as that. Not everyone's a grown-up when they're seventeen. Sad to say."

His temper didn't flare throughout his speech even for a second. I asked him about his kids.

"Two lads an three lasses. T' youngest is three. Lickle angels! An t'middle un, Kyle, plays fo't' academeh at Wednesday, which we're all reet prahd of."

The dawn was gathering pace. We'd sat in silence for a little while before he picked out an old CD from somewhere around his seat. It was a Rolling Stones greatest hits, with a razzing, gold tongue on its sticky cover declaring itself to the world. On came the opening strums of Street Fighting Man and as we began to turn northwards the burning top of the sun moved further and further towards the driver's-side window, irresistibly breaking over the smooth Midlands landscape.

After a while we reached a toll booth, and I understood that we were leaving the M42 to join the M6.

"Moneh grabbin bastards, orn't the'," he joked, rifling around in some hole or other until the bright chink of coins hit my ears and he pulled out his hand once more. He mulled the coins round and round in his small fist. "An we're onleh bloodeh on it for abaht four mahl!"

He pulled forwards gently and gassed for a couple of minutes with the tired-looking man in the booth, who bemoaned the fact he was on until six. I looked at my phone: 04.06. My driver waited until the barrier was lifted and we rumbled on through.

"On wahl six, luckeh bugger dunt know he's born. What yeh lookin fo'?" He'd seen me reaching into the money hole.

"A pen—you got one?" He produced a chewed biro from behind his right ear. "And any paper?"

"Christ," he grumbled, "Don' ask for much, duyyer? Back theeya mebbe, ave a look int map books."

Sure enough there were some old oil-splattered order forms in one of his road atlases. I took the cleanest one, smoothed it on the back of the book, and settled down to writing my letter to my father. I knew that for him to help me he'd have to receive it now, and at the earliest it was going to be posted in Sheffield, still half a day away with the detours. Still, he would know I was coming—ready at last to find him. As I slowly wrote I began to imagine his face. I couldn't picture it as any other than my own, this older, wiser version of me in creases of shock as I stood at his doorstep maybe half-alive from my voyage. What would he think? What would he do? What would I do?

I kept the letter short. He gave me some coins to buy an envelope and to post it with. Daylight had become broad by the time we swung our way through a potholed industrial estate. Gated entrances were either locked together by rusted, hanging chains or open for business; each drive and yard was filled-in with blackened rock and other rubble, giving the effect of the land being one giant, flattened slag-heap. Sometimes there was a seated, high-vis-clad yard worker sat in a plastic bucket-chair or on a set of boxes or pallets, reading a tabloid and tucking into a sandwich or rummaging with a Thermos flask, unshaven and unshirted in the rising heat of the morning.

But clouds were approaching, so my chauffeur said, and in anticipation already some of the workers were hauling tarpaulins over the more porous of their goods.

I left him to his business as he abandoned the cab in one of these yards. I cobbled a kind of makeshift blind out of doubled-up newspaper sheets which I hung from the sun visor and begun snoozing underneath the veil of breasts and football pages. I was brought to by the slamming of the cab door and the coarse voice giving goodbyes. I remembered his eagerness for company and stretched up.

"Don't worry lad, get yer ead dahn for some kip."

I fell straight back down into slumber.

When I awoke the landscape had completely changed. The soft hillscape of the West and Mid-Midlands, with its towns, roadside services and smooth, fast roads had gone: in their place was gorgeous and dramatic English hill-country, green and mossy, with ravines populated by silver birch and mud-coloured stones and drystone walls separating the narrow road from the downward drops, ancient and wet in the thick shade. Gone too was the sun. A solid, unmoving lid of dull cloud, ominously dark in places, had invaded the previously dry heat and replaced it with a sticky atmosphere made only slightly pleasanter when I wound down my window. The hawthorn in the fields was totally still.

"I ad to tek dahn them papers, the' were gerrin in me way. Dint bother you did it? Sun went in pretty shorpish lahk."

"No, not at all. Where are we?"

"Abaht six mahl off Ashbourne."

After navigating through that town we passed the national park boundary of the Peaks. We made slow progress, groaning and straining up hills in first gear with me willing it on like a gambler at the races. It was a long time before we reached Buxton down the two-lane road. Twice we had to pull in to let traffic pass, which he seemed used to doing. A light, straight-falling drizzle developed. We passed out of the town, heading east on the A6. The sharp ravines changed to open dales, more spacious and grassy, where white blobs of sheep were grazing.

At the village of Blackwell we turned into a small building site some way down a side road. A house, half-constructed, was set into a small hill and rounded off by trees. A few broad-shouldered men pottered about their jobs, lifting or smoking; one woman held a clipboard and leant on her Merc while talking to a dwarfish man wearing a chest-warmer. My driver yanked up the handbrake and rubbed his olive-skinned face; his expression was somehow both a smile and a grimace.

"Got nearleh allt' stuff off at Burton, so shan't be s'long ere, oreet."

I was about to say 'don't you worry' as a show of gratitude, but he'd already lightly closed the cab door and tramped off to wait by the officious woman and dwarfish man. I felt my aching body and wondered if I would get a book of site regulations thrown at me if I left the cab. But what the fuck, I opened the door and jumped down to stride up and down the length of the lorry, reviving my muscles while wondering at the straps that held the side sheet down.

I thought about Sheffield—the Prospect. A big city to navigate, completely unknown. Cutlery. Hills. Kes. Within ten minutes we were back on the road and bound for it.

Chapter Eighteen

My driver seemed full of a new lease of life as I asked him about the approach.

"W'll get rid o' this eap o' junk at Whirlow and there ah've me cor; so, where'd ah say ah'd drop you? Ah, Unter's Bar, course; cos from there ah'll tek Brocco Bank an you can appen gerron wun o't buses that run dahn theya. There's a shitload that run into tahn." He slapped himself lightly on the cheek. "Phew, can feel them pillehs, eh. Paggered."

He might have been tired but for me a wired energy was filling my head. The names Tideswell and Bradwell passed by. Around Hathersage the terrain became mountainous, with stark, sharp, silent outcrops of rock capping each rise, watching the land. My head turned fully until I could no longer see as each peak passed by, my mind boggling with the pure time they'd stood there: hard sentinels above the bleak and enchanting landscape. And then the view cleared; the skies expanded. Below, in the distance, there were high-rises. I saw the beginnings of Sheffield.

The road inwards was one long descent into the Porter Valley. We jumped into an old, low-riding Passat at the haulage yard and I suddenly felt like a mouse scurrying around at ankle-level. The steep road down got busy, and shops and pubs appeared at either side: The Banner Cross, Napoleon's Casino, a Co-Op. A grassy park appeared on the left as the road levelled out, and there up ahead I read the title 'Hunter's Bar' on the roundabout plan.

"So, this is the fabled Hunter's Bar lad. Lahk ah said," he continued as he indicated left and braked to a stop, "jus op on a bus fr'm this sahd an it'll tek yeh in. You can gerra train to Meadow'all once yeh've fahd t' station."

I offered my hand. "I can't thank you enough. You saved my life at Birmingham."

He looked almost offended. "Oh, it were note, honestleh. Cunt leave you there, cudda? Nahce to ave someone on board." He took my hand and shook it firmly.

"I never caught your name you know."

"Oh," he fretted, his look suggesting this was the first time it had crossed his mind to introduce himself. "Course fella. Sorreh. Andrew. Ah'm Andrew. Thissen?"

I froze momentarily to hear Cosmo's name. I stumbled.

"Gene, it's Gene."

I swung the door open and half got out. "Turrah, then."

"Aye, turrah! Tek it easeh, an good luck."

He gave another bulldog smile, his brown face looking worn-down and worn-out. I thunked the door shut. He muffledly shouted, "Gi't another shove!" then

"Pahl o' shit Passat!" over the rev of the engine, then he was gone.

The rain beat constantly and hard and I strode off down to the roundabout with my shoulders hunched against the drops. All there was was wetness, warm, earthy-tasting wetness, and the hunger in the pit of my stomach. I decided to find some shops before catching the bus. Two number 82's splashed by me as I crossed over from the azalea-bushed side of the unnamed road. On the other side were small cafés with open fronts, whose tables and chairs had either been stacked or abandoned; there was a betting shop, a pharmacy, a closed fast-food joint on the corner of an off-shooting road, and a glorious-looking sandwich shop. How much bar did I have left? My wallet made a sorry sight. I'd managed to save £5.12, plus the couple of quid I'd been given.

Inside the sandwich shop I ordered the cheapest thing on the menu and sat looking at the sheeting rain. I thumbed a couple of magazines, one of which had a poem entitled 'At Hunter's Bar' fittingly covering one of its middle pages. I read the poem twice and lingered on the last line until my call came from the attractive woman with tight black leggings. As she passed over the bag and then turned, I took another look at her back and then up at her pinned-back dark hair. For a second, she became Jo. And then I was out in the rain again. Just before a large car park which opened itself out to my right, I dived into a charity shop while I licked the mayonnaise off my thumb.

Two minutes later I'd parted with a pound and had crossed to the opposite side of the road in an oversized and overworn dark-green cagoule. The polyester stitching was shot along the hood's base and so my neck still felt the spatter, but it was an improvement. I sat in hope at the stop, with scenarios and silver-tongued sentences dancing around my head in the event of not being able to afford the bus. Before another minute had passed I'd handed over £1.10 and boarded a blue 83 into the city of Sheffield, leaving me with just one golden pound coin left in the world.

The first thing I can tell you about the Steel City is that the road into town from where I caught the bus is short. Being from Knaresborough, I am a walker. I judged the route would have taken 25 minutes, leading quickly into the smallish city centre.

The second is just that: the size of the place. Or lack of size. Humble—nothing like the straight, flattish arcades of Leeds: always snaking, arching with a hill, never seeming like it was about to give up its secret and burst into life. In Sheffield you are blinded by the hills and believe wholeheartedly that the city ends at the train station, and that, for all I knew, was the truth. My experience of the place is a closed book: wet, possibly charming, possibly with its own Selly Oak-style district of kicking parties and narcotic-fuelled forays by those free of an all-compelling destination in their lives.

I reached the M1 having stayed in the Don Valley by following road signs, passing the dark, groaning structures of its industrial past along the way. The motorway ran in two vertically-parallel carriageways, one on top of the other like grey piggy-backing elephants. It felt completely normal now to be thumbing for a lift, like it was a gesture I'd had to make all my life. I considered the effect that me looking like a drowned rat would have on the drivers with the traffic roaring from above and from the sides, and so I took off my cagoule, stripped off my t-shirt and wrung it out, replaced it, swept my hair about, and then threw a smile onto my patchily-stubbled face. I thumbed for half an hour with no success.

I burnt the time with imagining those I'd left behind. I tried to picture what their lives must have been like that morning, what fallout had occurred. But it was no use. Jo's image swirled around my troubled mind, coming and going like an ebbing tide. My mind slowly became consumed by the northering that I was intent on: the lift I simply had to get.

It was a midnight-blue Corsa that pulled up in the end. The slim-faced, long-limbed fella in the driver's seat wore a light, striped shirt and had his reddish hair cut short and gelled. He didn't look a lot older than me. He gestured to get in.

The car smelled clinically fresh, like his mum had Febreze-d it the night before. He was on his way to Leeds to visit his girlfriend and could take me as far as 'the interchange'. He seemed in awe of the various bits of my story that I told. He was always butting in with polite questions like: "So, where did you go after that?" and, "Wait, who was that fight with?" I felt at ease to put up my feet on the dashboard and sink into conversation, apologising now and then for being skint, and enjoying the escapism of his story. He led a normal life, that was all. But that was where I was: to hear normality was like drinking and laughing and forgetting, like listening to a song that spirits you away. Strangers had become my song.

He let me out at what turned out to be the East Ardsley interchange at just gone midday, telling me how he had to make it to Calverley so as to skim round Bradford, joining the M62 on the way. I closed the door quietly, wishing him well and checking for my cagoule as he held his palm out flat for some seconds in a kind of deferential farewell before cautiously pulling off. I was by the motorway once more.

The sky was still, a dull iron colour; the motorways growled all round, rumbling in the open West Yorkshire air. I was nearer to home. I could sense it. The old home, the rejected one, the old life. I sniffed inwards and could taste it.

As I darted between cars and crossed the roundabout to hook back up with the M1, confused, nonplussed looks dragged at the sullen faces of the drivers in their cars. Some were stationary, tapping at their wheels, while others dodged, darted and nosed their way in and out of lanes like terriers down burrows. In this part of the world the routes feel cramped, intertwining and hectic, and I could tell by the morose faces in those cars that no-one would bat an eyelid at a dishevelled teen disjointed on one of the arteries of the West Yorkshire town chain. No, all the bastards were on half-days from Morley to Dewsbury bent on getting home for a brew and Deal. I thumbed there for two hours, sitting down at intervals for a minute or so before my motivation would return and I would throw myself back out into the lonesome hard shoulder. But it was no use. I began to trudge northwards, determined to make it to the city of Leeds before night fell.

A few hundred yards down the hard shoulder, however, my luck turned. I saw flashing hazards, and a darkly-dressed male figure moving around a vehicle with his hand to his ear. A breakdown! As I approached and heard the man's soft voice read out his registration number, an older man climbed out of the passenger side and stretched slowly, looking up the road. He moved off to have a piss in seclusion against the hedge. I waited.

He finished. I walked up confidently.

"Hi there. I couldn't help but notice we're both a bit stuck."

He seemed unmoved. In fact, he didn't speak at all until after he had eased himself creakily back into the car's front seat: movements that suggested his body was beginning to decay but still enjoying the suppleness of an extended middle-age. I looked to the other man who was pacing around the car. He looked quickly away.

"Yes, we're sorting out that pickle now, thank you."

Hostility bubbled beneath the knitted, compressed BBC vowels. He reached to shut the door, but I quickly laid my hand on the frame.

"Look, if you're about to be picked up by a recovery van I'd be delighted if I could catch a lift with you."

I chose my words carefully, trying to mimic the old man's style. But not carefully enough.

"I'm afraid we don't give lifts to strangers."

"But, surely, if you've got space and we've an hour in which to..."

"No, I'm afraid we don't give lifts to strangers," he repeated, rocking in his seat for the door handle once more, "Especially not ones quite so objectionably brusque."

He wrestled the door from me and swung it shut.

"Well, fuck you then," I shot at the other man outside. He looked at me wide-eyed, afraid to say anything back.

I was spurred on by anger and quickly reached a suburb called Hunslet. I was entering Leeds proper. My stomach ached, longing for a hot meal, and this pain along with my tiring legs was fast turning my mind to theft. I trudged along a trunk road in hope of finding a supermarket; I was soon rewarded.

Over the tops of some houses on the left, around four hundred yards away, appeared a giant, beacon-like 'M' dressed in gold and green. It bobbed up and down in my view, ducking and surfacing amongst the terracotta rooftops. I took a left down Church Lane. My nerves jangled. I hadn't stolen for years. I passed through the sliding doors and I felt the blast of cool air shoot down on me, meeting with the lingering damp of my t-shirt and sending me into shivers.

The bakery section was at the back, and hair-netted staff bustled behind the shelves. I took up three rolls and a danish pastry, and then casually moved to the hot meat section to pick up the first bag I saw; then I disappeared to the tinned veg aisle to wrap them all in my cagoule. I'd regressed.

Once outside, I waited until I met back up with the main road to Leeds and then devoured the items, savouring their flavour and crunch like a roaring fire in Winter.

I'd gone back on my word to myself in doing this. They were hardly comparable, petty food thievery and auto-theft—that was what the social worker had called it— but my guilt followed me on the busying streets, all the way to the main train station where I stopped to take a seat and rest myself. I wondered at that period of my life, when I was fourteen, fifteen, where I had gone wild for a while: barely scraping my SATS, being caught red-handed driving to Harrogate with a few mates, then the change and the turnaround before it got too late. Now, I felt, all was creeping back.

I hopped the barrier to Leeds station toilets to use the hand dryers to finally relieve my body of the damp. Cagouled, a little restored, I set out to find the one-way system by the church that I could remember. From there, York beckoned.

Chapter Nineteen

I was hungry again. The day was waning. I headed back into town and found a Sainsbury's at Jackson's to perform my little trick once more. Then I traipsed back to the church with my food.

The sky had brightened somewhat, the sun was away in the west and, with my neck craned upwards at the clock, my eyes began to water. It was then that I heard a soft voice from behind.

"Quite an island in this sea of roads, isn't it?" I jumped. "It's a wonder to think they were only populated by horses and carts a hundred years ago."

I turned to look at the man who spoke, hastily trying to wipe away my tears. He was short—a vicar—with bristly, salt-and-pepper hair. He was the picture of stillness, even when he made to fold his arms and turn his eyes from the church to my face. "What's the matter dear boy? You're upset; I can see. Here, here are some tissues." He delved into a deep pocket within his long tunic-like clothing. "Fresh, I can promise!"

"Oh, no thank you, they weren't tears, it was just…"

I gestured towards the obscured sun.

"Ah, the light, the light."

"The light."

I wiped away the moisture with my shoulder. The old man took his hand from his pocket and offered me it.

"Sometimes we all need to look at the light," he chuckled, grasping my own hand in his loose palm. "I'm Simon, to my flock."

"Gene," I replied. "Sorry for the way I look—I've been away from home for a while."

"I can see. Did you live somewhere close Gene?"

"I used to but… things changed."

"They did, they did," he responded, as if he'd known my story all along. Now he grabbed my hand with both of his. "I saw your actions in the shop Gene."

It was nothing more than a whisper, and it sent shivers down my backbone. I suddenly felt like I'd slid into a cold pool.

"I…" He raised his hand to silence me.

"You must have been desperate to have committed that act. Desperate Gene. Why?"

I sighed. "It would take all evening vicar."

"I have all evening Gene, if you can spare it too. Won't you accompany me? We can take a cup of tea in my office."

"Yes," I nodded, beautifully warmed. "Yes, that would be good."

I told him everything. Simon's church was no ordinary church—it was Leeds Minster, replete with row after row of painstakingly-fashioned pews, numberless figurines of saints, and a grand organ rising up to the mezzanine floor. His office was small—we'd reached it by the staircase at the rear of the church and through a concealed entrance—and in it were those little, interesting features which breathe life into rooms: An ancient, polished bookcase carved with the images of angels and filled not only with religious texts but also, to my surprise, some John Steinbeck novels and 'The Millennium Trilogy'; a poster in rainbow colours with the CND logo, tacked at the side of a three-hooked coat rack; a picture of what I later learned were his two grandchildren—Mima, who wanted to be a firefighter at seven years old, and Johnny, a digger fanatic; and lastly, a row of plants, exotic, varied in size, and each kept to perfection, bearing the fruit or flowers of its species. As we spoke and the sky dimmed through the small, inornate window to a low dusk, I would look over to the plants, fascinated by their perfect symmetry. The vicar insisted they were just a hobby and got up twice to point out their faults embarrassedly to me like I was an authority, slowly stroking each one as he did.

We drank tea as I wound deeper into each one of the stories that made up the one Story. His face, unmoved and placid at all other times, turned slowly outwards as I narrated what drove me out of Birmingham to his old flaking ears; after I stopped at the point where I'd flown into the night, he put his mug down with a slow clunk and swallowed the last of his tea. Then, with eyebrows twitching like rabbits, he gave me his advice.

"I've always believed in premonitions Gene; there's too much space in between what we know and what we don't to take them lightly. Of course you wouldn't have dreamed of turning back in the park—nobody who'd been out drinking the same night and who had been taking drugs consistently over the last few weeks would. But listen to your gut; it's the gut that conjures these things you know." He sighed and loosened his collar.

I stroked at the soft stubble on my face. "I need you to tell me something Simon."

"What is it?"

"Did I do the right thing? Did I do the moral thing, running away like that? I mean, I left…" Words failed me, even as he raised his palm to quiet me. He took out a pencil from one of his drawers, inspected its nib, reached for a post-it note, and began writing in looping characters. As he did he pronounced slowly, "Don't let the ill deeds of others deter you from your path Gene."

He passed me the note. "Monsters can never sway you. Devils can never destroy you: only you have the power to destroy yourself from within. You are truly blessed if in the face of all that is evil you can douse the fire unburnt."

His voice, like a hand running through my hair, came back, "Let them stay on the dark side for now Gene, whatever they've done—your mother, your father, your friend. There'll be time for forgiveness in the future."

"Will there?"

"Yes, there will. In the meantime, what should be done? Your testament at a police station would be a beginning. Before that you would need to contact Cam, Jack, and Jo herself in order to find out what they are doing about it, about everything. Don't you think that would be wise?"

As soon as he'd finished delivering this uncomfortable, needling advice he rose and checked his watch. "Good grief!" he exclaimed softly, "It's half past eleven." He strode over to a small cupboard door underneath the coat rack and rummaged around inside until he had found a blanket and a cushion. "Gene, here you are. They've been used three times only—I think—yes, to keep a flock member warm during that cold snap in April. There you are. I would be happy for you to sleep here, in my office, for tonight, though I would have to lock you in. That would be okay, I presume?"

I nodded, trying to hide my delight. "I'm sorry that I can't take you home. There was a time before, my wife…"

I assured him of his generosity. "Where does the time go?" he pondered, slipping into his jacket.

"I know. Thank you Simon."

"My pleasure. Good night Gene. My my, half eleven…!" he trailed off as he closed the door and scraped the lock into place. I heard his footsteps echo off down the staircase and then I fell into sleep.

I was woken quietly early the next morning. Simon's watch read 6.30am. He explained, as he sorted out a coffee, that he had been up walking his dogs and doing his yoga routine. No wonder he could stay so still all the time.

"That's my morning therapy done with. Then there's Julie to come in in an hour to help set up the coffee tables—the trestles are still stuck in the vestry!—and after that we run an English class for the area's immigrants. Not that I'm rushing you out Gene."

I demanded to aid him with the trestles, and despite his protests I began to cart them into the church hall. I loved sniffing in the dust, seeing the particles become trapped in the shafts of light which penetrated through the stained-glass windows, and feeling the reassurance of the old stone underfoot. There was more walking again to be done today.

We drank our mugs of coffee at the entrance right where we'd met. It was a fair, slightly breezy morning. We embraced; and then I was on the road to York.

It was walkable in a day, but I found myself a lift at the big roundabout where the A64 meets the A1, right where an old ivy-covered house stands alone as a landmark. This time my saviour was a yellow Astra van, the type with only two seats and steeled-over back windows, driven by a plumber named Graham. Within the half hour, we were in York.

The plaque on the ancient stone gateway that towered next to me read: 'Micklegate Bar'. I followed the signs down the hill that led to the city centre, crossing the River Ouse as I made my way. The top of the Minster showed from behind the riverside bars and complexes. Below me the water flowed strongly on, its deep brown silty colour reflecting little of the overhead brightness. The river looked a greater, more engorged sister of Knaresborough's Nidd.

The main street was busy with buskers and tourists; I tossed a penny that I'd found into the fountain there, then re-read Simon's message. I couldn't call the others. They'd gone now, gone like clouds racing across a riven sky. I made my way to the Minster to stare upwards at its Gothic beauty instead, and there I thought only of my selfishness.

I asked an old local woman, the type with a wheeled tartan shopping bag, for the quickest way to the Bridlington road.

"Bah foot?" she asked with the faintest glimmer of a smile. I nodded, sharing in the real joke that she hadn't realised she had made. "Igh Petergate, King's Square, Colliergate, Fossgate, Walmgate," she laughed gummily. "Ere," she continued, holding my arm, "Down there, and keep going; you'll go through a little square, keep on, you'll cross ovvert River Foss, keep on, and go throught bar. That gets you too Ull Road bah foot at least. A'yeh parked up there or summat?"

I made positive noises, thanked the old woman, and then strode off with a garble of gates going through my mind.

In the square which she had mentioned there was a large crowd semi-circling a street performer who was on top of a stone-cut stage and shouting loudly. The twinkling fingers of green tree boughs moved near his head. I walked down a cobbled street and crossed the river: this one, much smaller than the Ouse, crawled with a turquoise tint to the waters, lily pads bedecking the surface.

I was hungry again and stole from a shop at the crossroads from which the University branched to the right, having passed through an old arch named Walmgate Bar. Within twenty minutes of this place I'd reached a dual carriageway, still in suburban York. From here, I thumbed periodically with no success until I reached Stamford Bridge in the mid-afternoon.

My feet had become two big blisters by this point. Drizzle had set in, and my cagoule became useful once again. I asked for a glass of water at a pub near the river and slipped through into the sheltered smoking area at the back, where two blokes were laughing away in loud conversation. One was supping on lager and the other on a cloudy, dark glass of something or other. Their matching Kangol hoodies were smattered in paint; the patterns weren't dissimilar from those that had been splashed on the TV stool in Jack's front room. One of the men had a dark gathering of stubble which had all but abandoned the sides of his face; the other's face was chubby and red, and he was broad in every sense except for his voice, which whined in a deceptively high pitch.

I sat on the only other bench.

"Don't suppose you're driving to Brid this aft fellas?" I ventured during a lull in their conversation.

"Y'what kid?" replied the dark-haired one rhetorically. He spoke as fast as an auctioneer. "Brid, nah. Why, yeh lookin fra lift?"

"Aye, but it doesn't matter."

"Well," began the other one, placing down his pint carefully, "We are off to Rudston later on, aren't we Dennis?"

"Aye, later on, yeah, once this job's done like." He turned away and spat on the floor.

"Would that do ya?"

After a minute of time-wrangling and learning that I would have to sit amongst the tools in the back of their van—this lift was also to be in a two-seater Astra—the two men had gone off to finish their job.

I milled by the river until around six, filling in the time by gathering and eating watercress that was growing there, and imagining the ghosts of the great battle that had taken place there nearly a thousand years ago. Then their van rattled up, a horn honked, and Dennis opened up the boot to let me in. I made an awkward and uncomfortable kind of nest between the toolboxes, dust sheets and tubs of acetone somewhere near the wheel arch, and off we clunked across East Yorkshire.

After some conversation with the two men I'd managed to wrap up a flathead and a crosshead screwdriver plus a hammer in my cagoule, which by now was proving invaluable.

It wasn't long before we'd passed into Rudston and the red-faced man had been dropped off. Dennis turned us back to the main street, nosed the van into a driveway and yanked the handbrake upwards

I uncurled myself painfully and hopped out. We shook hands—I was careful to hold tightly to my goods with the other—and I set off in the direction he sent me, which was somewhere away up the hill and beyond an old church.

The last leg. I could smell the sea now. I stopped for a few minutes on the way out of the village to hop a fence and look up-close at the giant standing-stone which stuck out from the ground in the churchyard there. It stood, staunch, still as though it was suspending time, out of the reach of time. Dark clouds were beginning to cover up the sun in the West, and I was cold; but a dim, blue sky hung above me and the coast.

Chapter Twenty

With my last pound I bought a plate of chips and sat on the seafront with my cagoule flapping noisily in the wind. It was almost dark now.

I was back. Everything in Bridlington was like I'd left it, though things had irreversibly changed inside since I'd last set foot in the town; I was staggered to think that was less than a month ago. All my experience—in Birmingham, Knaresborough, anywhere—all my knowledge, had led me here now in the search for my father. I went back to the harbour where I'd seen my boat. There it bobbed, still sparkling in blue and white, stout, like it had to be. Several black car-tyres and orange flotation balls hung over its side like moss on a rock, and onboard its small scrubbed deck lay lobster pots and other bits of fishing tackle. The sea-weathered cabin stood short, spanning the width of the deck with two spectacle-like windows facing seaward.

Nearby on the jetty I picked up a littered Sainsbury's bag and poured my tools inside. I walked back off the jetty to the concrete seafront and retraced old steps—an old escape route I remembered, amused—to take in the town one last time, for what it was worth, and to find the Tesco nearby the waste land where I could nick my food for the voyage.

It was well into the night when I decided to make my move. I'd been watching the boat from the hill that overlooked the harbour, tuning in to the occasional passing conversation until it seemed that the streets were empty. I turned on my phone. It was just short of 2 am.

I crept downwards, scared almost to make a noise with my footsteps though not a soul was awake in that Eastern-town. The slow wash of the calm sea reassured; as I paced along the jetty a soft wind began to make the small, luminescent orange balls which sat on the mast pole jostle around like fattened hummingbirds. I stopped.

Putting my first foot on board was an invitation for a different creature to make home, if only temporarily, inside me. Images of the car I'd once stolen flashed through my mind as I worked at the lock of the cabin door—a sticky fence, the deep smell of wet coal, a dog barking in a house across the way. The wrenching sound as I finally forced the lock reverberated off the hill. I ducked behind the side of the boat nearest the town. After a few minutes I poked my eyes above the parapet to look for any sign of life. But nothing moved. I was inside.

There was no steering column to pry off with my screwdriver, and so I spent a full quarter of an hour working away quietly at the thick wooden panelling below the wheel, finding a stake-like lump of metal next to the lobster pots to use for leverage before it splintered open. In front of me now was a small grouping of wires. Using my phone as a light and my hammer and flathead as a makeshift pair of pliers, I severed the two red wires connecting to the battery and stripped their ends. Then I twisted them together.

Some lights came to life on the dashboard. Good, I was almost there. My heart pounded. I severed the brown starter wires, stripped them too and took a long, deep breath. Sparks danced from the ends as I touched them together. The starter motor turned over. Then the deep, chugging engine rumbled into life.

Part Two

Chapter One

From Where Was This For

Andrew Chappell scratched at his hand once more as the morning sun shone down South Road. He was walking to work this morning, having eschewed the number ninety-five for the sunshine and fresh air that had been prescribed for his Pityriasis Rosea.

Pityriasis Rosea is a nasty, invasive condition which should be evaded at all costs. Andrew had allowed it to grow, ebbing and flowing seemingly arbitrarily across his body for the last four months now; and only last week had he finally booked the morning off work to visit the doctor. He had, like many men, a severe aversion to calling on the doctor to fix him. It was a fact he would discuss with Old Harry Delks later that night after work had ceased, after chasing up the annoying clients who had forgotten to put through their worksheets, and all the media-hotshot-wannabees that came through his doors had stopped self-aggrandising.

Like the men who once worked in the now dismantled heavy industries forty years ago, and the many men now who live with the hangover of their toughness, their mettle and self-reliance, Andrew still had a tendency to refuse to rely on anyone so organised as a doctor for his wellbeing. Neither him nor Harry would have known that, though; Andrew had always been more handsome than intellectual. But that was all he wanted— to chat to a friend with whom he didn't have to think too hard, after a decent day's work. Andrew was just seeing it through, life, and that was all.

As he descended down Commonside, the sound of the city got louder and some organised university students could be seen about, buying coffee or readjusting their tote bags as they too trickled down the slope into town in the thoroughly pleasant April morning. Shards of bright light were searing off the windows of The Arts Tower and, in the far distance, off the bright colours of Park Hill flats; the trees holding fast on the steep Norfolk Park slope to the right of the flats were just tinging with green, fresh and ready for another summer. Old Harry Delks would doubtless be waxing lyrical about how accurate his forecast had been when Andrew returned home later tonight, leaning on the wall opposite the library in Walkley, squinting through the evening like a tired dog at the crossroads he had never left in his life.

But he would perhaps miss Harry. There was no possibility of an early finish: Mondays were always full days at the firm, with young professionals having spent a prostrate hungover Sunday sending off their details to the relevant agencies in an extended loure of guilt.

He had taken a shortcut to avoid the West Street melee and now bore down on the square in which Media Village Recruitment was situated. Work lay ahead, bearable and well-rewarded, and the evening would most likely bring the streamed Sheffield Wednesday game (it being an away tie; he was a season ticket holder in the South Stand) and a healthy fruit smoothee, rather than the pub—doctor's orders again.

The itch of his Pityriasis continued all morning until Andrew made a conscious decision not to touch the back of his hand again. If he went near it, fingers twitching in anticipation of the cooling effect—cooling like dipping feet in water on a hot summer's day —he would add another minute until he could get a cup of tea. This had been scheduled, to begin with, at half eleven but was now due at eleven thirty-seven. He exhaled in annoyance at a badly-spelled reply in his inbox - journalist experience at a university newspaper, shadowed an arts editor for two weeks one summer. This one was right for Seren.

He forwarded the email smugly, knowing she would oscillate with ire behind their partition at being sent another journo. It was school leavers with extensive experience of technology that she needed for the Post Office Building. Still…

Until half-past five Andrew plugged away at filling some gaps in the new film company that had sprung up down Wicker, sifting through the chaff for some decent talent amongst the predicted heavy inbox. With a yawn he got up from his creaking swivel chair, ruffled his jacket on, and checked the others had left before locking up the back and then leaving through the customer entrance.

It was decidedly nippy outside. Yes, Harry would be indoors by now; and so Andrew headed up to catch the number ninety-five from West Street, satisfied also that he would not have to surmount the hill up Commonside. At the stop, he cheatingly rubbed his hand on the inside of his jacket. He used the upright at the side of the shelter to put pressure on the outbreaks on his ribs, too.

Through a gap in the row of bars and flats opposite he could see one of the great hills of Sheffield. Once, it had been home to a ski-slope. Now, though it had always looked somewhat barren from a distance, it lay to waste in the blowing South Yorkshire evening. It was a strange sight in a city so large, which in recent years had seen its fortunes change for the better. The futility of the heath and pockmark buildings on its shoulder was exaggerated due to its situation: it was a piece of industrial countryside, undeveloped and forgotten, in the middle of a sloping, humpbacked metropolis.

Andrew liked the hills. He embraced their mysterious quality, the quality which dictated that nothing which lay over the next hill could be viewed from the first, the screening of an expanse of geographically distinct districts all separate and yet under the unifying banner of Sheffield.

Most others found them a burden, a real hindrance. But Andrew loved them. He had grown up with hills, not of this scale but smaller, and he saw it as a natural progression to be living amongst them now. Occasionally he would venture out of Walkley over Broomhill, down to Hunter's Bar and then back up the hill to Nether

Edge, down into Heeley and Chesterfield Road and then back up another hill into Meersbrook, all to see his friend Pat. He did this on his moped, which he kept in a shed in his garden and which he refused to ride to work because of the helmet's effect on his hair.

He was vain, yes; he spent money on his appearance. He still had the vestiges of his handsome youth, but something in Andrew kept him on an unhealthy path, eating ready-meals, drinking beer, not getting enough exercise. Seven years ago he would have cycled his route to Meersbrook, and been proud of the sweat dripping from his exhausted brow as he parted the pub doors. Now, he was unhappy, overweight, but lacked any will to change things, comfortable in his unhealthiness. He hadn't exactly been helped by certain things, he told himself in all fairness: the ankle injury that put paid to his badminton on Tuesdays; the non-delivery of his trial spectacles which he knew he needed—the optician had known too—and his subsequent refusal to return to ask for another pair to be sent. As the weeks went by it was just another item on the backburner which nagged in a slow whisper, and which he didn't consider affected him in any considerable way; though, as with all these things that we deny and play the reactive part to, it did.

He was let off with a hiss in the middle of South Road. The curving Walkley high street was moderately busy, each shop flowing in and out with customers, some of whom were wrapped or zipped up against the breeze as they appeared on the pavement, but whose surprised faces looked as though they had forgotten the outdoor conditions they had only temporarily abandoned. Behind him stood the menacing Ebenezer Chapel with its great inscription that read Primitive Methodist. This was the only blemish to an otherwise average high street, where also there existed a local Asda, a pair of cheap-and-nasty looking barber's shops which Andrew had avoided since moving in, some takeaways, an Eastern-European food shop, and some more modern, sharper-looking shopfronts: a few sandwich places, a nice little Moroccan restaurant, and a greengrocer's. Walkley in 2024 felt economically slap-bang in the middle of Sheffield's districts.

The town-end of South Road lay up a slight incline, and left the great city shrouded to the residents of Walkley behind its slight shoulder. At the other end, towards which Andrew hastened now that his stomach had begun to protest at his choice of an early lunch, the library corner offered an obscured view of Hillsborough, whose tower blocks had changed little since their unwelcome erection, and of the East Peaks at Stannington to the left.

Down here, Andrew had made his home. Parsonage Crescent was his patch now. It had not always been so.

Whether this is Andrew's story or not doesn't matter here. We have replayed the central characters time and again, reconstituted her or him into a new soup on countless occasions. But Andrew's story is interesting. Here he is taking form, a clanking piece of machinery finding its groove once again, uncovered and dusted down. In his story there is work to be done. It should be told.

To call him unacademic is to use a frustratingly inadequate word. He moved to Leeds and lived amongst the students in Hyde Park; he drank at the pub of the same name; he took drugs. When the money had gone, and with his new-found friends now linked to him closely (too close, it had turned out), he moved to a squalid flat in Seacroft and worked at the Tesco in the precinct there. His poor school record didn't stop him feeling the utter powerlessness of working for such a monolithic employer. After this came redundancy, something which, he read, was the effect of the mechanisation of customer service. Things got worse, until the Jobcentre forced him to take a job at a recruiters in town. Barely able to iron a shirt, he made an inauspicious start but soon his health started to mend and with it his moral exactitude: a kind of smothering fog began to lift, and he saw his flatmates in all their worthlessness and manipulation for the first time. He escaped the flat, though not without disfiguring injury: as he scrambled for the door, a broken bottle flew through the air and delicately sliced his arm just so above his right elbow.

A promotion became available and he left the city, without much regret.

He had begun to grow older.

During this time, it was a strange fact that he had never been able to cultivate a meaningful sexual relationship. He was heterosexual although he had of course considered this against homosexuality; not carefully but quite slovenly, murmuring in the night on some occasions, speaking to the window for answers and looking at his thin body to consider the implications. He had been kissed by a man at an LGBT bar in Leeds once; he had kissed him back. Then came the damaging moment of feeling a rough hand round his waist, feeling the slithering wave of displeasure at its grip, and the reflex of shaking himself free; wide-eyed, he had turned his back swiftly.

And so the women in his life had been scant, save for a lucky night every few months. Many of these he had left before sunrise, once the act was over; speckled in his memory were prisms of walks home from various parts of Sheffield at contrasting times of year. Birdsong and waves of sweet new growth from the trees around were all that remained of Keira, as he passed the gates of the Botanical Gardens and ascended Collegiate Crescent. Howling wind and what felt like everlasting-numbness accompanied Jess on his way down from Park Hill.

It was as he neared the corner, still rubbing his hand with lessening patience, that Little Harry Brownlow, not to be confused with Old Harry Delks, jumped down from the library's outer walls and commanded:

"Stop, and get into line, you!"

Andrew arrested his momentum theatrically, planting both feet with a jump that forced him to wince as a twinge fulminated from his left ankle.

Harry was short for Harriet. She was a girl of ten who walked up from Langsett Road most days to visit her friend, Olivia.

"Liv's in for tea again, eh?" he replied, shaking his leg. A nod was the answer.

She pulled her hands together in the shape of a gun, with her little brown thumbs at the back as the locking mechanism.

"Can I walk you back to yours?"

"Walk me back to mine?"

"To yours," she interrupted.

"Well, it's only round the corner, but why not. You're a gent."

"A gentlewoman! Come on, follow me," she sang with a tone of resignation as she turned her back. "Superquick, 'cos she'll be finished soon."

"Oh."

They continued to the crossroads, Andrew in tow.

"Come on! We're losing enough time at the lights! You walk with such ineffinshency!"

"Do I!" he replied, amused by her vocabulary. "How long have you known that word?"

He made a noise to begin to correct her, then gutturally stopped short, not sure if he would cause upset.

"Aaaages."

The crossing bleeped.

"Watch me. You have to diagonalise. Like... This!"

As he crossed behind her he watched her weave from the textured crossing mat opposite to the slope which fell to the left down his street, Parsonage Crescent, robotically changing her direction so that she intersected each crossing angle with the shortest possible line—'diagonalising'. She did this all the way to his front door. In her mind it would have been unthinkable to have crossed in any way other than at the perfect angle; she could not, for example, have risked going across perpendicularly, mounting the curb, and then turning to continue along the correct side of the road. It wasn't, as she said, effinshent.

"Okay, bye," she said abruptly as she delivered Andrew to his lopsided gate, and she stalked off, her school uniform flowing under her cardigan.

"Till next time," he called bemusedly, shutting the gate. She was a little enigma.

Chapter Two

Of Course, You Have All Your Identification Papers

The working week had, by now, played itself out, and Andrew found himself enjoying a pint of Foster's on a beautiful, warm Friday evening with the sun dancing in his face. He was at the Walkley Cottage public house with John Gandah. Andrew licked his lips and surveyed the landscape from Bole Hill.

Iron ore had been smelted on that hill once; seventeenth-century alchemists had banked the existing hill up into containing ringlets; the fires of early industry had roared about that spot. Now, as he cast his eye northwards, Andrew could see Neepsend's turrets rising from the earth, set against the roll and sweep of housed-over hills. Some countryside remained in the view to Owlerton to his left. There one long row of white-windowsilled houses arced horizontally, kinked like a snake. The smell of new growth in the hedges filled the air around.

John looked up beyond Andrew and sniffed, having finished tying the lace of his heavy paratrooper boots. He was talking about Sarajevo again. Andrew turned his head.

"I wasn't aware there had been a war then; well, not one that long." A pleasant, light warmth had begun to unfrock his senses, the rivulets of alcohol beginning to merge with his bloodstream. It was one of those evenings where the atmosphere, the smiling weather and the prospect of no work on Saturday had conspired with the social lubrication of alcohol and the mutual temporary abode of the pub to force a joke or even an apology for someone's clumsy feet out of the most taciturn of regulars. He had chosen John Gandah's company over that of the work crew tonight and now he felt like talking.

"Oh yes oh yes; right in the middle of it I was. Boxed in for five years, dodging bullets and the rest."

"Hadn't the British withdrawn everyone from the embassy, though?"

"They had, aye, but I just stayed," John Gandah replied as though it were the most commonplace behaviour in the world. Yes, you stayed in a war zone, John, and I should hardly be surprised.

Gandah lifted his purple, fezlike hat and smoothed the sparse, wet-looking hair underneath it. He sat down, shuffled a tobacco tin out of his worn poncho, and set to making himself a rollie on one of the bars of wood which made up the outdoor picnic bench. Andrew removed his jacket, unsure of why he had brought it out in the first place, and then took the seat opposite; next to him sat Millat and his cohort of cronies, pleasant lads who, comically to the outside, thought of themselves as a bit of a pack, a crew who in reality were scared to walk around Hillsborough at night. They were drinking cider, Andrew saw from the glasses. Millat's excited tones rose a notch.

"Dere were people rahwnd the sdjreets of Newark with ord-ons whizzin off speed! I'm tellin yo'!"

"You're too young to know what speed is, Millat."

Millat turned jumpily, not a little shocked to hear the voice of his neighbour next to him on the bench. "Oh, oh nah den Andrew, yareyt mate?"

Andrew lifted his pint to his lips, smiled ever so slightly, and nodded. "Anyway, what do you fuckin' mean, Andrewman, I'm fuckin' seventeen!" laughed Millat. There was a sharp intake of breath from the youthful gathered near.

"Millat, man, whayudoin? Idiot! Keep it dahn!"

"Oh, shit."

Andrew looked away, smiled, and thought, the staff inside know, Millat, they're not stupid. Just not bothered. They'd rather keep you here than send you away to the park benches.

Gandah looked up from his rolling and also smiled as he addressed the lads to his right.

"God, where'd all this time go? Seventeen, you say? Millat, was it? I was seventeen just a few years ago!"

The group of boys did not understand, and certainly wouldn't for some years yet. Time was the one thing they were not worried about, so much of it remained from their vista; and yet it was already beginning to show. Carl resembled his old man so much it was frightening, and whoever the other white lad was had a permanent disdain about his face which suggested he'd just seen a boat full of infants being torpedoed and sunk. Time would catch them soon, Andrew thought as he finished his remaining half-pint more quickly than he would otherwise have done.

Andrew said, "I know, I know; where has it gone."

"Time," responded Gandah in a tone of wisdom once his tongue had been freed of its paper-licking obligations, "time is both of the essence and the work of the devil. We work in three dimensions; time is the fourth, many say. Whichever camp you're in, one thing's clear: that we're a slave to it—that we are slaves," he reiterated forcefully "—and happy in that slavery. Wasn't I in Sarajevo just last year? No. Time, you see: it dictates that it was a multiple of those units ago." He began to light his cigarette, hands clasped around a little black lighter he had dug out of a pocket somewhere. "I'm fucked if I know how to change that! You see, boys, you have to let the good times roll, and roll with them."

Andrew chuckled outwardly as the boys looked at Gandah with serious expressions, unable to offer any more than a sincere "mmm" to the ageing man's indecipherable ramble. They returned, after a respectful pause, to a discussion of Millat's trip to Newark.

"Anyway, ' Drew, I saw that teacher today," Gandah mumbled through his still-unlit cigarette

"Oh, aye."

"Oh, aye!" He raised his eyebrows as the first puffs of smoke billowed upwards from his head. "Down at the Forge Valley Community School." Swinging his lightly-clenched fist back and forth on these words, there was a deviousness in the old man's eyes.

"I'd forgotten if it was that or further down. Ideal for your rounds then."

"Exactly; and she's on her coffee break when I'm strolling around there. Perfect."

"Rather, John, you are on your rounds whenever she's having a coffee and a cig."

"Preposterous," he said in camp outrage as he swished his unclenched hand this time; "you get some funny ideas working over there in that city, Andrew, amongst all the slickers. I'm just an older man looking for conversation and, wherever possible, love."

"How was she? In conversation, I mean."

"Oh, fascinating. She told me she'd been asked to have Christian dissemination in her classes—exclamation mark!—and that she was fundamentally opposed to the idea of children being exposed to dogma in a secular, state-run environment. They should, of course, be in a position to access any materials of the like outside of such educative environments, but such adults around them at such a time ought to be very careful to provide a balanced outlook on religion to young minds."

"God, like honey to a bee."

"Pollen really."

"Yeah, pollen. I'm sure you had her late for class."

"I did, as a matter of fact. Oh, but it's not always about me, Andrew, when conversations flow on." Gandah had detected Andrew's inference. "We were of like minds, you see? She had as much to say as I. A nice bit of crumpet, too. Can you say that still?"

"Not particularly, but you're with me; I appreciate it."

Both men chuckled.

"You can always tell a chatter as well, can't you? She was… slouchey, in a good way. I knew we'd hit it off before the verbal comms began." John Gandah liked to throw the occasional piece of business or military jargon into his speech, and he continued: "Anyway, you were about forty clicks away when all this happened, making plans for tonight. Are the Office hitting West Street again tonight, hmm?" His tone dropped on the name of the city's busiest drinking strip.

"No, no. I only go every once in a while, you know; I'm really not there every week."

"Once is enough to bite and make forever shy."

"I like the manicness now and then. There's a certain…"

"Disquiet?"

"Maybe that's what I like sometimes." Andrew stared off, very unsure of whether he meant this. "But no, a lot of them are off to a kind of rave, not too far from here in fact."

John Gandah stubbed out the remainder of his fag. "Ooh."

"John, imagine you with me and my work lot in a blackened room somewhere listening to Detroit techno. The weirdest image ever."

"Wouldn't be so weird if we were off our heads. You know, Liz mentioned yoga this morning during our discourse…" He began to shuffle his legs around under the bench. Then Andrew's phone buzzed. It was Seren.

Andy come on come out tonight! I guarantee it'll be mint.
Bright's got some party stuff in and you'll be missing out.
These losers are fun but the office misses Big A. Drinking at
Walkabout then taxiing down Smithfield later. No worries if
it's a no. But come! X

He mumbled something, then slipped his phone away. John Gandah had in the meantime crossed his legs so that he balanced precariously on his seat; or, at least, it would have been precarious were it not for the fact that John Gandah had a supreme sense of balance, even as his joints creaked and his face winced a little.

"Anything interesting on the old dog 'n' bone?"

"Nothing."

"It didn't sound like nothing."

"I'm off to get another pint. What you supping?"

"Surprise me, sir."

Andrew got Gandah a shot of whisky and a strong ale.

Something had stirred in him tonight. Andrew didn't know if it was from reading that text, if it was from the presence, the otherness, of John Gandah, or from a deeper stirring that had been building within over the long years. If it was the text then was it the attention from Seren that was unsettling him? But he had long ago put his urge for her to bed. Was it resurfacing? Why was there this itch now? What was making the skin below his eyes hot with blood?

That something which had stirred was far more worrying than love or lust. John Gandah eyed the coppery liquid rippling inside the rocks glass for a few short seconds, gave thanks heartily, downed its contents, and then asked knowingly:

"Something troubling you, young man?"

"I'm not sure…" He gulped down the fresh lager, one, two, three mouthfuls.

"A yes, then. Come now, you can confide in old Gandah. Who was texting you?"

Andrew, in that short second cajoled by his friend's soft sonances, decided to come out and just say it all. John, he reasoned resignedly, probably knew half of it already. "It was work, mate. They're going to a big night later on, near here," and he drew himself in, not wanting Millat or his boys to overhear, "involving drugs. And usually I wouldn't go near that sort of thing, not now. Too much… baggage. I'd make every excuse in the book, I would. But tonight… I don't know… tonight feels…"

"Different."

"I don't know why."

Andrew sounded exasperated as the words fell off his tongue, dumbfounded by what was happening. A strong, unstoppable tingling developed inside. Then, his pityriasis inflamed sharply and made him feel like an invisible fire was licking at him. He jerked his hand upwards and gave a short gasp of pain. It was like the condition was attempting to remind him of a fact, the fact was that this was not him anymore. And yet. And yet. He wanted to blame John for this internal awakening, very eagerly indeed. But this was not some other person's chapter; nobody other than himself had any agency now, though he felt whisked away as if on the bore of a river, ripping him ungovernably away as he grasped at the reeds in futility, paradoxical and wonderful. What had made this so different to all previous temptations? All those other times he had been offered a way back in? The beer and the warmth of the night clung, almost like dew as it falls, to Andrew's senses.

There was something magical about John Gandah. Andrew could see it now, as he crossed his legs yogic-style on the pub bench, making a mudra with the fingers and thumbs which rested on his knees. There was a flame inside him, past his beard and through his cotton poncho; a flame which burned iridescent. It represented life.

Life, as he now was known, had observed Andrew's odd movements and collected everything he needed to know from them.

"We're about to have a ball," he murmured softly and deeply, his eyes half closed.

"Yes, yes we are."

Andrew's hand shook as he replaced his empty pint glass on the table. Night was falling. The city had begun to hum.

Chapter Three

Primitive Methodist

"All I'm saying, John, is that you swing—not all of the time, but some—between being a committed feminist—some of the time—and being a dog with two dicks."

They were continuing to recapitulate Gandah's sexual state of affairs as they strode in small drunken delight downwards towards the fast rush of Penistone Road, which was skirted by the feculent River Don. With his virtual map as a guide they were heading to Smithfield, an unvisited side street somewhere off the slope of Hoyle Street, where trams ran down the centre on tracks surrounded by white, rocky ground.

They were nearly at the main road when Seren called. Andrew answered quickly. The other end of the line was populated with wooping and shouting noises and with Seren's low, mirthful voice informing the two men that their group stood in the queue; that they had half a gram each waiting for them, and that they were so happy they were coming. Andrew absorbed the appreciation, still not quite sure of what he was doing or what was to come. Gandah talked reflexively about days he was too young to remember as they stumbled along the road.

Then Andrew came out and revealed another thing that, like the admission of his puzzled state at the Walkley Cottage, could not have been drawn out of him previously.

"Do you know about how set I've been, John? On settling, I mean. Settling in the fullest sense of the word. I haven't ever mentioned that. I've needed to grow old, John. I've needed to—here," and he pointed his finger passionately at the ground. "This is how I've been moulding my life.'

Interest pricked, the old man uttered a lengthy "Right."

"This is how I've shaped it. It's all been conscious—so very conscious. What I'm doing tonight, in a few hours, is picking it apart.'

"Picking it apart—like the handful of crumbs from a pie, or the million-and-one stitches from a knitted jumper?" Gandah asked plainly. Andrew made to answer, though he didn't know what he would say, but Gandah went on, louder. "I suppose what I'm trying to express is this: first, thanks for the whisky, it was lovely. Second, what are you holding back? I sense something's coming around up there, Andrew."

The younger thought heavily for some paces. "I'll know tonight."

Gandah stretched a slow, widening smile across his face, an expression which gradually crept, because he could not help it, onto Andrew's lips too.

Andrew had not disclosed anything near the gravity of what he was saying now for years upon years. His conversations had been default, his life glued to tracks like those of the tram which came rushing by now.

Interest, small and only piqued, had tickled Gandah. What was this new side to an old friend? he thought as he paced along, stealing a glance every so often at his companion. Where now, dear Andrew, are you about to suddenly swivel, I wonder? There was a sublime expectation in Gandah's heart that his companion was about to experience something beautiful, something worthy of transcendence.

Gandah also had vested interests. He had a world view, although it would do no justice trying to present all of the facets of that ideology here, so a line will suffice. Gandah wanted all men, women, and children to commune across the world, and to embrace these three things: Paganism, Working the Land, and New Housing:— and in Andrew, he saw the beginnings of a convert. This conversion, in these most basic terms, was what he hoped—along with Andrew's happiness—to propagate. But conversion was the last thing on the younger man's mind at present. Gandah resumed. "Then pick away. Pick it all away. You knew that would be my advice."

Smithfield was a tiny old side street not far from the centre, in Sheffield's finished industrial north. The great hopeless heath, the hill that could be seen from West Street, shadowed it now though the sky was almost completely dark and the district's amber sodium lamps were switched on. Around half way down the street's length there was an old archway gaping in one face of the otherwise unbroken wall from the days when the workshop, whatever it had been, had carted its goods out by horse, and it was outside this that a massing queue was being allowed entry, one by one, into its inner viscera.

Andrew commented on how loud the crashing beat was, even from there, as it filled the bricked streets around. All the while he was feeling little warm sensations he could not remember ever feeling. And now, in fact, he felt quite sick. There was a nervousness within him.

"I need you to stick with me tonight, John."

"I wouldn't dream of leaving," came the tender-sounding answer.

"Of course, of course. I'll ring Seren, see where they're at."

Andrew studied the queue as they slowly slipped down its length until halfway down he saw the full crew, all dressed up, laughing and shouting. The familiar, the sane. And how his heart vaulted when he saw them, tumultuous fever bursting forth.

"John, this is meant as no offence to you whatsoever, but they've all just reminded me of normality. Can you see them? There. God, I think we're going to have a good night. That's just reassured me. You can stop worrying about me.'

He nodded almost disinterestedly back at Andrew, who seemed to be gulping for air, and replied, "The suits! Andrew's suits!"

Andrew looked at them, dashing themselves about in the crowd. Here they were:

—Seren. Tallish, with tied-up dark hair that was dip-dyed at the ends, she had a delicate face. Her ears were always red; and her sparrowlike nose, with two strong lines of cartilage, pushed up her mildly tired-looking eyes.

—Bright. First name Neil. He was one of the younger bucks at the office, designer-stubbled, with flicked-upwards chestnut hair. He was good-looking. He was probably the same height as Andrew and Seren. He had those attractive, exactly proportionate shoulders which, Andrew had thought on a few occasions, could be heading chubby just like his own if he wasn't careful.

—Seeta. She really was short, with the unusual feature of having a nearly-circumferential band of fat around her sensibly-clothed torso; and she was an absolute barrel of laughs within the office. Andrew hadn't expected her out. Her family was Indian, maybe two generations back, and she spoke with a strangely seductive voice that was as South Yorkshire as the Pennines from Sheffield to Penistone .

—Mel. She was as short as Seeta, though much thinner. She was too thin, in fact, and there were things about her shape, unfair things which belied her incredible powers of observation and perception when it came to people—powers that made her very good indeed at her job. You felt there was an injustice done to her, with a body so weak and a mind so sharp. She had the type of body which suggested malnourishment either in the womb or as a child, limbs like outlines of a cage; she had a worn face, almost yellowing in certain lights, and thin drawn-in lips. Her hips looked too narrow to bear children, girl-like. She had made herself up with Persian eyes tonight, and was buried in her handbag, rooting slowly for something.

—Peter Noblood. His surname was so delicious you had to repeat it each time it was uttered. He was the eldest of the office, with the kind of craned body you would expect of someone much taller and more aged though he was, in fact, a mere thirty-seven. His ribcage had formed small and flat, as limited as a neat little filing box and as a result his white shirts, always perfectly ironed, hung off him like curtains. He never ceased to smile. Tonight he had dressed for the weather in a long-sleeved, wooden-buttoned, marl t-shirt, and looked surprisingly good to Andrew.

They all saw Andrew and Gandah at the same time and shouted out in joy.

"You made it!"

"Old misery-guts!"

"Join here, don't go to the back! Right here, just keep it shtum; eeya." Seeta spoke a little more quietly than the boisterous others, with a down-turn on her last syllable as if it were an 'o'. Disquieted faces looked on from the back, and Andrew tugged at John to integrate with the crowd quickly so as not to attract any more attention than his outlandish appearance habitually brought.

There was much back-thumping and kissing on the cheeks; introductions were made; the queue inched forward past a parked van. Bright handed out the drugs to the two newcomers, and Andrew's hand dropped, as if burdened by a substantial weight, as the small packet hit his palm.

So it was to be, he thought, with a perplexed heart beating away inside his ageing chest. Here, it happens again. His brain was uneasy. It was not the guilt of the act, nor the loss of control which gnawed away at him: it was the recidivism.

Andrew was bound on a course that all tread, indentured by one calling: that these events, these defining, thought-sticking events in a person's life will be repeated. Time guards this shrine as a headdressed Anubis, wary only of those who would disturb the pattern, who would attempt to divert this universal re-act, and only Time presides over eventful lives.

He and John Gandah plunged the contents of their packets down their throats with the aid of Seren's water. It was a full half-hour before they had edged to the front of the queue, and now each member of the group was the subject of a rigorous searching by one of the bouncers. Collars were turned out then in again, torsos were patted down, pockets were turned out and belt-bands ringed, legs were smoothed down, and finally ankles and socks were checked for any suggestion of drug-carrying. They all passed the test and were gestured mutely inwards into a beautiful courtyard lit by fairylights that hung tightly to vines and trellises.

Andrew's eyes took some seconds to adjust to the sparkling light. Before him people weaved between cushioned footstools and finely-crafted tables, the night sky squared above them by the quadrangled buildings above. Open doorways led to the old factory floors, four of them each with their own music and themes—Utopia, 20,000 Leagues Under the Sea, The Masque, and the Latin tea bar; next to these doors stairways led in turn downstairs to the unknown. Artwork hung wonkily on the stone walls, and all around there sounded a deep thumping, a repetitive beat with basslines underscoring it like river currents.

He was deeply impressed; his eyes gazed in conspicuous wonderment at the wall hangings and the people near him, unafraid of seeming new to everything. The work crew and Gandah took up some recently-vacated seats. He was about to sit down but then one man drew Andrew's eye, a strange man to look at, unattractive in face and body but oddly familiar. He had that build where muscles and veins hang off childlike bones, still giving his body a vigorous look like it could achieve a dazzlingly unexpected array of tricks at the click of a pair of fingers. He was osseous but moving, all thew and energy. Their eyes met—only for a second—and then the other man looked back to his seated friend. Andrew's eyes rattled, causing him to shiver as he began to grin though try as he might he could not place the man. The initial excitement of the daring act outside was still passing around him in a helix, focusing fiercely and arbitrarily on the unlikely-bodied reveller.

He used his experience to remind himself of the placebo, to remember that the real eye-rattle would come later.

And after cans of lager had been bought and the thin man and his friends had disappeared through the doorway at the furthest end of the courtyard Andrew looked around at his friends. Heads had begun to nod and eyes to open. He suggested they go down into one of these rooms, following the man. Bright looked around at his colleagues and then, always desiring to take the lead, he grabbed up both Seren and Peter Noblood and declared that Andrew was right, shouting,

"Downstairs! We need to dance! Come!"

It was simple—Bright only did simple. The doorway was heaving with bodies; there were people all around, but none pushed or shoved. The stairway was dusty and dirty and led downwards in just two flights. The first thing Andrew saw was a kind of antechamber, very dark and dusty, with sofas skirting its edges; the second, as he led on, mind beginning to truly buzz like the city around him, a concrete dance floor where throngs of dancers moved, almost threateningly, to some ear-shaking deep house.

As they began to dance, Andrew could sometimes see in everyone the same focused ecstasy that he was experiencing, sometimes hitting a trough in his emotion until he was lifted again yet higher. Gandah whispered—or so it sounded—that the DJ had grabbed him by the scruff of the neck, and as Andrew turned he could see the old poncho swinging about wildly and the man's old bearded lips set apart in joy.

After some time, he went and sought out the man who had fascinated him, compelled by some unknown force. He found him dancing near the furthest corner, twisting and often pirouetting with an astonishing freedom. And now Andrew saw it; he saw the uncanny unfolding before his eyes. It was as though an old friend was with him, moving in the shadows and streaked in light. He stopped and manufactured himself space on the dance floor, just as a new melody that had been introduced was beginning to make the pulse of bodies all the stronger around him.

What is it? his thoughts scrambled desperately. How could he be reminded of him through this body, this person in front of him now? He could not trace a single similarity between the faces of this mysterious, twirling man, and that of his old friend, Gene Bradley. And yet it was there, so strong that it was uncomfortable, like he imagined it would feel if a giant plughole was opened up beneath him as he swam in the sea.

He had been staring for a minute before he began to move closer, treading as warily as a deer. His mind see-sawed from second to second, wanting first to be filled with complete euphoria and then only to retreat and hide away, afraid of what it could find, of what could be uncovered deep within. He tried to lend his reason to it: his belief, struggling to assert itself, that bad things would happen if he let his addled state take him over in its wholeness and move him to talk to the man. And so he retreated.

The thought of Gene stuck there in his mind, but within twenty minutes the only thing that truly mattered was maintaining the movement of his body along to the bass.

Andrew awoke peacefully the next day. He lay on Bright's sofa in the corner of the flat that he owned in the West One complex, with his back softly caressed by the layers of furry blanket which had been lain down for him on top of the sofa's soft leather. He looked up at the unilluminated halogen lamps set into the ceiling. The flickering of the sun's beams could be perceived dancing prettily in their vertices. He turned his neck towards the source of the light and looked out onto the view. Devonshire Green was in its full Spring glory. The lawn and banks were already busy with bodies which were sitting or at play; beyond them, people sunned their arms and faces in deckchairs outside the Forum Cafe Bar. He smiled and a light happiness filled him.

He stood up to find that he was topless, only his loose boxers covering his genitals. At this, he cast around with an indifferent embarrassment to see if anyone else was in the room; he was, however, completely alone. He walked up to the flat's huge window and stretched, watching the little people below. One group of Chinese students from the nearby Victoria Hall had taken a frisbee out and were practising some exercise drills on the side of the green nearest the skatepark. They looked like little dots vibrating against the grass.

He ran his hands down his fleshy body, his palms, his finger-ends, his inside-knuckles feeling every patch of his soft pityriasis with an increasing creepiness. He looked down. His good mood in waking had been spoiled, this festering parasite which clung to his body reminding him of his ordinariness, his humanness. For a second he had been another person; now the decay of his own body brought him back to himself. The word 'decay' now swirled around his head. His mouth became watery.

He frowned and quickly put on his shirt, which had been hanging neatly on the back of a chair. That felt better. He was not so bared now. In fact, he felt surprisingly normal, despite the events of the previous night: the weekend had come, just as it had done so reliably over the last however many years. Had he been at home in Walkley now he would probably have been tidying his garden and sunning himself, though, despite having read on a Yahoo forum that sunlight helped slowly burn away pityriasis, he still would not have dared bare his chest in his garden at Parsonage Crescent. His fences were of the small picket type, utterly see-through except for the uprights themselves and the occasional bush on the Delks's side, and prying eyes could gaze in from most directions. To the other side, the fence remained unpainted: perhaps that was a job he would have tried to tick off the list today. A pearl grey, or maybe a military green, were two colours he had had in mind for the job.

He had, apparently, forgotten the inner revelations of the night before. He wanted to sit, watch the people play and drink a coffee in the comfort of Bright's spacious flat and so he walked over to the gleaming coffee maker near the cooker of the open plan kitchen (Bright was the type to take real pride in his gadgets) and set up the machine. He felt an ache in his legs all over, hitting its strongest each time he straightened his hamstring. He couldn't remember the last time he had felt that stretched, acidic soreness anywhere in his body. As the water heated with the machine's little dials and switches lighting up cheerily, he pieced together the night before with an increasing awareness of how much he had rubbed that pissing pityriasis, for now it burnt and itched more strongly than ever. By reflex his hand jumped to relieve the frustration pulsing on his body but he caught himself, quite literally, by grabbing the moving wrist with his remaining hand. The itch persisted with near-unbearable shimmers of discomfort.

He was distracted from his torture by two things: firstly, the memory of the dancing man's ineffable resemblance to his old friend, Gene Bradley; secondly, Peter's entry into the room. Peter was fully-clothed and coughed a grinny "Morning!"

towards Andrew before joining him at the whirring coffee maker.

"Morning Peter, you're sounding alright."

Peter smiled slowly. "Not so much mate. not. so. much. I need to sit down and to do absolutely nothing."

Andrew laughed, and then smiled that empathetic expression which avoids awkwardness when one person mistakenly states something to the other which they think cannot possibly be disagreed upon. Peter smiled unaffectedly back.

Andrew drank a coffee with Peter. As they spoke about the club and the music, his contentment flooded back like a soothing tide until the itch had vanished completely. Then he left for home.

So he had given in, he thought as he climbed towards Brook Hill Roundabout. He had submitted to the draw of an altered state and, more than that, he had enjoyed it. He was finished with his period of self-denial, of self-inflicted dullness. He'd been stagnant for so long! So long, now, that something had had to give, somewhere. He could see that now, see the need for reawakening. He welcomed back a part of his former self like a wise old friend, come in out of the cold rain of his exile. He felt the integration. He imagined shaking hands with his younger incarnation, his hair back then freer and lighter, his skin a nice brown and body a slim outline, wearing a pair of shorts and a ridiculous vest, so young and so brimming with that youth. The image made him smile again.

Fleecy daydreams of his face and body as a young man took up a happy part of his ascent up one of Sheffield's great hills. As he passed the chapel which bore that same forbidding inscription, Primitive Methodist, his thoughts shifted to the man he had not spoken to. What strangeness it had been; even now he could not get close to putting his finger on it, on what the uncanny had done to trigger his memory. Gene was there now, his slightly curly brown hair framing his somewhat soft face, with the obvious shaved patches and the beginnings of sideburns forming near his ears. He recalled the strong, oversized nose pointing proudly from his pale face. It was amazing what he could remember, these strange, little things.

Of course, this was not the only time his mind had wandered to his old friend over the years, but it was the first time he could, for definite, piece together parts of Gene's face. He had tried never to dwell on him before now. The dark spectres of Andrew's past ghosted around his image, this slowly-swirling, sharpening image.

The loss of a good friend had been his punishment for the crimes of the past. Gene was the irreplaceable, irreplaced. And now Andrew once again faced the mental torment he knew he deserved for those same crimes after so many years of peace.

He tried to block that out, desperate to hold onto what he remembered about Gene. The memories were so separated and distant now. They were reflections, growing weaker each time they were accessed, the connecting bonds dissolving yet further almost as if they were some way cursed.

"I woke up with Gene once. No, twice: one time in Knaresborough and the other… in Bridlington. Yes. And shouting and smashing and something about cheating, and a girl, a girl had found us. Was that Bridlington or Knaresborough?

I remember a pizza box, a cold morning, the nasty feeling of furry teeth, and my bed… a broken lat. My old house. And walking across a field, talking to Jack, finding out about Birmingham. Ahh, Birmingham… I'd forgotten. Standing on that concrete bunker and looking at the city with him. We were almost always together.

"We were at the beach.

"We went to a party in Coventry, or Aston.

"He was taller than me—that probably hasn't changed. He went quiet, sometimes. He laughed when I spoke, and I somehow found it funny too.

"Here it is, clearer. He deteriorated in our last days together. He would talk less and less, and he was nervous sometimes. Like something was at his back. I gave him my wallet.

"Bare legs, screams."

He stopped walking. The image of Jo being forced downwards by his own recognisable, straining hands had monstrously reared itself, filling the entire screen of his mind's eye. He fought back one solitary tear as he looked up at the abandoned church on Crookes Valley Road, with its boarded-over windows and Pennine stone facade, wondering at himself. He redoubled his pace for the rest of the journey home, longing now for the shelter of his four walls, scared that the world were somehow privy to his cursed memories.

He slammed his door and shook, gasping for air. Then he juddered violently along the hallway and felt his calves and thighs scream at their soreness. His vision grew dim and, purblind, he was shaking and slowly bending double, his eyes intent on the lightly-coloured objects in his darkened hallway as the band of colour narrowed in his eyes and began to die.

He staggered forward and grasped the doorframe to his left. A scream—the scream— suddenly pierced his head and raced around, causing him to spin. Then it shot, as if issuing from his ears, into the uninhabited house and reverberated on the close walls around before circling and striking into him, not through the ears this time but through his chest, and he fell forward and began to vomit. He was soaked in sweat. But even as he arched on all fours this expulsion, this vomiting, could not get rid of the gross feeling of disease inside. He pushed upwards and felt his body fall through the door into his living room, his legs almost lifeless and dead. Then, with one final, momentous effort, he climbed upwards onto the sofa. A weight across his chest; a flash of Jo's face, and then blackness.

Chapter Four

Counselling Marriage Politics Gender Language

How do you face a woman? How do you speak to these people day in, day out?

Many men harbour dark urges. For some, those urges come some shades paler. For fewer than that, they darken. And for fewer still, those urges are acted upon.

Andrew awoke on his back for the second time that day, wet with sweat. His body felt drained and unwilling to move. He had been dreaming; he had been dreaming of stairs, stairs all around. There had been no escape.

He still felt sick, all the way from his stomach to the outer membranes of his head. It was stiflingly hot in the room; the sun had been shining in all afternoon. Worse still, he could feel an erection pushing hard against his trousers, and it was aching painfully. He remained involuntarily prostrate and moved his penis so he could draw his phone out of his pocket. It was quarter to four. A groan.

His mind began re-imagining the stairs in a tumult of sharp images. In some images the steps had been bare and others richly furnished with different shades of carpet, some of which were a sweet cream colour and others as dark as though they were stealing the light from its very source. Occasionally he would see a wide, imperial, marble-hewn staircase sweeping upwards from the hallway of some stately home; all of them led upwards, away, towards. He dared not climb any, not even in his imagination. He knew exactly what he would find there. Immobilised, his eyes silently issued tears.

He lay quietly for a long time until his thoughts spooled in a different face. He began to think of Gene. His tears continued to fall evenly. Gene would have found him, he was sure, had he stayed at Jo's flat for much longer. His anger, his outrage, must have been great and terrifying.

He remembered the train he had caught from New Street to Leeds that night, how he had shaken and grown in panic and terror until he had risen and checked the entire train up and down to prove to himself that Gene wasn't there, waiting to pick him off. He had sat down with an easier mind, but still he could not sleep. At half past two he had caught a taxi up to Hyde Park, found a dealer, and resumed his truculent relationship with narcotics. The following years were like pieces of lost soul to him.

Now an echo of the relief that escape had brought to him gave him the strength to sit up and take stock of his surroundings in the front room. Everything was as it should be, his television still in the corner near the front window and his pair of plants shining verdantly on the windowsill. The calm and orderliness were almost foreign to him.

He blinked, once, twice, and then spoke in an unfamiliar, quavering voice:

—What happened to Gene, Andrew? Where is he now?

He continued to talk to himself, the words calming and strengthening him.

—He never came back to Knaresborough. I would have heard from Leeds if he had. Well, mate, what did he have left? Nothing really, did he? Yes, I know, you're right. He had that girlfriend didn't he? That one… didn't she go to London? That's right, she went to London. He probably went to London too, to patch things up with her.

There was no other way, his failing memory concluded. Where else would he have gone? What was there in the North for him?

His brain hurt from the effort of sifting memory like gold in a large pan. He hauled himself slowly from the sofa, planted his feet on the floor, and looked upon his lawn outside. There were the fences, unpainted; there was Harry Delks, old-bodied and topless, whistling as he repotted his tomato plants. A gust of exasperation flashed across him. Why do I think I'm so content, he thought, when really all I'm living is a half-life? With all the wounds now open and exposed to the air, why shouldn't I do everything in my power to heal them? Why do nothing?

He turned on his heel in disgust. Now he had a renewed strength.

—I resolve to find Gene and apologise for what I've done. It's the only way. I have to explain the past; I have to repair the damage done. I need absolution.

Questions and considerations mounted. How cautious would he have to be? Would Gene, transported back to the pain of Birmingham, become enraged at the sight of his old friend? Would he turn him in to the police? Or, worse for him now, deny forever his forgiveness?

He went upstairs for a shower then dressed himself in something fresh, and made some tea, feeling recovered. He had decided that caution and discretion were the best policy. He, his soul, neither could afford a head-on confrontation; even now he was too weak.

His research began. He thought he could remember Gene's parents' address; and sure enough when he tapped it in he saw it on Streetview, that little semi on Barbondale Grove. It had hardly changed except for the car on the drive. He checked for the phone number but it failed to yield a result.

He rang his dad up, who had since moved to Harrogate after the death of Andrew's mother six years ago. He was the only person who called him now. The old man sounded fainter every time.

"Son? How are you?"

"Not bad dad, same as ever. How are you?"

"Not too well." His voice was strained, as if the expulsion of air required some extraordinary articulatory effort from the muscles around his lungs.

"Oh." There was a pause. "Dad, I'll come to see you soon, I promise. But I'm ringing to see if you can remember a phone number for me."

"I can remember a lot of phone numbers, Nathan Andrew. Which bliddy one are you."

"Aye, I'll bet, dad."

"Aye, I can."

"Can you remember my old friend when I was a lad? He was called Gene. His dad was called Darren."

"Now then. Darren?"

"Yes. But my friend's name was Gene."

Andrew's dad mumbled on and off for a minute before confessing that he couldn't remember the number, nor really even a lad called Gene. Andrew asked him to find a local phonebook, and after another four or five minutes of dithering and of pages that refused to turn he had found the number of the Bradleys. Two minutes later, the two men had said their goodbyes.

He recognised the digits, not with excitement but with a small turn of his stomach at seeing the unexpectedly familiar pattern scribbled onto the inside of an old newspaper. He dialled the number.

There was no reply. He waited till the evening, not doing much except for moisturising his skin and leaving for the local Asda to buy a ready-made lasagna, then he tried again. This time a very prim-sounding woman answered.

"Hello?"

"Oh hello, I'm calling up about your son Gene." He was direct and even.

"Oh, I see." There was uncertainty in the woman's voice this time. "Who's calling?"

"This is John Barratt, Gene's old mathematics teacher. I'm organising a school reunion for the class of '09 and wonder if you'd have a contact number."

"Oh, I see…" she trailed off. "Well, erm, this is going to sound terrible—I don't."

"You don't?"

"Look, I know that sounds dreadful but no. It's a, um, private matter."

"Oh, okay. Well sorry to have bothered you either way."

She apologised several times for not being more help before they bade each other an awkward goodbye.

Andrew was amazed at how much older Jane Bradley sounded: not faint, like his own father, but grainier and more embattled. She sounded in a kind of misery.

In any case, she had been a dead end. He was no closer to Gene. He picked up his tablet and wiped off a stray fingerprint or two, and without any real expectation he typed the word 'Gene' into his search bar. He paused and racked his brains for a middle name. Finally he just typed in 'Bradley' and waited.

A board of results began to revolve on his screen, moving around nimbly as their text got greater or smaller depending on relevance. He stared blankly at

Gene Bradley
St. Louis Rams Linebacker
and

GBradley Aggregates (EIR)

He tapped at his social networks board to the left. His Swiftview, an engine that pooled together non-instant textual communication from email, Twitter, and Facebook, sat there with a few messages waiting for him. He had deleted his Facebook some years previously: it had, anyway, grown somewhat useless to him since his move to Sheffield. Instead he used his 7Pillars frequently, a kind of fusion between two of its forebears, Wikipedia and LinkedIn. The site provided general information on anything imaginable and then searchable biographical and contact information on 'Links'—individuals to whom you could send an information request. It was an incredibly useful tool to a recruiter.

It was on here that he searched that name again. A list of regions and figures burst into life. Twenty-two Gene Bradleys resided in London and the South East alone, and a hundred and fifty more lived elsewhere in the country.

He flicked through the first London entry, scouring the collection of photos in vain for any of the vestiges of Gene's face—the hair, the shy complexion, the softness in his cheeks. Then he moved to the second, and the third…

As the minutes and hours passed fruitlessly and as the unchecked regions began to dwindle his spirit for the search waned. He was puzzled that Gene was not in London; he had been so sure that he had gone there. He broke away to put his meal in the oven and to urinate, convinced that the task was an impossible one. When he returned and found that none of the entries matched his old friend he decided to change tack.

He zoomed out on the map of Gene Bradleys. A satellite image of the entire country was now framed in his small screen. There were little concentrations of lines pointing to the locations of various big cities. He zoomed out still further, curious to see if there were any on Orkney or Shetland or the Channel Islands. None appeared. He zoomed out yet further.

And something peculiar sprang out. Something very peculiar indeed.

There, on the west coast of Norway, lay one solitary line pointing to one solitary spot, somewhere near some snow-topped mountains. Andrew squinted, at first in disbelief. And then he knew.

He moved to Norway. He moved to be with his father.

He sat there dumbstruck for some moments, then said aloud to himself, "Of course, of course! And he clicked on the little red connecting line and looked at its owner's picture. Two blond children grinned eagerly at the camera as they surrounded a mature male figure. A white sea foamed in the background, blue sky edging in over the figure's shoulders. It was him. Gene's hair was longer, and with it the curls had flourished; along with his full sideburns and older face (which had lost some, but not all, of its softness) he cut a paternal figure of responsibility. He wore glasses now. His attire—a blue, woollen, crew-neck sweater —framed him well. My God, Andrew thought, he's a man.

He gulped hard, then lifted his finger. It shook like a thick, round blade of grass in a breeze. Moments passed. Then he tapped the screen, and in large, blue letters were the words 'Request Sent'.

"Well, the wheels have been set in motion now," he thought as he gazed off into his garden, only a little afraid of what lay ahead.

Friendship had all too often been fleeting in Andrew's adult life. Men's company he had found mostly dissatisfying; women's almost unbearable. His soul and mind and body had scarcely had outlet for years, damming him up and making his aura null, repulsive even; numb, null, and repulsive like a cracking pebbledash wall of an abandoned house in a forgotten seaside hamlet. His aura repulsed the women he desired, he knew, for despite his good looks they recoiled, slowly but firmly, from his presence. It was like there was a universe in which a great chasm of time lay between these two glowing forces, he and they. There was a giant, glowing strangeness, a huge distance, this dreadful, unobtainable emotion.

An answer to why this was so now flickered in front of him, as though light was dancing in through a previously opaque window which he had just wiped the dirt from. As a seventeen-year-old man he had marked himself for a lifespan in his act of violation. It had tainted the lens of his soul, not seeing with human eyes but with those of a wolf. He had been unmade by his lupine soul. He had seen Jo in every woman, and through it they had seen the wolf in him.

He felt alone, like an island.

He rejoined work on Monday having visited Pat and his wife, Cora, for a few gentle drinks on Sunday. There was a calmer half-peace within him now, though he still felt sick every time he thought of the response he was waiting for. He had been to the chemist's down Fargate in town and picked up some more moisturiser for his drying pityriasis. It soothed.

All week he worked diligently, patiently waiting for a response. He filed his new clients, called up placed ones, and swept out his desk. His anxiousness grew. Then late on Thursday night, as he lay sleeplessly, Gene's approval arrived.

Andrew's alarm sounded half an hour earlier than usual on Friday morning. It was a dull, humid kind of day even with the slight chill of the morning air fighting the stickiness. He selected a white shirt and a block-colour blue and orange tie. He made himself a coffee in his large Diamond Jubilee mug, and stirred in two sugars.

Then, the morning news caught up with, he jogged up to the bathroom. He moisturised the problem spots on his hands, then washed and moisturised his face. He stared into the mirror and observed the small wrinkles on the side of his mouth, smoothing them over once, twice with his fingers and thumb; then he moved a finger from both hands to a blackhead on the bridge of his nose, digging at it until the white pluke painlessly searched its way out.

He looked into his light-blue eyes. There was still a trace of handsomeness in him. It was strange that it should have been burnt away so brutally from the inside. The eyes bore back and removed him, taking him away to his young manhood, when time felt still and deep and his life had meant everything and nothing at the same time. He felt like that again now. He felt the wonderful return of life within his body.

He walked to work once again. He was the first at the little building behind the cathedral and so he opened up the entrances with a clatter of their noisy shutters, flicked the lights on and pressed the computers into action, and sat down at his desk.

The clocks, he reckoned, would be an hour further on in Norway and so it would be a more sociable time to receive a phonecall. He took out his tabphone and tapped in the number beginning 55 25. The office was quiet and still. He pressed call, closed his bright eyes, and held the phone to his ear.

Gene's soft, surprisingly deep voice answered.

"Is that you?" he asked.

Andrew stuttered. "Erm, it is, it is. I think." He was thrown off-balance by the question. 'This is Andrew. This, this is Cosmo, Gene.'

There was a silence, and a sound of shuffling down the line. Then, in a hushed, laughing tone, he replied, "Cosmo... I, I can't believe it. I just... is this really you? Andrew Chappell? That Andrew Chappell?"

"The same. Last time I checked, anyway," he laughed nervously.

"I should remember that voice of yours. It's just as deep and, well... It's Cosmo."

He was struck dumb. It was too strange to hear Gene, to feel just a grain of the bond he had forgotten, and to feel wanting, fishing for words. He cleared his throat.

"Listen, thank you for answering. And, and for responding to me in the first place.'

Gene struggled for words himself. "It did feel strange. But then there was this voice inside me saying, 'How can you not?' And I couldn't. Curiosity got the better of me—no, it was something much more. But where to begin?"

Andrew paused over Gene's accent, which had greatly softened. "Where do we begin?"

"Well, how have you been for the last god knows how many years?"

The two of them laughed at the absurdity of the question.

With glossy speed Andrew recounted his life in Leeds and Sheffield, and told of his job and house and street and how he was content and happy, though little of this rang true in his own ears. When he had concluded Gene began to tell of his own story.

"Well, I left Birmingham, as you know, and got back up North. Do you remember? I was looking for my father. Do you remember that from that time?"

"Yes, yes 'course."

"Mm. Well," he sighed, "I eventually managed to get to Norway. It was one hell of a journey."

"How did you manage it?"

"Oh, that's for another time. That'd take up a whole morning, and I have a list of jobs as long as my arm today."

"Oh, I shouldn't keep you then. Just, just one more thing...from the picture— you have children?"

"Ah yes, my boy and girl, Henrik and Agnethe." He pronounced the names in a distinctive Norwegian accent, sounding strange and new next to the tones Andrew remembered, then it struck him that, of course, Gene must now be near-bilingual.

"They're four and six. Growing, ah, growing up quick. I'm a proud and sometimes wistful father."

The conversation did not last much longer, only to arrange another call at ten a.m on Saturday coming; his phone had gone dead before a soul had yet entered the office. A rushing, ecstatic energy filled him from tip to tip and remained with him for rest of the day. He even took the entire office down to Tudor Square near the Crucible Theatre for lunch. Those who had been there a week ago knew that the ripple had turned into a whispering wave.

Andrew spent the waking hours of Saturday researching Norway and the city of Bergen. He assembled a set of questions in his mind that he burned to ask Gene, and then, nervous he would forget them, he wrote them in a neat, bullet-pointed list.

They spent almost two hours in a conversation that still left many stones unturned. They sometimes skipped to facts and conjectures of their presents and futures, only to return again to the anchor point of their youth, Knaresborough, school, Britain, even Birmingham and the strange characters they could recall, all characters except, of course, Jo.

Afterwards, with his feet up on the sofa, Andrew succumbed to the soporific effects of good talk and the light chatter of the wind, and South Road floating beyond his window. He awoke at nearly six, and felt two starts: one, that he had missed the Wednesday game, and the second that he didn't really care this time.

Chapter Five

To The Air

Over the next fortnight Andrew and Gene kept to their scheduled conversations almost religiously, re-arranging commitments to accommodate each other's lives, or to hear each other's voices and steal half-hours in the strangest of places. One morning, under the pretence of a research trip, Andrew had even dashed off to the old Post Office building where a giant gold sign bearing the words 'Fitzalan Exchange' was being attached to the sandstone exterior. Inside he dodged the joiners and shopfitters and called Gene as he drove from Bergen to Oslo on business, all for a fifteen minute conversation about what they were doing that day.

Gene worked as a regional manager for a Danish shipping company and he had done well for himself. He had provided for his wife, Hilma, a tall, radiant woman with Finnish ancestry, and for their children, though he had at first been reliant on Hilma's family's money and the goodwill of his now dead father. His father had given him a packing job in the long, rich harbour which lay at the city's heart. Gene became a fine employee, developing first his strength on the concrete harbour floor in the warehouses, and whenever hand-unloading was needed, inside the bowels of the enormous containers emblazoned with "Maersk Sealand' as though they were giant billboards floating gently alongside a motorway. He had developed his diplomacy and business knowledge to work his way up the company, away from the racket of the working Bergen men which he so adored, in order to feed his growing family.

Andrew continued to hear little flecks and dappled passages of the Norwegian Gene had acquired, the serious tone that sometimes filtered in. Perhaps it was the legalese too—for Gene handled a lot of contracts—but he had certainly matured beyond what Andrew had expected; but then fourteen years had seen them both age from boys to men.

The difference between the two languages and cultures fascinated Andrew. He began to spend more of his free time at the Central Library in Tudor Square, and at the semicircular Walkley Library which was just a stone's throw from his house, nose buried in travel guides and beginners' Norwegian books. He now went less to the pub, and focused less on the football (even the away Wednesday games) and on the pointless television programmes which had dominated evenings before now. Instead of trawling the results and trading knowledge in that strange, passive-aggressive pub table manner so many become accustomed to, he took walks out to Stannington and Oughtibridge.

Gene for his part began to notice the titbits of knowledge that Andrew occasionally threw in, and he mulled over the problematic nature of suggesting that he visit. So, so many problems courted that idea. So that they could meet again and he could experience the country, they were the beautiful reasons he wanted to feel independent of all others. But he realised that Andrew might be wary of him. Gene wondered if he would have to, or could, forgive him face-to-face. He wondered about whether Andrew had truly changed—like it felt he had—and whether he was the kind of man he could introduce to his home.

Gene waited until a month had passed before he felt as confident as he ever would. He had taken gambles before, and he had won.

Andrew was cooking tea when his phone rang.

"This is unexpected," he said loudly over the crackle of the wok as he crunched on some green pepper.

"I know, we weren't booked in till Thursday," came the reply. "Not too busy, are you?"

"Nah, fire away. What's up?"

"Well, I might as well put it out there completely—I was wondering if you wanted to take some time off work and come to visit? I've been thinking and—"

Andrew stopped chewing and tossing his sizzling chicken pieces.

"What, you mean come to Norway? To Bergen?"

"That's right."

"Well, I don't know what to say," came the surprisingly calm response. "I'm flattered. That's really—that's really good of you, Gene. Yes. Yes, I can."

"Are you sure?"

"Sure? Gene, I've wanted to ask you to have me over ever since we started talking again."

"Well, that settles it. Let me know when you can come and I'll clear my diary."

"Perfect."

The sound of a dead line filled Andrew's left ear as he stood, wok in hand, in the middle of his kitchen and stared at the little pieces of meat therein. A ginger, supine kind of feeling filled him slowly. His arm, lowering seemingly without choice, rested the wok back on the hob. He turned the ring off. Then he breathed out.

Much of Media City's recruitment push on the Fitzalan job had been achieved and, although there were always new projects coming in, Andrew saw a neat gap in the middle of May in which he could take his holiday. He spoke to Gene, who said he could fit in an extended weekend starting on the Wednesday. All was set.

The office grew curious at Andrew's mysterious plans. Most of them had noticed the change in his temperament and weight, and attributed it to one of those healthy pushes that people go for from time to time. Bright thought that he had a woman on the cards; Peter Noblood knew better. Seeta had asked Seren to pry by asking some awkward questions, but these had only yielded the considered response, "Nothing's happening in the love department. I'm just off home to visit my dad—he's quite ill." That had put an end to the desktop chatter.

It was true that he was in the best shape since his youth. He had been swapping crippling inertia for bracing activity at every juncture possible and it had brought out the fight in him. Now he was bright, confident, supple around the stomach and around his bones. His pityriasis was receding and, he thought, if anything should be a mark of the change it should be that. He would not have cared if it left a scar; scar away, he thought, like that bottle had in Seacroft. I want the memory for strength and resolve.

The weeks passed by and soon it was the night before the flight. He watched the news and chewed on some biscuits, which he enjoyed with the sweet chai tea that had been recommended to him by John Gandah. The bulging suitcase sat in his small hallway, waiting to depart. His tickets, passport, clothes and most of Sheffield's libraries' literature on Norway were packed safely away inside his black fifty-litre suitcase, which he had bought specially for the trip. He had his travel adaptors and his krone—a thousand pounds' worth.

He had met Gandah for a last hurrah at the Walkley Cottage. It was like parting permanently with a dear friend, even though he knew he would be back in little over a week. He felt he owed him a lot.

"What are you hoping to find there, 'Drew?" Gandah had asked him whilst he had been tying his bootlaces once more—they were always coming undone.

"I would say I don't know, John, but I think I do."

Andrew had stared out of the rain-streaked window to the green railings and their supporting poles which prevented them from falling down the hill. "Peace. That's all I hope for."

And John had given him a look as if to say, "So do we all."

John Gandah had not been the only character he had seen before his departure. Walking back from the very pub where he had bidden his old friend a whiskied goodbye, he had seen little Harry Brownlow—'the diagonaliser'—playing in the lengthening, but wet, May evening with her friend Alan Kivy.

Alan was a boy from over in Hillsborough. Andrew looked at him and shuddered sometimes. He bore obvious signs of neglect—his skin was pallid and his body thin from lack of proper food; his uniform, which he never changed out of, was ripped and filthy with food deposits. His face was lightly and evenly freckled; his mouth was sometimes thick with spittle; his cheekbones were thick and they stretched the skin; his eyes were of the most unearthly deep brown, almost as though he was not human but some kind of canine. They sucked in the light. He was one of Sheffield's tumbling underclass, those that cannot find their feet because they are stuck in knowledge deprivation.

But he was a very nice boy, and Andrew assumed that he must have walked the distance between Walkley and Hillsborough as regularly as he had because he knew there was light at the end of the tunnel which promised escape from his family's squalid flat. That, and he trusted Harry's judgment.

Alan and Harry had been playing on a patch of grass somewhere just up from Parsonage Crescent where a sharp bend turns the steep road into Walkley. Andrew waited until the two had finished playing a game of tig around the smooth, pearly-barked cherry tree there before saying hello.

"Where have you been?" came the typically contrite reply from Harry.

Alan Kivy delicately added an "Ay up."

"Me? Oh busy in the orifice as usual, Harry."

"My dad told me it's not really called an orifice, you know?"

"He did? Well, you got me. It's an office, isn't it?"

"Yes, it is!"

"What's an orifice?" asked Alan lightly, looking off across the hill.

"Have you been enjoying school?"

"Oh yes," her face lit up happily. "Well, most of it. We got to do tie-die today, that was my best bit this week."

"Sounds cool."

"It was, and I got told by Mrs Shipton that my handwriting was the second best in the class. What are you having for tea tonight?"

Mrs Shipton... Poor John.

Andrew, distracted and thrown by the sudden change in topic, had to think for a second. "Erm, probably summat quick and easy, I think. Pasta, probably. I need an early night."

"Why? I hate early nights."

"Me too," added Alan, this time with more fervour. Andrew looked at both of them adoringly.

"I'm flying tomorrow."

"Flying! Why are you doing that? Flying where?"

"Well, it's to see an old friend; and Norway."

"Norway! No way! That's where the Vinks are from," chimed in Alan, now becoming very involved in the discussion.

"NorwayNoWay..." giggled Harry, and the two children repeated the two words faster and faster until they tumbled madly over the words and had to stop, their sides splitting from the amusement.

When Harry had recovered, she began again but this time in her usual, strangely adult voice, "I don't think you should go to Norway, Andy." Her voice was like brass, warm but clanging.

"Really? Why not?"

"Because it's not a good idea!"

"What do you mean, it's not a good idea?"

"It's not a good idea!" Harry had become quite impassioned now, her face deadly serious and her voice clanging dangerously like a Tibetan singing bowl, brassy and hot.

"Harry it's fine, my flight'll be safe. Look..."

"I'm not bothered about your flight! I'm bothered about you! I don't think you should be going!" Her face had turned dark. She now walked towards Andrew. "You shouldn't leave."

Andrew stepped back slightly. He felt uncomfortable and hot, and the alcohol seemed to have disappeared from his veins. "Harry, I, I'm gonna be fine. I don't know why you're so worried." His voice sounded unnaturally high.

"You won't listen. I just don't like the sound of this, not one bit." Then in a childlike gesture which was a cut of relief to him, she crossed her arms in defiance.

"You've been watching too many spooky films."

He sounded entirely unconvinced by the words coming out of his mouth. There was something in the changed nature of Harry Brownlow which had thrown him utterly. There was a long, itchy pause.

Alan Kivy broke the silence. He said, "I want to play Vinks nah. You 'ave to be de quiet people fromt tahn an I get to wear orns.'

"Have fun. Goodbye Harry." Then he muttered, "Have faith."

Andrew tried in vain not to think anything of Harry Brownlow's turn as he sat there numbly taking in the weather forecast. If she had wanted to make him discomfited, she had achieved it. Now, as ever, she was an unreadable enigma.

His flight departed at ten a.m. He awoke at five thirty and took a taxi to Sheffield station, behind which the great amphitheatre, which had been developed and hewn into Park Hill at the end of the 2000's, stood majestic against the clearing early morning sky. His train was the first leaving for Manchester Airport.

He settled down with a coffee and a paper on one of the stiff, barely-padded terminal chairs. The runways at Manchester reminded him of being around nine or ten years-old and flying for the first time. One such time, the Chappells had flown to Egypt to see Giza and the White Nile. On the first night, Andrew's father was stung by a deathstalker scorpion and rushed to hospital. Andrew had caught a glimpse of that face as he sat waiting for the taxi in the hotel waiting room. It had been the first time he'd seen fear in his old man's eyes. He felt almost sad thinking of the same old man now, sitting in his home, on all levels of practicality simply waiting to die; perhaps looking fearful once again.

His morbid thoughts received a welcome interruption from the call to the departure gate. Feeling strong-limbed but with quavering squirms of lightness in his stomach, he boarded the flight with a flourish, even greeting the cabin crew with an unexpected "How do you do?"

Then he buckled in happily and listened eagerly to the in-flight procedures as they were explained by the stewardess with pinned-back-hair. He felt the thrill of the takeoff, then felt the roar of the engine curtail into a drone as his popped ears sent all sound underwater. After a while he looked at the sea below or what little glimpses he could snatch of it between the cloud, which had become thicker to the east.

The plane landed at Flesland Airport, some twenty kilometres from Bergen's centre, at just gone one o'clock. Norway's still pines and grey sky could be seen through the glass façade of the small airport. Andrew readjusted his watch to the local time as he stepped cautiously through arrivals.

The airport was fairly small and quiet: only thirty or so passengers were milling about, squinting at screens or sitting at cafes reading and sipping on tea and coffee. Large banners hung from the high ceiling bearing the word "Velkommen', and all around him Norwegian— the signs, the people speaking as they passed by. His senses began tingling as though an instinct was running through him. He was here in Bergen to see Gene Bradley, separated brother of fourteen years; he was here at last.

Andrew was wrapping himself up and ordering a coffee from a little, curly-haired trader outside the entrance in his most basic Norwegian—"Jeg vil gjerne ha en kaffe"—when Gene pulled up in a dark-green 22-reg Volkswagen Jetta.

He reached slowly out of the driver's door, stretched his long body out of the car, and strode across the waiting bay. He was smiling as he walked over; he recognised Andrew without a moment's hesitation.

Andrew shifted his bag off his shoulder and placed his coffee down. Neither spoke until Gene had stopped in front of him. Then they gazed upon each other's faces, drinking in the details of how each had changed so remarkably over the years. Gene thought how Andrew's face had rounded, his hair had receded, and how he had matured more than he could have expected. Andrew thought of how much longer Gene's hair was and how much thicker his sideburns, which framed his slightly aged face, had become; how his Adam's apple protruded and his glasses— there were glasses!—described his yellowy-brown eyes with calmness; and of how he had matured more than he could have expected.

But despite the myriad miniscule changes, to Andrew it was still the face of Gene before him, the face of the boy he had last seen in Birmingham, in England, forever ago. And Gene melted into the same wonderful nostalgia. It was almost too much for either man to take.

"Andrew," Gene addressed him gently. "You've come."

"I've come," came the sweet reply.

It was a twenty minute drive to Gene's family home, through a rolling pinescape which broke occasionally to reveal the sea on one of its winding encroachments inland. They crossed a bridge connecting two islands separated by one such sea fjord.

"Grimstadfjorden," explained Gene animatedly, "I travel across here all the time. Flesland feels like a second home."

They went via a small supermarket in what Gene explained was the suburb of Fyllingsdalen. Gene bought some wine and other odd bits and pieces for the house and Andrew bought a bottle of fruit juice. The odd nervousness around Gene and the excitement of seeing all the Norwegian signs had dried his mouth.

"Do you know that there's a place in the North York Moors called Fylingdales?" enquired Gene as they strolled back to the car.

"No, I've never been; we always went to the Dales or Norfolk."

"We went to Whitby quite a lot when we were growing up. I always loved the name. And now I'm here."

"One of those strange things."

"Not so strange now. Now I know why there was always the feel of a Viking heath round there."

The drive leading to Gene's house was a supreme, gorgeous mix of verges and embankments built up of spaniel-brown pine needles; and where the pines and cedars stood at intervals of several metres, the verdant bracken gave a pastel work of greens onto which the trunks' stringy and earthen bark applied itself, as though a painter's brush had selected the two most enviably matched colours in all the world and been swept across it.

Here on the hills to the south of Bergen, the city was invisible. Only brief glances of the waters belonging to the city's southern suburbs and of unknown steep hillsides could be snatched from the vista. The beauty of the surrounding woodland and the cleanness of the northern air, which Andrew sniffed in deeply as he got out of the car, left him spellbound.

"I know what you mean when you say it's home. I couldn't have imagined, way back when, that you'd be living somewhere like this. It's just beautiful."

"Nor could I," returned Gene as he popped open the boot and began lifting out his shopping. "It's been a long journey indeed."

Andrew turned away from the view and towards the house.

If the view down and across the valley had been spellbinding, then the view which confronted him now was extraordinary. A giant wooden structure, unlike any that had met Andrew's eye before, sat like a sloping mammoth amongst a combination of ferns, shale pathways, outbuildings, and water features which took up a larger patch of land than did Andrew's entire street. There was no mistaking that this was a Norwegian house. Two gigantic diagonal pieces of timber, the colour of coffee beans, began below the ground and intersected thirty feet in the air like two mighty arms resting on one another, each carrying on into the sky for a little distance before being cut off on the horizontal. They dictated the shape of the building—a long triangular prism—and down its length two more of the rabbit-ear-like protrusions made by the timbers were visible. It was more of a hall than a house. A balcony, on which were some decorations including a draped piece of burgundy cloth with cut-out pieces of paper forming the words Goddag Andrew stuck to it, indicated the first floor of the house. It ran across the entire front like one long deck on the side of a ship. Similarly, stepped decking ambled up to a large, squareish doorway on the ground floor. One giant thick piece of glass, dominating one side of the front wall, mixed modern with traditional. It gave an outsider a view into the interior, and had clearly been added recently, for some of the timbers on the house looked as though they had seen the weather of perhaps a hundred winters, the glass comparatively few.

To the left of the house stood a much smaller but still sizeable cabin, its wood a much lighter colour—beech, Andrew guessed. It was much wider than it was deep, and looked almost like a dormitory at an outdoor activity centre. As they walked up the final part of the driveway they passed a giant rhubarb plant neatly bordered off by an oval of small red bricks.

"Gunnera manicata," explained Gene when he saw the look of fascination on Andrew's face as he looked up into the plant's canopy. "I had it brought over with me on my last visit to France—beautiful isn't it? It's our experiment. I'm not sure it'll survive the winter, but they say it's a new breed they've cultivated."

They ascended the steps, their shod feet knocking softly on the solid wood beneath. Gene slipped his loafers off and put them neatly to the side, along with the brightly coloured wellies which belonged to his children and the two pairs of tall, navy blue wellies which must have belonged to him and his wife. Andrew followed suit, placing his dark lace-up trainers next to them.

"So, is anyone home?" asked Andrew, a little nervously and a little unnecessarily, as Gene reached into his pocket for his key.

"No, the kids and Hilma are out at Hilma's parents'. They'll be back about four I would think."

Gene grunted a little as he pushed open the door. "They'd usually be at school, all of them, but today they're shut."

"Ah right. Does Hilma work at the school that Agnethe and Hen, erm…"

"Henrik."

"Henrik go to? Does she work there?"

"No, she works at one a bit further away, at a place called Bønes. Agnethe and Henrik just go to the local one here."

"I can't wait to meet them all."

"They can't wait to meet you!"

"Yes, I saw the banner. How sweet of them."

They entered the house. The smell that greeted Andrew was fresh, the air mixed with the scent of the wood and of lavender. They walked through the hallway, past an exceptionally wide, blue-painted staircase, whose monochrome gave way at the very bottom to a riot of colours, colours which intricately covered a dragon's head on the bottom-most banister. The head was carved in the style of those which speared the prows of Viking longboats—a strangely rounded, almost feline shape. Greens and reds and yellows flashed across its notched, carefully shaped face, outlining each detail perfectly.

They passed a kitchen to the left, the rich smells giving way for a moment to those of bread and, vaguely, fish.

Now they came into the giant living room with sliding windows on either side following the sloped shape of the building and long planks of old timber which ran underfoot. Above them, great joists and beams criss-crossed, from which different colourful objects were hanging: patterned cloths, some with paisley or other foreign patterns on them; separate strings of bells and of pinecones; and some bones, giant antlers, and furs. The room was furnished with long, expensive sofas and a few chairs to the left of the doorway in which the two men stood. These furnishings gathered around an enormous wall-mounted television.

The wall divided the two distinct sections of the ground floor—the hallway and kitchen, and the living room. A grand central hearth in the latter hosted a log burner and above it the chimney breast must have led upwards to a stack somewhere in the centre of the roof, Andrew guessed. The burner crackled, and a small flame flickered away inside it.

They drank some mint tea and talked about the flight over. Gene told him about how the terminal at Flesland had been built—"In fact, I unloaded some of the ships which carried the steel structure over here. Made in Sheffield, some of it."

"Really?"

"Mm. There was uproar about it here, jobs going to foreign competition and all that." A knowing smile lit his lips. "But Maersk did well."

They finished their cups and Gene showed Andrew his sleeping arrangements. He was accommodated in the beech cabin beside the house, which had its own burner and bed and even a small kitchen.

"We use it for all sorts of things, little parties, guests; the kids use it as a snow fort sometimes. All sorts of things. And I have my own kabin all to myself further up the garden at the back."

"Is there a shower here?"

"Aye, just here."

He stepped across the bedroom and opened the door to a small bathroom, complete with large shaving mirror and double shower unit.

"What do you get up to in your other kabin?"

"I have all my books shelved in it, which I go to read a lot of the time. I can do work from home there on my computer too, and I have a telescope, some instruments, some maps… but look, here's Hilma and the kids. I'll have to show you it later.'

Through the window they saw Hilma and the two children pull up in an Audi estate. The children were the first to jump out of the back; they ran around, each holding up a mini hand-made windmill while blowing into their sails and calling loudly. Then the chirrup of little Norwegian voices was cut quiet by that of Hilma's.

"Shall we meet them?" asked Gene.

Andrew laid down his bags on the springy bed and followed him outside. He heard Gene call in Norwegian towards the giant rhubarb, behind which Hilma and the children were talking. It was now that Andrew realised how little of the language he could understand. Hilma replied something as she and the children emerged from the huge leaves. She had a small leather handbag with a brown strap placed across her shoulder, and a light-blue tube backpack hanging off the other that had notepads sticking out of the top.

The first thing which struck Andrew was just how tall she was: at least six foot. Andrew had never been tall and the way she looked down on him at a distance of ten paces or so reminded him again of it. The second was that she was deeply golden-skinned and had perfectly clear blue eyes, each with small lines which arrowed towards the pupil. Her naturally blonde hair was tied-back; in places it tumbled downwards.

She sang, "Andrew! It's so nice to meet you. How was your journey?"

She hugged him and kissed his right cheek. In the background, Henrik and Agnethe were chanting, "And-roo! And-roo!" with a little roll on the 'r'.

"It was wonderful thanks," he replied, smiling. "What a pleasure to meet you. And the little ones!" He walked over to Agnethe and said, "Hello young lady! Hva heter du?"

The children laughed at his short vowel sound in heter. To them he was really straining to say the words. Hilma scolded them in their mother tongue, then Andrew assured her that he was confident his speaking skills were terrible. She turned again to the children and reminded them that their guest was engelsk; then, to Andrew's great surprise, they chimed back "We know, mum!'

They headed up the steps and in to the kitchen, where Gene and Hilma had a conversation in English about her parents. They were doing well, and they had all walked along to see how the preparations for this evening were looking.

"What's happening this evening?' asked Andrew, curious.

"Hasn't Gene mentioned to you? Gene! Not telling our guest about syttende mai! Constitution Day, Andrew, is when we celebrate our constitution being passed in 1814—we call it syttende mai, the seventeenth of May. It's a very special day for Norwegians. We were making flags and food yesterday at school. Oh, Karl Thygesen even brought in his bunad, Gene, for the girls to look at."

Gene laughed.

"But I understand you work at a different school to the one which Henrik and Agnethe go to?"

"Mummy work in a school Bønes," said Henrik disinterestedly, his blonde head looking up to the worktop in search of food.

"Mummy works in a school in Bønes," corrected Gene.

Agnethe added, "I knowed that, daddy."

Gene spoke to them in Norwegian and they shuffled away. Before they had left the room Andrew called, "Thank you for the welcome message, Henrik and Agnethe. I feel very welcome."

Agnethe said something, then they ran off laughing and shouting after each other.

"Agnethe just explained what you said to Henrik—she's a bit more advanced with her English than he is."

"How old are they again?"

"He's four and she's six, nearly seven."

"They're wonderful."

"Thank you, Andrew," replied Hilma radiantly. "Now tonight...'"

Chapter Six

Norwegian Dream and So

It was still light but the sun had begun to wane by the time that the two cars, one containing Hilma, Henrik, and Agnethe, the other containing Andrew and Gene, pulled up gently outside the little wooden school in Fyllingsdalen.

The paintings, collages, and stories of the attendant school children hung from the corridor walls in which they were being welcomed by one of the teachers. The teacher, a dark-bearded, middle-aged man, wore traditional dress and had his hair specially swept back, with the effect that his ears had become the outstanding feature of his face.

The traditional dress—a 'bunad'—consisted of a white shirt that was fastened together at the neck by a small bright copper clasp. A green waistcoat with red trim fit tightly to the teacher's chest; over this he wore a smart black jacket which in turn was trimmed in green. His legs were clad in dark breeches which rumpled into white stockings, long white socks like those Andrew had seen along with kilts before. As he led them to the sound of voices chattering somewhere to the back play area his black shoes, which were adorned with an ornamental silver-coloured decoration - a kind of useless buckle - clacked loudly over the linoleum, and two knotted tassels coloured red, white, and green bobbed from his stockings as he walked.

For Andrew, it was like there was a newness to the world which had always seemed finished with, left not in another place but another time.

The play area was a woodchipped space that was enclosed on three sides by the U-shaped building. There were swings and halved tyres forming a semi-circle, walls, grass verges, and a football pitch. It teemed with children and parents, maybe a hundred or so, who either milled or ran around. Bright-coloured bunads were interspersed through the crowd, flashing like jays.

Above the volume of the crowd Gene said, "You've picked a very Norwegian day to arrive!"

"You have," agreed Hilma, her voice its usual happy sigh. "It's the time of year where we all get together and celebrate. It's wonderful, isn't it Gene? The boys and girls in their bunads, the light evenings, the celebration of Norway. Ah, it makes my heart…" she paused, then turned to them and sighed again, "so happy."

Gene mm-hmmed, then added, "Look, Hilma, it's Georg."

He continued in Norwegian, then concluded, "Andrew, come with me and meet Georg. He's got two barns here and he runs the local hiking club. You'll love him."

They pushed through the crowd towards a tall, clean-shaven, bright-blond man whose muscular shoulders and upper arms were covered by the long-sleeved shirt of his bunad, turned up to his elbow so that his expensive watch and tanned forearm were exposed.

Gene strode up and embraced him. Georg laughed like a stooping bird then turned to Andrew and, as though he knew implicitly that all this was alien to him, said, "Quite a scene for you, Andrew! We don't always look like this, ha. I'm Georg, nice to meet you."

They shook hands rather more firmly than Andrew was used to, then Georg continued, "Welcome in Norway." The tone to his voice, at the same time scholarly, playful, and almost impish, validated the welcome.

Gene spoke in Norwegian for a while about Constitution Day and enquired about the hiking club's fortunes. Their next meet was this Sunday.

"Well, we absolutely have to go, you and I, Andrew!" exclaimed Gene after translation.

"The club's always looking for fresh legs," agreed Georg, continuing the conversation in English. Then he leaned in, and spoke again in his impish tone, "and I'm sure everyone will enjoy the English practice." He clicked and smiled, stroking his shaven neck happily.

Teachers were encouraging the hoisting of banners in the packed playground and there appeared to be movement towards a large gate at its rear. A caterpillar-like line was forming and Hilma could be seen gesturing towards them with a smile lit across her face. She was incredibly beautiful, Andrew thought suddenly. She seemed wonderful.

Georg said his goodbye and went to find his children. Andrew and Gene caught up with the rest of the family and slowly filtered outwards at the rear of the crowd as it made its way down the road.

"We're going on the parade now," explained Gene, "we'll pass through the village and everyone gets to see the barns in their bunader." They still needed to speak at a half-shout to be heard over the mass of people snaking downhill.

"Ohh, they've made such a good job with their banners!" fawned Hilma.

"I suppose they're doing something similar at your school in Bønes, Hilma?" ventured Andrew.

"Yes, yes they are," she replied distractedly, "everyone's put so much work into everything. Ah."

Later that evening, after the parade had ended and the children had gone to bed, Gene made a fire in Andrew's cabin as Andrew looked on, eager to learn. "We still need a little warmth on nights, even though summer's here."

Andrew saw that the sky had not entirely dimmed, despite the time approaching twelve. "Sweet dreams."

Thursday brought with it much improved weather and the sky sparkled gloriously over Bergen. Andrew had arisen early and seen the family engaged in their usual school routine, though today the off-work Gene had walked the children to their school along with Andrew while Hilma had disappeared in the car to Bønes.

Gene led them on a different route back to the house from the one they had taken. They were now circumnavigating a very large pond.

"Orrtuvatnet, it's called. Fyllingsdalen doesn't have many other features I'm afraid—it's very residential. Hey, look at the way the sun's making the water look…"

It was like moving silver. "Y'know, we need to head down into Bergen so you can see the sea when it's like this."

They returned home in the morning's rising heat and ate a breakfast of cornflakes with some local unpasteurised milk. "Hilma makes me keep it on the top shelf so the kids can't reach it," laughed Gene as Andrew licked his spoon.

"It's the best bloody milk I've ever tasted."

Soon they were winding their way into Bergen. Andrew could see the small port-city shining beneath him for the first time, shining like shattered shards of glass under a lit microscope. Gene's face was written with excitement as they approached the harbour.

"So, like I said, first, we'll go to Bryggen," he declared while they stood at the parking meter, "there are the most wonderful, most Bergenser streets of anywhere in the city there. Then who knows? We have the whole day to explore. Anywhere you'd like to visit?"

A small piece of paper with a sticker attached to it popped out of the meter with a whirring and a thwup!

"Well, I've done a bit of research—as you know"—they caught one another's eye—"and Bryggen was top of my list, so yeah let's do that. I think I also wanted to see, and you'll have to excuse the pronunciation, the Schøtstuene?'

Gene barked, "Ha! Not too bad—I've heard worse—but you should say the first syllable as 'shirt'."

"Right, shirt-stoo-ner,' Andrew corrected himself.

"Good idea. There's plenty in there which explains the Bryggen fairly well. Do you know," continued Gene with a removed look in his eye, "I think that was the first piece of Bergen culture I took in when I moved here. Beyond the obvious, I mean. So, was there anywhere else?"

"Pronunciation again—Mariakirken?"

"Oh yeah, that one's always rammed with tourists. It's nice, but if it's a choice between that or the Håkonshallen then it's the hall every time."

"I must see your stave churches too…"

Gene had stuck on his all-day ticket by now and they had set off on foot into the town via a concrete causeway.

"You're my guide, Gene."

"Well, I'll save you time."

Andrew was feeling pained to only have a few days there. Then they looked at each other and laughed, and it was Gene and Cosmo, as if reanimated from their fossils. Both felt it now, and they had to turn away, still smiling, to look at the harbour. The sea glistened next to them like a magpie's nest full with bounty.

The wooden-floored street which ran along the front of Bryggen's shops was not so far from where they had parked. To their right was the harbour, wide, placid, and inviting for the container ships and other seacraft which were passing within its shelter.

Cutting through the harbour's flat waters were the wakes of the ships, which began as energetic, carving beasts but quickly dissipated into calm, foamy streaks as they criss-crossed like planes' vapour trails. On their left a long row of wood-clad shops and attractions drew the eye with their marvellous array of colours. At intervals, narrow passages and alleyways sloped gently upwards in between them, to what, Andrew didn't know, and all around a thick throng of tourists and locals moved about like a woven lattice of people, all enjoying the weather and the smells and Bryggen.

They had stopped before one maroon-coloured shop amongst the pastel work of colours and shades which made up the harbour front. At its entrance, sloping around the top of the doorframe like manufacture marks on a car tyre, were the words 'Sild Fisk Alfred Skulstad Schjøtt'.

"This is where they do the best herrings in the whole bloody city. Kept my bones in order the whole time I've been here. Do you want to try?"

"With a review like that, how could I say no?"

Andrew's unadorned response tickled Gene, who had opened the shop's door with a bark of laughter and a loud tinkle from the bell. He was feeling childlike.

A small, serious-looking man stood behind the fish-laden counter with his filleting knife lolling lazily in his strong brown hand. He wore a white t-shirt which clung to his compact, muscular frame. Small white hairs protruded proudly from the neckline, reaching up towards his stout neck, which reddened in patches. His face congruently looked as though it had no room in its world for pleasant conversation. Only business and compliance would do, from its neatly-outlined forehead to its dimpled, square chin, which was lightly dappled by grey stubble. The chin twitched as the pair drew closer, and the parrot-grey eyes darted between them.

It was because of this fearsome outward appearance that Andrew jumped when he heard the man call a singsong, "Goood daaag" as they stopped in front of him.

He began to spin his knife.

"I'll get us some herring," hummed Gene.

"Would you mind if I tried?" Andrew seemed excited at the prospect of exercising his Norwegian.

"What, to ask for some?"

"I think I can do it."

The fishmonger eyed the pair with a narrow curiosity and spun his knife at an even pace.

"Go ahead," replied Gene amicably. He wanted to see the result.

The fishmonger continued to spin the knife as Andrew stepped forward keeping his gaze away from the fishmonger and instead fixed upon the steaming ice-racks which bore vast quantities of unmarked seafood. Staring at a particular arrangement of fish and pointing his finger outwards, he asked, "Hva er det?"

The fishmonger's dimpled chin twitched. "Dette her? Sild." His attention had turned to Gene and now he asked softly, "Engelsk?'" in a tone suggesting Gene was his carer.

"Begge er Engelsk," responded Gene as he flicked his finger once between his chest and Andrew's back.

"Kan jeg få se på den?"

The fishmonger almost emotionally seized a large herring and held it forth on his curved hand and forearm with the tenderness of a father holding a newborn. Gene, wrapped now in his own thoughts, imagined that the fishmonger had been such a father many moons ago. "It looks good," Andrew continued, glancing at Gene. "Hvor mye koster det?"

The fishmonger's dimpled chin twitched again yet this time there was a different look in his grey eyes, a grudging respect which flew around their irises. "130 krone per kilo," he purred back.

Andrew produced a wad of notes and requested two. The fishmonger stopped spinning his knife and placed it with a tinny clang on the side.

Andrew breathed out, smiled, winked at Gene, and then folded his arms.

Gulls were calling screechily outside. A strange-coloured pigeon, the blue of whose wings lightened halfway down its proud chest into a brilliant white, flew up one of the alleyways leading away from the harbour.

"Aha," heralded Gene's voice, "this is our street for Schøttstuene."

They spent the next day revisiting some shops before they returned home to sand down some benches that Gene had made for the back garden, ready to be oiled.

Andrew found it amusing that Gene referred to it as 'the back garden'; it was a phrase more befitting of Parsonage Crescent than the grounds that Gene owned. Much of it was landscaped in dark shale and slate; ferns and more gunnera mannicata made up the bulk of the leaf before the garden went out of sight beyond a small hillock. Certain areas, the largest of which spread left to give the space its lopsided dimensions, were terraced. As the feet crunched slowly up these terraces, one almost felt as though one was ascending the steps of some ancient temple, so much so that to rush about in this still garden felt sacrilegious.

At the top of these dark steps was a single yew tree, unburdened by fruit in the season. Judging by the bark and the height it must have been growing for tens, if not hundreds, of years. It was around twenty feet tall, and within the bark nested little coves as if dug out by strong fingers within which dense spider webs had been spun. The bark cracked away like ageing, shedding skin. The tree provided shade on a day like today, and underneath it Andrew and Gene drank their fruit squash as they sat on two portable stools and contentedly overlooked the garden.

Andrew's shoulders ached from the sanding. Half dug-in azaleas and yet to be planted Japanese maple, Acer Palmatum, indicated Gene's ongoing project.

"I get inspiration from the gardens of the people who I've worked with around Europe," explained Gene passionately, "those who I've gone to visit. I'm amazed it hasn't ended up a complete patchwork if I'm honest."

"My garden's been one of my few hobbies over the years."

Andrew looked at the sky over the tops of some cedar trees and imagined being catapulted onto the lawn of his own small, sloping, well-kept garden. Just then, he felt as if that garden was the only thing in that rolling city to which he would have clung on.

"Wonderful places aren't they."

They slurped again on their glasses of squash. Andrew was wondering about this kabin of Gene's, and was about to ask its position when Gene plocked his glass down and said, "Let's finish the benches then go for a drive."

The evening brought with it a dinner of breaded herrings, boiled potatoes, steamed kale, and a rich onion sauce which Gene, having forgotten about it till the last minute, produced by throwing together a roux and chopping through two small onions with a razor-sharp knife which flashed like that of the fishmonger's. The pan nearly boiled over and Gene whipped it off to pour the sauce on the plates of the clamorous children, bashing their cutlery on the table like prison inmates. The sauce soothed the children and they ate away.

Hilma was wearing large, raindrop-shaped earrings that had three concentric circles of cobalt blue stones in their centres, making her eyes shine bright. Her simple, black, longsleeved top, Andrew noticed, hugged her body and for the first time he saw her well-proportioned waist giving way to her hips, which were covered by a straight, knee-length denim skirt. He had to look quickly away as she met his gaze, but she was looking beyond him in search of a cloth for Henrik's mouth.

Gene had been recounting the boats at Godvik. "Do you remember that we're up and away to the hiking club tomorrow, Andrew? I spoke to Georg earlier today when I'd gone out for the oil, says we're going to the Hardangervidda national park out east. Spectacular, I can guarantee."

"Ah, hiking! I'd forgotten! Excellent, when are we rising?"

"Oh, at the crack of dawn I should think. I'll come and knock on your door. I think Georg will have some boots—what size are you?"

"Nine."

"Yes, mine will be too big."

Then Henrik, peeling off from arguing with his mother about the household's lack of pets, cut in fairy-like, "Daddy have big shoes."

Upon hearing that phrase both of them turned firstly to the little boy and then to each other. The look etched on each face told of the memory which had hit them—That night in Bridlington, those women, Andrew's famous 'big shoes'. They shared a delighted, nostalgic smile, their thoughts filling with the warm air of that summer night and the imprint of wicker chairs, fairy lights, and waking in the flat on Cardigan Road.

"Now daddy, will And-roo come and play in the games room?"

"Oh, I'm sure," he wheezed lifting Agnethe up, "that Andrew would be more than happy to if you ask him nicely."

She wriggled out of his grasp and took Andrew by the hand towards the stairs while scolding Henrik in Norwegian for being slow. Gene and Hilma smiled on as they disappeared for a night of air-hockey, twister, and lego battles.

Chapter Seven

In the Kabin

The time was only approaching four o'clock when Gene knocked softly on Andrew's door. Andrew sat up feeling refreshed, peeled back the covers, and took a quick shower.

The dawn outside was a little grey as he crunched across the drive to the house. Gene had left the door open. Over an enormous breakfast of hard-boiled eggs, kippers, toast, and fried tomatoes, Gene assured him it was due to fair up later on.

"It'll get quite toasty out on the trail; in fact, we might want sun cream. Remind me to pack it. Oh, and you need boots from Georg."

Andrew nodded. "I'm sure this sounds a daft question, but do we need any protection? What kind of wildlife are we expecting?"

"Oh nothing vicious or life-threatening, no. Squirrels, mink, maybe the occasional lemming. But nothing to worry your socks about," he laughed as he grabbed Andrew's shoulder in a strong grip. "Don't stroke them, mind."

A sloppy piece of kipper fell out of his mouth.

The hikers' meeting point was at a place called Paradis, some way down the heathy hill and off the main South E39. It was a name apparently plucked out of nowhere; only a handful of ordinary shops, a crossroads, and the typically efficient atmosphere of Norway made up the village, not the angels or deliverance nor the bounty of a fulfilled life it suggested. They had pulled up on the shoreside just off the main road a little outside the village. He recognised Georg's figure striding about the stationary cars at the water's edge. Noticing the newcomers, Georg raised his arm, smiled, and tapped his precious watch. Andrew remembered it from their meeting at the Constitution Day celebrations, and returned Georg's beaming smile.

"Englishmen, I am nearly calling you! And how are you today?'

His tone hadn't changed from those first impish and welcoming words. "I think we have a lot of hikers today, plenty for you to meet, Andrew! I hope you enjoyed the sights of Bergen?"

"Yes, yes it's been lovely. We took in a hell of a lot, me and Gene, didn't we? I love it, you know. You have to be proud of your city."

"Most Bergenser are, yes," he agreed in a low birdlike hum. "Our drive ahead is like three hours," he continued, stroking his neck and looking up the road, "so I'm hoping the stragglers are arriving soon." He sounded both parental and amused, as though the stragglers would be in for an early bedtime if they kept them much longer.

Other members of the club were wandering about holding steaming drinks in flask lids and checking equipment. "Oh, Georg,' Andrew was reminded as he glanced at his light-duty trainers, "you wouldn't happen to have any size nine walking boots, would you?"

He had asked rather clumsily and Georg had to ask him to repeat himself more slowly; then, with a grin suggesting he had expected such a problem, he fished out a pair from his car boot. "Great grip. Sharp, too." He ran his finger along one of the sole's moulded plastic blades.

A few more vehicles had pulled up by the shore by the time he had laced up, and after a brief speech by Georg which was punctuated by sleepy calls from the group and gruff-voiced jokes, the convoy had rolled away along the Hardangervegen, past the lakes of Grimevatner and Haukelandsvatnet, through Espeland and past a gigantic golden fjord which hugged the left of the convoy, through a long dale and to Nordheimsund where an even greater fjord, Hardangerfjord, stretched its gaping jaws like a recumbent dragon. Here air changed too, becoming warmer and sweeter. Then it was on to Granvin, past which snow-peaked mountains loomed in the distance.

They chatted for the majority of the journey. There came a touching moment when Gene thanked Andrew for all his hard work in fitting in with the family. Upon this, Andrew came close to spilling that he was really so enamoured with the whole situation that he had a favour to ask; but he caught himself and saved it for later. He was nervy about more than one thing.

They hiked all morning, stopping once for coffee and fattigman bakkels, a type of Norwegian biscuit which was diamond-like in shape and had been fried instead of baked. The woodland trails had started tourist-friendly but had become more treacherous as Georg, Gene, and a counsel of others studied the map further, which led them down less-trodden paths. Andrew felt sometimes that the dark claustrophobia of the pines would never reach an end when suddenly another shimmering lake would burst spectacularly into view and open up the landscape again.

To fill these uncertain moments in the pines, when he was not speaking to the exclusively male and largely middle-aged members of the club and reluctantly correcting their English, he had been thinking of his departure. So soon it had come. He had been almost dreading it; his soul was against it. He mulled around in his head, as an assiduous kitchen porter sluicing the burnt-on contents of a deep pan, the hanging fact that he and Gene had barely scratched the surface with one another. There had been flashes of their recaptured brotherhood, and these alone would have sustained Andrew for weeks, perhaps even months on his return to the Heaving City that he felt like leaving behind for good; but there was that one thing he had set out to seek and which he had not found: he had not faced the demons of the past which his entire being needed to exorcise. This hung heavy, and while he thought of it he felt transported from his body as a thought into the dark universe, where he, the thought now, only the thought, wandered in the vacuum with a gross weight bearing down upon him. Only now to stop himself from falling under the dead weight he came thumping back into reality, stumbling through the bracken, and past the slow-eyed squirrels which darted lugubriously amongst the pines. He had concluded that they would speak tonight; it could not be any other way.

At mid-afternoon the sun was hot. They had been walking without shade on a mountain path overlooking one of the countless lakes, and now the hikers were weary. They stopped and sat on the grass next to some brambles. Some had stripped and created makeshift head towels, some were panting like dogs; all were in need of water. Georg decided that a group should set out to find a stream leading to the lake to fill their bottles and nominated some members of a search party. It was only now they'd halted their progress that Georg and Gene realised Andrew was missing.

Gene panicked.

"I'm responsible for him!" he said hurriedly and low to Georg, who was stood on a rock. "We have to find him immediately, before he wanders off even further." He let out a loud flare of hot breath from his nostrils. "What was I thinking, leaving him by himself?"

"Gene, Gene, calm now. He won't be gone far. We might have lost him somewhere near that last turning, maybe he stopped for a piss. We'll look for him together."

They tracked their way back to the turning, which was nearly a kilometre from where they had stopped. Georg continued his attempt to soothe Gene, who now was becoming more annoyed at than concerned for Andrew, remembering and cursing his doziness that seemingly hadn't changed.

They reached the turning. It lay perhaps a hundred yards from the forest, offering a fabulous first vista of the square lake below.

Gene was looking disconsolately towards the forest, convinced that Andrew was stumbling around alone within its confines. Georg was peering over the edge of a rock face in the opposite direction, on the other side of the turning. Then, with an apprehensive voice, he called the words, "Erm, Gene…"

Andrew was at the rear of the posse when he heard the animal crying; and what a strange, flesh-tingling cry it was: the combination of a duck's quack, a cat's screech, and the noise made when one holds one's cheeks and sucks inwards. It was undoubtedly in distress whatever it was and it was calling from somewhere over the large escarpment which led to the basin in which the lake sat. The two men he had been walking with, Fredrik and Håkon, were both wheezing asthmatics who only wanted to talk about cars and houses, and he had wanted to shake their company for some time. He held back ever so slowly, reducing his pace to a casual amble; they, with their limited vocabulary, reverted to speaking about their favoured subjects in Norwegian; and from his stationary position Andrew watched them wind tiredly on around the bend some forty yards ahead.

Now he was alone. He headed back towards the source of the noise, which continued in its frantic, almost human timbre. Still he could not see what it was, this ghostly call from below, and regardless of his safety he was clambering down a brush-covered track, sending stones tumbling down into the woods which skirted the water below. The shrill crying was getting louder with each yard he gained, reverberating against the bare face of rock.

He stopped on a large, level platform. There in its dusty middle was a dark, circular patch created by the animal's wriggling, and in the patch's centre lay a small lemming, its coat covered in reddish dust, its miniature beaver-like teeth protruding high, and its rear left leg crooked and broken.

It continued to shriek horribly as he neared it. This was the first time he had seen a lemming and it surprised him how its head seemed to merge with its shoulders like a squat lampshade, making its appearance curiously combative. He kept a little distance; the pained calling was almost menacing. Three punctures in the lemming's broken leg indicated that a bird of prey had had its talons wrapped around it before something had caused it to drop its prize upon the table of stone. The bird had not caught it cleanly and perhaps there had been competition for its meat. Andrew slowly unlaced his boot, all the while staring at its writhing body, fear and fascination branded across his face.

"I can hardly bear to look," gagged Gene. "It's disgusting."

Georg stood there motionlessly, staring at the spatchcocked corpse, while Gene stood with his legs apart staring with a look of accusation etched onto his face.

"I was putting it out of its misery," said Andrew quietly.

"What was wrong with it?"

"Broken leg, and, and a big gash down its body. I just used this," he held up his boot earnestly, "and then this," he demonstrated towards the lemming.

Its entire body had been opened and around it lay the various organs which had once functioned inside. The whole corpse must have lain only an inch from the ground, so flattened was it.

"This happened? You hit it and this happened?"

"Yes! It just sort of exploded. Look at me," Andrew pointed to his trousers and t-shirt. Blood had also splattered high up his right arm.

"Look," said Georg, holding up Andrew's other boot. Entrails hung from its sole's grip. He muttered something else in Norwegian.

"Disgusting, I know."

A thin buzz of flies had gathered around the baking body and were laying eggs in its flesh. Georg shot a look towards Andrew, and dropped the boot onto the rock.

"Come, we need to find water and clean you."

Despite Georg's fierce expression and Gene's disquiet, they, Andrew, and the hiking club spent the rest of the afternoon happily plodding around their circular route having found plentiful cool water to slake their parched mouths. By the time they had reached the cars again the heat of the day was on the wane and Gene and Georg were laughing heartily along with Andrew over a story he'd told. It was about a visitor to his offices, and it went like this:

"A big fat audit officer came to visit us for the day. He had one of those nail-scrubber moustaches pasted to his philtrum like a fridge magnet. Musta been about twenty stone, fat sod. He'd just given Seeta a roasting in the supply room, all sorts of shit about some hotshot who thought he'd been ripped off and who'd run to them—that's the thanks we get from these people for getting them a job. He, the auditor, had a vagina-shaped sweatmark on his back all day, I seem to remember.

"Anyway, he was hanging around at the back late on, writing his report up. Well, we've often had a problem with pigeons flying in through the vents—we're near the cathedral where there's loads of 'em—and suddenly three blokes in Amey jackets and baseball caps, all carrying bloody fishing nets, burst in chasing one! The auditor waddles out to check out the fuss, face like a slapped walrus, and these three blokes don't see him at all, they just come charging through, not only knocking him over but sending him tumbling down the back steps. We got a bad write up."

It was a bright, starry night in Bergen. Andrew was nearing the end of his stay. The children had been packed off up to bed and the three adults were sat in conversation, drinking red wine and listening to Hilma's vinyl collection. Blondie's Parallel Lines had just been set to spin.

"And Fredrik really couldn't carry on after the scramble, so we rested again; but we were still quite quick round the trail," Andrew was describing to Hilma, who was listening with attentiveness to their delineation of the day's events. The incident with the lemming had been omitted. "About eighteen miles in eight and a half hours?" he checked with Gene, who nodded and poured them all some more wine.

The two hikers turned happily somnolent, a hush descending as the thumping opening to Call Me crackled into the room. Then Hilma flicked her hair to one side, lay down her glass, and said,

"You know, I was listening to the radio earlier today. It was that woman Jorffdal, the one we've seen on tv? Yes, giving her opinions on education again. And she was comparing our system to yours in Britain, Andrew. Apparently she's coming to the university for a talk soon."

"Interested to hear what she thinks 'bout the mixed-age classrooms we have to have,' said Gene through a yawn.

"You have to? Why?" asked Andrew.

"Well, the population's so much sparser than that in Britain or elsewhere that there often aren't enough children to make up six or seven classes. They're thrown in together and the teacher has to cater for the mix of abilities and interests. It's an interesting difference."

"And one that I'm not sure would work in Britain, beyond the obvious reasons. I visited a few schools in Wimbledon as part of my teacher training, and the red tape…" Hilma elucidated the topic further until, reaching her real point and curious about what Gene had mentioned over the pillows about the fishmonger's, she asked, "Would you ever learn Norwegian properly, Andrew? In a classroom, I mean."

"Possibly," he replied hesitantly, "I mean, I'd definitely do it if there was cause to. Perhaps that'd be if I was to visit again, eh? I mean, I love the language, the sounds and the words I know."

"I learnt Norwegian alongside Finnish as a child," Hilma continued. "It's a nice feeling, that feeling of being at home in more than one tongue. Like you have twice the family, almost. It's a strange language, Finnish: very few are in its own family. You know, I feel very… old, when I speak it. Almost as though I was a cavewoman!"

Gene barked a laugh.

"It's pretty strange when you just become a part of a language," he said, leaning toward Andrew. "You never, ever think about it and then one day you're thrown into this world that would understand you but doesn't, can't. You have to stay afloat at first, before you can sail properly. Very odd…"

"But you both managed."

The hush descended again as Andrew began to think.

Then Hilma slowly rose and announced her bedtime. "I'll see you before you fly, Andrew. Sweet dreams."

"You know, I might follow suit," stretched Gene, "but feel free to stay up and watch the telly mate."

Andrew was about to fall into complicity with Gene's suggestion when, jogged unpleasantly by Hilma's reminder of his departure, he sprang up.

"Oh Gene, can't we stay up a little longer? You still haven't shown me your mysterious kabin. I can't leave without having seen it."

"Ah!" Gene berated himself hoarsely as he headed to the kitchen, "You're right! Hang on, let me grab another bottle and we'll wander up." His voice echoed down the hallway.

Andrew saw Gene and Hilma exchange a goodnight kiss next to the dragon's head at the foot of the stairs before she sleepily disappeared, her dress hems flowing behind her and ankles clicking softly. Then Gene walked unsteadily back through the hallway clutching his glass and a dust-covered bottle of Malbec.

"If you don't mind me being a little arrogant, you're in for a treat."

They shuffled out into the night, the stars' blazing aura lighting their way up the garden and beyond the hillock to the kabin. The shale crunched underfoot like grass under a hard frost; occasionally a piece of granite or some other reflective material caught the light from above and dazzled their eyes like they were, for a brief second, staring into the glare of the midday sun. There was a faint background noise of cars whispering in from the hills around; above this the calls of owls echoed not far from them, as well as the periodic trickle of water and the rustle of small mammals.

"The garden's even bigger than I thought," puffed Andrew as the path began to incline upwards, "And… oh… wow."

They were both out of breath by the time they had climbed the formidable rise on which the kabin stood. Andrew's mouth hung open. "This isn't merely a kabin, Gene."

Standing tall against the indigo sky the 'kabin' looked more like a home in itself. It was about ten metres square and was intersected by enormous horizontal tree trunks, except for the corner to their right which was made of glass integrated with the timber. In between the trunks little slats of back-boarded bamboo had been added as cladding, so that it seemed almost like a medieval armoured Japanese barracks. The kabin had been lifted by a series of legs to support it where the slope fell away and in the gap lay an ordered collection of sledges each with a rope on either side which, Gene explained as he fumbled in his back pocket, were used for wood storage in winter and could be slid out and under with ease. Inside the interior lay in darkness, yet unknown.

Gene creakily unlocked the door with a large mortice key. The smell of old libraries met the back of Andrew's throat with an inviting, beckoning finger of familiarity as he continued to catch breath. He lifted his feet over the threshold as if drawn inwards by the finger; a smell so steeped in time and wisdom and experience that he flared open his nostrils to better imbibe it. Floorboards creaked underfoot as he made his way blindly through the hallway in Gene's wake.

Gene opened a door leading to a large room. It was pitch black inside. He illuminated a thin strip in front of them by the light of his phone. Then he moved about, switching on lamps at either end to throw light on its contents.

A short, wide window would have offered a view onto the path leading up to the door were it not for a blind covering it. Two walls had been recessed so that they accommodated vast bookshelves.

Gene smiled at Andrew's astonished expression upon seeing this, for within them sat seemingly neverending rows of books; battered old covers mixed with glossy new, some thin as sticks, others wide and fat; the occasional volume laid on its side, too gigantic even for these capacious lodgings. At intervals there were features which broke up the lines and cast small shadows—a fruit bowl (empty), a small statue of a hunter with a stag slung across his shoulders, a pair of scales, a microscope, some crystals, an incense holder and a pack of incense, an old cowbell with a fur-upholstered stick...The items, too numerous to count, ran onto wheeled book racks and onto two more hand-made shelves. These shelves were sliced into vertical cross-sections of the trees they had been cut from, varnished, and bracketed to the wall.

The floor was made of a mixture of materials. Firstly, there was the bare floorboarded underlayer—the same as the hallway had been, Andrew assumed. The boards were long and thin and the extra effort had given the effect of making the room appear wider than it was. In the room's centre lay a square rug, deep in pile and woven in the Berber style. It was a stunning sight. In its centre was a golden box, a red and blue star ablaze inside. A blood-coloured square was wrapped around it, containing images of double-ended canes, each with antennae at their ends like those of magnified ants. A thick-lined, snow-white octagon framed this further, and as the rug spread outwards its Near-Eastern patterns and colours grew increasingly intricate and rich, its emeralds and ochres and cobalts lapping at each other.

As Andrew's gaze broke from this he turned and saw the floorboards give way to shining black and white marble, which rose in small grades to a fireplace with a large basket lying upon a simple trivet inside it.

Above floor level there were two pieces of seating: a large brown sofa with its back to one of the bookshelved walls, and a bucket seat. Glossy white on the outside, and matt crimson inside, the latter had the appearance of a pod from a spacecraft.

It was into this that Andrew slid. The stem leading to the legs was air-cushioned, and sighed lightly as he settled himself inside its clutch. Gene took a seat on the sofa so that they faced each other, the prismatic rug lying between them.

"So, this is the kabin—my sanctum, my place of rest and work, my illumination."

Andrew gazed around, still stunned. Only now as he swivelled in his chair did he notice a wall of maps which, like the books, seemed to span the ages.

"I don't know what to say.'

He had turned to face Gene again.

"That'll come, I'm sure. You know, I wasn't going to let you leave without seeing it; I was going to make my excuses to Hilma after I'd gone up with her, but you were too quick off the mark."

"Oh, I didn't…"

"I'm not telling you off! Haha. No, the opposite, complimenting you. Complimenting your memory and your forthrightness. You know," Gene continued heavily, "I can't believe you're leaving."

Gene placed down the two glasses he had brought, filled them with wine, and handed one to Andrew "Here's to friendship. Lost friendship, found friendship."

"Reignited."

"Reignited." There was a deep sound of satisfaction in Gene's response, then a brief pause. "Yes, that's how it feels. Like a flame I'd forgotten could live."

"I've got to thank you for today, Gene, and for the whole stay. It's been…"

Gene saw emotion well up in Andrew's face, and interjected, "Don't feel you have to say it. Maybe later, eh. Why don't we talk about the past? About the good times?"

"Yes, okay, later," agreed Andrew as he wiped at his eye. He quickly pulled his knees up to his chest within the comfortable chair. "I like to remember what we were like when we were young."

"Me too. I think about it more often than I'd like to admit."

"Those days by the Nidd, when I think about them now, they were the foundations of us, weren't they? I'm not saying life's perfect now, but that whole time… That whole life in Knaresborough, that unknown shelter before the growing up and the changes and the slow but unstoppable peeling back of your comforts until you're out there on your own, and you realise the voice in your head is still the same, it's still you. Forgive me, I think I'm rambling with the wine, but…"

"No," interrupted Gene again as he threw his arms up, "no you're not. It's as clear as day to me. I remember feeling that, remember feeling it in stages, where you've reached a level of grown-up but you're not quite there, and yet you know that there is a marked-out, uncrossable division between the old you and the new. It's like shedding skin, like a snake. Ah," he sniffed before taking a sip of the wine. Then he stopped. "We grew up too fast, didn't we."

"You had your back to the road behind, so to speak—You made it out early, old friend—childhood and Britain. I... I had my own issues."

Andrew stopped, sensing with a prickle of dread that he was at the precipice, beneath which the memories of Birmingham had been arranged bleak and menacing, waiting to be crashed into, finally and head-first. Despite its inevitability he feared that the undressing of the whole sorry scene would come now, too early, too early, though it had to come soon.

"Now Gene, what I've always, always wanted to know is how you managed to get over here. Did you save up the money? Or did your father pay?"

Gene's mouth widened into a broad grin; he appeared unruffled, as though he hadn't noticed Andrew's trepid tone. "I thought you'd ask," he said with a quiet mystery about the words, "and I'm not sure you'll believe me. I sailed here. By myself."

His simple tone wrongfooted Andrew, who could only gasp "Right."

"Yes," Gene continued to grin, "that was how I did it. I'd come back up North and was utterly penniless, but I'd had this plan the whole way. I found myself in Brid, eventually, and had found a boat in the harbour; and—I'm not proud of this, by the way—one night I stole it."

"Stole it!" exclaimed Andrew, "how?"

Gene clicked and rolled his eyes with childlike pleasure. "Well, I'd just had a bit of experience shall we say."

"And you sailed here?"

"Look, maybe this will explain better." Gene had pushed himself off the sofa and was now perusing a section of the bookshelves. "Where's it gone?"

He spent the next few minutes flicking through the rows of books as Andrew watched on asking questions all the time until with an "Aha!' he picked a slim tatty-looking pad from between two larger volumes. "This is my log. It documents nearly the whole journey."

He tossed it to Andrew and it fell in his lap. He opened the yellowed pages gently, ever so slightly scared they would break off and crumble despite knowing that they were barely fourteen years old.

He stopped at a random entry and read.

18.08.10

Have sailed for over a week now. Still haven't been able to pick up a radio signal and I think it's best to leave it and instead work on the condenser. The compass though is working fine and there's a definite nip to the air, hopefully means that I'm working my way north.

The entries continued in their short style. Some were too water-damaged to be legible.

.10

Un   *not sure when*   *st*   *Managed to bail most of it out. Why am I*
writing   *log? I can't face goi*   *there, need rest. Just for a minute.*

"So you made it? Across the entire North Sea. You. And a boat." Gene nodded. "I'm staggered."

"Not as much as me! I was nearly dead by the time I'd landed at Kristiansand! How fucking stupid was that?" Gene laughed loudly. "Ridiculous! Hotwire a boat and sail the North Sea with no prior experience, you'd think I was suicidal."

Andrew smiled open-mouthed at Gene's flippancy. "No, looking back I was a lucky fucker, seriously lucky. I'd never take a chance like that again… but I suppose that's the beauty of it, youth. If I wasn't seventeen once upon a time, I wouldn't be where I am now. You'll do anything, you have no brakes, everything seems possible."

"Yes, no fear—not for you apparently! So, in a manner of speaking, it was youth that brought you here? Yes, it makes sense. But I think there were limits also, weren't there? Limits that the gaps in your knowledge fed. Limits imposed by the absolute way in which you think. I do sometimes wish I could pick up my past self and shake him, shake him about decisions, about the petty and false ideas I had, about the things I got so wrong! You look at how far you've come, and it's hard not to want to disown that person, that you."

"But I think we can be harsh on ourselves through the lens of hindsight. We do have that narrative voice swimming in our heads, the one that never changes through your ages, the one that's always been you, like you said… In fact, I've been reminded of something. Maybe this will cheer you up. Julian Barnes puts it better than I ever could.'

Andrew was nearly overheating from the words that would not leave his mouth.

Gene arose and rifled through a neat section of books nearest the microscope, which Andrew, as he choked back what he'd been about to say, could see from the titles was reserved for fiction. His neck was dripping.

"Here."

The novel Gene had produced had a preternatural colouring to its closed pages along their edges, as though they had been sprinkled with coal dust and gilded with gold. "Give me a minute… Right. The character's called Tony Webster, and he's been reflecting on a friend of his, who ends up dying. Ahem."

"I'd been examining my younger self, as far as it's possible to do so.
Of course I'd been crass and naive – we all are; but I knew not to
exaggerate these characteristics, because that's just a way of
praising yourself for what you have become."

They both meditated on these words for a moment as one of the lamps in the room gave a faint flicker.

"Of course, he's right, Julian whoever," conceded Andrew, having taken it in and wiped his neck with his sleeve. "We're bound by fate to be our own cheerleaders. I suppose if that bond breaks then that's the boundary drawn-out between life and suicide."

"Yes, yes; I couldn't have put it better." Gene hung his lip on his glass in thought as he took his seat.

"What's troubling you?"

"I've wondered,' he replied with a start, as though he'd been mesmerised, "just what it was that spurred you to find me, Andrew? I'm just... interested."

Andrew measured up the question. The answer came slowly. "Well, you see that's an interesting one. It was a re-enactment of youth, I suppose. I had an epiphany, put it that way."

"An epiphany? What does that mean exactly? Come on, Andrew, I'm interested, I told you."

"Well," he repeated, a little uncomfortably, "I've wanted to talk to you about the ways we used to alter our minds. You see, after those experiences we had together, after we lost contact... You escaped the cycle rather sooner than me, I'd guess. Yes," he continued, noticing the search for explanation in Gene's eyes, "the drugs. I lived a fairly reckless lifestyle in my early twenties. It kept a hold on me, Gene."

"It did? I had no idea; I assumed you just slipped into recruitment. I suppose the time after Birmingham is a grey area for us both, another gap in our knowledge. You see, they never stop. Well, you're right, I did escape—I quit it after those few times. I got pretty disillusioned early on. But you carried on? I feel like that's the detritus from our use together, like I..."

"Oh don't be ridiculous, Gene, I had no one to blame but myself for my abuse. I got in with the wrong crowd, you know how it goes. That's a case where I can make a fair judgment on my younger self, with hindsight. But abuse—it's an interesting word we use for it, isn't it?"

"It's the right one."

"Okay, so we're coming round to what I was getting at. The outcome can only ever be bad?"

"The outcome can only ever be bad if you fool yourself into thinking what you're feeling is truly real. I can remember the places we took those drugs and we felt that ecstasy, I remember them well. Your... your world is perfectly ordered then. I haven't forgotten a gram of that experience. There are... certain truths; yes, inalienable truths which you wouldn't possess without having seized that experience—is that what you meant? But it all depends on what you want to believe.

"We're talking about life now. You can choose to believe that our paths are mapped out in the stars and that our ancestors are up there in the ether, watching over us. You can choose to think that your actions are really of no consequence to life here—in essence, that you are a fatalist. I was never a fatalist, Andrew; I took on what I needed to and changed my course.

"On a footing to fatalism is the decision to believe that what you think, and feel, and taste, and touch, and smell while you are on drugs is real: that it is you connecting with a higher truth.

"And for a time that might be true: I felt once, maybe twice, that this was it, this was my path. This was Inner Peace. But there you uncover the sham of it all—that your peace is derived from waging war on your mind and body."

"I felt the Inner Peace too," said Andrew, "and I knew enough people who thought that the MDMA was the only path. I was with them for a while, and not just MD, any altered state— 'Altering your mind is the only way to inner peace'—it's a sound enough concept with everything considered."

"Everything being?"

"This world, the horrors and disappointments within."

"Which ignores the wonders and the beauty quite neatly."

"My point exactly. That's why I had to break out of it eventually. And the inner peace? What happened to yours—the imagined one?"

"I swapped it for something real." Gene looked at the Berber rug with a far-away expression. "I suppose, old friend, that eventually all rivers must change their course."

Both men let the words settle. There wasn't another sound that penetrated the room. Andrew felt easier now.

"Your answer to my original question, then, was a no," Andrew smiled. "You've put into words what I never could, a reflection on your library, I might add. So there are certain advantages to be had. Does that answer your question about why I got in touch?"

"I'm seeing where you're going. An epiphany indeed. How did it feel?"

"Hmm, you never really forget it. When it hits again its like it's never been gone, it grips you in just the same way. You have to understand that it was a complete indiscretion, the first time I'd done it since I escaped the bad life in Leeds that I'd been living. But I can't say that it was a bad or wrong thing to do. The high has wonderful qualities; it focused my thoughts and feelings on the life I'd swapped it for, made me realise there were things still left for me to do."

"I'm glad to know the reminder was timely. From all I've heard from you, it sounds like a getaway to an old friend's was what you needed."

"I'd been in a rut, spiritual and social. But let me change the topic again. You know, I hope we haven't vitiated our youth completely. Those experiences were one of those stages I mentioned, weren't they, a piece in the ever-changing puzzles of us, if I can speak for us both?"

"And things did change…"

Gene only realised that his words had had an unexpected effect on the man sat opposite him when he noticed Andrew's chair tilt perilously backwards. He sat up and called him. He could see his friend go grey in the face, all colouration fading to a deathly pallor, and watched as he struggled to replace his wine glass on the small chest of drawers next to him as though the glass was suddenly made of lead.

"All things were leading to this." There was an unknown grimness in Andrew's deep voice.

"Andrew, you don't look good. I didn't mean, maybe I started too strong, we don't have to…"

"I have to explain, Gene." He looked as if in a trance. "Just let me."

"Take your time, then."

Andrew sat there unable to look his friend in the eye, speaking with a voice that was shaking like a cornered animal.

"All I can give you is my memory which is doubtless distorted and mangled like the mind it's sitting in, and hope you can fill in the rest."

"Just take your time.'

"I'd better go from the start. Right from the start, in fact. Aiy. Do you remember that autumn that we first met? I'm surprised. We'd been by the Nidd, remember? That first playing-out of the year after dark. We found a nest of tadpoles. Yeah. And mine died, but you raised one, one survivor, didn't you? On a diet of boiled-up cabbage. I envied your achievement. When I came round I saw that it was going through its transformation, growing its legs and its lungs. It was, now I think of it, going through one of its own many stages; it was probably at the same stage as us. We were really just growing legs and lungs in the grand scheme of things. Still so much to come. Ah, now you remember. I couldn't stand the thought of you having that thing, just owning it and keeping it. It was mad, childish jealousy."

"Wait Andrew. Are you comparing your jealousy of a tadpole to jealousy of her—Jo?'

Andrew shuddered when he heard that name, like an entire knot of tadpoles were wriggling inside his spine. His voice broke as he answered,

"No, no. I just think… that was what I had in me then. It came from the same despicable place. It was a hail of hate, of sickness, when it happened. I was ill."

He took a moment to compose himself. Gene had crossed his legs now and was listening intently with a deep frown upon his brow. "Besides, ahem, I'm not in any way suggesting that we own women like we own animals, Gene. I hope you understand that."

"Oh yes; well, I do now."

Gene's placid voice suddenly snapped into a snarl: "You should have faced the consequences of your actions."

"I know!' Andrew cried, "I know I should but I ran, I ran too, just like you'd done."

"Don't make another off-key comparison! It was nothing like my running! You defiled a woman and stripped her of her humanity—that's actually what you did. I was too busy trying to find and kill you. Now are you going to admit what you did?"

"Gene? I…"

"Did it happen?!" he roared. "Did you rape her?"

"Yes! It happened. Oh…" Andrew began to sob uncontrollably. "I hate myself, I really do, I hate myself forever. Please forgive me, Gene! I needed to tell you, I needed you to know. I had to end it, end the lie! I have to have your forgiveness!" He continued to moan quietly in the chair.

"You have to."

Gene sat there and smiled a troubled smile. He took a moment and tried to calm himself. His voice still shook. "I don't know what to do. I finished with my anger for you a long time ago Andrew. I've ended my spite. But I don't know what to do."

Then, after a pause of minutes the length of which neither man could count, it came.

"I know that my forgiveness is here for you. If it wasn't then you would never have made the trip." It came simply. Gene nodded to himself and knew it was right, it was right to let the past go forever.

Andrew's tear-streaked face looked up with the thankfulness of a child, the mercy only a child could feel, and he murmured, "You've saved me. That's the lifting of the knife, my life given back. You know if I was in your position, Gene, I'm not sure I'd have the same compassion."

"You wouldn't? Look at it this way, Cos, you've had the balls to find me, the grace to be a pleasure to me, my family, and my friends, and finally and probably above all, you've shown your real and lasting remorse. You say you hate yourself; we say that life comes in stages, that we alter, and I can't hold on to the past any longer, I can't deny my friend. Come here mate."

He rose from his seat, laid down his glass and pulled Andrew up, overjoyed to have him in front of him again as if rewound to that threadbare room in Cardigan Road in Bridlington. The confession had erased the darkness. He hadn't even registered that he'd slipped into the old form of address.

They embraced tightly, then with their arms slung across each other's shoulders Gene walked Andrew over to a cabinet in the far-corner of the room.

"I still have this. I wonder if you remember giving it to me."

He slid a drawer open and rummaged around in what looked like a collection of scrolls, his shiny, slightly worn hands searching nimbly through. He pulled out an old wallet which had a pattern on it that was at the same time new but strangely familiar to him. As he raised it into the light Andrew, thrilled by nostalgia, recognised that it had once belonged to him.

"My old wallet! But how?"

"It was the one I went to buy beer with! Here, it's yours."

He passed it to Andrew who excitedly flipped it open and revealed two pouches just as they had been, one with a Lloyds TSB bank card in it, expiry date 06/11, and the other filled with a King James's sixth form I.D card, and then he looked to the right and saw his slim, handsome seventeen-year-old face staring back at him from the surface of a green provisional driver's licence. "Blow me away."

He popped it into his jacket pocket and patted it. "But what are these?" he pointed to the scrolls.

"Some are letters and memories from my dad, anything he wrote to me and that I kept. These on the left are the things he wrote down in hospital before his death." Gene was matter-of-fact, but still he could not hide his longing, sombre expression.

"I had no idea he wasn't with us anymore. I'm sorry. You grew quite close?"

Gene sighed. "Very. But I won't go into it. It's nice to have these memories. You know best that I might never have had them. Hey," he breathed, his tired face lighting up, "why not come and see what else is in the kabin?"

He led them through the door and along the corridor into the room with the glass window at its corner which they had seen from the outside.

"This is where I look at the stars."

A huge telescope took central position in the room, pointing outwards at a forty-five degree angle. With a flick of the light switch a third giant pane of glass was revealed which occupied the ceiling, completing Gene's astronomical observatory. A fridge, worktop, sink, and kettle hugged one of the walls. On the linoleum was the outline of a hatch with a ring to pull it up – a secondary fire escape. "Now we'd better have dark."

The light was switched off, and the coruscating stars overhead showed their flux once more. And now Andrew felt a strange conviction which he kept secret, a conviction that somewhere up there, in the swirling masses of gas and flame, John Gandah was watching over him and thinking "That's my boy", or some other paternal remark; and though he was inclined to think that this idea was nonsense, it was that type of conviction which, despite the attempt of logic to wipe it away, remained strong and upright, like they can in our thoughts. He smiled gently.

"I only take an amateur interest," said Gene. He was sitting at the telescope. "But I've learnt how to set it up. Ah, there."

He removed his eye from the lens and gestured for Andrew to look into it. "You can literally see the worlds apart."

After a few minutes of Andrew fiddling with some of the knobs and Gene teaching him how to swing the device around and refocus, Gene continued: "You know, I never wholly felt at peace in that town of ours, even before it all came out about my dad. Even when I was young I felt I would make sense of myself in some other place, some other environment."

"Do you mean you were always running, even before you knew it?" responded Andrew, eye still fixed to the viewing lens.

"That's a neat way of putting it...and yes I suppose. But, Cos, you were born a runner too, don't forget."

"Now that I think is where we depart. I became a runner, remember? I had to catch up with you. As you fled Knaresborough so I fled Birmingham." He had taken his eye from the lens now and was looking at Gene, who stood in the small kitchen. "And now, it seems almost uncontrollably to me, I'm assuming the role once more, the role of fledgling - the same kind of flight from safety that you made that time, the breathless plunge into uncharted waters. Gene, I don't want the old life I've crafted for myself. I want this, I want Norway."

Gene knocked on the worktop twice with his knuckle, then softly folded his arms. "I think I knew that. Go on, ask."

"It's a huge favour to ask and one I don't expect you to do. But Gene, if I left work a message tomorrow saying I won't be coming back, would I be able to stay here?"

A curled, almost condescending smile lit on Gene's face. "Andrew, if that's what you need then sever the ties. You can call this your home from now on. "

They returned to the room with the rug and the bucket chair and chatted excitedly about breaking the news to the family. Then with the night wearing on into the early hours they lit a fire in the stove above the magnificent marble hearth and explored Gene's collection, Andrew handling every item with the vigour and the vitality of the reborn soul he had become. Intoxicated by his giddiness and by the extra wine which Gene had run off to get, he declared from his seat, "I could remain here forever, in this kabin."

Chapter Eight

To the Sea

The following morning Hilma and the children heard the news. Henrik clambered over the table to give an overwhelmed and somewhat teary Andrew a hug, swinging round his neck like a heavy, blond-headed pendulum. Hilma swept over and, embracing them both, said that the entire house had been made the richer and that a special roast was going to be made tonight to mark the news.

Gene clapped his friend on the back again, delighted and secretly a little relieved that there had been such a good reception from his wife. Hilma had never been a matriarch, it was true, but the household was one of an equal partnership and Gene had known that the act of taking on a lodger indefinitely had posed a risk to the relationship's fine balance. He had been up since dawn plotting speeches and coercions.

Before the roast took place Gene and Andrew caught a bus into town and met Georg at a small tavern away from the exposed harbour area and from the garishness of the nearby Rick's complex.

It was another clear day. The two Norwegians were wearing wraparound sunglasses and dark-green t-shirts as though they had deliberately co-ordinated. Andrew hadn't thought to pack sunglasses and had opted for blue jeans and a plain white t-shirt, a little baggy from the weight he had lost in recent months.

The sidestreet in which the tavern was situated reminded Andrew of the lane they had taken to reach the Schøtstuene: cobbled, with irregular and sharply-angled stretches of timber reaching from the ground to the roofs for support. It was pervaded by a feeling of homeliness; it milled with people strolling in between its bars and other attractions—souvenir shops, off-licences, music shops, craft stalls and food stalls, the latter of which kicked out a series of wonderful, mouth-watering smells as varied as lemongrass from the Thai stall to meaty crackling from the spitroast. A soft wind was blowing through the crowd and it sent steam and smoke towards the sea.

The chairs in which they sat were low. They gathered around an old halved barrel at the side of the tavern's barriered streetside annex. Behind Andrew and Georg, Gene could hardly see the commotion on the street because of several thatch palms standing tall in their terracotta pots.

Having been inside to order three beers, Andrew took his seat and looked through his shades at Gene. *I'm between stages again,* he thought, *I'm out in the world and this doesn't feel real.* The street with its steam and smoke felt like a mirage.

A young thin waiter slipped the half-litre glasses of lager, which bore the golden hop 'Hansa' logo, onto their mats and then whisked back away into the busy tavern.

"So, it wasn't just a short affair, how do you call it, a fling with Norway!" Georg chuckled to the table, then lowered his voice. "I love it, Gene, when our national pride is justified by this kind of thing. So Andrew, tell me, we need a toast. First, we call skål! Then, how about to new beginnings?"

The other two raised their glasses in agreement and repeated Georg's toasts. Andrew drained half the glass and placed it back down giddily. The gas came back up in one tremendous belch and the crackliness of the lager twisted his face around, making the two Norwegians snort. "Well, if there's any time for indulgence, it's now eh," he burped.

"I couldn't agree more," said Gene wiping his mouth, "and you Georg? I trust there's none of your work to tidy up before tomorrow?"

"There is, but it can wait. I prefer beer - and indulgence," he clucked stroking his neck, which seemed to have gained an unnatural amount of stubble since yesterday.

"What do you do for work, Georg?" asked Andrew, also wiping his mouth.

"Oh, my job? It's very dull. I work for Norwegian government, watching some departments for tax."

"It's important then?"

"You could say so, but like I said it's very dull, though it is a lot of responsibility. I like that."

He slipped back into his playful tone. "Hey, now you're staying, are you thinking about what you will do? Where you will work, live?"

"Oof," he blew, "I'm not sure about that yet, but I'm glad—happy—that you asked. I do need to think about that, I suppose…"

Gene listened with increased interest as Andrew gazed off at the rooftops. "I suppose what I'd really like is some time off, just like I've been having, and to do my own thing. Don't worry, Gene, I know you've got things to run and you need to get back in the thick of it. Maybe I'll travel around a bit, see Norway."

"Well I've always said, if you wanna see Norway, get a car," opined Gene. "The public transport's great, granted, but if you're driving around you can stop off anywhere; it's always those little tucked-away points which are the best to admire the view from."

"Then maybe that's what I'll do, I'll get a car. I've got some money saved, I'm sure I can find something."

"And what about that house of yours? Did you say it was worth something?"

"Oh, it's worth a good amount alright. Mortgage is a bugger—I can ditch my mortgage! Yes, when you're out tomorrow I'll make some calls, put it out on the market. This beer *is* good," he finished, wiping his mouth once more.

"I can't remember if you always drank like a fish or if that's something new."

"Something new."

"Drink like a fish!" grinned Georg, "A good English saying."

"We'll be calling another skål in a minute."

Promptly enough the thin lively waiter had just returned, having seen that the patrons' glasses were running low and sensed with his waiter's intuition that the three of them were sat down to a real session. Andrew's slightly wobbly eyes noticed the waiter's red waistcoat and its brass buttons as he placed down three fresh beers, then worked their way up to the waiter's face. He was dark-haired, with a narrow, boyish head, the forehead home to sparse freckles and the rest of the face similarly marked. Perhaps Andrew had been staring too long or perhaps the waiter had sensed that the special occasion centred around the man in the white t-shirt with waxed, sandy hair, for he quickly met Andrew's gaze and smiled politely. Then he saw the man in front of him give a flicker of something, some unreadable but strongly-present emotion, and he paused for a fraction of a second with his tray under his arm. Then he recalled the million and one jobs he was juggling in his head and he whisked back into the bar once more.

Andrew's eyes turned back to the table, insisting that the start he had just experienced was nothing more than the dazed feeling from the beer he had just gulped down. But then there had been something in that face, a flash of uninvited familiarity…

"You know you're welcome for as long as you need though, Andrew…. Andrew?"

He had been absent as Gene and Georg had been joking about house prices in Bergen.

"What? Oh, yes, thanks mate. It really means a lot."

"The beer's gone in his head, eh," clucked Georg loudly, while really he too was reeling from the alcohol.

They called another skål, and Gene continued. "You know with all that time off you could work that kabin over, see if you can find any treasures. You said yourself that you could live there."

"I did," Andrew laughed, "and that's a great idea. Though I might still sleep where I am, despite how comfortable that rug of yours looks."

"And how do you feel about learning Norwegian?" asked Georg, curious as Hilma had been.

"I want to do it is the short answer. I've got some basics, but probably not enough to get by on, and all self-taught. I hate to think of what the accent's like."

"Knaresborough-Danish, with a bit of Sheffield thrown in," mocked Gene.

"There you go. I'll put that on my growing list for tomorrow, ring around some language schools and get enrolled," Andrew mimed onto an imaginary pad.

The beers were being drained with all the vivacity of the first.

"When will you like to work again, Andy—never?"

"Oh no, Gay," Andrew mirrored, "I can't do that."

Gene thunked his glass back on the table. "Well, when the time's right I can see what I can do at Maersk, maybe manufacture you a little position if the skills are there," he smiled.

"I can't take any more kindness, please."

"Then perhaps a little pain, Andy. Gene and I have a little trip to Oslo planned next Saturday - just business - but we go out on the night, so that's fun. Maybe if you have a car you'll want to get some practice at driving on the wrong side of the road?"

"Ooh yes, a chauffeur," purred Gene.

"Of course, sounds a riot. I'll see to it that I'm on the road before then."

"And you'll be able to check out Oslo, the big smoke, while we're attending to business."

'Then it's decided."

The roast that evening was nothing short of splendid. The two drunk friends came home on the bus to a feast laid specially upon the larger living room table, which had been wheeled out into the centre of the vast floor. It was bedecked with the tastiest trimmings, from roast parsnip and goose-fat potatoes to different cabbages and leaves mixed with pine-nuts, and in its centre sat two giant racks of lamb sprigged with rosemary and thyme. They thanked the tired-looking but still sparkling Hilma for her efforts as the children lay waste to their plates of food, a show of appreciation the men soon followed.

Later they were washing up in the brightly-lit kitchen. Gene had gone to the toilet, which he had been doing regularly all day, and Hilma wandered in to sit and read at the table in some company. Today she was wearing a black, woven shoulder-cardigan and underneath a darkish purple top. On her bottom half was a pair of black leggings, and on her feet some flip-flops.

Andrew put down his teatowel carefully.

"Hi," he began in a high voice, "thanks again for the tea."

"Oh," she replied dismissively, "it was nothing. Besides, I love to cook."

"I just wanted to ask if everything really is okay with me staying? It's just that I understand it's a lot to ask; and don't worry, I will pull my weight, I assure you. You have your family here, the kids especially, and it seems unfair on them and you for…"

"Listen now, you're being silly. Of course it's fine for you to stay."

"Honestly?"

She rose. "We've all really enjoyed your company, and to be honest—and don't say I mentioned anything," she confided, "but I think you have really done something good to Gene. He was okay before you came but maybe a little *down*, and I think you've turned things around for him."

"That's…. I'm touched." He put a hand on her shoulder. "So things are fine?"

Hilma touched his hand gently. She smiled and looked down at him with her radiant eyes. "Yes, they are."

She took her seat and resumed flicking through her magazine.

Andrew let himself into the family's empty house the next day and by noon he had arranged for three different estate agents to borrow the spare key from his neighbour Harry Delks—who sounded as perturbed as he ever had done in expressing a measured 'Ohh' at the news of his permanent departure—in order to value his house for market. He expected a decent increase on the £170,000 he had spent on it, but he could only imagine how that increase would be swallowed up over here with something as simple as the beers the afternoon before costing close to £350. The offer of a paid position in Gene's department was looking an attractive proposal for the not-too-distant future.

But first, things for himself. He had informally enrolled at a private language school right in the heart of Bergen, and was meeting the director tomorrow to complete the process. He had also browsed some second-hand motors after baulking at the price of new, and bookmarked some pages so that Gene could contact the owners when he returned from work.

An hour or so after making himself a lunch of ham sandwiches he rubbed his stomach and turned his mind to exercise. He stared at his bright blue eyes in the mirror, smoothed his still-slim face, and then lifted up his shirt. He could feel the excesses of the last two days sitting uncomfortably in there, swilling around in his bloated midriff; so he donned his running outfit, hoping that the pain he had managed to expel from his left ankle was not lurking to make an unwanted return, and jogged to the fjordside at Bønes. It was not just the fear of putting weight back on which concerned him, it was what he would look and feel like if his pityriasis was to resurface again from all the boozy and mental toxins of inactivity.

The next day his house was on the market with one agency at £230,000 and he had been to see two different cars, the latter of which he purchased. It was a small, black, 15-plate Yaris with a dented wing and 30,000 miles. It sat near his cabin to the side of the *Gunnera Manicata* and it made him smile every time he peered out of his curtains, whenever he took a moment from Wiggins's *Needs, Values, Truth* - borrowed from the kabin's vast library. He was yet to insure the car and wanted to leave the logbook and policy to Gene or Hilma, whose Norwegian he would need.

Because he was still short of being on the road he hopped on the bus again to make his meeting at the *Bergen Språkskole* with the Director of Studies, who was only too happy to enrol him fully at the school for the following Monday. He took another wander around Bergen. He felt utterly at peace for the first time in a long time. He headed home.

"Tuesday's the night that Agnethe and Henrik go to Hilma's parents, so we usually go out and do something in town," explained Gene after he had suggested going to the cinema. They were in the living room, looking at the furs and other items which hung from the joists as Harald, Hilma's rheumatic but smiling father, was upstairs drawing with the children.

"What's on?"

"Oh, I've no idea," coughed Gene. "But there'll be something interesting. And it's always lovely to get out in Bergen at night."

And so with the children gone the three of them dressed up, Gene in a blue-striped Ralph Lauren shirt, whalebone cufflinks, a pair of dark, slim-fitting jeans, and dark brown loafers, Andrew in a black shirt with pearly white buttons, blue chinos, and plain black shoes, and Hilma in a magnificent white maxi-dress which had the brown print of a single lily running up its folds, silver and wooden jewellery adorning her neck and wrists, sandals her feet, and her hair pinned upwards with a few tendrils falling about her neck.

She drove them down the slopes of Fyllingsdalen and on into town, parking away from the harbourfront. The film they had gone to see was a re-screening of an old Mexican film called *Y Tu Mama Tambien*, at a cinema named *Bedehus*. In it two Mexican boys competed for the love of a Spanish woman called Luisa, and promised her the idyll of a beach named *Boca del Cielo*, which Andrew translated for himself with his little Spanish as 'Heaven's Mouth'. He could not understand any of the dialogue because of the Spanish audio and Norwegian subtitles, but he understood all the same that Luisa was leaving an imprint of herself on the worlds of the two boys, and that at the same time she was really helpless in making her decisions when she knew she would eventually die.

They came out of the film sombrely and took a seat in a nearby bar. They ordered coffee instead of alcohol. Hilma was especially impressed at how deep Andrew's understanding of Luisa seemed to be as he meticulously described the film he'd just seen. And as she sipped at her latte slowly she wondered at how he had never found a partner in this world.

After they got in Gene went through the Yaris' logbook. Then the pair sat down together and insured the car at 5,000k.

As the weary married couple ascended the stairs to bed with the clock chiming eleven, the husband enquired about what Andrew would do the next day.

"Oh, with the car sorted and ready to go now I think I'll take it for a spin. Where do you think I should go, any recommendations?"

"Erm," he yawned, "you mentioned the sea and the fjords… see if you can find Herdla. It's gorgeous."

"Beautiful," agreed Hilma.

"Goodnight."

He took it slowly on the drive north to Herdla on the island of Askøy; he wasn't used to left-hand drive and often came close to opening the car's door when he meant to change gear, setting his heart racing each time he did.

When he got there he took a stroll along a beach towards the end of the island, a little away from the village. The whipping wind chilled him as he trod along the rough white sand. He looked north over the water to a small island in the distance. Some rocky skerries littered the foreground, causing the waves to fizz as they buffeted into them.

He breathed in the sea air and could taste the pureness and the northern chill which clung on despite summer's onset. To his left rose a tall cliff at a sharp angle with a path running to its rocky top. At the cliff's bottom lay a series of razor-sharp rocks, some with the shattered remains of lobster pots strewn across their backs. The cliff's looming face appeared grey even on this bright day; and indeed beyond it there appeared to be a weather front coming in, some ten miles out to sea, broodingly emphasising the strange grimness of the craggy rock.

Up a little track which ran opposite the small, homely harbour in the village he found a church. It was painted a brilliant, beautiful white and its steeple was slated in grey so that it looked like a long, tall hat overlooking the island's inhabitants.

Andrew tried the door but it was locked. He stepped back down the gravel drive to look at the east façade and saw that three dates had been mounted in steel along its painted stone: 1863, 1935, 1950. What life stages had that place known? The people it had seen, the ages it had watched? And he imagined that its character had never once changed, not once among the years hanging in front of him. Here, he knew, there was a constant—an unfickle heart amongst the flux of humankind.

The weather did indeed take a turn for the worst for the remainder of the week, and an unseasonal low sat deeply over the west of Norway. Not that Andrew's buoyancy could be fettered; he had already gained two bidders for the house (both under valuation, but expected to be pushing upwards) and was enjoying the anticipation of the Oslo trip, not to mention the delights of Gene's collections in the kabin. Buoyant, that was, until he unearthed Gene's sea log again.

He had just experienced another uncomfortable meeting with Hilma, with whom there had been an awkward few days, neither really knowing what to say to each other when they were alone. But for Andrew it was not just this, not merely a lack of communication, which felt odd. He felt a difficult flutteriness around her, like the shyness of a timid teen around a friend's parents. He had taken to stealing uneasy glances at her like a child doing wrong, and had convinced himself that she took the occasional reciprocal glance when he wasn't looking, for a reason opaque to him. He tried not to let it trouble him and indeed he forgot about it completely whenever the whole family were together. He was, in any case, more focused on his projects: His car, his house, his reading and wandering.

In the kabin now in order to steer clear of her, he had raised the blind of the window which overlooked the path and permitted the day's grey, wet light. He lay backwards on the library's sofa, wriggling to get comfy. In his hand he held the log. Its front had, he could see, been quite attractive once; its green cover was made of a thick pleasant paper and in its middle a title box bore the water-stained words 'Northern Soul Incident Book'. He opened the book at a random, undamaged page and travelled backwards in time.

13.08.10

The sea's placid for the minute so I've got time to write.

Here I am, sitting on Northern Soul's deck and soaking in the sun and I can't enjoy or stand a second of it. I know that my mind should be on the journey ahead, on finding my dad finally, but this hate and this anger are just coursing through me and it's impossible to enjoy anything. I'll welcome a storm. I'll probably read this back in, well, whenever and cringe, but right now all I can do is write in this book and shout to the open ocean, so it'll have to do.

I suppose what I'm most furious with is myself, that I could be such a bad judge of character. Andrew – I won't do him the friendship of calling him Cos any more – that short-arsed, shit-eating cunt, I want to have him on the floor where he belongs and to be smashing his face in, the coward.

I should have fucking known there was something up with him when he moved us to Jo's out of nowhere, but I missed that one. I also missed the fact that he probably arranged for her to come back when he went to get the keys from the takeaway, and all he had to do was get rid of me on a booze run. STUPID STUPID STUPID. If we ever meet again, one day distant from now, I'll make sure that I ruin his pathetic worthless life. He won't have a thing left in the world which he loves. I'm making this promise to myself.

He closed the book, dropped it to the floorboards, and stared at the stove above the marble hearth. *He won't have a thing left in the world which he loves.* Is that so, Gene? Not a thing? There's plenty I love now, you bastard.

But, turning over the words in his head, he reasoned that Gene had had every right to make that entry, every right to have shown that vitriol, and yet there was something in the phrasing, something visceral that cut a nerve of his in those final sentences. He remembered Gene's description of the items in his kabin. *Treasures,* they were to him.

He went to make a cup of tea in the astronomy room kitchen. Then he found some matches near the stove and burnt the treasured book outside.

The morning of the drive to Oslo had come. It would take six hours and with Gene and Georg's meetings scheduled to begin at one o'clock it made for an early start. Andrew, however, was up and about and delighted to be taking in a whole swath of Norway on the drive east such that it was he who was chivvying Gene out of the door and into the car, paternally checking that he had everything he'd need.

He was tapping at the wheel as they pulled into Georg's drive, which was overlooked by a vast house in quite a different style to Gene's. Everything about the exterior of Georg's home was flash and new, unlike the traditional theme of the Bradleys'. Shop-fresh white PVC framed each window, and sharply-defined black marble plantpots led in ascending rows up to the keycoded glass front door. A freshly-shaven Georg emerged after a couple of minutes with a small suitcase and a packed laptop bag and briefcase, and then they were away across the Rv40.

He dropped them off at two central locations and then parked up. Left to his own devices he wandered around the streets of the capital and took a tram up to the Ulleval Stadium and the adjoining Football Museum, which he found closed. He couldn't tell exactly why he had chosen a football stadium to visit of all things in Oslo, though he knew somewhere that a small part of him missed the Saturday afternoon devotion in Hillsborough and the pubgoing relaxation of it all.

He circumambulated the ground, seeing nothing noteworthy but feeling something stir inside, something of the old him. Afterwards he headed back into town to enjoy the Munch Museum; and after that he watched the people traversing the Jernbanetorget and wound down the hours until Georg's and Gene's appearances as he sat drinking coffee and reading a British newspaper.

He met them in the lobby of the Radisson hotel, not far from the Jernbanetorget, at around five. Both seemed in high spirits from their day's work and after showering appeared eager to go out into the Oslo night.

"We should drink heavy, boys," Georg clucked as he appeared in a white dressing gown at the door; "Not so often to be away from the family hey?"

Gene ordered up three daquiris to show his share in the enthusiasm, yet even with the strong sweet flavour of good sugar cane in his mouth Andrew couldn't muster much excitement. He showered himself in order to re-energise; really he was keen to keep up the good impression, really he was just feeling a bout of homesickness and deep down he couldn't waste his first night in Oslo in a fit of introspection. He called for another three daquiris before choosing a shirt and sitting down to his hair, a long process which far from proving a nuisance to the other two actually provoked their own vanity, Georg testing out different colognes and Gene spit-shining his shoes, as well as an open conversation about their dressing habits; the kind of conversation which gives men such unaccustomed release.

The city looked stunning by night. Its buildings were saturated by a kind of yellowy light which reached upwards till it met the strange indigo sky which refused to dim in the north. Packed streets of people were moving around in the semi-darkness and creating a constant murmur which was overborne by the city's busy trams and the music of bars, restaurants, and clubs playing out onto the streets almost like a celebration of the strange twilit summer-sky.

They hopped around a few bars in the Grünerløkka district becoming steadily more merry and noticing, among other things, the wealth of fit women who were out for the night's revelry. One woman, her face like a young Catherine Zeta-Jones, asked them for a light; none of them could satisfy her request. She swept on, dissolved in the beauty of it all, this night, the drinks, her cigarette; smiling quietly by the doorway in her red dress, she could only have been nineteen. Through the glazed eyes that the cocktails had brought on, the three men could only think of how lucky she was. Nights like these really belonged to her, really to those who still made the right kinds of mistakes.

By twelve they had settled in a pool bar and were taking badly-aimed shots over the baize in a two-v-two game with a Physics student while discussing Georg's experience at the Universitetet I Oslo. He boasted that he'd slept with upwards of thirty women in his time there, "And always at their place, never mine. I left when I wanted to; too much fussing with a girl at yours," he clucked as he missed an easy black to middle.

"Hey," whispered Gene in Andrew's ear as he passed his cue to the chuckling, gawky Physics student, "this brings back memories. Reminds me of when we used to go out together, the women-chat, the falling-over drunkenness…"

He slung his arm around Andrew and gathered the attentions of the other two, who were eyeing the spread on the table. "This is my mate here," he declared, "and I've missed him terribly."

He slapped a kiss on the cheek of Andrew and they embraced, happily at first until Andrew cut short the affection and turned away. The student had missed his shot.

"Lerrus make the pot," he explained quickly.

The other two had faces of iron as they made their way back across country to Bergen, and Andrew's spirits were not much higher. At around four he dropped Georg off, who was determined that he was returning to his bed with a hot chocolate, and only once they had kicked off their shoes and were recumbent on the sofa did Andrew venture to say that his car was a good buy, and that it had done well for fuel. Gene's spiritless response of "It did" was a reflection of how much he'd had to drink, itself indicative of how demanding the catch-up work in the wake of Andrew's stay had been.

Parsonage Crescent sold on Monday to everyone's surprise, not least the excited estate agent, who was set to make an unexpectedly quick fee from her client. Once all the necessaries were out of the way a handsome sum of the full asking price would sit nicely in Andrew's account. This buoyed him after a taxing first day at the Sprakskøle, in which he found he was not nearly as competent as his encounter with the fishmonger some time ago had suggested. Perhaps he was a little shorn of confidence without Gene at his back; in any case, his teacher had repeated 'Time and constant practice outside the classroom" as his prescription over the coming months.

Gene, still working overtime on pushing through the deal he had set up in Oslo, remained at the office well into the night and so it was that Andrew and Hilma spent another quiet, edgy evening together watching television and reading, neither able to shed their politeness nor converse without this strange constraint upon them. At one point Hilma made him jump by asking if he thought there was anything else on the television, and it was after this that Andrew silently decided enough was enough and drove down to watch the ships passing quietly in Bergen's dusky harbour.

He felt just as adrift the next day at school. Not just because things were proving trickier than he'd anticipated, no; all the time in that class he couldn't help thinking of Gene in the office, occupied, calling the shots. He could only picture that soft, sideburned face as that of the seventeen-year-old Gene, not like now but like then, in that harbour at Bridlington, on that boat with that log and that pen.

To make things worse he received an unwelcome piece of news later that afternoon after he had got back to the empty house. An email from the estate agents confirmed that his buyer had pulled out, for reasons unknown. But this was just a small thing, a trifling layer on top of the deep carpet of dirt. Something else was on his mind. He stalked up to where he had burnt Gene's book the other day, kicking at pieces of shale and thrashing at encroaching ferns on the way. The book's ashen remains were barely visible on the soggy floor behind the kabin. He looked at them in dismay, remembering the words on the page, remembering Gene's pathetic devotion to Jo. A terrible boiling was pulsing through his brain and into his body, not like that of an overheating fever but like that of someone growing hot and powerful, like someone communicating with a hidden soul, a lurking emotion. He felt it pulsing with pleasure and heat and anger and felt the strange familiarity of it, the recapitulation of past events. The incident with the lemming had been no freak accident, no unwillful turn; he had meant it. He had enjoyed taking the life from it. He had enjoyed the power. And in this house he felt powerless. In this house and near this man he still felt wanting, still felt an old jealousy.

He looked around at Gene's kabin and at his beautiful grounds, and saw in the distance the smoking chimney stack of Gene's beautiful house, where his happy family would sleep tonight. Hilma had arrived home.

Hilma was preparing something in the kitchen, humming one of the tunes they had been learning in class earlier that day. The kitchen door opened behind her.

"Hmm, hmm, oh hello Andrew, how are you? Just look at these new potatoes, delicious-looking hey? How was your day at school?"

"Pleasurable," said a level Andrew, "much better than yesterday."

"I'm glad to hear it. We knew you'd settle in, it just takes time. So—*hvor er du?'* Andrew found himself laughing. '*Oh, Jeg har det bra takk.'*

Hilma tinkled a laugh. 'Very good! Oh, now I have you, would you mind grating up some carrot for a salad? I'm thinking something light tonight."

"Of course not," he replied rolling the sleeves of his brown shirt up. "And afterwards, could you help me with something? It's something at Gene's kabin, something that's puzzling me. That's if you're allowed up there," he added jokingly.

"Well, I don't think he'd mind. A puzzle hey? I like puzzles."

DNO had been pushing all day for the distribution end of things to be wrapped up by the end of the evening. Their man was satisfied with the way things had sounded on Saturday but now delays from the Bergen office were frustrating the process and causing a hold-up. New licences were being granted steadily with the growth of the oil fields outside of Alvheim, and they could ill-afford to be stalled upon.

Gene had decided that he needed a break, just for an hour, and was driving homewards for dinner before heading back to the office to look again at the figures.

His Volkswagen crunched up next to Hilma's Audi. He pressed the ignition switch and composed himself for a second so that he could enter in a better frame of mind than he felt. A mask, a small sacrifice, such as one of the many one has to make in a marriage.

He called out, "Hilma, Andrew!" as he stepped across the threshold, catching his black brogues on the step. He wished that his children were home for him to see, and not at their grandparents'. In his mind he felt exhausted, but there was an end soon, he knew. He passed through into the kitchen where the radio was playing, expecting to see them busy cooking—enjoying themselves, he hoped. A deep pan sat on the hob, and as he peered in he could see some halved, starchy-white new potatoes sitting there without water. "Hello?"

She must be in, he thought, and Andrew too for his car was visible through the venetians at the front. He checked upstairs, his tiredness beginning to be forgotten and his pace becoming faster. There was no one in the rooms up there. Why this strange uneasiness? The work, surely. He had to switch off just for half an hour. But for whatever reason, he could not.

He scoured the vast living room, half-wishing that they were waiting to play some trick on him, some prank they had concocted after school. Then he stepped briskly outside, wandered over to Andrew's cabin, and flung its door open. He found himself shouting not Hilma's name but Andrew's. The sickening imprint of a memory he thought he'd forgotten began to slide to the front of his mind, the memory of being in that flat in Birmingham as he flung open more doors and began breathing heavily, adrenaline taking a foothold in his blood, readying him for what he didn't know yet but which he sniffed. He looked around in the narrow entrance of the cabin at the bed to his left, the deserted bathroom in front of him, then back to the bed. He hoped using all the might he possessed that he was wrong, that there was some rational explanation, and yet he felt that now, only now, he knew his old friend too well for there to be a way out. Then he stopped twisting his head from side to side in his frantic search for clues and heard the words ring within, the words he'd said which tolled dreadfully:

"I could remain here forever, in this kabin."

His vision tunnelled as he charged up the shale path; a branch whipped his face, cutting it from temple to jaw. On he ran. He made the summit of the hill where the kabin stood and flung open the heavy door. A woman's muffled shout sounded from the library door to his right. He kicked it open, a hot sickness rising like a burst oil well up his throat, and then he saw her.

Hilma had been tied at the wrist, gagged, and stripped from the waist. Her face was purple from the weight that had been upon her, her eyes saturated with tears. Small strands of vomit hung from the gag to the floor. He rushed forward to release her but, finding the knot too tight, he crashed open a drawer somewhere across the room and found a knife to cut the bond and the gag. Hilma gasped and let out a guttural sob. He clung to her, rocking her gently. Then he looked up, stirred by a movement through the room's small window, which had had its blind raised.

Andrew was sprinting down the path in a torn shirt, having escaped through the trap door next to the telescope.

Gene tore out of the room. Andrew had evaded him once; *not now, not again,* his insides screamed. The knife used to cut Hilma's hands free was still in his hand as he barrelled down the hill and onto the path where Andrew's crashing steps had revealed the clay layer beneath. His quarry was out of sight; it had got a good head start. He leaped up the steps to the portico at the rear of the house and tore through the long living room, anticipating that Andrew had gone straight for the kitchen to arm himself. He made the hallway and span into the kitchen, knife raised, adrenaline thumping through every sinew of his body. No one was there. Then he heard the roar of a car engine and the slam of tyres hitting gravel from the front of the house.

Instinctively he slapped his pocket for his keys, ran past the dragon-head bannister and jumped down the porch steps to his Volkswagen.

There were no mistakes in the gear change now, no thoughts or feelings or consciousness other than to get away from Bergen as though the devil itself was behind him. Andrew looked at the clock hitting seventy as he sped down the winding road into Bønes. Suddenly the fjord and the bridge towards Flesland and the airport burst into view. Then he despaired. There was no hiding from Gene at the airport, no easy getaway. He was overtaking lorries and cars, not daring to check his mirror as oncoming horn-blaring traffic missed him by a whisker. Then, as the bridge grew closer, he had an idea. It was the only idea that he could imagine.

He reached a large roundabout and accelerated into the right hand lane. Without looking he screeched off onto the first exit, the car feeling like it would tip over with its high centre of gravity and the g-forces compressing Andrew's head. He shrunk to think of what would happen now on the open road if Gene was behind him in his much faster car. He was on the long, straight 557, heading for Herdla.

The departure board at Flesland showed no sign of a flight to any UK airport. Frantically Gene rushed from one airline counter to the other, demanding to know if any were flying in case the board said wrong. Most staff were taken aback but answered 'No,' others turned to their computers or told him to wait while they checked. Each time he tore off madly. But in his heart, he knew that there were none.

He dashed back through the main atrium and into his car. He clubbed at his steering wheel with his palms, a miserable but potent moan issuing from his lips; then suddenly, he stopped. If Andrew ran to Oslo he would know that he'd be caught. He wasn't seeking to run; he was seeking to hide.

His car took off the entire door of a parked Volvo as he reversed through the empty space behind him. The owner peered through her windscreen with a dumbfounded look at Gene, whose fuming features now faced her. He slammed into first and swung left, crunching her bonnet skywards as he did so. The barrier at the entrance to the car park was rising but was not elevated enough to avoid the same treatment and it went spinning off its mounting onto a grass verge as Gene's Volkswagen careened though it.

Though he had nearly come under the lethal crushing force of an opposing lorry two or three times upon the way Andrew had made it to Herdla, with no sign of Gene in pursuit.

He wasn't satisfied that Gene would fail to remember his own recommendation and forget about Herdla, and so he sped past the small harbour to the right and the white church to the left, its weather vane spinning in the wind like the blades of a helicopter, and onwards to the beach at the northernmost tip of the island over which he had wandered only a few days before.

His mind rang after he had cut out the engine, the pitch of the ringing rising and the volume growing until he could hear nothing else. He left the car and stumbled out into the bitter wind. There was nothing he could do to prevent Gene's coming, he knew. He sat on the low dune which ran the length of the beach and looked at the swirling cloud above.

It was only a short time before Gene arrived. At the first sight of Andrew backing his way slowly towards the sea Gene's rage surged freshly. He flew out of the car with his knife and down the dune, then stopped twenty or so paces short of Andrew. The man Gene had twice loved and trusted looked a wreck, his shirt ripped and back bent, with his clawed hands in front of him as though ready for a schoolyard fight. Gene advanced as Andrew began to cry; and Gene too began to cry.

"I gave you everything!" Gene's hoarse voice rang across the beach. "I gave you my home, my family! I gave them to you! And I gave you me."

And, irreverent of his sorrow, with a leaping roar he charged at Andrew with his knife low, ready to sink it into his abdomen and spill his blood across the sand.

Andrew turned and fled into the shallows where the skerries lay and then whipped around, almost ready for what he knew must come. Gene was upon him. His instinct kicked in. With a reflex movement he sidestepped Gene's frothing, taller form and punched the knife from his hand. Gene tumbled forwards but kept his footing. The waves crashed inwards, erasing all trace of the knife. Emboldened by his sudden strike Andrew knew now that he was not there to run or to hide but to survive, and kill to that end, like a wolf cornered by a hunter. He landed a right hook around Gene's ear which sent them both toppling into the water. Gene rolled on top, first pinning him down even as he felt warm blood surge out of his ear and drop to the waves, then letting both his fists fly furiously downwards. His punches were loose and wild; an ape trying to murder the curled up body beneath him. But then Andrew kicked upwards under the hail of bone-cracking hits and landed a shoe firmly in Gene's testicles. Gene slumped off, whimpering; and he was turning on his knees ready to ignore the pain and finish the job when Andrew took a hold of his head and ran with him sideways. He kicked out the legs from underneath Gene, then twisted him so their faces were within an inch of each other. Both looked into their tear-strewn eyes. And then Andrew gasped, "No, no."

For there were the eyes which had followed him around, the eyes of the man in Sheffield on that fateful night with John Gandah, the eyes of the waiter too. He looked into Gene's eyes and saw the dark brown centre, flecked with yellow and eventually rimmed with the same gold hue, ring-like. For a second he loosed his grip, unsure of whether he could do it. Then he remembered he must, and with all his strength he threw the side of Gene's skull against the rocky shore of the nearest skerry and heard it crack.

He made it up the beach to the dune before collapsing in a moaning heap. What more did he have in the world now? What had he become? Juddering, he pushed himself up.

"What have you always been?"

He wished Gene was there to answer him, to snuff out his life forever.

He turned and looked up at the tall cliff face to his left. The sea lashed at its bottom, sometimes blanketing the rocks which crowded around it like chicks around their mother, sometimes menacingly revealing their short, sharp crowns. The sky seemed to be wrapped around the clifftop, blue-grey and pulsating. Slowly he limped to the path at its base, then began the ascent.

He looked down from the summit and felt sick. As he shuffled forward his knees nearly gave way as though they knew what was to come, and as he steadied himself a small rock unlatched from the clifftop and tumbled down noiselessly into the churning sea below. His tears had dried. At the skerry away in the middle of the beach Gene was slowly pulling himself upwards onto its rocky shore; but Andrew's gaze was fixated on the rocks beneath and the sea sloshing amongst them. The sky swirled grey. The wind whistled all around.

Aaron Smith

I was born when my parents lived on the road but soon I had settled with my mum in York, which was to become my hometown. My dad settled nearby in rural North Yorkshire and I would see him on weekends. I remember spending a lot of my childhood digging ditches or getting water from the well (and no, this wasn't in the 18th century), and making up very unstructured but kind of real stories as I did – real in the most childlike, most involved, most imaginative sense of the word.

But for the most part I grew up with my mum and brother and we held together as a small family in the shadow of Terry's chocolate factory in south York.

I oscillated between wanting to be a cricketer, a journalist, a farmer, and a writer before settling on being an English foreign language teacher. I write now in between my work and my busy social life, and when York City F.C aren't playing. I write because I know I have these sweeping stories to tell, and because it's much easier for me to express ideas on paper than through speaking!

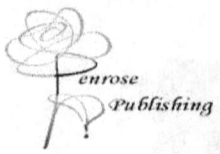

Penrose Publishing

Available in English, Paperback, Kindle, Kobo and PDF formats

See our website: www.penrose-publishing.co.uk

See also books from our other authors:
Grace Harding
Devon Volkel
JR Smith
Aaron Smith
Les Bill Gates
David Palmer
Joshua Mercott
Susan Mehra
Richard Lyon
Stuart Yates